THE LAST OF ALL
POSSIBLE WORLDS

and

THE TEMPTATION
TO DO GOOD

THE LAST OF ALL POSSIBLE WORLDS

AND

THE TEMPTATION TO DO GOOD

Two Novels by
Peter F. Drucker

PAUL DRY BOOKS
Philadelphia 2016

First Paul Dry Books Edition, 2016

Paul Dry Books, Inc.
Philadelphia, Pennsylvania
www.pauldrybooks.com

The Last of All Possible Worlds: Copyright © 1982 Peter F. Drucker
The Temptation to Do Good: Copyright © 1984 Peter F. Drucker

Author photo courtesy of The Drucker Institute of
Claremont Graduate University

Printed in the United States of America

Contents

THE LAST OF ALL
POSSIBLE WORLDS

Preface

This is the first of my nineteen books that admits to being fiction. Its length makes it a "novel." But in structure it is akin to chamber music—to the deceptively simple quartets perhaps which Antonín Dvořák, contemporary and countryman of some of the book's characters, wrote only a few years before the events described, or to the *Sinfonia Concertante* a century earlier, in which each movement features as its soloist a different instrument of the same small ensemble.

Most of the action of *The Last of All Possible Worlds* takes place— largely in London—on a few June days of the year 1906. None but a few, a very few, nonagenarians still survive who were adults then. For the rest of us that time and its world are as remote as the Egypt of the Pharaohs or the tourneys of mailed knights, for all that there were automobiles and telephones and electric lights. Yet this is not a "historical novel"; no one says "Egad," wears ruffles, or draws a sword. Historical personages are mentioned—Bismarck, Marx, and Disraeli, Gustav Mahler and John Pierpont Morgan. But they do not even have walk-on parts, existing entirely offstage, mentioned only as they might have been mentioned in the conversation of contemporaries. The characters are inventions altogether. If they matter at all, they matter not as "personages" but as people.

The title of this book is, of course, a play of words on "the best of all possible worlds" of Voltaire's *Candide*. But whether it refers to the Edwardian Age, that shimmering twilight before the First World War, or to old age, I leave to the reader to decide.

P.F.D.

1. Sobieski

Henrietta
Margit
Josefa
Lord Owen
A Tale from Goldoni

Henrietta

Only twice before—and then decades earlier—had the Prince Sobieski experienced such a wave of euphoria and bliss as engulfed him when the art dealer yesterday afternoon had lifted from its crate the new Claude Monet painting, the facade of Rouen Cathedral in exploding blues flecked with russets and with the great rose window radiating carmine light. Euphoria and bliss engulfed him anew every time he looked again; indeed, even when he did not look but thought of the painting with eyes closed.

It was the same ecstasy of tenderness that had suffused him forty years ago in his twenties when he had first met the long-legged eleven-year-old who years later was to become his wife, and who then, still a complete child, had trustingly put her hand into that of the stranger, a distant cousin she had never seen before nor probably even heard of—and who had dragged him off for a long walk through the dusty streets of an Austrian garrison town to pour out her loneliness, her despair, and her shame over a gambling-crazed father and an embittered, secretly drinking mother.

It was the same ecstasy of tenderness that had suffused him, a few years later—just before he turned thirty—when he beheld his firstborn, his natural daughter, only a few minutes old, the child of his mistress in Paris during his days as an apprentice diplomat at the court of the third Napoleon.

And now, on the threshold of old age, the ecstasy, the tenderness, the well-being and harmony had returned. "For the last time?" wondered Sobieski.

The sense of well-being was heightened—or, Sobieski thought, "sharpened" was the better word—by his enjoyment of Dr. Wegner's discomfiture.

The Monet painting had been put on an easel in the downstairs "library," once the ballroom of the eighteenth-century mansion Sobieski had bought for his London residence when first appointed ambassador to the Court of St. James's, and now his office and reception hall. And so, to be in the painting's presence, Sobieski, on the spur of the moment after coming out of his bath and the massage following it, had decided to take his breakfast there instead of in the upstairs sitting room, something he had never done in all his twenty-seven years in London. This meant that Wegner, the private secretary, instead of being ensconced behind his upstairs lectern, had to read the daily presentation standing in the middle of the big library: the Prince's schedule for the day and the evening; the overnight dispatches from the Foreign Ministry in Vienna; the *Court Circular*; the main news and lead editorials from *The Times*, *The Morning Post* and—two days late—the Vienna *Neue Freie Presse*; and the daily business telegram from the Director-General of the Sobieski Estates and Enterprises. This had so rattled and confused the man (usually a model of efficiency) that he began to stammer, mispronounced the familiar names of senior diplomats in the Austrian service and of Sobieski-owned timber companies and sugar refineries, and might even have forgotten the *Court Circular* altogether had not the Prince peremptorily reminded him.

It was then that into Sobieski's memory suddenly flashed an old schoolboy tale as to how the sternest and most tyrannical of schoolmasters could be thrown off balance by the students' looking fixedly at the fly of his trousers. In his own youth Sobieski never had occasion to try this. He had been taught by private tutors save for two short years when, aged sixteen and seventeen, he attended the Jesuit academy for the high aristocracy at Kalksburg near Vienna. The Fathers, of course, wore ankle-length cassocks, and anyhow were never seen walking or standing but always formally enthroned on a high podium or behind a big desk. On a sudden whim Sobieski fixed his eyes on Wegner's fly—and the private secretary blushed to the roots of his sparse sandy hair, dropped the papers he was holding, and wriggled in embarrassment. His sufferings were real, yet so comical that Sobieski, feigning concern, asked: "Are you not feeling well, Dr. Wegner?"

Years before, at some grand royal dinner at The Hague, Sobieski had been served a very sweet East-Indian chocolate dish into which the cook had put grains of exceedingly, almost unbearably hot red pepper, the sudden sharp burn of which only heightened the chocolate's sweetness. Similarly, the torment of the self-assured, arrogant, pompous Wegner exquisitely sharpened for Sobieski the tenderness, the harmony, the serene perfection of the Monet painting and the ecstasy of his yielding to its embrace.

Altogether it had been a singularly good morning. When he left for his daily two-hour horseback ride, the fog was so thick it was still dark, even in June. This was the London he loved: the eerie stillness with all sounds muffled or swallowed up, and the surprises when the fog swirled to show for an instant familiar squares in new fantastic shapes or to reveal unexpected features and vistas. With the fog and the heavy rain that had preceded it, the park was so empty Sobieski had it almost to himself. As so often when he rode alone, Pauline was riding beside him, just as she had done every morning of their enchanted love in the castle of his long-lost youth, deep in the endless Polish forest, he Prince Charming, she his Sleeping Beauty. He could almost smell her fresh, young body over the sharp odor of the horses and the even stronger stench of the big city: the coal dust in the yellow fog, the exhaust gases of yesterday's automobiles, and the millions of unwashed bodies crowded together in filthy tenements.

On the ride back, the sun had begun to pierce the fog with lances of silver and gold, the first patches of blue sky peeking through the rising mist just as he turned into Atherton Square.

Then, thanks to a new American masseur whom Hinton, the banker, had discovered and recommended a few weeks earlier, the shoulder which he had wrenched falling from his horse eons ago while trying to teach Pauline how to jump on horseback had become pain-free for the first time in months. The telegram from his Director-General in Vienna had reported that the stock market issue of the shares of the Polonia Brewery in Cracow had been a huge success, netting several millions—pounds sterling, at that, not Austrian crowns, and a sizable fortune by itself. To make this all the sweeter, the founding of the Polonia and the sale of its shares had been Sobieski's ideas, pushed through by him against the skepticism of the bankers, Hinton in London and Mosenthal in Vienna, both of whom had said: "There's already too much beer, there are too many breweries and far too many brewery shares." They had both been wrong.

Finally, the day's telephone call to Margit at Horne Abbey had assuaged the worry with which he now awoke each morning. The Princess, the tone of her voice told him at once, was still secure in her relationship with Owen Rhys Nevis, still sure of her lover and of being loved by him. It couldn't last, of course—she was fifty, after all. Sobieski dreaded the day when the *affaire* would be over and she would have to face up to no longer being a *jeune fille* fresh from convent school. She would then surely look to him as she had looked to him ever since he had first appeared to a lonely child as the knight come to rescue her, the answer to her girlish prayers for a miracle. What could he do? What could anyone do? But for the moment at least the Princess was at peace, happily pratting away with the backstairs gossip that so innocently amused her.

It was a singularly good morning—or should have been. But Henrietta's letter had marred it.

He had been able to put the thing out of his mind for some of the time, when, for instance, he looked at the Monet painting or thought about it, or when he made Dr. Wegner wriggle in embarrassment. But otherwise, ever since he had first glanced at the letter, he had been aware of an unease, a malaise, a dim but persuasive foreboding, and the dread of a crisis ahead.

He had so far had no time to do more than glance at what Henrietta had written. The letter had arrived in yesterday's afternoon mail. No sooner had he opened it than the art dealer called with the new Monet, followed by a fussy bureaucrat from the Foreign Office with a nonexistent problem about a Manchester businessman suspected of being a fence for stolen goods but claiming diplomatic immunity as the honorary consul of some Balkan kingdom, so that Sobieski, as doyen of the Diplomatic Corps, had to be informed and consulted in endless detail. Then he had had to rush and dress for an official dinner the Foreign Secretary was giving for the ambassadors and ministers to Great Britain, a dinner of empty speeches and inane toasts that lasted until midnight.

Of course these were the routines of his profession, and Sobieski had been taught, forty years ago, not to complain about them. He still remembered vividly how he had complained to his first mentor, the Austrian Ambassador to France, Prince Richard Metternich-Sandor, whose *élève* or trainee he had just become, how terribly bored he had been at his first four-hour state dinner. "Wasn't there anything you enjoyed?" Metternich-Sandor had asked.

"Oh yes, I very much enjoyed hearing Franz Liszt at the piano," he had answered; "but he only played for twenty minutes." "Don't you realize," Metternich-Sandor replied with a chuckle, "that Liszt has to practice the most boring scales at least four hours every day so that you can enjoy twenty minutes of his playing?"

And Sobieski had also learned, as every diplomat must, how to survive a two-hour briefing or a four-hour dinner without falling asleep, without yawning, without picking his nose, and without being bored to death. Last night he had done it by mentally surveying his entire collection of Impressionist paintings. In the new Monet, he had known at once, Impressionism reached ultimate perfection. It would therefore be the last painting he would ever buy, and the crown of the collection that he had started, forty years ago, with a small Degas— a gouache of a dancer at ballet practice—which he had bought more to please Lucille, Henrietta's mother and a ballet *élève* herself when he first met her, than because he particularly liked it or knew how to look at it.

But still the thought of Henrietta's letter broke through his defenses again and again, and when it did so he was seized with anxiety and felt almost ill. He had forced himself not to look at it until after Wegner's morning presentation, so that he would have two or three hours in which to read, to study, to analyze and to think. There was nothing on his calendar until one, when he would walk over to the embassy to preside at the luncheon of his diplomatic staff as he did every day when he was in London. Of course he had already gained an "impression"—probably a reliable one, as he had been trained to remember word for word documents once read. But—and this, too, Metternich-Sandor had taught him—to trust "impressions" was an unforgivable sin for a diplomatist, the one sure way of making mistakes.

Years later when he had moved to London, by then an ambassador to a great power and a senior man himself, he had gotten to know the Duke of Avila, already for ten or twelve years the Spanish Ambassador to Great Britain, and had learned to appreciate him as the master-diplomatist of his generation. When they became friends a few years after that, Avila showed him in confidence the treatise on *The Craft of the Diplomat* on which he had been working for twenty years. "It's almost completed," he had said ("and," thought Sobieski, "he's still working on it twenty years later, well past eighty, retired and half-blind"). The very first chapter cautioned: "Don't trust impressions. Read word for word, and analyze."

Now that Wegner was gone and he was alone—except for the two Cuirassiers who stood sentry outside the door and at the head of the stairs, and the three or four pageboys on their bench just inside the door ready to run his errands—now at last Sobieski opened the private drawer in his desk and took out Henrietta's letter.

First, as Metternich-Sandor had taught him, he looked at the handwriting. It was Henrietta's normal hand, the slanting, French schoolgirl hand that looked so legible but was in fact almost impossible to decipher. Next, the envelope. It read:

> *His Royal Highness*
> *Jan Casimir IX, Prince of Sobieski*
>   *and Duke of Przemysl*
> *Ambassador Extraordinary and Minister*
>   *Plenipotentiary to the Court of St. James's*
> *The Austro-Hungarian Embassy*
> *Londres, Angleterre*

And in the corner it was marked "Personal," with the initials H.D.S. (Henrietta Duguit-Sobieski), which told Dr. Wegner that this was a family letter, not to be opened by him.

This was how Henrietta always addressed her letters, completely correct to the last detail. And it was also Henrietta's habit to mix English and French on the envelope. He had once teased her about it. "But Papa," Henrietta had said, "I have to write your name and titles in English. The clerks in the London Post Office can't be expected to read French; and I have to give the city and the country in French—

for the clerks in the Post Office in Paris can't be expected to know English."

"Henrietta," he had protested, "you are inconsistent. You address your letters in French only for the few weeks I spend in Austria each year."

"But, Papa," she had come back, "every Austrian clerk knows that French is the language of civilization and wouldn't dare admit that he can't read it"—and she was right, of course.

This was Henrietta's inimitable logic; she called it "being practical." She had inherited it from Lucille, her mother, a Flemish peasant who by "being practical" had clawed her way through the jungle of the demimonde: as artist's model who had run away to Paris from some hamlet near Dunquerque when only fifteen with the painter for whom she had modeled for a summer; as an understudy in the ballet; as small-time courtesan. Until finally being practical had made her a Prince's mistress and, using the money Sobieski had given her when they parted, established her in bourgeois respectability and marriage with a widowed textile manufacturer in Tourcoing or Roubaix or some such provincial place. And it was "being practical" that made Lucille as dutiful a wife to an elderly textile manufacturer, and as good and dutiful mother to his children, as she had been a good and dutiful mistress to a young, madcap prince and, undoubtedly, a good and dutiful companion to impoverished painters for whom she modeled during the day and with whom she slept at night.

This "practicality" was a cold and remorseless logic, totally amoral: it had shocked the young Sobieski in his mistress as it frightened an older Sobieski in her daughter. It had shocked him to find out that Lucille was taking a 30 percent commission on the paintings she picked for him to buy from her friends, the young Impressionists—for it was Lucille who had the impeccable eye and who had taught him to see. "But," she had explained, "I charge less commission than an art dealer, and I make you pay the painters more than an art dealer would. You still get the best pictures and get them dirt cheap."

Only last night had he realized how right Lucille had been.

For in reviewing his collection in his mind, he had also reviewed what he had paid for each painting—and compared it with what the dealer now asked for the new Monet. He had never bought paintings as an "investment," but because Lucille had made him see them and love them. Yet he had made as much money collecting Impressionists as he made out of the Polonia Brewery or even out of his great financial coup, the shift of his large Bohemian and Moravian estates from wheat growing, in which they could not possibly compete with the Hungarians, let alone America or Argentina, into sugar beet, and the subsequent launching of what was now the largest sugar refinery in Central Europe.

Henrietta had shown the same "practicality" during the Dreyfus Affair ten years ago. Pierre, her husband, then still a captain and recently transferred from the cavalry to the French General Staff, had been obnoxiously loud in his denunciation of Alfred Dreyfus as a "traitor" and a "dirty Jew for whom shooting was much too good." Sobieski had said quietly to Henrietta: "Make Pierre restrain himself. The evidence against Dreyfus is hardly conclusive."

"But, Papa," she had protested, "everybody on the General Staff knows that Dreyfus is innocent. Indeed, Pierre always wants to tell me the name of the real spy. I am much better off not knowing it, I tell him.

"Of course," she continued, matter-of-fact, "the truth will come out in a few years. Far too many people know it for it to remain secret long. But the generals can't afford to have Dreyfus found innocent; they are committed to his guilt. Any junior officer who doesn't shout louder than they do is considered disloyal and his career finished. When the truth does finally come out, maybe a Minister of War will have to resign. But the only officers who'll suffer will be the ones who haven't been loud enough in denouncing Dreyfus. And what good would it do anyhow for a nobody like Pierre, a mere captain, to play Don Quixote?"

It had turned out that way, of course; and Pierre, whose intellectual gifts were barely visible to the naked eye, had made it to lieutenant-colonel on the General Staff, though Dreyfus's innocence had now to be admitted even by the generals. This ruthless, remorseless, amoral practicality—the practicality of the peasant and the courtesan—shocked and frightened Sobieski. But it also fascinated him, it was so utterly free of hypocrisy.

It was this very "practicality," this hardbitten, self-centered candor, that had first attracted him to Lucille. Owen Rhys Nevis's father was the one who introduced them. He was then still only Lord apRhys and heir to the earldom. He was also not yet finally separated from his wife. Indeed, the last attempt at a "reconciliation," as a result of which Owen had been sired (he arrived in the same week in which Lucille gave birth to Henrietta) took place several months later. ApRhys was then living in Paris to be away from his wife and had had himself appointed *élève* to his cousin, the British Ambassador to France, despite his age—a good ten years older than Sobieski. He was known all over town as the "Mad Lord," out to set a new chorus girl record. He and Sobieski became friends through their common devotion to horsemanship. They were in the habit of taking their early morning rides together—That's how I learned English, Sobieski recalled. One day apRhys had invited Sobieski to a picnic in the Rambouillet Woods and had asked his chorus girl of the moment, a rising ballerina at the Opéra Comique, to bring along a younger colleague. She had brought Lucille.

"You two ought to hit it off," apRhys had said in his barbaric French. "You're both *élèves* and both in comic opera. You," turning to Lucille, "in the Corps de Ballet, and you," to Sobieski, "in the Corps Diplomatique. And you need each other." Sobieski was still young enough to be embarrassed, but the girl—she looked hardly more than a child—only laughed.

"What did you come here for?" Sobieski asked her.

She looked him full in the face and said: "To find a generous protector."

No, the envelope of Henrietta's letter was only an envelope, a carrier, not part of the message, and could safely be dismissed. And now for the letter. Sobieski read it through slowly in its entirety:

"*Monseigneur, mon Père*," it began, as Henrietta's letters always began ever since she had been made to write her first letter of birthday wishes to him when she was six or seven years old.

Monseigneur, mon Père:

> *In three weeks we shall be in London with you. We are only waiting for Pierre's return from the spring maneuvers, which he is attend-*

*ing as a special aide to General Martineau—it's a very great honor
indeed and usually reserved for officers far senior. And as always,
our stay with you will be the high point of our year. You know, I am
sure, how much we depend on your wise advice and counsel.*

*This year we shall be more in need of your counsel and help
than for many years past. Pierre is at a critical point in his career.
What needs to be done is quite clear, I believe. But it is something
totally out of Pierre's and my reach—and yet it would be simplic-
ity itself for Prince Sobieski, his Apostolic Majesty's Ambassador to
London.*

*Pierre will be forty this coming year. He is still quite young for
his rank and for the responsibilities entrusted to him by the General Staff. And yet in another few years he'll be just another middle-
aged cavalry officer waiting out his retirement. If Pierre were to
transfer back to the Line, he would probably get command of a
regiment immediately and with it a colonelcy—and we would be
willing to suffer the tedium of some horrible garrison town in the
provinces if it would help him. But that would be the end for him—
fifteen years of drilling recruits and signing sick-call reports. With
the wicked Socialists daily gaining influence and out to destroy the
Army, the number of general officers is not going to increase; even
existing vacancies are left open for unconscionable periods in the
name of "economy." Of course the war will change all this, and we
all know it is bound to come. But by then Pierre may be past fifty
and past promotion.*

*Pierre often accuses me of being too ambitious for him. But it
is not for Pierre Duguit that I am ambitious; it's for Pierre Duguit-
Sobieski! When you in your love and generosity acknowledged as
your daughter the child of a humble farm girl, and when you then
later added to your generosity by permitting us to join the illustri-
ous name of Sobieski to that of a notary's son from Toulon, you set
us a standard I am committed to and determined to live up to. It
is not a matter of ambition for me, but of honor. I shall not dese-
crate the name of Sobieski, the name of a race of soldier-kings, by
being your guest and sitting in your salon as the wife of an aging
mediocrity who could not make it beyond a colonelcy, but yet bears
your name.*

There must be a way out—and, my dear Papa, there is a way out, but only with your intervention. There is one military appointment for an officer of Pierre's age and rank where lack of seniority is not an absolute bar. You will, of course, have guessed already; it's assignment as military attaché to an embassy. This appointment is made not by military people but by the chief of personnel of the Diplomatic Corps at the Foreign Ministry. The chief of personnel at the General Staff has a veto power and expects to be consulted in advance, but he should be no problem as he is favorably inclined toward us. Pierre has the one qualification that is considered most important for a military attaché: languages. Thanks to our annual trips to London to visit you, he is fluent in English; and having grown up on the Côte d'Azur, he has an adequate command of Italian still.

A French military attaché is automatically promoted to colonel within a few months of his appointment and then advanced to général de brigade when his tour of duty nears its end. And he is almost assured of being promoted to général de division three or four years later. When war breaks out—and it is, of course, a question of "when" rather than "if"—the former military attaché can be sure of an important assignment. If he has served with an ally, he'll be the Liaison between two high commands; and if he has served with an enemy, he'll be the expert adviser on intelligence.

My beloved Papa, you have done so much for us that I hesitate to come to you again with a request for help, even though last year when we first talked about Pierre's future, you so generously promised all the help you could give. But as your natural daughter, my beloved Papa, I cannot depend on your name or on the august family of Sobieski. I can only hope for the help you can give in person and through your exalted position.

I can hardly wait till I can kiss your hand again, my dear Papa—it's only three weeks. But by then, I am sure, you will have found the way out of my troubles and difficulties as you always found the way out of the troubles and difficulties of your little girl.

Your loving daughter,
La petite Riri

"How clever," thought Sobieski, as he put the letter down after reading it a second time. "She could give lessons in diplomacy to the most accomplished practitioner."

She had meant him to be touched by signing herself "*La petite Riri*," and he was. When she was very small and couldn't pronounce "Henrietta," she had called herself "Riri." He had liked it and went on calling her that even after she had learned to speak her name. The baby-name had released all the tenderness and affection in the young and doting father which he himself, as he then realized, had craved in his own infancy. He had never received it, either from a mother who hated the Polish forest into which her marriage had banished her or from a father who had eyes only for his horses and his harem of gypsy girls, nor even from a grandmother who had warmth for and interest in the little boy, but was the prisoner of her pride as the daughter of the Royal House of Saxony and of the court protocol that hedged her as a granddaughter of the Habsburgs.

But Henrietta had come to dislike "Riri." "It's the nickname of a *cocotte*," she had once complained. To sign it to this letter was not only meant to please him; it was a cri de coeur, a declaration of need. He was indeed touched and moved, and felt sorry that she had had to humble herself.

And how skillfully she delivered the threat. Of course, it wasn't much of a threat. He had no illusion that Henrietta loved him; she loved no one but herself. But as long as he was alive and she could hope to get money out of him, she'd court him and "sit in his salon" whenever he invited her. Still, she also knew how dependent he was on her affection—and without using her claws had managed to remind him of it. "She is the only human being I love," thought Sobieski, "and she knows it."

How thoroughly she had done her homework! She had all but drafted the letters for his signature. If his Italian was no better than his English, Pierre was not much of a linguist. Still, it was the one qualification that could justify appointing him over the heads of a dozen seniors. And how in heaven had Henrietta wangled his appointment as General Martineau's aide? She must have spent quite a few weekends in Biarritz with the vain old man. He liked to be seen in the company of fashionable women. Something like that undoubtedly also explained why the personnel officer at the General Staff was "favorably inclined." "After all," reflected Sobieski, "she's not a courtesan's daughter for nothing."

Of course, Henrietta was right: appointment as a military attaché was the only way open to Pierre, whose career was blocked less by want of seniority or by the stinginess of the "wicked Socialists" (of which Sobieski heartily approved), than by lack of any trace of intelligence. Pierre de Duguit—his grandfather, a real estate speculator, had purchased the middle "de" from Louis Philippe in 1842—had been the typical *beau sabreur* young cavalry lieutenant when Henrietta brought him to her father as her intended, very nice to look at sitting on his horse, with his long, carefully waxed mustachios, and very good at ogling the nursemaids in the Bois de Boulogne. Today he was middle-aged, gone to fat, and still with no assets beyond his waxed and now carefully dyed mustachios. But lack of intelligence was surely no handicap for a military attaché, Sobieski thought.

Sobieski himself had never been a great admirer of the military, nor impressed by its virtues. To be sure, he was hereditary commander of the most prestigious of Austrian cavalry regiments, the Sobieski Cuirassiers. As a young man of nineteen, he had even taken part in a military campaign, the Austrian war against the Italians of 1859. But he had been utterly bored as much by his fellow officers and their drivel as by the camping out in endless autumn rains.

Of all the military, he respected least the military attaché, who was neither soldier whose job it was to get shot at nor diplomat whose job it was to make sure that no one altogether got shot at. He was pure popinjay. Sobieski thought the military attaché the least happy of the nineteenth century's inventions and had long fought against having one. When he had finally been overruled and forced to admit one to the London Embassy, the appointment only confirmed his prejudices. Vienna had sent him a count of very old lineage and very young money—he had married one of the Wald-Reifnitz daughters—who did nothing at all except send an embassy messenger once a month to the bookstall in Victoria Station to buy copies of *Bradshaw* and the *ABC*, the British Railway guides, which he then had carefully wrapped in oilcloth, stamped "Top Secret," and sent in the diplomatic pouch to the Ministry of War in Vienna. Somebody must have told him that railways were strategically important.

Well, if stupidity and indolence were the qualifications for the job, Pierre possessed them and could be recommended with a good conscience. Sobieski wondered anew what Henrietta had seen in the blockhead, and then remembered the conversation he had had with her at the time. "Why do you want to marry such a lightweight?" he had demanded.

"Precisely because he is such a lightweight, Papa," she had answered. "I want a man whom I can manage, direct, dominate." As simple as that, and just as direct as her mother, who had said: "I want to find a generous protector."

Henrietta was right, once more. She had to have her father act for her as long as he was alive and still in office. The Sobieski name would only be an obstacle after he was gone. Margit had always been jealous of her, and his legitimate children pretended that his natural daughter did not exist. None of them could ever forgive his acknowledging her at birth, nor would ever understand why he had done anything so quixotic and unnecessary.

"Surely," his legitimate daughter, the wife of Prince Wottawa-Sonthofen, had once said angrily to her mother in her father's presence, "giving the brat enough money to live on would have been ample for a bastard from the gutter."

Henrietta was also right in her assertion that to get Pierre appointed a military attaché should present little difficulty for her father. Of course, of the French embassies, the only ones that qualified were the ones that really didn't matter: Madrid and Rome. One look at the *Diplomatic Almanac* showed Sobieski that they must have been the posts Henrietta had in mind. In both, the incumbent French military attaché had just been promoted to *général de Brigade* and was thus ready to return home, according to Henrietta—and in such matters one could rely on her. This also explained the reference to Pierre's Italian, of which Sobieski had never heard before.

The rest should be easy indeed. The personnel man for the French Diplomatic Corps was an old acquaintance who owed Sobieski a heavy debt. He had been a junior in the French Embassy in London ten years ago and Sobieski had bailed him out of a stupid mess when his pretty but giddy wife had signed some IOU's for gambling debts at usurious interest and was being blackmailed. One word to Hinton, the banker, and the IOU's were returned in an unmarked envelope. He did not personally know the man in charge of personnel on the General Staff. But the French Army list showed him to be a Segur-Ponchivy. It was his sister therefore (or maybe a cousin) who was married to one of the Sonthofens of the cadet branch and had become a cousin by marriage of Sobieski's son-in-law, Wottawa-Sonthofen. So he could write directly to Segur, addressing him as "*Mon Cousin.*" Segur would surely be flattered to receive a personal letter from so exalted a personage as the Duke of Przemysl and be recognized as a kinsman by him. Again, thought Sobieski, how clever Henrietta was. She surely knew all this and had worked it out to the last detail.

"And she did indeed, as she claims, prepare me for her request. The fact that I didn't understand it is not her fault." He recollected clearly the conversation with Henrietta the year before to which her letter referred. Henrietta had come to him for money, as she always did before the end of her visit. As in every year, the sum she asked him for staggered him by its size—more than enough to keep a French officer and his family in comfort for the rest of their lives. These annual gifts came, of course, on top of the princely sum he had settled upon her at her birth and of another, even more princely, one she had gotten when she married, not to mention the monies he had set aside for each of her two boys when they were born. Thank God Henrietta did not know how rich he really was!

And when he had written out for her a check that was almost twice what he had expected to give, Henrietta had said: "Papa, next year I shall have to come to you about Pierre's career. Can I count on your help?"

He had of course said, "Yes," only it had never occurred to him that she would want anything but money.

But now she wanted a good deal more than money. She wanted his active intervention. Yet she had the right to ask for it, and he an obligation to grant it. This was, after all, what one owed one's children, especially a natural child. The legitimate ones could ask in their own name with all the Sobieski connections at their disposal. His natural daughter had nothing but his protection and good will.

Why then was he so upset, so agitated, so disturbed—to the point where even looking at the Monet *Cathedral* no longer gave serenity, happiness, or peace of mind? Why, above all, was he so apprehensive?

"Are you a pacifist?" one of the bright Austrian General Staff officers had asked in a surprised voice when he had opposed a proposed move as "warlike provocation" during a joint diplomatic-military conference last autumn, just before his return to London.

"No, General," he had answered, "I am not a pacifist, but war is much too risky to be taken lightly. I do not subscribe to the famous Clausewitz epigram always spouted in your General Staff schools: 'War is the continuation of diplomacy by other means.' I see it as the failure of diplomacy."

And he had then tried to tell the man how impressed he had been a few weeks earlier when his younger son, who was as absorbed in mountain climbing as Sobieski had been in horsemanship at the same age, had taken him to meet a famous guide in the Dolomites.

"The first rule of climbing," the guide had explained, "is never to move forward until you're sure you can go back. And the second is not to move one member, arm or leg, until the other three are firmly anchored on secure holds."

"That's the best definition of diplomacy I've ever heard," Sobieski told the general. "Compared to it, war is like jumping off a mountain top hoping that God will provide wings.

"Actually," Sobieski had continued, though the general was no longer listening, "I am not opposed to war because it is unpredictable. I'm opposed to it because its aftermath has become only too predictable. Who will win or who will lose is indeed as unpredictable as jumping off a mountain top, despite all the maneuvers and war plans. I have lived through five or six wars since my campaign in Italy almost half a century ago, including the Boer War the British bungled so ingloriously only a few years back. And not one of them has borne any resemblance to what your smart officers in their well-tailored uniforms had predicted. But regardless of who wins, the loser in this world of ours is bound to be plunged into bloody anarchy—and perhaps the winner, too. Whoever wins, civilization is lost."

And Sobieski thought again of the months when he was the only diplomat left behind in the Paris of the Commune during that terrible year of 1871 when the Prussians were besieging a city in which the mob ran riot. In those dreadful months when hatred, mindless violence, and lawlessness ruled, he grew up; the playboy became a man. But it was also during those months that his career began and the *élève* became a diplomat. When the old women with bloodlust in their eyes and the young men bent on rape and pillage tried to storm the Austrian Embassy in which he had given refuge to a few hundred hapless German civilians (tailors and bookbinders, commercial salesmen and a physician or two and some very frightened wives) and when the Revolutionary Militia assigned to protecting the building had turned tail and ran, he had faced down the mob alone, appealing to it as a Pole and a friend of France.

They almost lynched him—he had never been so close to death, he knew—but at the last minute they had wavered and broken. The English and American newspapermen who were still in the city published the story after the regular troops of the French government had stormed in a few weeks later and suppressed the Commune— with as much brutality, as much savagery, as much raping, shooting, and looting as the Communards had committed in their turn. And he had become a hero!

He had also become so highly acceptable to the Germans—the old Emperor sent him a handwritten letter of thanks for saving the German civilians—that as a young man, still barely thirty, who had never held a major diplomatic post before, he was sent a few months later to the brand-new German "Reich" in Berlin, not yet in the top spot but with the personal rank of ambassador and the trickiest assignment: the relations with Austria's old allies, the former independent German principalities, now submerged in Bismarck's Reich.

The Commune experience had also earned him the London appointment a few years later. Bismarck, then at the peak of his power and reputation, had asked Sobieski in alone for a long evening during which he pumped him about the Paris of the Commune. It was then that Sobieski—to his own surprise—heard himself saying for the first time that modern war, the war of large conscript armies, had become socially too dangerous. It could lead only to the dissolution and destruction of the bonds of civility and community in the losing nation, with the distemper easily infecting the winning one as well.

Bismarck had apparently been impressed. For when Disraeli, the British Prime Minister, and Lord Salisbury, his Foreign Secretary, had come in 1878 to the Berlin Congress, Bismarck suggested to them that they talk to Sobieski about the Paris Commune. And that, in turn, had led to Salisbury's asking for Sobieski's appointment to the vacant Austrian ambassadorship in London.

Of course it was fashionable now to explain the Paris Commune as "class war." Sobieski had read with growing surprise a whole treatise by Karl Marx, the prophet of the Socialists, painting the Communards as revolutionary heroes and harbingers of a new perfect world of love, peace, and brotherliness. Alas, he knew better. He had seen them; Marx had not. There was neither love nor peace nor brotherliness in the mob that wanted to hang those frightened Germans on the nearest lamppost or hack them to pieces. There were only the basest of animal passions; hatred and self-loathing, envy and the mad lust to kill. Those poor Germans weren't "class enemies" or "exploiters"; they were simply proletarians who did not have the money to flee the city. Needless to say, the wealthy ones were long gone.

But no one any more believed the lesson he had learned in those months in the Paris of mob rule. No one believed how fragile civilization was, how thin the overlay of humanity over the brute, how little it took to unchain the savage.

Once when he discussed his experiences with the Duke of Avila, the older man had said, "I am not the old reactionary the Freemasons in Spain and the liberal newspapers depict me as just because I don't believe that a secret handshake and a licentiate's degree in jurisprudence or economics are all that is needed to usher in the earthly paradise. But they are right: I am not much for 'progress.' We are already living in the last of all possible worlds. It can only get worse, not better.

"Now we can still have kings, and they may matter all the more for being constitutionally restrained. There are still the likes of us, the aristocracy. We still have a pope and bishops; but if you want to be an atheist, no one is going to burn you at the stake—not even in Spain. And the bourgeoisie is growing richer every day, absolutely secure in its property, as no bourgeoisie has ever been before or is ever likely to be again. Look at the peasants—even in my poor Andalusia they use oxen instead of their wives now to pull the plow. The proletarians form labor unions and elect deputies and get Sundays off and are even agitating for a fifty-hour week.

"It's the last of all possible worlds where all these groups and classes can live together without slitting each other's throats and plunging into civil war. Change it, and one group must dominate— it doesn't matter much whether it's the rich who buy the military to shoot the poor, or the poor who take out their envy on the rest of us. There would be nothing left of what makes life worth living, none of the balance and diversity, the tolerance and choice, we call civilization."

To be sure, Avila *was* a reactionary; and yet he was right. They were all—kings and bishops, dukes and bankers, peasants and laborers—balanced on a frayed rope over an abyss. It had been proven again only a year ago when St. Petersburg and Moscow erupted after the Japanese had beaten the Russians in a war every staff officer in Europe knew the Russians were going to win. And that the Czar's government was now channeling the mob's bloodlust against the Jews, trying to unite workers and peasants, church and nobility, in the madness of pogroms, was hardly an improvement.

But no one was willing to listen any more. A few months ago Sobieski had thrown the caution of a lifetime to the winds and committed the one unforgivable sin for an experienced diplomat. He had risked making an enemy in a high place by warning the British Foreign Secretary, proud architect of the British alliances with France and Russia, of the danger of civil breakdown and anarchy that a war entailed.

"You don't know the English," the Foreign Secretary had said icily.

"But maybe *you* don't know the Irish," he had answered.

He had drawn blood. A few weeks later the King said to him half-laughingly: "I hear that you treated one of my ministers rather roughly, my dear Sobieski."

But of course he had not made the slightest impression on either the Foreign Secretary or the King.

And now his own Austrians—the ones least able to afford a war, even a victorious one—were joining the rush to suicide. The old general in Vienna, who for so many years had made sure that the lessons of all those wars Austria had lost in the mid-nineteenth century would not be forgotten, had been finally forced into retirement, defeated by age. The leadership was passing into the hands of the archduke Francis Ferdinand's men, the bright, eager saber-rattlers determined to prove to their "friends" in Berlin, and above all to the archduke's "great friend," the German Emperor, that they too could be "manly" and "sharp." Conrad von Hoetzendorf, the general who had asked him whether he was a pacifist, was, he heard, slated to become the next Chief of Staff. And Aehrenthal, the "activist" Austrian Ambassador in St. Petersburg whom everyone considered so "clever" because he used such fashionable terms as "calculated risk" and "preponderance of power" in every other sentence, was, so Sobieski's few remaining friends in Vienna told him, almost certain to be the next Minister of Foreign Affairs.

No, he could not blame Henrietta for taking war for granted. She was surely right. He could not blame her for trying to prepare for it; he could not blame her for seeing it as her husband's opportunity. And he certainly could not blame her for preferring to be the wife of a general safely behind the front to being the widow of a colonel who had died a hero's death.

And yet could he, Sobieski, be the instrument through which she accomplished her end? Could he act as her accomplice without betraying all that he stood for, all he was known to stand for?

The moment he asked that question he realized that it was this that had caused his malaise, his profound unease, his near-terror. He had long accepted that he had lost his cause, been defeated. He knew that his life's work had been in vain. But at least he had not given in, had not joined the enemy, had not tried to gain personal benefit from what he knew to be criminal folly, irresponsibility and madness. And now Henrietta was asking him to help her turn the ruin of civilization into her husband's advancement.

"I am totally irrational," Sobieski said out loud. "There are not many people to whom I could even explain what upsets me.

"What difference could it possibly make whether Pierre Duguit is military attaché in Madrid or Rome, or stays a middle-aged colonel sitting on a big horse and performing useless heroics? If Pierre doesn't get the job, some other colonel will, and anyhow, whoever makes history it isn't military attachés. They write reports which nobody reads or put railway timetables into packages marked 'Top Secret.'

"Ambassadors don't make history either, of course—at least not now that we have the telegraph and the telephone. All ambassadors do nowadays is sit through endless dinners ignoring pompous speeches, even those they make themselves. Henrietta probably knows nothing of my convictions and my politics; why should she? But if she did, she'd be only rational—she'd call it practical—to dismiss them as the foibles of an elderly eccentric and ask me to do what I, her father, am supposed to do: advance her interests and protect her, precisely because the catastrophe is imminent and coming closer every day."

He suddenly thought again of the Duke of Avila. "The thing that makes a gentleman out of a man of birth and breeding," Avila had said in one of those interminable discussions about that elusive word "gentleman," "is that he cares far less for what other people think of him than for what he sees when he looks at his face in the mirror in the morning.

"I know," Avila went on, warming to the subject, "that nobody thinks it unusual for an ambassador to have ladies of easy virtue entertain his guests at a stag party—even royalty, I'm told, does it all the time. But I still wouldn't want to see a pimp when I look at my face in the morning, nor would anyone *I* should call a gentleman."

What would he have to call himself, looking at his face in the mirror, if he did Henrietta's bidding and wrote the letters that would make her husband a military attaché?

How long Sobieski sat there in deep gloom, he did not know. All he did know was that he had rarely in his life felt so miserable. He had a duty to Henrietta. Or rather, it was a duty to himself, which he had assumed at that very moment thirty-eight long years ago when he had told a surprised (nay, shocked) midwife: "Cross out the 'Unknown' you've already inserted in the father's column on the birth certificate, and put in my name and titles instead."

She was so surprised that she came back a few hours later to ask again, and then again the following day.

Lucille, practical as always, had been equally surprised—and by no means pleasantly. "A well-paid-for illegitimate daughter without further obligation is one thing—and there are convents and orphanages to take care of such mishaps. But a duke's acknowledged natural daughter, whatever her financial endowment, is a burden and a liability I would be just as happy not to have to take on."

But he had been adamant, without quite knowing why, except that his heart had gone out to that helpless, squalling creature. The promise he had then made to himself, the obligation he had imposed on himself, was just as much a duty as the obligation not to betray the beliefs, the convictions, the sacred honor of his professional public life.

It was then, after he had gone through all the arguments for the fifth time or so, that the solution suddenly struck him. A man of honor was supposed to do his duty, in this case, to intervene for his natural daughter—and then resign. That was what a minister did who had to carry out a government policy with which he disagreed in conscience. And that was what a senior officer in the army was supposed to do when he could no longer, in conscience, carry out the orders of his superiors.

Sobieski knew immediately that this was the way out and the right answer, if only because the marvelous facade of *Rouen Cathedral* suddenly began to glow again before his eyes.

He had hoped to stay on as ambassador to London for three more years until he had served three decades, or perhaps for four more years until he reached seventy. But twenty-seven years in one post was not a bad record, either. There were few diplomats who could match it and, to his knowledge, none that had done better; and sixty-six was a perfectly respectable age for returning to private life. There was so much he wanted to do and could not as long as he was chained to the embassy and had to preside over staff luncheons at noon and sit through inane dinners at night. Robert Mosenthal, head of the Austrian Court and State Archives, one of the famous "Mosenthal twins" and the banker's younger brother, had many times asked him to help edit the Sobieski papers on the First Partition of Poland. And he himself had long been wanting to spend some time with the letters, memoranda, and diaries of the only one of the Sobieskis who really had made history.

The sole time Henrietta had shown genuine interest in his work rather than feigning it was at his mention of his hope that one day he might study this "one Sobieski who has really made history."

"Oh, Papa," she had said, her eyes lighting up, "was that the Soldier-King who is in all the history books for his great victory under the walls of Vienna in 1683? The one who removed the Turkish threat from Europe? How I'd love to know more about him—he always fascinated me most among our ancestors."

He had had to disappoint her. "Jan Casimir the First, the one in all the history books, was a *beau sabreur*, not unlike your Pierre, and a featherweight and a puppet whose strings were pulled by his clever, ambitious, unscrupulous wife. And forget that famous victory! The King of Poland couldn't have done anything more idiotic than try to remove the Turkish threat to Europe. Without it his country was finished, done for—no one needed an independent Poland except as a buffer against the Turks.

"No, the one Sobieski who really did make history is not in the books at all. He took good care to stay out of them. He is the Soldier-King's great-grandson, Jan Casimir the Fourth—I'm sure you've never even heard of him—secretive, crafty, ultra-private, calculating, and totally unheroic. Seventy years after the Soldier-King, he understood that there was no chance for Poland to stay independent and that his countrymen could survive only under the umbrella of the Great Powers, and especially the one Catholic power, the Austria of Maria Theresia. So he set about to conspire, bribe, and negotiate, until he managed the partition of Poland to come out as Austria's premier noble with a dukedom and estates, wealth and power, for himself and his descendants."

"How I envy your knowledge of history, Papa." Henrietta had forced a tight little smile while she firmly squelched him.

Well, now he'd have time for Jan Casimir IV: to delve into his papers and his secret correspondence, and into the mind of the one truly successful diplomatist (other than Henrietta) of the Sobieski lineage.

But above all he had yearned again and again for time to work on the Sobieski Estates and Enterprises. Nothing in his diplomatic career—even in those first years, when there was still the thrill of knowing secrets and being privy to affairs of state—had satisfied him so much or made him feel so productive as the work for three years, under the tutelage of old Jeidels, on the Sobieski estates, their accounts and the planning for their future.

Suddenly Sobieski remembered that it was not twice before that he had felt the euphoria, the bliss experienced again yesterday afternoon on first beholding Monet's *Rouen Cathedral*. There was a third, even earlier time—when old Jeidels had blessed him as he sent him out into the world.

Sobieski was twenty-three when he returned to Przemysl and Sobieski Palace. At sixteen, he had been sent with his governor and a household of twenty servants to Vienna to study with the Jesuits at Kalksburg. Next, he had spent some two years with his regiment, the Sobieski Cuirassiers, including his service in the 1859 campaign in Italy. And then, as was the custom at the time for young noblemen, he had been a private student with famous professors at the University of Vienna, reading law and economics, philosophy and history—although, Sobieski smiled wryly, he probably had spent more time with girls than with his books or in the great scholars' famous lectures.

But at twenty-three he had greatly surprised his father by proposing that he return to Sobieski Palace in the Polish forests and apprentice himself to the Prince's administrator, Jeidels, the old Jew, to learn estate management and become familiar with the Sobieski properties. Now, of course, it was the proper thing for young noblemen to do; even a Habsburg archduke had done it. But in Sobieski's days it was unheard of.

Right away he met Pauline, at the welcoming reception and ball the senior Sobieski staff gave for their returning young master. There she stood with her widowed father, the German forester, a tall, willowy, white-blond girl with luminous blue eyes. He had waltzed with her as duty demanded—and so enjoyed it that he risked gossip by asking her to dance with him once more.

At the end, when he was walking her back to where her father sat, she blushed and asked in a whisper: "Shall I see you ever again?"

And he had answered on the spur of the moment: "What about tomorrow afternoon?" never expecting that she would take him up on it.

But there she was in his study the next afternoon, half-hidden behind an enormous bunch of cornflowers that exactly matched the color of her eyes. He had had sense enough not to let her go back but to keep her there and then. Not that she had resisted much.

And so began the three happiest years of his life. In the morning he would ride out with Pauline, whatever the weather. Then he would put in three or four hours of hard work with Jeidels, who meticulously took him through every ledger book, explained every property, dissected every balance sheet. Late afternoons and evenings were spent again with Pauline. And which made him the happier, the four hours with Jeidels and the accounts, or the evenings and nights with Pauline and her wild, passionate lovemaking, he would not have been able to say.

Then, inevitably, there came an end and an awakening. His father died suddenly in the remote Hungarian castle where he had spent the last five years carousing with his gypsy girls—a fall from his horse after he had ridden out in the early morning, quite drunk, of course, following a flaming row with his current favorite. Sobieski made the long trip in midwinter to the Carpathian Mountains—they had no railway then, and it took forever to get through the snow-drifted roads—to bring his father's corpse back to Poland and go through a state funeral in Cracow Cathedral with hundreds of dignitaries and relatives, followed by the entombment afterwards in the Sobieski family church.

He was away more than four weeks. When he returned, Pauline was gone.

But Jeidels was waiting for him. "I took the liberty," he began, "of suggesting to Miss Pauline that she return to her father's home. Your Highness is very fond of the young lady, I believe. You had better not see her again. You will now have to travel for several months to introduce yourself as the new head of the House of Sobieski to His Imperial Majesty and to all the family's noble kindred. I have the list here—it's the same one, brought up to date, that was used when your late father, God rest his soul, succeeded His Highness, your grandfather, eighteen years ago. You would not want to take along a young lady of whom you are fond. She would only be insulted and humiliated in a false position.

"Then you will have to spend another six months traveling to the main Sobieski estates to introduce yourself as the new master and meet your local representatives and administrators. Again, it would be humiliating and embarrassing for the young lady to be with you.

"Of course, you cannot marry her. Even if you considered anything so inadvisable, the young lady would never consent as, I believe, she herself has told you. If she stays here with us she will be honored as the young woman whom our beloved Prince ennobled with his affection, respected by all of us. It would be much better, Your Highness, if you were not to try to see her before you leave . . . it can only make it that much harder for you and for Miss Pauline.

"Altogether, Your Highness," continued Jeidels quietly, "I trust that I am not overstepping the bounds of my position when I bring up the question of your future. You have learned from me all I can teach you. Indeed, you are a better administrator than I ever was or ever will be, a better one than my son will be when Your Highness puts him into my place upon my retirement in a few years—Your Highness will remember that we have discussed this several times. I have trained my son for more than twenty years. Your Highness will not take it amiss, I hope, when I say that I know no one with as good a head for business as your own.

"Yet it would be totally inappropriate for a Prince Sobieski to become an administrator of estates and a businessman—it's surely not the right place for Your Highness. And you would also not be content with a life of aristocratic leisure. You knew that yourself, I think, when you asked to spend these years here with me, learning estate administration.

"May I respectfully suggest, therefore, that you try the diplomatic service? It corresponds in the public domain somewhat to the administration of a very great property in the private domain. Of course, Your Highness will make your own decision. But I have taken the liberty of writing to the private secretary of Your Highness's kins-

man, the Prince Metternich-Sandor, the Austrian Ambassador in
Paris, and from all I hear considered the most accomplished diplomat in our country's service today—a worthy successor to his father,
the great Prince Klemens."

Jeidels bent to read from a letter already in his hand: "His Grace
the Prince Metternich-Sandor would be delighted to welcome his
cousin, His Highness the Prince Sobieski, Duke of Przemysl, as his
élève and personal aide at the Paris Embassy at any time . . ."

It was then that Sobieski realized that this old Jew with his skull-
cap, his limp and cane, the trace of Yiddish in his careful High German, was the only person other than Pauline perhaps who had ever
cared for him, had ever seen in him a human being rather than a title
and a uniform, had ever loved him. And in a sudden transport of
emotion he had asked the old Jew for his blessing. When the old man
raised his hand to intone the sonorous Hebrew words of the incanta-
tion: "May the Lord make His Countenance to shine upon you," his
own eyes were brimful of tears, and so were Jeidels's.

He had left the palace the same week without seeing Pauline
again. Eight months later he presented himself in Paris to his distant
relation, Prince Metternich-Sandor, as the new *élève*.

But he had never lost his interest in the management of the estates. Indeed, Jeidels had inculcated in him the ideas and principles
that had made him a very rich man, worth perhaps ten times what he
had been worth when his father died and he had inherited the estates.

It was Jeidels who had preached to him that the future lay with
the railways. "Your noble colleagues, Your Highness," he would say,
"hate the railway and fear that it will bring subversive ideas. But the
ideas will come in anyhow; they are being carried by the wind. Railways carry goods, Your Highness, not ideas. They can make a valuable commodity out of the timber in your forests that is now rotting.
They can create markets for the coal on your domains. They will enable you to send grain to Vienna, and to have the hides from the cows
on your Hungarian grazing lands turned into shoes. What are now
farmlands will become industries once you can ship your products
to market. And the expensive, unproductive palaces which the Sobieskis never use—in Vienna, Cracow, Prague, Budapest, and a dozen

other places—will become valuable real estate, space for office buildings and apartment houses. The cities will grow with the masses the railways bring to them.

"Indeed," Jeidels went on, "I have anticipated this and have bought up all the urban real estate I have been able to get at a decent price in the main cities of the monarchy ever since the railway line from Vienna to Prague was begun thirty years ago. That real estate alone is worth six times what we paid for it."

It was Jeidels who had made him receptive to Hinton and Mosenthal when they first came to him with the proposal for the Bank of London & Austria which had become one of his most profitable investments. Indeed, thought Sobieski, Jeidels had had, fifty years earlier, the ideas and the vision that have since made Hinton Europe's greatest banker.

It was also Jeidels and his teachings who had made him welcome the offer from the two real estate barons, Perkacz and Wald-Reifnitz, to merge his city properties with theirs in the First Austrian Real Estate Company—a move hardly less profitable than the Bank of London & Austria.

But this meant that he had to continue in active management. To be sure, Jeidels's son had been a competent administrator, and so was the present Director-General, the husband of old Jeidels's granddaughter. But the big ideas, the big ventures, and the vision had to come from him; the administrators confined themselves to execution and day-to-day matters.

And so, inappropriate or not, he had never lost touch with the Sobieski Estates and Enterprises, and had also never lost his enjoyment of business affairs. Indeed, his only regret had usually been that he did not have enough time for them.

Now he would visit every one of his main domains and every one of his major factories immediately. He would meet in person every one of his managers and administrators—beginning with a stay on his Polish properties and in the palace to which he had not returned since he had said goodbye to old Jeidels forty years ago.

It would take a few weeks until Pierre had his appointment. Then he would submit his resignation to the old Emperor right away—at the latest when he called on him on his birthday in August as he did every year—and, a day later, to the Minister of Foreign Affairs. By September he'd be an ex-ambassador—able to look at his face in the mirror in the morning and like what he saw.

But, and the thought pierced him with physical pain like an arrow, what would that do to Margit?

Margit

It was a few days—or rather, a few nights—before the Parisian mob attempted to storm the embassy that a noise woke Sobieski as he lay in heavy slumber in an airless servant's room under the eaves, the only space left in an embassy crammed with refugees. It had been an exhaustingly busy day—every minute filled with appeals to him to find food and water and toilets and a place to sleep for frightened, terrorized people. And when word got around that the Austrian Embassy was offering asylum, there was a near-riot outside the gates, desperate men and women trampling each other out of the way in their frenzy to get behind the protection of the walls. Sobieski was worn out, above all by the emotional strain of denying asylum and safety to all but the Austrians, Germans, and Swiss his embassy represented and who, therefore, in international law, he could allow into sanctuary. Finally, well past midnight, he had gone to bed and sunk at once into a deep sleep.

But he was wrenched out of it—or was it just a dream?—by a voice calling insistently: "Cousin Sobieski! Cousin Jan-Casimir!"

Slowly, heavily, he dragged himself back from his stupor. When he at last got his eyes open, he thought: "Surely I'm dreaming." For there, next to his head, stood an apparition—a girl?, a woman?—lit dimly by the flickering candle in her hand. The light reflected glitters of deep red from the hair that was piled high up on her head—the identical red of the hair of the girls and women Renoir painted. (Was that the reason why there was not a single Renoir in his own collection?)

With her other hand the apparition clutched the hem of a nightgown—and what a nightgown! It was the kind then favored by cheap Parisian whores, pink frilly lace that revealed more than it covered, with a deep décolletage in front through which the cleavage of young, firm breasts was clearly visible, and slits along the sides to reveal the thighs. The kind of nightgown, reminisced Sobieski, that was now advertised in *La Vie Parisiènne* and referred to with a salacious leer by junior clerks and schoolboys as a "naughty nightie." It made the child, whoever she might be, look like a little girl playing "grownups" who had put on her mother's clothes.

"Cousin Sobieski," said the apparition in a small, little-girl's voice very close to his ear, "don't you know me? I am Margit Balaton, your cousin. I want you to be my lover. I've wanted you to be my lover ever since you took me on that long walk in Baden a few years back. Don't you recognize me?"

And then Sobieski remembered.

When he had come back from that long walk with the little girl— it was during his tour of introducing himself as the new head of the House of Sobieski to the noble families of his kindred—her mother, the Princess Balaton-Balat, had taken him aside and with much hemming and hawing, asked for a loan. "We are temporarily embarrassed," she had said, "and need the money to send Margit to school."

He was already prepared. The itinerary which Jeidels had written out for him said, in the old Jew's small, clear hand: "Prince and Princess Balaton-Balat will ask Your Highness for a 'loan.' If you decide to grant the request—and I suggest you do so only if the amounts are small and the purpose clearly stated—do not make it a loan. You will never get the money back and it will only cause bad blood. Make an outright gift. And do not give the money to the Prince or the Princess; it will only be gambled or drunk away. Instruct them to send the bills to me and I shall pay directly."

He had agreed to pay the girl's school bills—after all, her mother was a Sobieski, the daughter of his grandfather's younger brother and thus a first cousin to his late father; for her not to be able to keep her daughter in a decent school would have reflected adversely upon him, the head of the House, and on the House of Sobieski altogether. And so for several years now (four? five?) the young cousin's bills from the Sacred Heart Convent in Paris had been paid directly by the Sobieski administration and reported to him twice a year.

Still he rarely, if ever, thought of his young cousin. But he had thought of her earlier that day when he admitted the Sisters of the Sacred Heart and two dozen pupils into the embassy grounds after a mob had set fire to their school. It was the one exception he had made to the rule that only Austrians, Germans, and Swiss would be allowed in. The headmistress of the school had come to thank him. But when he offered to go to the stable, which was all the shelter he could offer, and make sure that she and her students were reasonably comfortable, she had declined rather haughtily. "We do not admit men into the schoolgrounds." Then he remembered Margit. "Is my cousin, the Princess Margit Balaton-Balat, with you or has she managed to get out of Paris in time?" he asked.

The elderly nun had been icy. "You surely know that we can give such information only to a pupil's parents or her guardian"—making Sobieski suspect, of course, that the girl was there. But he soon had other things to worry about than a schoolgirl cousin, and had promptly forgotten her.

"I may have done the headmistress an injustice," flashed through Sobieski's mind; "she may know more about adolescent girls, or at least this one, than I gave her credit for. How, in God's name, did the child smuggle in this awkward, vulgar nightie? And how did she learn where to find me?"

Just then the child, in an even smaller voice, barely audible, asked: "Do you want me to take off my nightgown?"

Sobieski was so startled that he answered without thinking: "No, don't do that. You'll only catch cold."

As soon as he heard himself say this, he knew that he was fatuous—but also that he was endangered. He held his breath, waiting for the child to say the obvious: "But you'll keep me warm"—and he often wondered what he would have done or said then. Only the child just stood there in an agony of indecision, nibbling at her lower lip.

It was absurd, comical, farcical. Sobieski could hardly keep from laughing. But it was also sultry, heavy, risky. For while the girl had a child's face, a child's gestures and a child's voice, the body—only too visible under that dreadful nightgown—was that of a fully developed, fully ripe woman. It radiated such sensuous appeal that Sobieski felt desire rise almost irresistibly within him. He knew that he could not have held back had she but touched him. Yet she remained standing there, one hand clutching the candlestick, the other the nightgown's hem. He fought down the urge to reach out and pull her to him.

It was then that he suddenly knew himself committed to making sure (he didn't know how) that this child-woman would not be harmed by him, and to keeping all harm away from her. He was committed to her trust in him. It was not that he felt an obligation to her parents, though there was one of some sort there. It was not that he would have hesitated to make love to one so young. "She must be sixteen, after all, and I have had plenty of girls younger than that in my bed without any compunction on their or my part."

It wasn't even that the absurdity of the situation made him laugh so hard inwardly that he wondered what would have happened had he taken her in his arms as she wanted him to do. It was something he could not define: a feeling of honor, of chivalry, perhaps, or of awe at her innocence.

For despite the reckless foray into his bedroom, despite her offering herself and despite the whore's nightgown, even despite the dreadful hackneyed phrases the child must have picked up from some of those near-pornographic "shockers" which somehow got past the nuns to be read avidly under the bedclothes by teen-age girls whose lurid imaginations were constantly inflamed by the nuns' harping on the "sins of the flesh"—despite all this, the child was innocence itself.

Suddenly he was no longer a young man at all. Until then he had always been "Mr. Jeidels's pupil, the young Prince who is learning estate management from the old Jew"; or "Prince Metternich's élève who is learning diplomacy from the old ambassador"; or "Lord apRhys's young friend who is learning lechery from the English milord." He was, of course, still only thirty-one. But in that night in Paris he ceased to be "our young man." He matured, became an adult who took responsibility and set example. Above all, he became the older one, the trusted one for Margit . . . "and," thought Sobieski, "that's what I've always been for her ever since."

It took him the best part of an hour to get the young woman to be willing, indeed quite happy, to leave. Perhaps she was, after all, relieved that her adventure stayed "romantic." Whether she really knew what would have happened had he let it go further, he very much doubted. She finally left, giving him a chaste, sisterly peck on the cheek after he had promised to let her write to him, had promised not to marry anyone else, or at least not to do so without first telling her, had promised that he would indeed become her "lover" if she only finished school and became a little older, and had altogether made so many speeches in the mock-heroic vein of the romances she was clearly addicted to that he felt himself almost ready to switch from diplomacy to politics as a career.

Three years later he had married her. As the head of a great princely House, he had the obligation to beget heirs—and that meant marrying someone of equal rank. The Balaton-Balats had sunk low through the improvidence of Margit's father and grandfather; but theirs was still a great name, almost as great as that of the Sobieskis. They had been Hungarian grandees long before the Turks overran the country in the sixteenth century, and then semi-independent lords under the Ottoman rule. In the seventeenth century they had thrown in their lot with the Habsburgs, which led to their becoming princes and being endowed with the richest estates the defeated Turks vacated in western Hungary. And for four generations they had been intermarrying with the Sobieskis and their kindred. Assuredly a Princess Balaton-Balat was an eminently suitable match for a Prince Sobieski.

But also there were Margit's weekly letters: amazing letters in their passion, their physical details, their declarations of desire and longing. How she smuggled them out, he could not even guess. Later on he realized that they must have come to him through Josefa, who by then had left the convent. They arrived punctually every week and made him hot with mixed embarrassment and longing whenever he read them—though they made him laugh, too. Above all, the picture of Margit's ripe body under that flimsy nightgown intruded again and again into his thoughts, his fantasies, his encounters with other women.

And so, a few years after he had moved to Berlin, when Margit was nineteen and two years out of the convent school, he had made good the promise given to her that night—just to get rid of her—and Margit became Princess Sobieski, Duchess of Przemysl—as she, for her part, so she told him much later, had always known she would be ever since that walk with her Parfit Knight as an eleven-year-old child, lonely and unloved.

Margit's body did indeed fulfill the promise it had signaled that sultry night in the Paris garret. It was sensuousness itself. It responded eagerly to his every lead. It gave the more, the more he demanded and demanded the more, the more he gave. If introducing Pauline to the delights of love had been bliss, introducing Margit's body to them was high adventure.

And Margit's body also lived up to the promise of marriage: the production of heirs. In their first five years of married life—the years in Berlin—Margit's body gave him three healthy children, two boys and a girl. Pregnancy and childbirth came easily to that body. Indeed, Margit's body was never more appealing, more voluptuous, more radiant than when it carried.

But the face, the gestures, the voice remained those of a *jeune fille*, of a child just coming into adolescence, and so did her clear, unselfconscious, pealing laughter. Her relationships with people were those of a temperamental fifteen-year-old. One moment she would call you the closest of friends and shower you with endearments; the next she would pout, sulk, and refuse to speak to you—only to make up again within ten minutes amid tears and laughter. Everyone treated her as a lovable, adorable, slightly spoilt child. Young people in particular thought of her as a contemporary rather than a grown woman, a great lady, the wife of a duke and ambassador and the mother of three children.

In their early years in England, in the 1880s, they spent a good many weekends at the Marquess of Salisbury's great house in Hatfield, especially when the Conservatives were out of power and the marquess therefore out of office. Sobieski himself would spend long hours closeted with the marquess in discussions of politics and international affairs. Margit meanwhile would romp with the marquess's children—that vivacious, loud, enchanting brood of young Cecils— acting charades with them, leading them in a raucous treasure hunt through the big house, or playing Cowboys and Indians with them in the woods. The young Cecils soon ceased to treat her as a great lady, a grownup, or a visitor, and began to call her "Margie." And while their father, the marquess—who in all these years of friendship never called Sobieski anything but "Highness" or "Duke"—reprimanded his children for such improper familiarity, he again and again called her "Margie" himself.

Even her own children came to treat their mother as a contemporary, an older sister perhaps. Margit was not particularly interested in them; she gladly let wet nurses, nannies, governesses, and tutors look after them. But still they were close to her. Sobieski himself knew that while not scared of him, as he had been of his own father, they were not at ease with him. But when, for instance, their younger son, at around twenty-four or so, had fallen head over heels in love with a Viennese operetta singer ten years his senior and wanted to marry her, he went at once to Margit to confide in her. Margit, of course, already knew of the *affaire*—one of her maids had heard about it from the young man's valet and promptly told her mistress. She also knew, well before the son came to her, what the singer had not told him: that she had a husband, the coffeehouse proprietor in the provincial town where she grew up, and there was thus no question of marriage and no danger of a *mésalliance*.

Everybody always told Margit everything about people. Gossip clung to her the way iron filings cling to a magnet. Her maids told her all the backstairs tattle, and so did the hairdresser and the masseuse and the coachman's wife. But so too did the ladies in the country houses and the embassies. Margit never read a newspaper—she read little altogether. Yet she always knew a week or two ahead whom the Prime Minister would nominate for a vacancy among the Knights of the Garter, who was to be appointed Bishop of Ely, and, above all, who slept in whose bed or no longer slept there, whose child the newly born baby of a royal duchess really was, how much the rascally valet stole from the rich young lord, his master, and how much commission the artists' models paid him to get them into his master's bed.

Every morning, after her cup of coffee at ten, she'd be on the telephone for two hours—her telephone bill, thought Sobieski, is an outrage, larger than that of the entire Austrian Embassy. When she finally put down the receiver around noon to call for the maids to help her get dressed, she knew more about London society than those great gossips, the duc de Saint-Simon and Samuel Pepys, had known about the court of Louis XIV or the London of Charles II respectively.

Yet she was totally indiscreet—as indiscreet as a child. And no one seemed to mind. Indeed, her greatest charm lay in the manner with which, amid great peals of laughter, she talked of bedrooms and backstairs, of *poules de luxe* and homosexual liaisons, of titled swindlers and family intrigues. The old Earl of Cardiff—Owen Rhys Nevis's grandfather—whose great pet she had been in their early years in London, had once said jokingly to Margit: "You should publish your stories under the title *Tales from Goldoni*." Of course the joke lost all its sparkle when it had to be explained laboriously to Margit, who did not get it anyhow, for she had never heard of Lamb's *Tales from Shakespeare*, though every English child was raised on them. She had never heard of the commedia dell'arte, the dramatic form popular in eighteenth-century Italy, which achieved vivacious hilarity by putting everyday stock figures: the adulterous wife, the lecherous old man, the thieving servant, into predictable, everyday situations. And, of course, she had never heard of Carlo Goldoni, the playwright, who had been to the commedia dell'arte what Shakespeare was to world literature.

Margit was totally, irremediably illiterate, for all the years of expensive schooling with the Sisters of the Sacred Heart in Paris. No school would have made any difference. That Margit was born uneducable dawned on her husband when he heard her say at a dinner party—also in Hatfield, as he remembered—to her neighbor, a distinguished mathematician: "I don't think it nice to discuss multiplication at the dinner table," and realized that for Margit "multiplication" was something to do with begetting children. Margit simply had no ability for ideas, for abstractions, for policy and diplomacy or for books and theories of any kind. She only saw, heard, took in people as individuals, as men and women and children, in their most elemental behavior—their love lives, for instance.

But she was not stupid; far from it. She loved the theater, coming up to London from Horne Abbey, their country seat near Maidstone, three or four times a month to go to a play. She disliked Ibsen, whose plays had been the rage ten years earlier, in the nineties. "He has no real people," she'd say, "only talking ideas." She had, however, become very fond of the new playwright, George Bernard Shaw, and would attend the first night of every Shaw play.

"But Mr. Shaw is even more a playwright of ideas than Ibsen— and such bizarre ideas, feminism, vegetarianism, total abstinence, and socialism," someone would argue.

"I know that," she'd return, "but his characters always get the better of his theories." Mr. Shaw, Sobieski thought, might not appreciate this remark. But it was not the remark of a stupid person. Rather, it was the penetrating insight of an intelligent child. And that was what Margit really was: a highly perceptive child, endowed with a woman's sensuous body.

"But then," mused Sobieski, "real, live men and women are rarely as simple as the stock figures of the commedia dell'arte or Margit's *Tales from Goldoni*." Margit herself was the best proof. There were hidden dimensions to her, riddles that teased and could not be solved, but defied any formula.

There was, for instance, her indifference toward the Evening Parade.

Sobieski was around twelve years old when a woman first shared his bed. His valet must have reported evidence of "wet dreams." For one evening after he had said his prayers with his governor and been sent to his bed, a woman was there waiting for him. She was probably no more than seventeen or eighteen years old herself, Sobieski now thought, a simple, illiterate Polish peasant and one of his governor's maidservants. But she appeared mysterious, sophisticated and mature beyond imagination to the twelve-year-old boy, both delicious and frightening. From then on, there was a young woman in his bed every week, though never on the same day of the week and never the same woman twice in a row, lest he form an attachment.

At sixteen, when he was sent to the Jesuits in Kalksburg for two years of formal schooling, he was told that henceforth he would have an "adult household." He did not know what that meant until the first evening in his new home, the former summer villa of some Viennese nobleman. After dinner he walked to his sleeping quarters alone (the first time without his governor accompanying him) between two valets, each carrying a candelabra with many candles. The servants were lined up in the hall, the men on one side bowing, the women on the other side curtseying. When he reached his private suite, one valet asked: "Would Your Highness want any of the girls to attend you in your bedroom?"

This was the "Evening Parade," which would be performed routinely from then on every night, as it was performed routinely in great houses throughout eastern Europe, but also in Sicily and southern Spain or wherever aristocracy had lived in close proximity to the Moslems and their harems.

Pauline was disgusted by the Parade. "I shan't live in a bordello," she had said, and had banished all women servants below stairs. Lucille, while not saying anything, had done the same. But Margit was utterly indifferent. "When you are with me, I demand all of you," she had once said. "When you are not with me, what difference does it make?"

But above all there was Margit's Josefa.

Josefa

When Sobieski was appointed to London, Margit was pregnant with their third—their last—child. She had repeatedly told him that she was bored with the official life of a diplomat's wife and hoped he would soon resign to live carefree in the palace in Vienna and on his estates in Poland and Bohemia. But when he went to tell her instead that they were moving to London, she was jubilant.

"Now I can ask Josefa to join me as my lady-in-waiting and companion!" she had exclaimed. "I've wanted her to live with us ever since we got married. But she hates Germany and the Germans and refused to come to Berlin, even though she's quite unhappy as companion to that cold, stuck-up countess in Scotland. She likes London, though. I can hardly wait till we move and she's with me again!"

Sobieski had heard, of course, of Josefa—the clever, beautiful, accomplished Josefa—who had been Margit's one friend in the hostile convent school in Paris, her best friend, and the person whom, next to her husband, Margit loved the most. The name, Josefa Kaleska, was familiar enough. The Kaleskis were a respectable family in Austrian Poland with a lineage going back two hundred years. They were even "barons," though they lacked the resources to live up to such pretension, so that they hovered precariously between minor gentry ("Peasants with a title in lieu of a handkerchief," his grandmother had sneered) and genuine nobility. Indeed, one of the Kaleskis—he turned out to be Josefa's oldest brother—was an officer in the Sobieski Cuirassiers. Sobieski was delighted that Margit, in a new, strange city where she did not even know the language, would have someone near her whom she loved, trusted, and could talk to. And so Josefa had joined the Sobieskis within a week or two after their move to London.

Sobieski well remembered the evening when Josefa was first presented to him, curtseyed, and tried to kiss his hand. He was unprepared and quite overwhelmed. Margit was pretty, very pretty, with her Hungarian coloring: her red hair, chalky-white skin, and sparkling green eyes. But Josefa was a classical beauty, a Greek goddess modeled by a great sculptor, with raven-black hair, skin the color of rich cream, and long tapering fingers—the face saved from classical insipidity by high Slavic cheekbones that gave it animation and piquancy. Like Margit she had a soprano voice. But whereas Margit's tended to become shrill when she got excited, Josefa's voice had in it a deep undertone like dark honey. What struck him most strongly, however, were her movements. All the pupils at the Sacred Heart Convent were taught how to walk, how to sit, how to get up. Margit had often amused him by strutting with two books on her head or showing him how to sit down in a chair and get up from it without moving shoulders or head. But Josefa moved with the grace of a trained gymnast.

When Margit noticed his admiration, she was overjoyed: "I knew you'd adore my Josefa; she's the most adorable creature in the world." But Josefa, while smiling pleasantly, had not responded, had indeed paid no attention to him at all.

He was therefore utterly surprised when, a few weeks later, upon entering his bedroom he found Josefa in bed waiting for him. "The Princess has sent me," she said. And her voice forbade his questioning so extraordinary an announcement. Next morning Margit asked: "And did my Josefa please you?" When he in bewilderment asked back: "Why did you send her?" she said only: "We vowed in the convent to share everything."

From then on, for four years it was Josefa who represented Margit in his bed, Josefa who performed the conjugal rites, Josefa who substituted for Margit, was indeed Margit's alter ego and *Doppelgänger*. For somehow he always knew that he was never Josefa's lover, that in truth she never was his "mistress" in the usual sense of the word. Josefa served him in his capacity as her mistress's husband, and was tied to him through her tie to Margit. She never again said, "The Princess has sent me." But without the words being uttered, that surely was how both she and Margit understood the relationship, and how it actually worked out even when Sobieski and Josefa were alone, indeed, even in their most intimate moments together.

But what of the relationship between the two women? What was the tie between them?

Several years before Josefa joined them, in the early 1870s when Japan was opened up to Westerners, the first travelers reported a strange and—to European ears—barbaric custom, which they said prevailed among the country's former rulers. The wife of a lord was expected to find a concubine for her husband, to instruct her in satisfying her master, and then to substitute the concubine for herself in the lord's bed. Years later—indeed, quite recently—Sobieski had mentioned this to the Japanese minister as they sat next to each other at some interminable function—a royal wedding, or perhaps a royal funeral.

He had called it "an ancient custom." But the Japanese demurred: "Not ancient at all," he said; "very much alive. Present Empress, wife of Meiji Emperor, finding herself unable to bear children, searched for and found concubine for Emperor, trained her, and closely supervises her performance both as her husband's bedmate and as mother of her husband's children. Very excellent custom. Greatly improves marriage."

"Indeed," Sobieski thought, "it did do that for our marriage, Margit's and mine." It had restored the relationship to something akin to the perfect trust an eleven-year-old child had given when she put her hand into his without hesitation.

"Still, the analogy with the Japanese Empress doesn't quite work," thought Sobieski. "Margit did bear my children, after all—three of them." Did she begin to tire of him? Or did she fear his getting tired of her? True, when she was forced in the later stages of her third pregnancy to deny him her bed, he hardly missed her and was quite content with whatever the Evening Parade had to offer.

"The Japanese story," thought Sobieski, "might also explain why Margit pushed Josefa into my bed; but not the relationship between the two."

That they had been lovers in convent school, Sobieski believed possible, if not probable. It was what happened between adolescent girls in a convent school where there was only a thin line between kisses, hugs and vows of eternal friendship—all perfectly normal—and erotic stimulation, and between erotic stimulation and erotic fulfillment. However much frowned upon, such schoolgirl affairs were, Sobieski knew, not considered particularly harmful and, at worst, a lesser evil.

He recalled talk of a lesbian scandal in a fashionable school at a dinner party in Napoleon III's Paris. The irrepressible Princess Pauline Metternich, wife of his chief, the ambassador, and the *enfant terrible* of Paris society, had said in her clear, carrying voice: "How much better at that age than an *affaire* with a man!"

Whenever the Princess Pauline said such things, everybody pretended not to hear—only, of course, to relate her gaffe next night at the next dinner party. But the way the ladies (most of high Catholic nobility and themselves convent-schooled) had looked, they knew perfectly well what the Princess Pauline was talking about, and several of them, to judge by the smiles around the corners of their mouths, from personal experience.

Still, the bond between Margit and Josefa was stronger and more enduring than the tie of Eros. It went to the very core of their personalities.

One clue as to its nature, but only a clue, was what Sobieski over the years could piece together about Josefa's early life. Josefa had been the youngest of five children, the only girl, born ten years after the last of her brothers. Her mother had died when she was very small. She thus grew up the only child, in effect, of an aging widower, himself a failure both as a minor civil servant and in managing his pitiful estate. Josefa had proved a brilliant student and had won a much-coveted scholarship to the Sacred Heart in Paris, where she acquitted herself with high honors as a student of languages and history, as a musician (she still played the piano beautifully and sang well), and as prefect in charge of the smaller girls.

She had finished the four-year course in three, and her father then wanted her to come back home and look after him. But she knew that she would have to earn her living and begged him to let her stay a few more years in Paris—with the offer of a new and even better scholarship—to be prepared by the nuns for a position as governess or companion.

Three months later her father shot himself. He had not told his daughter, but he realized that he was dying of paralytic palsy—the affliction the English call Parkinson's Disease—and was rapidly becoming senile in mind and body. Of course, Josefa could not have cured him, could not even have helped him. In fact, he would hardly have known her much longer. But she must have blamed herself, must have held herself responsible for her father's death, and reproached herself bitterly for her selfishness.

"And," Sobieski thought, "she still does. Such imaginary guilt, no lapse of time and no amount of reason and logic can ever assuage."

It was then that Margit arrived in Paris: a lonely, frightened, awkward youngster, just past twelve, abandoned, ashamed and overawed by the accomplished young women from great houses among whom she was suddenly cast. That the two girls, both from far-away frontiers of civilization, both without money, both totally alone, were drawn to each other, was not surprising. And that Josefa earned the eternal gratitude of the child whom she protected, mothered, caressed, sheltered in an alien and hostile world—the first person perhaps in the child's life to offer solace and affection—was not surprising either.

But perhaps Margit did even more for Josefa than the older girl could do for the child. "Even then," Sobieski thought, "even when I first met her a year earlier, Margit had animal vitality, radiant joy in life, and a natural exuberance that shone through her sorrow and her shame. If anyone could have lifted Josefa's depression, her guilt feelings, her self-loathing as a parricide forever stamped with the mark of Cain, it would have been the effervescent, irrepressible Margit, with her gossip, her observant eye and storyteller's tactless tongue, and above all her almost pagan, amoral candor. Josefa could dry a small girl's tears. But Margit could restore laughter and joy to a despairing, lost adolescent."

This perhaps also explained what had from the beginning been to Sobieski the most mystifying element in the relationship between the two: that Margit was the leader, clearly in command. It could hardly be explained on a rational level. No one was more conscious of Josefa's superiority than Margit—her superiority as a student and a linguist (for where Margit butchered every one of the very few languages she knew, Josefa was mistress of half a dozen, perfect in each, without a trace of accent); of Josefa's superiority as a musician (Margit could not carry a tune); of her beauty and the elegance with which she wore even the simplest frock. And Josefa was already an accomplished young woman when Margit first arrived in Paris.

"By now," thought Sobieski, "it makes no difference that Josefa is four years older. But to a twelve-year-old, shapeless, conscious of buttocks that are too big and breasts that are too small, and with the pimples of puberty, the sixteen-year-old Josefa must have seemed a being from a higher world—just as the sixteen-year-old peasant girls appeared to me when they came to my bed when I was twelve.

"Yet finally it is not reason but power," Sobieski reflected, "that counts between human beings. And the power to make the despairing laugh is greater even than the power to give solace and comfort and rock a child to sleep. To restore the despairing to laughter is to restore them to life." That was the power, he speculated, that Margit must have had, even at twelve.

Josefa with her exquisite manners well knew the distance between a poor baroness and a wealthy duke, and between an employee and her employer. She never treated Sobieski except with greatest respect and punctilious courtesy. But she was totally without subservience. She called Margit "Your Highness" when there was company or when the servants were around. But it was "Margit" when the three of them were alone, and the two usually called each other "tu" when they spoke French together, as they liked to do. Still, she deferred to Margit on every decision, waited for Margit to open a topic or to close it, accepted Margit's opinions especially on people, and, it was clear, completely trusted her—very much as if Margit had been an older sister.

But while Josefa thus accepted Margit's authority, she knew that she had by far the better mind—and so did Margit. When it came to matters of the mind, Margit stepped back and Josefa took over. This was a very different Josefa from the one who served her mistress's husband in his bed at night; a Josefa who was her own person, independent, indeed sovereign.

The years of Josefa were the years in which Sobieski almost became what the *élève* of Prince Metternich-Sandor had thought a diplomatist could and should be: a power in the affairs of nations, a maker of history. It lasted only a short time. But during those years he was, he knew, considered the most influential and most remarkable among the younger diplomats, and the one most likely to make a name for himself.

For Sobieski had arrived in London with a firm resolve to build what he called in his mind a "special relationship" between England and Austria—an alliance if possible, but at least an understanding and a counterweight to Austria's dependence on Imperial Germany. Looked at with the hindsight of 1906 this was a pipe dream. But it had by no means been unrealistic twenty-five years earlier. After all, next to Portugal, Austria was England's oldest ally, the two nations having been on the same side in every European conflict since the late seventeenth century. There was then no area of rivalry or even of friction between the two; Austria had no colonial ambitions and neither the desire nor the means to become a naval power.

Yet he had failed, totally. Not because of opposition—there was almost none. Everybody in Vienna and London and even Berlin had thought it a good idea; but no one was willing to act. Only Sobieski had doggedly worked on the plan for four or five years, worked harder than he had ever worked before or since, and long past the point at which there was the slightest hope of success.

During those years it was Josefa with whom he discussed his ideas, his hopes and his fears, his strategy and tactics, and with whom he again and again sat down to appraise his progress. She was realistic; she never thought his chances of success as great as he did in his optimistic moments. But she was also enthusiastic about the plan. Passionately Polish herself, she hated Germans and Russians with equal fervor and saw in Sobieski's alliance the one protection against both, for Austrian Poland, for Austria, and eventually for Europe. Josefa and he would discuss diplomacy in the evenings, with Margit sitting by quietly, listening but saying little or nothing, and then only words of encouragement for her adored Josefa or for him.

The Duke of Avila, recently widowed and lonely, would often join them. He greatly admired Josefa, her knowledge of history and her understanding of politics, her quick ability to cut through rhetoric to the salient point, and her perception of people, most of whom—Salisbury, for instance, or Bismarck—she had never met. Avila, Sobieski thought, would have proposed marriage to Josefa, but for his reluctance to disturb what he realized was a delicate and quite unusual bond between the three of them.

But the duke, normally so astute, had been wrong when he talked of Josefa's having a "man's mind," though it was meant as a compliment. Josefa had indeed a first-rate mind, one of the best Sobieski had come across in all his life. Yet it was very much a woman's mind—as Josefa was all woman, body and mind. She was not a bit "feminine" in the sense in which people spoke of Margit as being "feminine," and surely neither "cuddly" nor "dashing," to use the terms the younger generation (his sons, for instance, or Owen Rhys Nevis) used when they talked of a "womanly" woman.

"No, she is a much older type," Sobieski thought, "the eternal woman who, in Greek drama, remains behind when all the men are dead and gone to chant, dry-eyed, of human vanity and human folly and to renew the race. And," mused Sobieski, "she also reminds me of the most womanly of Shakespeare's women, Portia in *The Merchant of Venice.*" Of all Shakespeare's plays, he thought *The Merchant of Venice* to have the most preposterous plot: no judge, however befuddled and blind, could possibly mistake Portia for a man, despite her lawyer's wig and gown and her false beard. But still, while the plot was as absurd as any Italian opera, Portia was totally believable—and totally woman. Whenever he recalled Josefa's voice, that silvery voice with the dark honey-colored undertone in it, he thought of Shakespeare's Portia.

The liaison with Josefa came to an end when she conceived his child. It was Margit who brought him the news.

"Josefa is carrying your child," she said. "She is quite sure; she has missed two periods. She is ecstatically happy—she always wanted a child. And I am happy, too, that the child she is carrying is your child.

"But," Margit went on calmly, "we don't want any more 'natural' children. One is enough. And Josefa is a lady, not a slut from the gutter. She must not have a child born out of wedlock.

"We have therefore arranged (we did so, actually, some time back, just in case) for her to marry the officer commanding the embassy's military guard, Lieutenant-Colonel von Goellner. He is a widower, middle-aged, with grown children, poor and perfectly willing to appear as the father of Josefa's child. I have told him that you and I will make Josefa and the child financially independent. I have told him, further, that you will get him promoted to colonel right away and to major-general five or six years hence. I'll be the child's godmother and will convey to it one of my Hungarian estates at the baptism."

What neither Margit nor Josefa told him was that this would also mean seeing the last of Josefa.

She remained Margit's closest friend, and, as with the Japanese, the child, a daughter, became Margit's child, as Josefa in his bed was meant to be Margit in a different body. Josefa came to stay with Margit at Horne Abbey every year, but only when he was on the continent. And while she always brought her daughter with her, he never once was shown the child between the day she was baptized in the embassy chapel and the day she was given in marriage nineteen years later, in a country church in Austria.

Five years after Josefa had married him, Von Goellner died—a few months before his promotion to major-general was to come through. Shortly thereafter, Margit found a second husband for Josefa, another widowed, elderly officer, this one already a major-general, whose first wife had been the sister of the chamberlain of Margit's brother, the Prince Balaton-Balat.

The daughter's marriage, a few years ago, was surely arranged by Margit, too. Just as the bride was the illegitimate daughter of the Duke of Przemysl, the groom was the illegitimate son of a Habsburg archduke and of the woman with whom he had been living for thirty years, but whom, being Grand Master of the Order of Teutonic Knights and thus a Catholic priest, he could not officially marry. (Legally, she was the wife of his master of the household who, as everyone knew, was interested only in boys.) Only the wife of the Duke of Przemysl, he thought, could have arranged the marriage of a Von Goellner to a son of the Habsburgs. Nobody else could credibly warrant Josefa's daughter to be a Sobieski by blood.

Sobieski knew that the two women intended Josefa to join Margit for good and to live with her once Josefa's husband, the elderly general, should have died. But Sobieski was completely excluded from his daughter's upbringing, from any say in respect to Josefa's future, from any contact with his former mistress and his youngest child. He did not know whether Margit had planned it this way from the beginning, let alone why. Had it been the two women's idea all along, to give Josefa a child and a husband and the money to achieve both? Was this their way of carrying out their youthful vow to "share everything"? Or was it Margit's way of making sure that she and her beloved Josefa would remain tied to one another? The more he thought about it, the more confused he became. Josefa, he thought, he might be able to figure out. But Margit?

And why had Margit sent Josefa away—only to abandon herself to lovers?

They were always the same: presentable, ineffectual, forgettable young men, usually idle, the younger sons of great families and younger than Margit. Most lasted a few months, a few a year or two. "They meant no more to Margit," he thought, "than the girls I chose at the Evening Parade meant to me—and I could barely remember a girl's face or name a week later. They were affairs of the senses, nothing more."

But then came Owen Rhys Nevis.

"I can't, I mustn't hurt Margit," Sobieski almost shouted aloud, "nor her happiness with Owen."

Lord Owen

"I can't, I mustn't hurt Margit," Lord Owen Rhys Nevis said to himself at almost the same moment, and as he had said to himself countless times these last two days. "I can't, I mustn't hurt Margit—if only because of the Prince."

Never before had Margit been so passionate, so amorous, so ardent. Never before had she excited him so much, demanded more, and given herself so fully or so wantonly. Yet when he made his way back to his own rooms in Thorne Abbey in the early morning hours two days ago, Owen had known for a certainty what he had suspected for some time now: his seven-year liaison with the Princess Margit Sobieski had come to an end.

Of course, she was fifty. Yet she seemed to him more seductive, more desirable, more embraceable than ever. That the skin, especially around the eyes, showed the first signs of aging—even though face and figure still glowed in the bloom of young womanhood—only made her seem more interesting, *piquante*, deliciously naughty. Certainly he never would have guessed the strength of their mutual attraction when they began what he thought was a mild flirtation at the small dinner party her husband had given in Owen's honor—it seemed an eternity ago—after Lord Salisbury had appointed him a Junior Lord of the Treasury in the Tory cabinet. And Margit had shown him pleasures, happinesses, delights—dimensions of his own erotic nature he could not even have guessed at before. Yet it could not go on, it had to be over.

"Tomorrow I'll break it off," had been his last thought, before, back in his own bed, he had fallen into exhausted sleep. "It can't go on," had been his first thought when his man had woke him up with the morning tea and the drawing of the bath a few hours later. And

"It can't go on," had been his thought when, shivering in the grayness of a foggy June morning, he had taken his seat in the Rolls to be driven up to town. As the car rounded the turn into the long beech-lined drive that led to the London road, he had asked his man to stop and had taken a long look at Horne Abbey.

"I shan't ever see this place again," he thought. Then he realized that he had spoken out loud when he saw the startled look on the face of the man who had been driving him to the Sobieski country place almost every week for the last seven years.

But it wasn't just Margit who had been the center of his life these last seven years, to the point where he had neglected the political career that had seemed so important to him at the beginning. In fact, it was not even a liaison with Margit alone. Somehow her husband was also part of it. Both Owen's grandfather and his father had held out the Prince to Owen as the very model of *grand seigneur* and gentleman, and had urged him to cultivate the Prince's friendship. And the Prince, though old enough to be Owen's father ("Of course," thought Owen suddenly, "I always forget that he's sixty-six, sixteen years older than she is") had welcomed him with open arms and made him his companion on the long rides in Hyde Park he took every morning when in London. When the *affaire* with Margit first started, Owen felt therefore quite uncomfortable. But soon, very soon, it became clear that the Prince knew about it, had indeed known that there would be an *affaire* before Owen did himself, and perhaps before Margit did—and that, far from feeling betrayed, he took an almost fatherly pride in the happiness of what he called "you young people."

Everyone in London knew that Prince and Princess had long ceased to be married in any but law and name. There were three children, to be sure. But they were grown up, the oldest only a few years younger than Owen. All three lived in Austria and rarely came to London. And the youngest, the only daughter, was herself married to some nobleman as grand as the Prince himself, minor Bavarian royalty or such, who had been a diplomat and Austrian Ambassador to Spain. Indeed, Prince and Princess lived pretty much apart, since he went to Horne Abbey only for weekends while the Princess did not often come up to London. And that the Princess had had lovers, without making great efforts to be discreet about them, was as

much common knowledge in embassies and country houses as that
the Prince himself was an indefatigable womanizer.

But what first surprised, then disturbed, and finally enchanted
Owen was the Prince's attitude toward his wife. It was not love; it
was concern and care. He was clearly very fond of her, the way one
is fond of a charming child. When they were under the same roof—
if she was at the Sobieski townhouse in Belgravia or he came for the
weekend to Horne Abbey—he would always pay a formal call on her
in mid-morning, having taken his two-hour ride. She would just be
getting up; he would sit with her while she sipped her morning coffee and gravely ask her how she felt and what he could do for her. He
never went so far as to act the Mother in a French farce and say to
Owen: "Be good to her, my son." But he had conveyed the same feeling more than once, saying for instance, seemingly offhand, "I am
delighted that the Princess looks so well and seems so happy."

And yet there was nothing comical, let alone farcical, in this curious relationship. Rather, there was dignity and a sense of humor, genuine affection and, of course, exquisite manners. The Prince was at
every moment what Owen's grandfather and father had called him:
the most gentlemanly of aristocrats. Neither Owen's grandfather, the
eighth Earl of Cardiff, nor his father, the ninth, had been overly fond
of foreigners. They had felt a strong, somewhat old-fashioned resentment of the American heiresses and the German bankers who had
begun to push their way into English society in the last decades of
the old Queen's reign. And though they themselves were inordinately
proud of their ancient Welsh name and lineage, they still sneered
at the clever Irish barristers with their glib Celtic tongues and their
political ambitions. Yet they had admired, indeed embraced Sobieski,
despite his outlandish name and his distinctly un-English marital
and extramarital arrangements.

The Prince, for his part, held the House of Rhys Nevis in equally
warm affection and regard.

"I've had three close English friends," he had said as they walked
together out of the churchyard at apRhys Castle after the funeral of
Owen's father. "Lord Salisbury, whom I first met when he accompanied Disraeli as Foreign Secretary to the Congress of Berlin in 1878,
and who then suggested that I be appointed Austria-Hungaria's Am-

bassador to the Court of St. James's. Your grandfather, who opened his heart and his home to me when I first came to London. And your father, who treated me like a brother. Those three men made me love England and feel more at home here than in the Poland of which my ancestors were kings or the Austria which I serve as ambassador. And now that all three are gone, I feel alone."

And then the Prince, with a gesture of intimacy that was unexpected in so reserved a man, hooked his arm into Owen's as if to say: "But I still have an English son," and added in his usual conversational voice: "I hope you'll be able to come to Horne Abbey this weekend despite your bereavement. I am not yet sure I can make it; but the Princess too mourns your father's death."

And yet the *affaire* with Margit had to be finished, and at once. Whatever her physical attractions, he simply could not stand being with her except in bed. That childish prattle of hers, in the somewhat primitive English with its baby talk and its sprinkling of French words from her convent school days in Paris as a *jeune fille* and the faint Hungarian accent that had charmed him, amused him, aroused him for so many years, now grated on his nerves. The flirtatious manner in which she greeted every male—half shy child, half *cocotte*—had come to annoy if not disgust him. And her conversation . . . he did not think he could stand another evening alone with her, nothing but foolish gossip of liaisons, jealousies, and clandestine assignments. No interest in art or music or nature, no mention of a book or an idea, nothing but the backstairs gossip of ladies' maids.

"But how, how do I break it?" Owen had asked himself as the car sped through Kent toward Croydon and Waterloo Bridge.

He was still asking the question when the car stopped outside his flat in Carlton House Terrace. He could not hurt Margit. He no longer loved her, however much his body longed to possess her still. He no longer could bear her company, no matter how much he craved her caresses. But he was fond of her, the way, he thought, with a wintry smile, the Prince must be fond of her.

"For his sake alone, I cannot, I must not, hurt her. But how, how, how?"

The question still loomed two days later—but he knew then that he could not go on asking it much longer. He had forced himself to go to the House and sit through two evenings of interminable debate about some expenditures of the British Army in India and other equally dreary drivel. He had spent hours in his club listening to the chatter of bored young men. And all the time he kept on asking himself: "How, how, how?" Now it was Thursday, and Margit expected him at Horne Abbey for Saturday dinner. "The Prince will be here this weekend," she had said, "and you know how much he enjoys your company—and I need you." Surely he could wait no longer without being a cad.

For a moment he thought of writing her that he was sick, or perhaps telephoning her, Horne Abbey now having a telephone connection to London. But she would surely come up to see him right away; and anyhow this feeble lie was just a coward's way of postponing a solution. Perhaps the best thing was a formal wire:

> Lord Owen Rhys Nevis presents his compliments to Her Highness the Princess Sobieski and deeply regrets that urgent political business prevents his joining the Princess and His Highness the Prince Sobieski this weekend at Horne Abbey.

This was polite yet unambiguous, final and dignified. But could he be so cold to a woman who had been the center of his life for seven years and who still loved him? And would the Prince ever forgive him for treating his aging child-wife with such cruelty?

By now it was mid-morning. Owen was almost ready to send the telegram as the least of all evils, then bury himself on the back benches of the House of Commons where no Sobieski could reach him, and sit through another evening of inane debate.

"I sound like Orestes seeking sanctuary from the Furies when all I am is a middle-aged man who has become tired of his mistress," he chided himself, and sat down to write the telegram. It was at this moment that his man, who had carefully stayed away from his master ever since they had returned from Horne Abbey on Tuesday morning, came in with a card on a salver:

> *Sir Montgomery Bramlett presents his respects to Lord Owen Rhys and requests ten minutes of His Lordship's time on a most urgent matter.*

Now what could the quack want of him, Owen wondered? "Most urgent"—it sounded ominous. He'd better see the fellow.

"I trust I find Your Lordship in good health," Bramlett began, as pompous, as unctuous as ever. "I am sensible of the intrusion on the time of a busy politician," he continued, greatly increasing Owen's already considerable irritation, "but I would not have come without good reason, although my mission is an unhappy one. I have this morning returned from apRhys Castle. I was called there by your sister-in-law, the Countess of Cardiff, at the urging of my local colleague, Dr. Evans, whom Your Lordship may remember as attending your late father in his last illness. We trained together at Bart's Hospital and I know Evans as a competent and thoroughly trustworthy practitioner.

"Tell me, Lord Owen, have you seen your brother lately?"

"Not since my father's burial four years ago."

"Then you can't know of the recent deterioration in his physical condition. He has been losing a good deal of weight these last months and has become progressively fatigued and weak and listless. Dr. Evans became concerned and urged Lady Cardiff to ask me to come down. I did so and gave the Earl a complete physical examination—and the result, Lord Owen, is far from reassuring."

The doctor stayed silent for a few moments, then resumed: "I have, of course, told neither the Earl nor the Countess. But your brother presents an advanced and, I fear, quite rapid case of Diabetes mellitus, the sugar disease. I see Your Lordship knows what I am talking about and I do not have to explain. Medical science, I am afraid, does not as yet fully understand this insidious condition. But we do know the disease is incurable and irreversible. And in someone as young as the Earl—not yet forty-five—a case of Diabetes mellitus which deteriorates rapidly does not allow for much hope. I am afraid, Lord Owen, that your brother cannot expect to live more than two years at the very most, and I do not myself expect him to be alive even one year from now.

"With this disease"—here Sir Montgomery put on his most unctuous mien and steepled his fingers over his ample abdomen while his voice sank to a confidential whisper—"the patient is likely at any moment to sink into a deep coma from which he never awakens."

"Is there anything I can do, Sir Montgomery?" Owen broke in. "I take it there's a reason for your coming to me with such urgency."

The physician was again silent for several moments. Then "I am reluctant to bring the subject up," he began slowly, "but I feel it is my duty to do so. Your brother has three daughters but no male heir. In his present condition he is quite unable to perform his conjugal duty. Within a year, at most two, I am certain you, Lord Owen, will have become the Premier Earl of Wales, will have assumed the name and dignity of Earl of Cardiff and with it the responsibility for heading and perpetuating one of Britain's noblest, most ancient, and wealthiest houses."

Owen was seething with rage at the man's impudence when the doctor left. To dare tell Owen in so many words to ditch his mistress, mount the first marriageable filly, and start making babies. Who was he, an unknown tradesman's son and hardly a gentleman himself, for all his being the King's physician, to lay down the law to a Rhys Nevis? And then to sound like the phrase book of a German *Oberlehrer*—"conjugal duty" and "begetting offspring"—by the *plume de ma tante* indeed! And the pompous poltroon had still got it wrong in the end: the Earl of Cardiff was not the Premier Earl of Wales; he was Premier Baron as Baron apRhys.

Still, Owen had to admit the fellow had a point, for all his impudence. Of course the title would not become extinct even if he were not to leave behind a legitimate male heir. There were some cousins, descendants of his grandfather's younger brother, perfectly respectable chaps who would look no sillier in ermine than Owen would. But as Earl of Cardiff one did have the responsibilities of a great aristocrat; and breeding was what aristocracy was all about.

Now, he suddenly realized, he had the perfect excuse for the break with Margit. Dynastic, family duties—which a European aristocrat married into a former Royal House would surely understand even better than an English girl.

Yes, the Margit problem could now be solved, though he didn't like having to pretend to her as he would have to do.

But what of the Prince? What would the Prince think of him if he threw over the woman he had so long professed to love so as to keep title and estates in his own line? After all, even without the Cardiff estates he was rich enough, thanks to his mother's property. And could he lie to the Prince?

It was really the Prince, Owen suddenly saw clearly, who mattered, no one else. He could stand the titters and the gossip and even the congratulations of the rest if only the Prince would understand. And then the solution came to him and with such sudden force that he stood motionless for a good ten minutes as in a trance.

"Why don't I go and ask the Prince how to break off with Margit? The Prince is as fond of her as I ever was, perhaps fonder. He'd understand that I cannot hurt her. But he'd also understand why I have to break it off—after all, he clearly fell out of love with her years ago himself."

The Prince with his old close friendship for the House of Rhys Nevis would also understand why Owen had to take seriously the responsibility for being soon its head. Above all, no one Owen knew would better understand the delicacy of being a gentleman and the importance of behaving like one than the man whom the Earl, his own father, had so often called "the first gentleman of Europe."

But go to her husband? This wasn't a French bedroom farce after all, wasn't something by Scribe or Sardou with music by Offenbach and called "My Mistress, Your Wife." What should he say? "Sir, I no longer want to be in bed with your wife." Or, worse still, "Sir, all I want of your wife any more is to be in bed with her." And yet, hadn't some wit said that life does not imitate art, it imitates the bedroom farce? The very thought of going and talking to the Prince had suddenly lifted from Owen's shoulders the weight that had crushed him down for days now.

With a violent lunge he jumped for the bell rope and called his manservant. "I shall need the motorcar in twenty minutes to drive to Prince Sobieski's house in Atherton Square."

And he had the intense satisfaction of seeing, for the second time within a week, indeed, for the second time in the ten years the man had been in his service, a look of total surprise break through the mask of the perfect manservant's imperturbability.

A Tale from Goldoni

"I can't, I mustn't hurt Margit," Sobieski repeated, "and I can't, I mustn't endanger her happiness with Owen."

From the beginning—probably well before Margit knew it herself and certainly long before Owen did—Sobieski had realized that this *affaire* with Owen would be different from all of Margit's earlier ones, different on her side and different on his side, too. From the beginning, he had somehow known that this *affaire* made sense: for Margit, for Owen, and for himself, Sobieski, as well. For while he did not think Owen outstandingly bright or attractive—he was just a nice, well-mannered, pleasant young man of excellent family, no different from dozens of others—he had always had a liking for him, a special regard, and felt toward him something of the same selfless fondness he had felt toward the child Margit. And apparently both Margit and Owen too felt that there was something special to the relationship, something transcending either the raptures of the body or the mutual dependence of the two sexes. They were deeply, touchingly, in love with one another—and at the same time close to him, dear to him, confident of him and trusting him. This was why he could not hurt Margit, could not endanger her precarious happiness with Owen, nor jeopardize her trust in his, Sobieski's selfless devotion.

Yet Margit, he thought, was bound to be hurt—and, he feared, very soon. In all her earlier liaisons, it had been she who decided to break off. "But this time it is Owen who will tire of her first and desert her. He's so much younger, and at their respective ages, the difference in years becomes greater with each passing day. Then Margit will need me, will have to be able to put her hand in mine again and pour out her sorrow and shame to me as she did when being too young rather than growing old was her burden."

If he answered Henrietta's request, then resigned, as he would have to do, he would forever forfeit Margit's trust in him. There were, he knew, situations in which he would resign his ambassadorship regardless of the impact on Margit and her *affaire* with Owen Rhys Nevis. If indeed the saber-rattlers, the courtiers of the heir to the throne, the archduke Francis Ferdinand—men like Hoetzendorf of the General Staff or Aehrenthal of the Foreign Ministry—were to come to power in Vienna, he would resign in short order. Of course they could not dismiss him—at least not as long as the old Emperor lived. But they could make it impossible for him, a Sobieski, a Prince, and a Duke, to serve with dignity and self-respect; and they would surely try. Margit, who cared nothing about abstractions, might not understand that he could not serve as a false front for policies he despised as thoroughly as he despised the policies of the war-lovers. But she did understand honor.

A resignation under such circumstances might not even force Margit's *affaire* with Owen to an end. It was just barely possible that she could and would stay on at her beloved Horne Abbey and see Owen as before while he spent a year or two—until Owen broke it off, perhaps—by himself, touring his domains and estates. No one would expect a lady Margit's age to suffer what despite railways and motorcars and central heating would be strenuous, uncomfortable and dreadfully boring business trips. But even if his resignation for reasons of policy and honor were to lead to the end of the *affaire* with Owen, Margit's trust in him would survive. It would give her pain—pain that was bound to come anyhow. But she could blame the politicians in Vienna and lash out at them as her enemies. She would not blame him; on the contrary, she would be able to see him as the victim and the one to be commiserated with.

But if he resigned for Henrietta's sake and consequently broke up Margit's relationship with Owen—and his resignation *would* break it up, he knew—there would be no excuse, no forgiveness, and no possibility of her ever trusting him again. It would be the ultimate betrayal.

Margit had never been jealous of any of Sobieski's women; she was completely indifferent to them. But ever since she had first learned of her existence, she had been jealous—fiercely, unyieldingly jealous—of Henrietta. At that time, when they were first married, Henrietta was no more than six or seven years old—and of course Lucille had been paid off and left years earlier. But before she ever laid eyes on her, Margit hated Henrietta, fought her, feared her. And Margit was quite right—her instincts usually were. None of the other women mattered.

"Henrietta is the one human being I love," thought Sobieski. "I'm very fond of Margit and I think she knows it. But except for Pauline for a few years (and that was long before I even met Margit, still a child), I have never loved anyone except Henrietta. Margit sensed it at once when Henrietta, still almost an infant, was brought for her annual visit the first year of our marriage and told to curtsey to Margit and say '*Son Altesse Royale*' to her. Margit never again allowed Henrietta into her presence. She knows that she never even came close to being a serious rival to Henrietta in my affections. I realize that Henrietta is cheap and vulgar, greedy and totally cold . . . yet I love her. And Margit cannot, and will not, forgive her for it.

"Of course, she'd know immediately of Pierre's appointment as military attaché—where Henrietta is concerned, Margit's hearing is doubly acute. She'll realize immediately who brought about the appointment—it won't be a secret, anyhow. That's all right: she knows I look after Henrietta and is resigned to it. But she could not accept my choosing Henrietta over her, destroying her happiness to satisfy Henrietta, betraying her for Henrietta's sake. And that is what my resigning to comply with Henrietta's request will seem to Margit. It can only mean I am abandoning her to satisfy Henrietta's greed and assuage Henrietta's burning resentment at being the baseborn brat of a strumpet."

But what was the alternative? Sobieski knew that he could not turn down Henrietta. He had made his decision and could not unmake it. The commitment had been made, after all, much earlier, when Henrietta was born, long before Margit had entered his life. And he had made it to himself, not to Henrietta. Still, he had learned to examine the alternatives before saying "Never." Would it make any difference if he ignored Henrietta's request and stayed on as ambassador until he was forced out? Would it help Margit and his relations with her? Would it help him?

On reflection, he thought not. Certainly, it would irreparably damage his relationship with Henrietta. There would be no rupture—

Henrietta was far too greedy to give up even one penny she might get out of him. But what was now greed would turn to avarice, what was now amiability would turn to hypocrisy and falsehood, what was now willingness to suffer his affections would turn into the prostitute's barely concealed scorn for her customer. He'd prefer an open break, but he knew he would demean himself rather than endure one.

Yet it would not help Margit or his relationship with her; it would not help at all. The bond of trust would snap, if only because he could not but blame Margit for losing Henrietta. And somehow—he did not know how but was sure of it—the bond between Margit and Owen would rip apart too. Then he would have repulsed Henrietta for nothing. And when Margit's hour of need came (and it was surely imminent) he would not be there to help her, to take her hand in his and be again her Parfit Knight.

If Owen's mistress had not been his own wife, Sobieski would long ago have told the young man to make an end of the business, the way the old Jew, Jeidels, had told him, forty years ago, to end his *affaire* with Pauline. Every day of dragging it out meant in the end more pain, more suffering for Margit, and more humiliation. To be sure, once in a very great while a love affair between a younger man and a much older woman lasted into their old age. Disraeli was the only recent example perhaps, with a wife as much older than he as Margit was older than Owen, his devotion to her outlasting forty years of marriage and even her death well past eighty. But Owen was no Disraeli, no great romantic; he was thoroughly conventional and without imagination, and would soon want a home and children and a wife to keep a great house for him rather than being satisfied with his bachelor flat and weekends with an old mistress and her even older husband.

Still, Owen was not his concern. Whatever wound he might suffer—and Sobieski did not think it would be a deep one—would heal soon enough.

Margit was his trust, and Margit's trust in him. This precluded his speaking to Owen. If he did so, Margit would know it at once and would rightly consider it as much a betrayal as his sacrificing her to Henrietta.

Was there then no solution, no way out? "Of course," thought Sobieski, "there usually is one. But usually it is also a solution 'in theory' only, like my Anglo-Austrian alliance of twenty-five years ago."

There *was* one solution acceptable to Margit and befitting her temperament. If she could see herself as sacrificing herself for Owen, "the man she loved," if she could act the romantic heroine grandly renouncing happiness, youth, and love for the sake of Owen's future, for his honor and to make him happy—that, Sobieski knew, would be the one solution Margit could accept.

She would welcome such an end to the *affaire*. In her *Tales from Goldoni* there had been too many liaisons between older women and younger men for Margit not to know how the tale usually ends and not to welcome a different ending for herself.

If only this *were* one of Margit's *Tales*, with its stock characters and its happy third-act curtain! There the rich uncle died at the right time, the handsome shepherd was revealed as the lost prince who could thus marry the princess who had so faithfully loved him, the clever servant smuggled in the lover disguised as an aunt or smuggled out the hero's beloved disguised as an elderly notary. Yet such endings happened only in the *Tales from Goldoni*.

"For me and Margit and Owen and Henrietta there is no rich uncle, no prince in disguise, no clever servant, and no solution," thought Sobieski. "At least I can't see any. And yet I have only two days in which to find one. It's already Thursday. Tonight I have to go to another official dinner. Tomorrow night I'll give my own small dinner party for the two dignitaries from Vienna. And on Saturday morning, I must go down to Horne Abbey to spend the weekend with Margit and Owen Rhys Nevis. By then I'll have to decide."

The repeater watch in his waistcoat pocket rang out. Twelve-thirty already. Time to get changed and walk over to luncheon at the embassy. Sobieski was so weary and felt so weighed down with years that he was greatly tempted to forget all about lunch and the embassy. But the long years had disciplined him; he forced himself, almost dizzy with the exertion, to get up from his chair.

As he was putting Henrietta's letter back into the secret drawer, his valet entered the room carrying a tray with a card on it. "I apologize for disturbing Your Highness," the man said; "but His Lordship insisted."

The card read: "Lord Owen Rhys Nevis." Underneath his name, Owen had written:

I must see you for five minutes.
It is extremely important.

2. Hinton

The Panic

He knew it as soon as he turned off Jermyn Street and into the passage to the Square between the coach houses. He smelled it as he crossed the Square's private garden, over the heavy scent of the French lilac in bloom, the French lilac which had been her favorite and which he had planted for her when they first moved in, more than twenty years ago. He felt it, whether tremor or sound, before he mounted the three broad steps between the hitching posts. When the door opened, before he could even touch the bell, the moan engulfed him. It was not human, more elemental even than the wail of an animal in agony. It seemed to issue from the very walls—low, pounding, pervasive—carrying with it the stench of putrefaction and decay, of death and pain and fear. He had no need to read the note, written in a stiff schoolgirl hand, which his valet wordlessly held out to him on a salver:

> Sir, Madam's pain has begun. I sent for the other nurses as arranged. I sent for Sir Montgomery's assistant, who came and examined Madam; Sir Montgomery himself will come in the morning. I would suggest your coming up to Madam's room when you get home. Respectfully, Nurse Rogers.

Hinton let the moan carry him up the two flights of stairs to the apartment she had refused to leave since he first brought her to London, but which—the thought flitted through his mind—she would have to leave soon, dead. Stairs and halls were glaringly bright. Nurse Rogers had lost no time in replacing Melissa's dim, mysterious candles with the brightest electric lamps, as if light could push back death and suffering. But the bedroom was so dark, only one night-light burning in a corner, that he had to wait until his eyes adjusted. The bed had been moved into the middle of the room.

And there lay a something, no longer a woman but a pulsing moan. Just a few months earlier, when he had left on his annual trip for America, she had been so grotesquely, so obscenely fat that her flesh rose like a mountain out of the bedclothes. Now he could barely make out the shrunken body under a blanket which the nurse had tucked in as tight as a winding sheet.

Next to the bed still sat Anna, as she had always sat since the first moment so long ago in the tawdry nightclub dressing room: straight-backed, motionless, soundless, with her cat-green eyes that glittered in the dark fixed unblinkingly on her goddess, her mistress, her dying sister.

A tug at his sleeve; a nurse whispers something urgent. But he is swamped by panic, he flees blindly, unseeing, down the garishly lit stairs, past the valet who seems not to have moved at all, through the green baize door into the womb of his study. Panting and trembling as if from extreme exertion, he drops into his chair. Only then does he notice that he is still carrying his umbrella, and wearing top hat, coat, and gloves.

Then his fingers encounter a piece of paper in his coat pocket. He has to look at it a long time before he recognizes the familiar shape of a telegram. Somehow he knows that he has seen it before, somehow he knows that it is important. But he is like a man who dreams that he must wake up, dreams indeed that he has woken up, and yet cannot open his eyes. It takes supreme effort, seemingly for an eternity, before his eyes make out his own name, "McGregor Hinton, Esq.," on the piece of paper. And he has to focus deliberately, like a man in a drunken stupor, before he can read: "Traveling up on evening train. Please meet Lady Bancroft, Sheldon, Hinshaw, Eldridge, myself, Bancroft Terrace ten tomorrow morning, Bancroft."

Then, all of a sudden, he is fully awake and the day comes rushing back at him in full spate.

Freddie Bancroft

Since his wife had become so ill, Hinton always waited at home for the doctor's morning call before going off to the office. Today in the morning—or was it already past midnight and had become "yesterday"?—the doctor—not Sir Montgomery Bramlett but one of his assistants, as Bramlett had been called to the country—had taken longer than usual. And when he finally came down he looked grim.

"I fear the morphine is becoming ineffective. The lady's pain will soon be controllable no longer." (Hinton noticed with wry amusement that the doctor, though by now a regular in the house, still said "the lady" rather than "Mrs. Hinton" or "your wife.")

"Nurse Rogers has instructions and knows where to find me," the doctor continued. "Tomorrow morning Sir Montgomery is expected back in town and will call himself."

Then, just as he was about to step into his motorcar to be driven back to the Bank, Hinton had been called to the telephone—something quite unheard of. The Bank had orders not to call him, and no one else was supposed to know that he had a telephone.

"Sir Roger Smithells has telephoned," said his private secretary at the Bank, "and requests your immediate presence at the Foreign Office"—and Hinton could hear how excited the man was. "Sir Roger asks that you not tell anyone."

When Hinton reached Whitehall twenty minutes later and was immediately ushered into the Assistant Secretary's office, he found two other visitors already there: old Mr. Eldridge, who had served three generations of Bancrofts as solicitor; and a tall, heavy-set man, whom he knew he had met but could not place at first.

"This is Chief Inspector Brayton from Scotland Yard," Smithells said.

And then Hinton remembered. He had met the policeman when the Bank of England discovered six weeks ago that some of the hand-made paper for its twenty-pound notes was missing, and had called in Scotland Yard's Special Branch for a hush-hush session with the Bank's Governor and Court. He had met Brayton again a week later, when the Chief Inspector reported that the retired supervisor of the Bank's paper stores—who was supposed to live in a Richmond cottage and grow roses or cabbages—had disappeared without leaving an address.

"I am afraid, gentlemen," Smithells said, "that the Chief Inspector has very bad news."

The policeman pulled a piece of paper from his briefcase. "This telegram," he said, "came in cipher around three this morning from an inspector of mine attached to the Sureté in France and currently on the Riviera. It reads:

AT EIGHT O'CLOCK LAST NIGHT, WEDNESDAY, A UNIT OF THE SPECIAL BRANCH OF THE Sureté, ARMED WITH A SEARCH WARRANT ISSUED BY THE *Juge d'instruction* AT NICE, RAIDED THE VILLA OF LORD FREDERICK BANCROFT, OLDEST SON AND HEIR OF LORD BANCROFT OF BEECHHURST, HONORARY CHAIRMAN OF BANCROFT BROTHERS, MERCHANT BANKERS IN LONDON. THEY FOUND IN THE CELLAR OF THE VILLA A PRINTING PRESS OF THE LATEST DESIGN, A LARGE QUANTITY OF SPECIAL BANKNOTE PAPER ANSWERING IN EVERY PARTICULAR TO THE DESCRIPTION OF THE PAPER FOR TWENTY-POUND NOTES MISSING FROM THE BANK OF ENGLAND, SPECIAL PRINTING INKS IN TUBES WITH BANK OF ENGLAND MARKINGS, A COMPLETE SET OF ENGRAVERS' TOOLS, AND 973 BANKNOTES OF TWENTY-POUND DENOMINATION WITH NUMBERS NEVER RECORDED BY THE BANK OF ENGLAND AND IDENTICAL WITH THE COUNTERFEIT NOTES ALREADY IN THE POSSESSION OF THE Sureté. APPREHENDED IN THE VILLA WERE LORD FREDERICK HIMSELF; CAPTAIN RICHARD HUMBRETH, YOUNGER BROTHER TO SIR WILLIAM HUMBRETH, BARONET, OF HUMBRETH HALL, WARWICKSHIRE, AND LORD FREDERICK'S CONSTANT COMPANION FOR THE LAST SEVERAL YEARS; TWO MALE SER-

VANTS; AND A PERSON WHO GAVE HIS NAME AS SMITH BUT IS BELIEVED TO BE ANTON MEES, FORMERLY ENGRAVER AT THE RIJKSBANK IN THE HAGUE AND SOUGHT ON COUNTERFEIT- ING CHARGES BY THE POLICE FORCES OF SEVERAL EUROPEAN COUNTRIES. LORD FREDERICK DISCLAIMS ANY KNOWLEDGE OF THE PRINTING PRESS, THE ENGRAVERS' TOOLS, THE PAPER OR THE BANKNOTES. BUT CAPTAIN HUMBRETH AND THE SO- CALLED MR. SMITH HAVE DECLARED IN SWORN STATEMENTS, GIVEN THE POLICE IN MY PRESENCE AND THAT OF THE BRIT- ISH VICE CONSUL IN NICE, THAT LORD FREDERICK INITIATED THE PLAN, ENGAGED BOTH THE MISSING NOTEPAPER SUPERVI- SOR OF THE BANK OF ENGLAND AND THE ENGRAVER, BOUGHT THE PRINTING PRESS, AND MASTERMINDED THE CONSPIR- ACY, IN WHICH IT WAS PLANNED TO PRODUCE £100,000 WORTH OF COUNTERFEIT TWENTY-POUND NOTES. THE ARRESTED MEN ARE BEING HELD OVER THE WEEKEND AND WILL BE ARRAIGNED BEFORE THE *Juge d'instruction* IN NICE ON MONDAY AFTERNOON, WITH THE Sureté RECOMMENDING THAT THEY BE REFUSED BAIL UNTIL TRIAL.

"Surely," Mr. Eldridge interjected, though his voice lacked strength, "the French police can't suspect the oldest son and heir of an English peer of counterfeiting. It's absurd!"

"I am afraid, sir," the policeman replied, "that they not only sus- pect him. They have enough proof to be sure of conviction."

"The Riviera police have been concerned with Lord Frederick and Captain Humbreth for some time," Chief Inspector Brayton contin- ued. "And, since it is my job, as Sir Roger knows, to work with con- tinental police forces, the French have repeatedly talked to me about the two gentlemen ever since they first settled on the Riviera four years ago. Of course, after what happened here in London earlier, the two were not allowed into the Monte Carlo Casino—I presume you gentlemen know what I am talking about. But there were rumors of very peculiar goings-on at Lord Frederick's villa, involving both men and women. The French police do not, of course, want any scandal on the Riviera. They have therefore been wondering for some time how to prevail upon Lord Frederick to move elsewhere. Frankly, they have been worried about some of the nastier stories getting to the sensational French or American journalists, of whom there is always an abundance on the Riviera, especially during the winter season. And I myself have been worried even more about a blackmailer getting his hands on some of these stories, especially as a prominent banking house such as yours, Mr. Hinton, is so very vulnerable.

"But, of course, no one suspected anything like counterfeiting. Indeed, both Mr. Humbreth and the person who calls himself Smith assert, according to a second telegram from my inspector, which came in just before I called Sir Roger this morning, that it was precisely the belief you voiced, Mr. Eldridge, namely, that Lord Frederick Bancroft would be above suspicion, that made the idea appealing to the gang.

"A few weeks ago, shortly after the Bank of England called me in the first time, the madam of one of the *maisons privées* in Nice came to the police with a particularly ugly story. A woman in her establishment had been hired for a week by Lord Frederick and returned to the house brutally injured. I shall spare you the details, gentlemen, though I am afraid they will come out at the trial—they are the most revolting I've heard in my twenty-eight years on the Force. Of course, these women are being paid for such things, and I suspect that the madam knew very well what kind of entertainment her customers had in mind, and the girl too. Still, she was so badly injured that her life was feared for for several days, and she'll bear scars the rest of her life. The madam was afraid the girl would die, so she came to the police with her story, and also admitted that Lord Frederick, when she had gone to him to complain, had given her a hundred pounds in twenty-pound notes to keep her mouth shut.

"The notes looked all right, but this was just after we had informed police forces in major resorts of the missing twenty-pound banknote paper. The French checked the numbers on the notes the woman received from Lord Frederick and found that seven of them had numbers which the Bank had never recorded.

"They were the cleverest forgeries I've ever seen"—and here Hinton thought he detected a faint note of admiration in the policeman's voice. "We sent our best expert down and he had a hard time at first finding anything amiss. But they are definitely forgeries.

"Then, of course, the Sureté in Paris took over, and we detached one of my men to work with them. Regular surveillance of Lord Frederick and of everyone in the villa was begun, and within the next three weeks Lord Frederick and the other inhabitants of the villa passed another twenty of the twenty-pound notes with numbers unknown to the Bank of England. Several of them were passed by Lord Frederick himself, which will make it difficult for him, I'm afraid, to convince the judge at the trial that he knew nothing of what was going on."

"And what will happen now?" Smithells asked after a pause; Hinton had thought it better not to say anything himself.

"French law allows the police to hold a suspect incommunicado for three days, and Sundays don't count," Brayton answered. "That's why the raid was made late on a Wednesday. The French police can keep the five arrested men without publicity over the weekend. But on Monday afternoon they will have to announce the arrest and tell the story. Fortunately, it's off-season now; there are few visitors and even fewer reporters on the Riviera in June. But they'll be down there like flies after honey within forty-eight hours—and every newspaper in the world will have the story. Even if the details of the orgies at Lord Frederick's villa don't come out when those vultures of the press go to work (and I don't see how that can be avoided), they will, of course, be trumpeted at the trial. You can trust a French prosecutor to make the most of stories of perversion in high places, especially if an English lord is involved."

"And what do I tell the family?" quavered Mr. Eldridge, suddenly sounding like a very old man.

"I'm afraid the family had better be prepared for a shock," said the policeman grimly. "Lord Frederick, if convicted, will be deported to Cayenne and Devil's Island as a common criminal."

Hinton had spent the rest of the day in futile efforts to concentrate his thoughts. He did not want to be at home, and he could not go to the Bank. After dropping off Mr. Eldridge at the solicitor's office, he had himself driven to Kew Gardens, where since his earliest days in London he had done his most focused, clearest thinking. But though it was early June, the best time of the year, with rhododendron, iris, azalea, and lilac all in full bloom and a cloudlessly blue early summer sky, Kew had failed him.

He knew intuitively that it was not Freddie Bancroft, his past misdeeds or his future punishment, that he needed to think through, needed to resolve. Yet he could not tear his mind away from the wretch. The news had stunned him; but it had not surprised him. Freddie Bancroft had been aiming himself with deadly accuracy at self-destruction and catastrophe for far too many years for his ruin to cause surprise. The only thing one could not have predicted was the specific—and, Hinton thought, singularly imaginative—form that his latest outrage had taken.

Otherwise, Freddie was only too predictable, had indeed been predictable since adolescence when he was regularly expelled from school after school amid dark rumors of homosexual gangs, senseless cruelties to younger boys, and outrages against kitchen maids. After three years at Oxford, he had been sent down without a degree. An old friend of Hinton's from undergraduate days, who by that time was a senior tutor at Freddie's college, had hinted guardedly at a satanic cult, with Freddie as its high priest, at black masses with sexual orgies, the drinking of human blood, and ritual whippings of prostitutes from the town. The Bancroft money then bought a commission in the Guards—military discipline, Freddie's father had hoped, would "straighten the boy out." But four years later the same stories reappeared—plus a new one of cheating at cards—and Freddie was asked to resign his commission.

Another try, this time as a junior attaché at the British Embassy in St. Petersburg: if Freddie Bancroft had not enjoyed diplomatic immunity, the Russians would have tried him on a murder charge when a woman prostitute engaged for one of Freddie's orgies died from a whipping he had administered. It was then, at Mr. Eldridge's urging and despite Freddie's mother's tearful pleas, that the Bancroft wills had been changed. Freddie, though the eldest son, was excluded from inheriting any property, was debarred from any share or position in the family bank, and was put on a fixed, though still generous, allowance.

Shortly thereafter he teamed up with that other scoundrel, another cashiered officer, Captain Humbreth, whose own family had disowned him. Three or four years later came a scandal which even the Bancroft money and the Hinton influence could not entirely hush up. Freddie Bancroft and Captain Humbreth were caught at White's with several sets of loaded dice and marked cards on them. Only speedy flight to the continent saved the two from arrest, prosecution, and jail sentence.

By now, Hinton had to agree with Mr. Eldridge, nothing could save Freddie. And Hinton also had to agree with Mr. Eldridge that there was still worse to come.

"Take my word for it, Mr. Hinton," Mr. Eldridge said, when, on leaving the Foreign Office, they drove together to the solicitor's office, "Lord Frederick will survive Devil's Island. Then, as those ex-convicts do, he'll marry a black prostitute in Cayenne and have children by her. I can't face it," Mr. Eldridge wailed; "a black son of a convicted felon and a Negro whore taking his seat in the House of Lords as Lord Bancroft of Beechhurst!"

Why had Frederick Bancroft, gifted, indeed brilliant, handsome as the Fallen Angel, beloved and adored by his parents and especially by his mother, and so full of charm as to be all his life the darling of men and women alike—why had he, from boyhood on, been filled with a manic rage to revenge himself, bent on destroying himself and his family?

Hinton had discussed the riddle of Freddie Bancroft with Mr. Eldridge scores of times before.

"In these enlightened days," Mr. Eldridge had once said, "we no longer believe in moral insanity as my father's generation did. Now we speak learnedly of brain damage, which sooner or later science will be able to cure through corrective surgery. Or we speak of some profound psychic shock in the womb or early infancy, which sooner or later psychiatrists will be able to repair through corrective education."

"But, Mr. Eldridge," Hinton had replied, "these are futile attempts to cover the horror of the unknown with whatever figleaf suits the prevailing fashion. We know just as little about the Freddie Bancrofts as we did when we called them 'possessed' and tried to exorcise the Devil in them with bell, book, and candle!"

"It's because of the Freddie Bancrofts," Hinton added, "that men need a religion, a sense of the supernatural. It isn't because of death—

death is a natural event we share with all creatures. There is wisdom in the German fairy tales which speak of 'Gevatter Tod,' 'Godfather Death,' who is with us and looks after us from the moment we are born to our natural parents. It's evil that haunts us—an evil that we cannot explain by nature alone." And Hinton had long ago concluded that Freddie Bancroft presented a deeper mystery than any he, Hinton, had ever had to unravel; a deeper one, indeed, than he, for all his trained analytical skill, could hope to unravel.

And yet, sitting under his favorite copper beech in Kew Gardens, he had also known that it wasn't Freddie Bancroft he needed to think about. The catastrophe of which Freddie was both villain and victim, both cause and effect, would go on to its foreordained end—not as a tragedy, but, as Mr. Eldridge had divined, as dark, bloody farce. Freddie and his fate were not central, not the issue that needed to be resolved before Hinton could sit down with the Bancrofts on the morrow. It wasn't even the terrible hurt and injury Freddie's disgrace would inflict on the person who loved him so passionately, his mother, nor the mud that would bespatter anyone connected with the Bancrofts—Hinton himself, first of all, as the head of Bancroft Brothers. No, all this was somehow secondary, somehow peripheral. But what, then, was the real issue?

In mid-afternoon Hinton had himself driven to his club to await the telegram from Lord Bancroft, which, as expected, summoned Mr. Eldridge to the family meeting with Freddie's parents, Lord and Lady Bancroft, and the two family partners remaining in the Bank: Freddie's cousin, Lord Sheldon Bancroft, the oldest son and heir of Freddie's uncle, Viscount Claymont, who, in his eighties, was retired from bank and public life alike; and Freddie's younger brother, the Honorable Hinshaw Bancroft. It was to him, Hinton, that all of them would be looking for the way out, as they had been looking to him in every crisis since he had been recalled from Vienna to London, almost a quarter of a century ago, to save family and bank from bankruptcy, scandal, and disgrace. Yet he still could not seem to concentrate, could not define the central issue; and he was just as unable to concentrate when he left the club in the long June twilight to walk back to his house and the dying woman who was legally his wife.

Riemann's Mantra

"Don't define a problem, organize the set," Georg Friedrich Riemann, the great mathematician, had said in the first Goettingen seminar that the awkward young McGregor Hinton with his brand-new mathematics degree from Oxford had been permitted to attend. It was held in Riemann's bedroom, as the master, slowly losing his fight with the phthisis that was to kill him three years later, was already too ill to lecture.

The simple sentence, delivered in the hoarse whisper of the very sick, had struck Hinton with the force of the lightning bolt that smote Saul on the road to Damascus. He would never again see the same world through the same eyes.

Years later, Hinton chanced upon one of the tawdry Theosophical tracts that littered Melissa's apartment and read of the mantra which the Indian swami bestows upon his disciple. He then realized that Riemann's saying had been his own mantra all along—though it was a Western rather than an Eastern mantra. The Indian sage gives the mantra to the disciple to meditate on so that he may understand himself. Riemann's mantra was Hinton's tool for action rather than for meditation, and for understanding the world rather than for understanding himself. But whenever he needed to think, to understand, to decide, he forced himself to define the set rather than define the problem.

Hinton knew that Riemann's mantra had made him a better banker, and a more successful one, than all but two men of his generation: John Pierpont Morgan in New York, and Georg Siemens, already dead, in Berlin.

To be sure, Julius von Mosenthal in Vienna, with whom thirty years ago he had founded his most successful venture, the Bank of

London & Austria, was better as a negotiator. Hinton was amazed anew every time by the uncanny prescience with which Mosenthal, before even sitting down to negotiate, knew to the last penny and the last footnote what the final agreement would be, and by Mosenthal's intuitive feel for the slightest nuance, the slightest shift in the other side's position, the slightest sign of any disagreement among the other side's people. And Ernest Marburg of Maimon & Marburg, Hinton acknowledged without envy, was greatly his superior in structuring a financial deal—a genius in using different financial instruments to create what Marburg called a "financial symphony."

Yet these two men, perhaps because they were virtuosi, tended to work on the individual problem, the individual transaction, the individual deal, rather than on the "set," the basic long-range strategy, or what Georg Siemens had called the "entrepreneurial mission." "Siemens," Hinton thought, "is as unknown to the general public and even to most bankers as J. P. Morgan, the Banker-Prince, 'Il Magnifico,' is trumpeted and has become the very symbol of money and power. But Siemens had been an even more successful banker. The public thinks Imperial Germany is Bismarck's handiwork. But it's just as much Georg Siemens's creation. Through the Deutsche Bank he founded in 1870 to industrialize a still agricultural Germany, he has created the industrial and technical Great Power without which Bismarck's Germany would be hollow bluff. And Siemens, from his earliest days on, always treated the individual problem, investment, or transaction, as an element within a configuration, part of a whole, a specific within his 'set.'"

Hinton knew that his own entrepreneurial missions were not nearly as bold as J. P. Morgan's vision of an industrial continent or Georg Siemens's goal of creating through industrial development national unity, economic strength, and a liberal society. Still, like his two masters, Hinton had based himself on organizing the set, on defining his entrepreneurial mission, rather than on being clever. Indeed, whereas both Morgan and Siemens had only one set, one entrepreneurial mission throughout their lives, he, Hinton, had had two.

When he first joined Bancroft Brothers as a very young man and hardly more than a clerk, although he had an Oxford degree and a doctorate in mathematics from Goettingen, he had invoked Riemann's mantra. He realized then that the traditional merchant banks like Bancroft Brothers were being made obsolete by their own success. In the generation before Hinton, Freddie Bancroft's grandfather, the first Viscount Claymont, had daringly used traditional merchant banking—the financing of international trade and international investment—to convert his inherited small firm of sleepy Baltic timber merchants into a financial giant, overshadowed only by the very wealthiest, the Rothschilds or the Barings. But, as Hinton soon saw, its very success had made the traditional merchant bank outgrow its financial base. No matter how rich the partners were, the resources of a family bank were no longer sufficient to finance international trade and investment. To do what the merchant bankers had done successfully in the first half of the nineteenth century required, as the young non-banker Hinton soon realized, a very different vehicle in the second half of the century. It required the resources of the emerging middle classes, made wealthy or at least comfortable through the growth of world trade and world investment.

Georg Siemens in Berlin—also a non-banker, though a legally trained civil servant rather than a mathematician—saw the same shift. He founded a new bank to channel deposits from the public into industrial development and international trade. But Hinton already had a bank, Bancroft Brothers, and so he defined his "set," his "entrepreneurial mission," as the use of the resources of a successful merchant bank such as Bancroft to found and to control banks created in the image of Siemens's Deutsche Bank. He was going to be the banker's banker. Thus, it was only logical for Mosenthal to come to Hinton with the idea of starting such a bank in Vienna, through which to develop industry in Austria, and to do so by taking into partnership the enormously rich but totally illiquid great nobles, such as the Prince Sobieski, for instance, with their estates as the bank's first clients.

Fifteen years later, when Hinton returned to London after five years in Vienna during which he and Mosenthal successfully built the Bank of London & Austria into one of Austria-Hungary's most profitable financial enterprises, he realized that his original entrepreneurial mission had made itself obsolete through its very success. It was then that, again using what Riemann had taught him, Hinton delineated his second, even more successful "set": a world economy with the Western countries as center and market for the non-industrialized, raw material-producing, colonial world.

Hinton had once said to J. P. Morgan: "Our generation has seen not only economic but above all social change. Europe—with America traveling the same path not far behind—has been transformed into an urban industrial society. When we began, Europe was still primarily rural, primarily pre-industrial. Goettingen was still a village when you and I first went there as graduate students in the fifties and sixties—fields and woods only a few minutes' walk from the town's center, houses like the one where I boarded, with a thatched roof still, and a pump in the yard as the only water supply. Just fifteen years later, when I stopped over to spend a few minutes at Riemann's grave, Goettingen had become a city. There were trams, some already electrified, running on the main streets; half a dozen or so of those massive, arrogant bank buildings the Germans love rearing their five or six stories on a new, busy *Bahnhofsplatz*—and most striking of all, factories and towering smokestacks all around the town where you and I saw only wheatfields and apple orchards."

It was on this visit to Goettingen, Hinton concluded, that he suddenly had a vision of Europe as a giant maw, gulping the products of the non-industrial world, with an exploding urban population and an exploding manufacturing industry demanding ever more food and fibers, metals and industrial materials. It was then that he first perceived a new "entrepreneurial mission": to use finance to create the supply to the new industrial world, its urban population, its factories.

J. P. Morgan had immediately grasped Hinton's entrepreneurial mission. Indeed, he adopted it for himself, though he always gave Hinton credit for the successful ventures in which he organized the raw materials, the pre-industrial resources of his own country, to feed the burgeoning millions of America's exploding cities in the East and Midwest and to supply her fast-growing manufacturing industries.

Georg Siemens also understood what Hinton was after, but could not really use it himself nor even fully grasp it. He was a German, after all, and could never quite accept the sea as a highway—he always saw it as a barrier, always remained landlocked.

To the end of his days, Hinton mused, Siemens remained hypnotized by the will-o'-the-wisp of the Baghdad Railway. He knew that it faced almost insurmountable obstacles in its terrain; wild, impenetrable, roadless mountain ranges and burning deserts. But at least the rails were laid on firm earth and held in place by hard, solid spikes. Siemens also knew that his Baghdad Railway was a monstrosity economically, politically, even militarily. Still, he could never quite accept that one troopship could get more soldiers to Baghdad faster and more reliably than his railroad could ever deliver them there. Then too, being a continental, he could not accept that importing is a legitimate economic function. It was no coincidence, Hinton thought, that the German banks financed all of Germany's exports—with Siemens's Deutsche Bank probably carrying a full third of the total or more—but that they still left the financing of German imports to the bankers in the City of London.

Still, Georg Siemens, while he could not share Hinton's vision, could at least understand it. Most of Hinton's fellow financiers couldn't. Even Ernest Marburg, the brightest of the lot, and increasingly his partner in working out the deals, saw only that Hinton went into a wide and to him bewildering variety of ventures: docks and ports and shipyards; jute plantations and jute mills in Bengal; railways to take cattle to the stockyards of Buenos Aires and Canadian wheat to the Great Lakes or to Montreal; power plants; copper and gold mines in Australia, Africa, Chile, and the American West; and finally, after the Germans had first begun in 1900 to use petroleum to fuel their merchant fleet, oil exploration and pipelines and tankers, in Burma and Indonesia, in Mexico and along Russia's Caspian Sea.

"Why don't you specialize in one area: grain exports or metal mining or ports and docks?" one of his fellow members at the Court of the Bank of England—a Baring or a Goschen or some other of the old-established merchant bankers—had once asked him.

"Bancroft Brothers," Hinton answered, "does not invest in grain or livestock, in ports or in copper mines. We invest in the industrialized world as a market, in its exploding urban population and its exploding factories, with grain, livestock, ports, or copper mines simply the vehicle, the channel, by which to reach the market." The fellow had shaken his head in total bewilderment.

But even his critics—and Hinton knew that he had many—had to acknowledge his success. They had to admit that he had made Bancroft Brothers into the financial leader in London, and, next only to J. P. Morgan & Co. in New York, undisputed leader among the world's private banks all told.

And Hinton's entrepreneurial mission, his "set" based on Riemann's mantra, had also made him personally an exceedingly rich man, though he doubted that he was indeed "the richest man in England," as some American journalist had printed.

A few years ago, at a Congress Hinton attended, Georg Cantor, Germany's leading mathematician and Riemann's acknowledged successor, had said: "There is no applied mathematics."

Hinton had gone up to him afterwards and said: "You are wrong, there is applied mathematics. It's called banking."

Cantor had looked at him as if he were demented. Riemann, Hinton thought, might have understood.

To the Riemann injunction not to define the problem but to organize the set, Hinton also owed in large measure his career at Bancroft Brothers, and with it access as a penniless clergyman's son to the resources for effective banking. He had done quite well during his first two years at Bancroft Brothers, even though his ideas (then, of course, quite unformed) tended to frighten the traditional bankers who were his superiors and associates. Still, he was hardly more than a middle-level clerk when Lord Claymont—having just come into the title—called him in and said, "There's a Mr. Morgan in town from New York, you know the name, don't you? And you're aware of the tariff problem we have in New York with my late father's Canadian venture? I think Mr. Morgan may be able to straighten it out for us. I understand that he, like you, studied mathematics in Goettingen. Did you meet him there? I see he was before your time. Still, you have something in common. Why don't you go and call on him?"

Morgan was then no more than thirty-eight, a few years older than Hinton. He had started his firm in New York only a few years earlier. Still, he already shone in the financial world as a rising star of the first magnitude. He had quit Goettingen without taking a degree, but had left behind, like the tail of a comet, a memory of rare talent as a mathematician and considerable wonderment as to why he had forsaken the brilliant university career that was assuredly his for the asking for something as humdrum as banking.

He received Hinton courteously, promised to take care of the tariff matter upon his return to New York (which he subsequently did), and said: "You got your doctorate in Goettingen, didn't you? I didn't, as you probably know. I hear you were one of Riemann's favorite students at the end. I was a great disappointment to him, I fear. Tell me, what did you learn from Riemann?"

"Not to try to define the problem but to organize the set," Hinton shot back.

J.P. gave him a long, searching look out of those extraordinary hooded eyes of his—the one striking feature in what was otherwise a coarse, ugly, heavy face, permanently disfigured by a diseased purple nose—then said very quietly: "So, you too learned this," and dismissed him.

But three months later came a cable addressed to Lord Claymont, offering Bancroft Brothers a partnership in an immensely important and immensely lucrative financial syndicate Morgan was putting together, on condition that McGregor Hinton would manage the European end. Bancroft Brothers had little choice but to make Hinton a partner, a junior partner at first, then a full partner after three or four more Morgan deals. And thus, Hinton knew, Riemann in the end also procured his career for him.

But it was Riemann too who, acting through J. P. Morgan, earned Hinton the dislike and the jealousy of Mr. Armistead, ten years his senior and until Hinton's rise the only non-family partner in Bancroft Brothers. And Armistead's hostility and hatred some years later—just when Hinton thought himself at the very pinnacle of success—would force him out of Bancroft Brothers altogether. Not to put too fine a point on it, Armistead had him sacked.

Everything had been set for him to split his time for a few years between London and his partnership in Bancroft Brothers, and Vienna and the chairmanship of the newly founded Bank of London & Austria. Then came a most attractive offer from Mr. Morgan to Bancroft Brothers: to form a syndicate of European investors to buy one third of the capital of a new, big coal-mining venture in the American Midwest, in such remote and indeed almost unknown places as Kentucky and West Virginia, Indiana and Ohio. Mr. Morgan made only one condition: the investors must bind themselves not to sell their holdings on the open market for at least five years.

"You and I," he wrote Hinton, "have seen too often the damage premature greed can do. This time we'll keep control till the time is ripe to go public."

This seemed eminently reasonable to Hinton, was indeed something he had been urging all along. But Armistead objected violently. "We need profits much faster than that," he said; "we aren't going to lock up capital for long years, no matter how attractive the investment."

"But, Mr. Armistead," Hinton had argued vigorously, "this violates the elementary theory of merchant banking. Merchant bankers become truly profitable when they have enough routine business to earn their overheads and a stable dividend so that they can invest their own capital long-term for extraordinary returns. That's how the Rothschilds got to where they are. That's how Georg Siemens is making his bank the continent's financial leader. And that's what J. P. Morgan in New York is doing so successfully."

"Mr. Hinton," Armistead had replied icily, "merchant banking was devised in England, by practical men without doctor's degrees. And we haven't done so badly, I should say, that we need lessons from Jews and foreigners."

Two days later, Lord Claymont called him into his private office, where he also found the other Bancroft brother, Dennis.

"Mr. Hinton," Claymont began, "Mr. Armistead has convinced us that you should not split yourself between Bancroft Brothers in London and the Bank of London & Austria in Vienna. The new bank will need all your time and energies. Of course, you will remain a partner in Bancroft Brothers in all but name, and are welcome to return here whenever you think it proper. My brother and I are as one in hoping it will be soon—your contribution will be missed. But for the time being you had better concentrate on the Vienna assignment, with your partnership in Bancroft Brothers held in abeyance. My brother and I have therefore decided to buy you out."

Claymont offered a sum that staggered Hinton, being more than twice, indeed nearly three times what he himself at his most optimistic would have thought a fair price for his partnership. Still, however obscured in honeyed words and money, it was the boot. Armistead must have said: "Either Hinton goes or I go," and the Bancrofts had chosen Armistead.

For months he was terribly bitter. He had been driven from the only home he had ever known, had been orphaned again. But gradually he came to admit that being forced out of Bancroft Brothers was the best thing that could have happened to him. He invested every penny the Bancrofts paid him in the American coal mines and thus became the biggest European shareholder in the most profitable of J. P. Morgan's ventures. It was the foundation of the Hinton fortune; when ten years later he finally sold his mining shares, he found himself a very rich man.

But more important, he also immediately became his own man and a financial power in his own right instead of being merely an "associate." "If I hadn't been pushed out," he once said to J. P. Morgan, "I would always have remained 'that clever young man of the Bancrofts.' " Instead, both Georg Siemens in Berlin and Sir Solomon Maimon of Maimon & Company agreed to join me in the coal-mining venture as minority partners and accepted me immediately as the European leader for their future transatlantic deals."

"And that too," thought Hinton, "I owe, however indirectly, to Riemann's mantra."

The chair into which Hinton had dropped at the end of his panicky flight was his oldest possession and the one piece of furniture he had bought in his four years at Goettingen. Though reupholstered countless times, it remained stubbornly what it had started out to be: cheap, monstrously big, monstrously ugly, overstuffed, and thoroughly Teutonic, calling to mind the German students' Meerschaum pipes redolent of the harsh tobacco they called "knaster," big beer steins, and even the tasseled smoking caps German students of the mid-nineteenth century affected. Yet it somehow did not look out of place in the formal eighteenth-century elegance of the Adam library where it now stood—the library for the sake of which Hinton originally had bought the house on the Square, and which he had lovingly restored to serve as his working and thinking room.

Across from the chair, separated from it by the room's entire width, was the neoclassical mantel around which the Brothers Adam, a hundred and fifty years earlier, had designed the room. Above it Hinton had mounted his most precious relic: Riemann's death mask, given him as one of the master's last and closest students. Beneath it was a copy of the inscription which Hinton and a few other students who had still occasionally been admitted into the dying man's presence had written for Riemann's tomb (the authorities had, of course, turned it down as being obscure and probably blasphemous):

Sein Leben war zu kurz um das Gebaeude zu vollenden doch lang genug um dem Weltall ein neues Fundament zu ermauern.

(His life was too short to finish the edifice but long enough to lay the universe a new foundation.)

On each side of the mantel hung portraits of the other two deities in Hinton's pantheon, the other two founders of modern mathematics. On one side was an autographed steel engraving of Carl Friedrich Gauss, Riemann's friend, teacher, and predecessor. Hinton had bought it before leaving Goettingen ten years after Gauss's death; he had lived on potatoes for three months to pay for it. On the other side hung an India ink drawing of Sir William Hamilton, the founder of modern algebra, which Hamilton had signed with a key equation for his quaternions and his own name—Hinton's old Oxford don had given it to him as a parting gift. On either side of these two portraits stretched the bookshelves as the Adam Brothers had first designed them. They were still empty except for the fourteen volumes so far published of the *Monumenta Mathematica*, "M. Hinton, Editor": five volumes of the *Opera Inedita* of Riemann (papers, notebooks, letters), five volumes of the *Opera Inedita* of Gauss, and four volumes of the *Opera Inedita* of Hamilton, the last volume off the press only a few weeks ago.

This was Hinton's sanctuary, into which the Furies of Life could not enter. Here he was in direct touch with pure reality, with ultimate truth, and with the laws of the universe, which existed before any of the gods were born and will live long after the gods are gone: the perennial, unchanging, ultimate truths of pure mathematics, of number and form, of symbol and ratio, which as every mathematician since Pythagoras has known are the true universe, the true *Weltall*—all else being mere illusion.

Except for Hinton, only the valet was allowed to enter the room, once a week, to dust. Even the young mathematicians whom Hinton had hired to assist in finding, culling, winnowing, and editing material for the *Monumenta Mathematica* had never set foot inside, never even seen inside. They put their work through a slot in the wall onto a table in the far corner.

There was quite a bit of copy there already, as Hinton saw. It must be the first batch for the next series, the mathematical papers of the seventeenth-century giants, and almost certainly the first batch of the mathematical letters of Leibniz. Hinton thought Leibniz the greatest mind the West had produced since the ancients, but also the prickliest, most obscure, most challenging, and most difficult. At any other time he would have dropped everything to go to work on these letters. But today Leibniz would have to wait. First he had to organize the set.

Now at last he was ready. Now he could think, applying method, rule, and order.

Riemann had been much too sick to work on what he himself had called "*Das Gebaeude*," the edifice (the theorem that would express the ultimate logic of all sets in one algorithm), the algorithm that, Hinton thought, would have made the harmony of the spheres accessible to the human mind and open to perception, analysis, and proof. But when his fever abated enough to let him see a few favorite students, Riemann had always talked of "the method": the formal order in which a set had to be organized.

The first step was always to make yourself see. List systemically all the phenomena that do not fit the way you approach the problem, and especially the unusual, the strange phenomenon, the phenomenon that, as you perceive it, cannot possibly belong to the same set as the problem you cannot define.

Well, that was easy enough. The phenomenon that could not possibly fit the set in which Freddie Bancroft was a problem, the phenomenon that at the same time was most unusual and least explicable, was surely Hinton's panic a few minutes ago in the dying woman's sickroom upstairs. Hinton had never panicked before. He had been frightened, shocked, disgusted, hurt, upset—but panicky, never. There was also absolutely no surprise in his wife's condition; it had been anticipated and expected for weeks, and Hinton was fully prepared for it.

When he returned from New York a little over three months ago, he had called on Melissa as usual—she did not appreciate it, hardly noticed it, but still she was legally his wife. He had seen at once that she was sick. Her face had a deadly pallor that was only accentuated by the heavy cosmetics she had smeared on it; she looked bloated and yet curiously shrunken; and she gave forth a strange, fetid odor. Even Anna, who always blocked anyone's access to her mistress, seemed relieved when he suggested the doctor be called. The physician took one look and immediately sent for Sir Montgomery Bramlett. Then Hinton knew that his wife must be very sick indeed; he had often enough heard the jest current among London doctors: "If the dying patient is a Roman, send for the priest. If he has money, send for Bramlett."

Sir Montgomery's examination took a long time. When he finally came down from her rooms, he said: "The lady is very ill indeed. I would suggest you immediately inform her relatives." And Hinton, to his own surprise, heard himself say what he had always believed he would never say:

"She has no relatives except me. The lady is my wife."

He could feel Bramlett recoil—the rich, the great, the powerful Mr. Hinton secretly married! And not to an Englishwoman, not even to a European, but a person with more than a touch of the tar-brush! But the physician had said only: "Then I have to give you the facts. There is a massive malignant growth in the female organs. It has progressed much too far for surgery to be possible, let alone successful—it probably would never have worked anyhow. By now the malignancy has spread throughout the body. The lymph glands in the neck and armpits are greatly enlarged and painful. And there is

suspicious enlargement of the organs in the abdomen and great sore-
ness. Only death can relieve the poor lady's sufferings. It is not too
far away; at most, I would estimate, another three to four months.
All you can do for her, Mr. Hinton, is pray that her sufferings will
soon be over. All the physician can do is to deaden her pain. I'll send
nurses and I, or one of my assistants, will come every day to take
a look.

"But, Mr. Hinton," and the physician lowered his voice to a whisper, although there was no one around to listen, "there comes a time
when even the largest dose of painkiller we dare administer no longer works, and when the pain gets out of control. Fortunately, the
end then follows fast, in a matter of days, within a fortnight at most.
But it is a dreadful time for the family—I always advise all but the
very closest relatives to leave. They cannot help; they only suffer, and
they suffer more, I feel, than the dying patient, who is not conscious
except for brief moments, does not usually want anyone around, and
cannot generally recognize anyone any more. I, or my assistant, will
give you ample warning when the patient approaches that time."

A week ago Sir Montgomery had told him that what he called
"the terminal period" was close at hand; and then that very morning
Sir Montgomery's assistant had told him that it had arrived. There
was reason to be sad, frightened, even enraged at one's impotence in
the face of such suffering and one's inability to help. But panic—why
had he panicked?

Was he ready then for Riemann's second step: "Assume that the
unusual, the inexplicable phenomenon is part of the same set to
which the unsolved problem belongs. What set could that be?"

There was only one set, only one field into which both Freddie
Bancroft and the panic in his wife's bedroom could possibly be fitted.
The only dimension they had in common, the only point at which
they touched, the only universe to which both belonged, was Hinton
himself and his own life.

Hinton immediately knew this to be right. He felt the aesthetic
pleasure, the almost physical euphoria, which organizing the set
always produced.

"You may later discover," Riemann had said in that first seminar, "that it still wasn't the right set despite the feeling of enlighten-

ment, of vision. But without it, it never is the right set, at least not for me. When you feel it, you must therefore assume you are right and go ahead."

Then Riemann noticed the young Englishman who had called that very morning with a letter of introduction from his Oxford tutor, and had turned to him: "Herr Hinton, what then is the next step?"

"Define what is truly unique about the set," Hinton had answered, almost without thinking—for someone who had been nourished for the last three years on Hamilton and his quaternions as Hinton had at Oxford, it was the obvious answer. Riemann beamed—and from that moment on he had accepted Hinton, admitted him, singled him out.

What then was truly unique about the set McGregor Hinton? That he was male, English, and sixty-three, he shared with thousands. That he was a banker and very rich, he still shared with some. Even his mathematics degree, though uncommon for a banker, at least in England, was surely not unique. Nor was it unique to have a wife dying of cancer.

There was only one feature unique to the set McGregor Hinton: "Every one of my life's decisive moments, every turning point, has been marked by embezzlement or major financial crime. Marked, mind you—not caused, but marked. Not crimes I committed, not even necessarily crimes committed against me. But embezzlements or similar financial misdeeds committed around me and having an impact on me. And there have been, counting Freddie Bancroft's counterfeiting, three of them.

"According to Bernoulli's Law," Hinton said aloud, "the probability of three such unusual events being coincidences is practically zero. They must be part of a pattern, a configuration. They surely are the unique feature of the set. And to understand the set, applying what Riemann taught me, I have to reconstruct every one of these events, think through every one of these vortices, those turning points in the configuration that is John McGregor Hinton's life."

Goettingen

First, of course, came Goettingen: the time, 1867.

Because of his brilliance in mathematics, Hinton, after attending a minor public school, had received a scholarship to Oxford. His father had grudgingly consented to continue his meager stipend for three years, though he complained bitterly about the burden on a poor vicar's slender income. Then when Hinton had received First Class Honors in the Mathematics Tripos, his father, at the urging of Hinton's tutor, had agreed to extend the stipend for another four years.

It was barely enough, £50 a year. But one could subsist on that sum in the Goettingen of those days, which was still Hanover and not yet Prussia, still a village rather than a town. But then, just at the time of Riemann's passing, his father had died. His stepbrother did not tell him for several weeks, and Hinton was not surprised. He was close neither to the father who was an old man when Hinton was born, nor to the stepbrother who was almost twenty years his senior and already high up in the Colonial Service. The stepbrother then wrote to inform Hinton that the check for £25 which he was enclosing with his letter was the last remittance; his father, as Hinton undoubtedly knew, had not left any property behind.

By that time Hinton was almost finished with his dissertation. Riemann had wanted him to write on Hamilton's quaternions. Hamilton, of course, had done his work on the quaternions decades earlier. But Dublin, where Hamilton had lived and worked, was then so far away from Germany that very few people in Goettingen had heard of him, let alone studied his work. Riemann immediately saw its importance, immediately saw that applying Hamilton to Riemann's own areas of set theory and number theory would produce important new results—what now, Hinton thought, they call matrix algebra, which has become all the rage.

So Riemann invited Hinton to write a paper on quaternions for the seminar, then urged him to develop the paper into his doctoral thesis. He was right, thought Hinton—it would have been at least as good a thesis as those produced twenty years later when Hamilton was finally "discovered" on the continent.

But by then Hinton had already become interested in the history of mathematics, and he decided instead to write his thesis on the history of the inscribed square, which had fascinated mathematicians, alchemists, magicians, astrologers, and philosophers from Pythagoras to Athanasius Kircher, the Jesuit mathematician of the seventeenth century. "That thesis of mine," reflected Hinton, "is now considered a 'classic,' reprinted in anthology after anthology. Today the history of mathematics is fashionable—and I was honored as the pioneer of a new discipline at the same Congress at which Cantor declared there is no applied mathematics. But then few people were interested."

And so when he came to his Goettingen professor to talk about jobs, the answer was discouraging: "It's hard enough for a young mathematician to find work except as a high-school teacher. But for a historian of mathematics, I don't see any university position in Germany. I might be able to get you an appointment as a librarian—not in Goettingen, I'm afraid; there are too many here like you. But the Technical University in Hanover might have a job for you. In a few years you'd undoubtedly be appointed *Dozent*, and in another few years you might even get the title of Professor. But I do hope, my dear Dr. Hinton, that you have independent means. All the librarianship will ever pay is something like a hundred of your English pounds; and I consider a paid professorial appointment to be quite out of the question."

His old tutor in Oxford was just as discouraging: "I am reasonably sure, my dear boy, that I can get you elected junior tutor—you'd have a roof over your head for three years and your food at the High Table. We should be able to get you appointed curate at one of the university churches if you're willing to take Holy Orders—that pays twenty-five pounds a year and all you have to do is to conduct a few services when the rector wants to go away on a Sunday. But beyond that, Oxford, I am afraid, isn't much interested in mathematicians. If you can hang on for ten years things might work out—that's what I did. But I wouldn't recommend it. Those ten years of ingratiating myself, paying court to masters and deans and senior tutors, all to get a fellowship, have broken me.

"I should have done a good job as a mathematician. I'm not as good as you are, never was, but I was competent and William Hamilton's pupil to boot when I came here. I have produced nothing. And yet at least I had a reasonable private income. If you want me to, my dear boy, I'll go to work on that junior tutorship, and in the meantime you'd be welcome to stay with me and keep an old man company, though you'd find me very rusty—I haven't had anyone to talk mathematics to for a long time. But I really can't encourage you if you have any other opportunity."

Then the old man, with tears in his eyes, had taken Sir William Hamilton's pen portrait from the wall of his sitting room and said: "Remember me by this. But now go and look for a decent job in which you won't have to beg your bread as you would have to do here."

Hinton had gone straight up to London and called the next morning on Lord Oliver Bancroft (the present Viscount Claymont, then the head of Bancroft Brothers) to whom his stepbrother, who had been at Oxford with him, had given an introduction. Lord Oliver called in his brother Dennis (the present Lord Bancroft) and they hired Hinton on the spot. He was to be private secretary to the partners and in charge of correspondence in foreign languages—he spoke fluent German and passable French—and they offered him £150 a year, a princely sum for Hinton, who had never had more than the £50 from his father.

A few years later—just about the time Lord Claymont sent him to J. P. Morgan—he received a letter postmarked Glasgow and written in a strange, uneducated female hand. Hinton had never forgotten a word of it. The letter, signed Margaret McGregor Clawson, read:

You probably never heard of me. I am your mother's distant cousin and grew up with her in the Hebrides; she was my only relative on the McGregor side. I would not come begging to you but for being a widow and poor. My only child, a daughter nineteen years old, is sick and the doctor says she will die unless she has an operation and treatment that will cost £50. And you now, I know, have all that money from your dead mother, the friend of my childhood, and can surely spare £50 to save the life of your only cousin . . .

Hinton had scraped the money together. But in his accompanying letter, he pointed out that he had no legacy from his mother or anyone else and was living on a bank clerk's salary.

Instead of thanks, he got back a sharp reprimand:

Don't pretend, McGregor Hinton. I know that your mother was left £1,800 by that rich great-uncle of hers, the ironmonger in Carlisle, when he died while she worked as housekeeper for the Reverend Hinton, who then married her. We were all surprised—we did not even know of the existence of that great-uncle . . .

Hinton was at first inclined to dismiss this as the ravings of an old woman, but one should never treat lightly what a Scot says about money. So he went to Somerset House and looked up his father's and mother's wills. His father had left all he possessed (it was not much) to his two children by his first marriage, Hinton's stepbrother and stepsister. But there was a curious additional sentence in his father's will: "I leave to my older children the settlement of my obligation to their stepbrother, John McGregor Hinton."

And his mother's will, made a few months before she died of the phthisis when he was not quite eight, stated specifically:

I leave and bequeath to my beloved only son John McGregor Hinton the sum of £1,800 which I inherited from my great-uncle William McGregor in the year 1841, with said son to receive the income from said sum for his support and education, and the principal of said sum upon completion of his education but not before reaching the age of twenty-one.

So, the income which his father had so grudgingly remitted, the income he always pretended Hinton was taking away from him, had been his, Hinton's, all along, and was actually half of what was due him—for the £1,800 would have produced an income of at least £100 a year.

And now of course he realized why his father had married his mother. His father, he knew, had never loved her and had always treated her as a servant; he himself had always resented it. The only reason his father had married his mother was to get his hands on her money: he had married her less than three months after she received the unexpected legacy.

But still, his father had not quite dared to embezzle all the money, only half of it. His stepbrother and stepsister had had no such qualms. Of course, they had never accepted their father's second wife, let alone her child, openly showing their contempt for both. They shared the same father, the son of a small tradesman in a cathedral town but become ordained priest and thus a gentleman. But his mother, as they reminded him only too often, was a crofter's daughter, while theirs had been a gentlewoman, daughter of the local squire, who had had the poor parish in his gift and appointed his son-in-law to the living.

That they wished him no good, Hinton knew—indeed, he had been surprised when he received the letter of introduction to Bancroft Brothers from his stepbrother. But he still had never dreamed that they would unblushingly steal from him. In fact, but for the letter from Glasgow from that distant relative of his dead mother, he would never have found out.

When Hinton discovered this brazen theft, he had trembled with fury. But he soon realized that he could do nothing. At first he thought of bringing suit. He would have ruined both of them, even if they got off without a jail sentence. But he would also have ruined himself— for by then he had seen enough of bankers to know that they do not cherish scandal and do not love troublemakers. If he brought suit, Bancroft Brothers would get rid of him fast and no one else would want him either. The money was surely gone, anyhow; his stepbrother and stepsister had both been in debt, and neither of them had a penny except for the £1,800 they stole from him.

But what would he have done had he received the money while he was still in Goettingen, still expecting to become a mathematician? A hundred pounds a year was not very much, to be sure. Yet, together with what the Germans paid a librarian, it would have been enough to live modestly, and equal to what smaller German universities paid a professor in those frugal pre-Imperial days.

A hundred pounds wasn't much in Oxford, either—indeed less than in Germany. But with the room and board a junior tutor got, and the few pounds picked up as a curate, he could have got by, at least for the three years for which a junior tutor was usually appointed—and after that, who knows? There might have been a lectureship at one of the provincial places, Manchester, Leeds, Durham, or Birmingham, all of which were then building universities and might have been willing to have on their faculty an Oxford don and former student of the great Riemann, to drill calculus into undergraduates' heads at £250 a year.

By the time he found out, Hinton already knew that banking was to him more exciting, more challenging, more satisfying than academic life and the pettiness of the University High Table could possibly have been. By that time he knew that banking was for him the way to apply mathematics. But would he have known this if his stepbrother had not embezzled his legacy? Would he even have used the introduction to Bancroft Brothers? But of course he never would have received it. His stepbrother only wrote it because he had a bad conscience. However ironic, £1,800 was surely a cheap price to pay for that letter of introduction and the job at Bancroft Brothers it had procured.

Melissa

Fifteen, sixteen, years later he had come to the next turning point, with the second embezzlement; with Melissa, Armistead, and Elaine; and with his return from Vienna after five years away from Bancroft Brothers.

Hinton had forgotten how he came to walk past the third-rate cabaret in one of Vienna's outer districts beyond the Ringstrasse one spring evening, or why he went in—perhaps it was the name "Melissa" on the playbill as the cabaret's star attraction, with its evocation of thyme and wild honey. Nor could he remember why he sent his card to the artiste's dressing room after her bored and lackluster performance of a routine belly dance and her singing of a few risqué French ditties in a tired voice that could barely be heard over the clatter of the beer-swilling customers. But she and he both took it for granted that he would walk home with her, with Anna following a few steps behind, and that she would take him straight into her room and into her bed.

Then it had happened again, as it had happened every time he was with a woman. At the very moment of fulfillment, the memory came back—and with it such disgust, shame, and revulsion as to make him unable to finish.

He saw himself again as a fourteen-year-old in the third-rate public school where his mathematical proficiency had won him a scholarship, and where he was immediately singled out by the mathematics master for tutoring in advanced work. After two or three sessions in the master's rooms, the man had edged toward him, put his arm around him, pulled him ever closer, undressed him, and then violated him. He had been paralyzed with disgust and pain, but also with fear; there was something in the master's manner that told him the man would not hesitate to use force should he resist. The worst, the very worst though, was that he felt himself respond ever so slightly—and he knew that the master had also noticed it. When the man let him go, Hinton rushed off and was violently sick. He was sick for weeks thereafter, could hardly eat, and vomited whenever he encountered the man. But nothing was ever said; the following term the master was gone.

Yet thereafter if Hinton was with a woman the memory of that dreadful hour—its shame and disgust, its pain and its rotten, putrid excitement—arose in him and maimed him. He was sure the women he was with must have noticed; they were professionals and experienced. In any event, they got paid and so chose not to say anything.

But not Melissa. She stopped immediately and asked: "Did I do anything wrong? Did I hurt you? Did I upset you?"

And he had blurted out the whole horror to this total stranger whom he had not even met until an hour or so earlier. He did not know what to expect—disgust, pity, or outrage. He certainly didn't expect the reaction he got.

"*Ce pauvre homme!*" she said. "No, I don't mean you. You just got initiated the way most of us do, man or woman, by the wrong person and before you were ready. One gets over that. But that poor man, that teacher, to have to violate little boys who don't respond to satisfy his needs. What a barbaric country that England of yours must be, where there is no way for such a man except to risk shame and losing his job and blackmail. In my country—*Je suis Grèque, vous savez, mais j'étais née en Egypte*—we know how to provide for such needs discreetly and properly. But now, forget that poor man," she said, putting her arms around him, "come back to me and finish." And he did.

She had lifted the curse from him. He still felt disgust and shame and revulsion, with black bile rising in his gorge whenever he thought of that evening so long ago. But it never again unmanned him when with a woman. And so, more out of gratitude than affection, he began to pay the rent on Melissa's and Anna's apartment and became their protector.

And, as he soon learned, their savior too. Another few weeks and the two women would have been over the precipice. Melissa in her

youth had been attractive and successful, he found out—as successful, that is, as a demi-mondaine can ever be—as an "exotic" dancer
and *chanteuse* in cabarets all over the Mediterranean and Central Europe, in Genoa, Barcelona, Budapest, Constantinople, and
Vienna. She must have made a fair amount of money. But she had
not kept one penny—"spent it all on men," Hinton thought; she was
a born victim. And by now she was middle-aged, getting wrinkled,
getting fat, and if she had ever had any voice it was cracked and gone.
Her contract in the third-rate cabaret in which Hinton had found her
only ran a few more weeks, until the place closed for the summer,
and was not going to be renewed. She would literally have been out in
the street; and, thought Hinton, dead within a year, killed by syphilis, liquor, opium, or a pimp's knife.

Melissa's was a common enough story, Hinton knew. But who
or what was Anna, who night or day, ever-present and green-eyed,
sat silent, unblinking, outside Melissa's dressing room or bedroom,
and who was always there when Melissa wanted to give her a tongue-
lashing or needed someone to pick up her handkerchief?

He could not find out from the two women, of course. Anna
wouldn't talk, and one could not believe a word Melissa said. But he
had come to know some officials among the Viennese police, and
the police everywhere know all about people like Melissa and Anna.
From them he learned that the two women were sisters, daughters of
the same mother, a Greek belly dancer and demi-mondaine, but by
different fathers: Anna, the daughter of an Irish ship's chandler in
Alexandria, which explained her green eyes and milky-white com-
plexion; Melissa, the child of a Levantine merchant who himself had
a Nubian from the Sudan for his mother, which accounted for Melissa's Negroid hair and lips.

What had happened to the mother, no one knew; she might have
run off with another lover, been thrown out by the Egyptian merchant or killed by him. But the two little girls (Anna the older by five
or six years) grew up in the Egyptian merchant's house—neglected,
ill-treated, probably sexually abused, but at least fed and allowed to
sleep wherever they could find a place. Anna had become the guardian, the watchdog, the protector of her baby sister, had defended her,

trained her in their mother's trade, and made looking after Melissa her life's mission. And now, but for Hinton, they would have gone to their doom together.

He soon tired of Melissa—and she, he thought, had always been indifferent to him, indifferent indeed to anybody and anything. But he kept on paying the rent, and he continued to visit her from time to time, though less and less frequently. He had already decided to pay Melissa off by settling on her a small annuity when, one day, he found her in hysterics, crying and laughing and throwing her arms around him.

"I'm pregnant!" she cried. "And, Mr. McGregor" (she always called him that, probably didn't even know that he had another name) "do let me have the child. I have always wanted a baby, always dreamed of being a mother. I've been pregnant before, but every time the man made me get rid of the child. Oh, please, Mr. McGregor, let me have this one! I promise I'll go away and you shall never hear from me. I won't be a burden. But, please, Mr. McGregor, let me have this child. I know I'm getting too old to have another one. Oh, Mr. McGregor . . ." and she went down on her knees before him and tried to kiss his hand.

When he had calmed her, had convinced her that he would let her have the child, that indeed he would get her a doctor and take care of her during the pregnancy and would afterwards set up a fund to support them both, the poor woman cried so hard that he found himself sobbing as he had not done since the pain and sorrow of his own mother's death when he was a little boy, suddenly lost and orphaned in a hostile world. Even Anna, that stone-faced Gorgon, for once softened and curtseyed, kissed his hand and said, "May God bless you."

Melissa had had a difficult pregnancy. He called in Dr. Augsburg, whose daughter had just then married Mosenthal and who was considered one of Vienna's best physicians. But while Melissa was far from well, it was also a happy time for her—she grew girlish, gay and radiant, and one could see in her again the femininity that had made her the toast of waterfront cabarets all over the Mediterranean fifteen or twenty years earlier.

For him, her pregnancy served as the deadline he had needed. He had been in Vienna five years—hardworking, challenging, and successful years, which he had thoroughly enjoyed. Now he was ready to leave. Mosenthal hardly needed him any more and the Bank of London & Austria was established, set on its profitable course.

He could have stayed on, taking life easy and growing rich and fat with an Austrian barony his for the asking. But he was barely forty, not yet ready for retirement, however comfortable and cozy it might be. Now he knew he'd stay in Vienna only until Melissa had given birth to his child. Then he would leave. He was not quite sure what he would do—or rather, he could not quite make up his mind which opportunity to pursue. But he would leave.

The most attractive opportunity was not available to him: to join Sir Solomon Maimon as a partner in Maimon & Company. He knew that the old man would have wanted him, and he in turn was fond of Sir Solomon and had respect for him. In all London there was no better banking firm and no older one, either; Maimon & Company had been started by the very first Jews allowed back into England by Cromwell, all of two hundred years earlier. But Sir Solomon could not imagine a partner in the firm, let alone a successor to its leadership, who was not a member of the family—and he could not possibly accept any but a Jew as a son-in-law, husband to one of his five vivacious, attractive daughters.

"Times have changed," Hinton mused. "Both the daughters Becky Maimon bore Ernest Marburg have married into the aristocracy, the youngest one no less than the grandson of a royal duke. But that's twenty-five years later. Then all I could do was find Marburg and introduce him to Sir Solomon. It has worked out well: Marburg is a baronet, the King's banker, and a good and trusted friend. But he, not I, owns Maimon. It's Maimon & Marburg now."

However, there was no such obstacle to a partnership in J. P. Morgan. All Hinton had to do was to send Mr. Morgan a telegram:

I AM READY TO JOIN YOU AS A PARTNER.
WHAT ARE THE TERMS?

He knew (everybody knew) that Mr. Morgan never offered a job, let alone a partnership, to anybody who worked for a firm with which he did business—and he did more business with the Bank of London & Austria than he had ever done with Bancroft Brothers while Hinton had been there. But he had also been openly courting Hinton. Morgan had come to own banks of his own in both London and Paris. Still, he regularly entrusted to Hinton in out-of-the-way Vienna the management of his most important and biggest deals in Europe. And whenever Morgan came to Europe, which he did at least once every year, he summoned Hinton, usually to Paris, for a few days of good talk and then always finished up by proposing a major joint venture.

On this last New York trip, the one from which he had returned to find Melissa dying, Morgan had confirmed what he had guessed twenty-three years earlier: he had wanted him as a partner then and was only waiting for Hinton to take the first step.

One evening last February, while sitting in the exquisite library Morgan had recently built for his art treasures and looking together at one of the illuminated manuscripts he loved so much and knew so well, Morgan had said: "The one mistake you made in your career, Mr. Hinton, was not joining me when you were ready to leave Vienna. I had already written out my acceptance and was only waiting for your cable. I think I would have made a more stimulating partner for you than the Bancrofts.

"But then," Mr. Morgan had added with a chuckle, "you and I may see more of each other during the six weeks you come to New York every year and we spend all our evenings together, than we would have done had you joined me in New York and shared an office with me during the busy day." For Morgan monopolized his evenings in New York—in his private corner in the Metropolitan Club or, lately, in the Morgan Library—talking about everything: art, mathematics, the world, but rarely about banking.

"Indeed," thought Hinton, "the six weeks I spend with J. P. in New York every year and the six weeks I spend in Vienna are my real life, other than the *Monumenta Mathematica*. In London, I dine out; in New York and Vienna, I live out—with Morgan in America, with Mahler conducting at the Opera in Vienna or at the Baroness Wald-Reifnitz's musicales. I couldn't have known this twenty-three years ago when I was almost ready to send off the cable to Mr. Morgan. It was in my desk already written out, just as Mr. Morgan had written out the answer to it."

But then a second opportunity had arisen: it was far more difficult, far harder work, but also meant being his own man instead of Mr. Morgan's second in command. To organize and run the International Industrial Bank in London.

He had discussed the idea with Siemens and Maimon. Both were interested and would have come in for 30 percent of the capital each. So would J. P. Morgan, he was sure. Hinton would then have kept the remaining 10 percent and been chairman and managing director of the world's first international bank, which would pool the resources and entrepreneurial talents of the world's best bankers.

"It was the right idea," Hinton had often said to Mr. Morgan; "and I should have followed through with it. When I didn't and the various banks started, ten years or so later, to do it on their own, they did well—Siemens perhaps best, with the bank he founded to develop northern Italy, then the one for northern Spain and the one for South America. And Maimon are doing well, especially in Argentina with their Bank of London & South America. But now the great banks are competing against one another, fragmenting their efforts, and have to take on a lot of donkeywork to earn their overheads, whereas I could have concentrated on the really big, important tasks of development."

Yes, the only decision he had had to make then in Vienna when Melissa got pregnant was whether to join Morgan or to start on his own. Otherwise he was ready to go as soon as Melissa had had her baby. He had already told Mosenthal in confidence that he was leaving Vienna by the end of the year.

It was just a few days before Melissa's time was up that he received a cable from Dennis Bancroft, the present Lord Bancroft and Freddie's father.

COME TO LONDON IMMEDIATELY AND WITH UTMOST
DISCRETION.

He had almost entirely moved out of the Bancroft orbit. Officially, Bancroft Brothers were to accept him back as a full partner any time. Actually, he had left and been paid off.

Lord Claymont and his brother Dennis together owned all but a tiny fraction of the firm's capital. But neither was active. Claymont was then at the peak of his career as Chancellor of the Exchequer, in the final years of the Conservative ascendancy. Bancroft, the younger brother, had also gone into politics, was sitting in the House of Commons and had become a junior minister (a parliamentary private secretary or such), so that he was busy whenever the House was in session.

Armistead was thus in charge—and Armistead disliked Hinton just as much now that he was in Vienna as he had disliked him when they sat in the same partners' room in London. He in turn did not like the little he saw or heard of the way Armistead ran the firm: very clever, very greedy, and not a bit intelligent, Hinton thought. Also Armistead never had had much use for the Bank of London & Austria, had opposed the proposal to set it up, was forever grousing that the dividend was too low (the profitable years for the Bank of London & Austria were, of course, then still in the future), and would have been delighted to get rid of the shares and with them of Hinton altogether. And Hinton had already decided that he would buy out Bancroft Brothers. Should he join Morgan by placing the Bancroft holdings in London & Austria with Maimon—both Sir Solomon and Marburg wanted them; or should he start the International Industrial Bank by buying the shares himself.

Nonetheless he took the first train from Vienna to England. To his immense surprise, Dennis and his wife Elaine met him when the ferry docked at Dover, sent his luggage on to London with a servant who was instructed to pretend to be "Mr. Hinton," and whisked him off to a small hotel in a back street. There in an upstairs room Lord Claymont and Dennis Bancroft were waiting.

"Armistead is dead," Elaine immediately said—the two men seemed paralyzed. "The coroner will rule that it was an accident, but he shot himself; and he has looted the Bank. You must come back immediately—you alone can save us!"

Bancroft Brothers was bankrupt. The partners' capital was gone in its entirety, and there was not enough cash even to cover current liabilities, many of them overdue. Worse, Armistead had dipped deeply into trust funds—funds of the Church of England of which the viscount was lay treasurer; funds of Oxford colleges, of London hospitals, and colonial governments.

Worst of all, however, was that morally at least Armistead was not the culprit—the Bancrofts were. Little if any of the money Armistead had taken out of the firm went into his own pocket. Most went to satisfy the boundless demands of the Bancrofts. Viscount Claymont had always lived on a scale befitting the great statesman he fancied himself to be. During those years as Chancellor of the Exchequer he saw himself as a future Prime Minister and spent accordingly. The real spenders, however, were the younger Bancrofts, Dennis and Elaine. It was not Armistead, Hinton suddenly saw, who had forced him out five years earlier. In reality it had been Elaine, when he objected mildly to her demands for more and more money from the firm.

Elaine had pushed Dennis into politics. She had bought the huge Tudor mansion at Beechhurst in Wiltshire, twenty-five miles from Claymont where her father-in-law, the first viscount, had built his Victorian pile. There she had begun to play political hostess and to spend her ineffectual and retiring husband into political prominence and a peerage in his own right.

"And she succeeded," thought Hinton wryly, "though it took her much longer than she probably expected. It's less than six months since Dennis became Baron Bancroft of Beechhurst, when the Liberal tide in the winter elections swept out the Conservatives and retired him permanently from politics."

Faced with Elaine's ever-increasing demands, Armistead had begun to speculate on the Stock Exchange; in commodities; on the bill market. When he lost, he had plunged in even more wildly: into pepper futures and selling Sicilian quicksilver short; into buying and selling hog bellies in Chicago. Legally, the Bancrofts might wriggle free, although of course they were liable for the money. But morally the Bancrofts were guilty—and everyone would know it.

There was only one way out: liquidation. The shares of the Bank of London & Austria were the sole major asset Armistead had not pledged or sold, perhaps because he was afraid of Hinton. They would cover the trust accounts and thus prevent scandal, exposure, and criminal prosecution. As for the rest, the creditors could be prevailed upon to hold still for a year, and then they might be paid enough not to scream. The Bancrofts, with the resources they had from outside the firm, might still salvage a sufficiency—though both Beechhurst and Claymont would have to go, and political careers would have to be forgotten.

The two men were resigned; they must have reached the same conclusion themselves. But Elaine denied reality, refused to accept it. She argued that Bancroft Brothers could and should continue business as usual rather than be liquidated, and that, with a little luck, the firm could be saved.

It was just barely possible, Hinton thought. But it was extremely risky. One mishap and they would all be in jail for fraudulent bankruptcy, deservedly so. And even if it could be pulled off, it would mean spending the next five years of his life saving the Bancrofts from the consequences of their irresponsibility, greed, and unspeakable negligence, instead of doing his own constructive work.

He had all but decided to say "No," and tell the Bancrofts that all he could do for them was sell the shares of the Bank of London & Austria for enough cash to avoid criminal prosecution, when he found himself alone in the Bancroft partners' room with a pale, haggard Elaine.

"I'm afraid it's all over," he said. But she reached across the table and put both her hands on his: "McGregor, don't ever say that. Don't you forsake me and my child; don't you forsake me and Frederick!"

Never before had she called him by his given name, never before had she touched him. He was deeply disturbed, deeply moved, and found himself mumbling something inane like: "Don't you worry, it'll be all right." And he immediately saw that she thought he had committed himself.

But he was not at all sure that he had—and he left her as soon as he could.

When he got back to the inconspicuous hotel in which they had arranged for him to stay, he found the telegram from Vienna. It contained the code message he had given to Anna to let him know that Melissa had had a child, that it was a boy, and that both mother and child were doing well. But it also contained in clear uncoded German the words: "You are needed immediately, please return at once." And it was signed by Dr. Augsburg, not by Anna.

He left on the morning train, wiring Lord Claymont from Victoria Station that he would give his decision within forty-eight hours. From Vienna's Westbahnhof he went straight to Melissa's flat.

Anna did not want to let him in, but he brushed past her into Melissa's bedroom. She was lying in bed with a face so swollen by tears that he hardly recognized it. Next to her, in the cradle which she had so lovingly prepared, lay a horror, a monster: a huge deformed head, its eyes covered with a gray film, and a twisted misshapen body. When Melissa saw him, she screamed and pushed him away . . . and since then she had never again let him come near her, let alone touch her.

"This is the punishment for my wicked, sinful life," she sobbed. "Don't come near me. I am accursed!"

"It happens sometimes," said Augsburg gently, "when a woman has her first child at such an advanced age. Fortunately, they don't live long."

But Augsburg had been wrong. The poor monster for whom the Doctor found a foster home with a farmer north of Vienna would not die until eleven years later.

That same day he decided to marry Melissa and to take on the Bancroft rescue job. Two weeks later, he was back in London. In another six weeks, after he had found and rented the house on the Square, Melissa and Anna arrived. Both women seemed to have lost all will to resist, all faculties of their own. But Melissa would hardly speak to him again and never once asked about the baby. When he told her that it had died, she did not even listen. She refused to leave the top floor of the house and never set foot outdoors. She grew layer after layer of fat, as if to build a wall of flesh against the outside world, and brought in a growing army of Greek priests, Indian swamis, Theosophist ladies from Boston clad in flowing sarees, astrologers, palmists, and spiritualist mediums.

Hinton, for his part, immersed himself in work. For five years it was touch and go, and he rarely got away from the office before ten at night at the earliest. He could not have pulled it off but for the dividends from the Bank of London & Austria. These were the years in which the industries Mosenthal and he had started ripened and became ready to be sold to the public at ever-increasing share prices: sugar-beet mills and a big, extremely profitable timber company to exploit the enormous Bohemian forests owned by those great nobles, Sobieski and his son-in-law Wottawa; two or three paper companies to utilize the pulp from those woods; woolen and cotton mills and a shoe manufacturer and a fast-growing chemical company to supply the textile mills with dyestuff and mordants and the paper companies with caustic soda and chlorine.

In one banner year—three years after the crisis—the London & Austria paid an unheard-of dividend of 800 percent, which enabled him at one fell swoop to pay off all the Bancroft creditors. He also got help from his friends, from J. P. Morgan and Georg Siemens and Maimon & Marburg. He did not know whether they suspected what was wrong. But they threw business his way whenever they could and supplied what Bancroft Brothers needed even more than cash and profits: prestige and credit.

Within five years he had turned the firm around, and in the process had become Bancroft Brothers' main owner. When he had agreed to take over, he demanded one third of the bank and an agreement that the Bancrofts could not sell any of their shares without offering them to him first. He knew better by then than to trust either the Bancrofts' good faith or their judgment.

But they were even more irresponsible than he had feared. For a short year they did indeed try to control their expenses. Then they went back to their lordly ways as if there had been no crisis at all. And then, too, Freddie began to be a drain—early in one year there were claims for almost £15,000 to reimburse the Guards officers whom Freddie had fleeced with marked cards. And Elaine was once again pushing her husband's political fortunes, acting the political hostess, making Beechhurst a haven for political hangers-on, journalists, younger members of Parliament, and whoever else could further Dennis's pallid career.

The only way the Bancrofts could get cash was to sell shares in the bank. Even without the clause in his contract, there was no one they could sell to but Hinton. Anyone else would have demanded to see the books, and that would have been the end of the sale. Hinton therefore found himself under pressure to raise cash to buy what were then still worthless Bancroft shares—so much so that during most of those years he was almost as poor and lived almost as frugally as he had done twenty years earlier as a penniless student in Goettingen. But by the end of the eighties, when Bancroft Brothers was restored to liquidity and profit, when indeed the income from the investments in Hinton's second "entrepreneurial mission" (in copper mines and Chilean nitrate for fertilizer, and grain terminals and slaughterhouses overseas) were beginning to roll in, Hinton owned more than two thirds of the firm, with the Bancroft family holdings reduced to less than one quarter.

Since then he had been Bancroft Brothers. Dennis, the present Lord Bancroft, had effectively left the firm for politics, though he retained the chairman's title until he joined the cabinet in 1899. Lord Claymont retired even earlier.

The two younger men, Sheldon and Hinshaw, were partners in name only. Sheldon rarely even came in, and then only to use the firm's telephones for whispered conversations with whichever demimondaine he was buying diamonds for at the time; otherwise, he lived for his racing stables and for the hunt of which he was Master of Hounds. Hinshaw came in most days and stayed faithfully from ten to five. He would have made a good branch manager, Hinton thought, perhaps in Bayswater or Ealing, granting fifty-pound overdrafts to local tradesmen. As it was, he worried over trivia, remnants of traditional banking such as letters of credit, which Bancroft kept on to keep him busy and which cost more than they produced.

Lately Hinton had made Wyndham a junior partner and begun to train him as a banker. Then there was Lovell, a chief clerk really, but given the title of "partner" and a tiny stock participation so as to have an extra signature when Hinton was away on his frequent travels.

"Why haven't I done what Marburg did and changed the name at least to Bancroft & Hinton?" he asked himself suddenly; he had never thought of it before. "And why haven't I got rid of those incompetent Bancrofts? Freddie's crash wouldn't have been such a problem then, and I've known for years that it was bound to come."

But he knew the answer as soon as he asked the question—Elaine.

Elaine

"I've been in love with her for forty years," Hinton suddenly said out loud, "ever since that evening when I was first invited to the Bancrofts' for dinner, just after I was made junior partner following the first Morgan deal. She's known it all along, of course. And so has everybody else—everybody else, that is, except me."

No wonder that she knew he was committed when she appealed to him not to forsake her and Freddie; he was committed before. No wonder that he had been so disturbed, so moved, even overwrought by her placing her hands on his and leaving them there. She had offered herself to him . . . and he had not even noticed it.

Suddenly Hinton heard himself laugh, was convulsed with laughter, doubled up with laughter until he was gasping for air. So he had been Ritter Toggenburg all along—what superb, what cosmic irony!

To the Goettingen student a future as professor at a German university had, for a few years, appeared the ultimate bliss a human being could attain. So he'd set out to become an educated German, "*ein Gebildeter Mensch.*" He mastered the language to the point where people in Vienna took him for "Reichsdeutsch," a German from the north, and were surprised to learn that he was English. But he had also faithfully read up on the German classics and especially on German poetry. To an English boy steeped in the Lake Poets and the seventeenth-century Metaphysicals, German poetry had been thin beer: shallow, didactic, sentimental, and belabored by a mechanical rhyming that to him sounded like the clop-clop-clop of a lame man's cane on a wooden floor. But then, his ear was probably at fault; after all, German was not his mother tongue.

But even if he had been German, he could not have made himself like the Schiller ballads which his German friends all knew by heart and quoted incessantly. Compared to the passionate, violent Scots ballads his dead mother had read to him when he was quite small, Schiller was trite, pious and contrived. Worst was a ballad called "Ritter Toggenburg," the tale of a *Ritter*, a knight of chivalry, who so worshipped his unattainable lady that he built himself a hut outside her castle where he sat for decades gazing at her bedroom window until he finally died there, still sitting, still gazing.

Hinton had thought it sentimental twaddle—a perfect example of what the Germans call *Kitsch*—and totally false. The lady, he thought, must soon have tired of that stolid admirer sitting there like a bump on a log and left through the back door with another lover—and Ritter Toggenburg was too befuddled, too full of his importance and suffering, to notice the big "For Rent" sign over the castle's front entrance.

His German friends were appalled. To make fun of Schiller was *lèse majesté*; probably still is, thought Hinton. They were shocked by what they saw as his callousness and his cynicism. "So very much like the English," his closest Goettingen friend had said, "that nation of shopkeepers, no poetry in their souls."

But, as Hinton now realized, he had not been cynical enough. The lady had been waiting for Toggenburg in her bedroom—his slippers warming by the fire, the pillows on the bed all fluffed up, and the champagne cooling in the icebucket—and he had been sitting there, gazing at the wrong window, probably the storeroom for the castle's ledger books or its spare halberds, and had not even noticed her when she leaned out of the bedroom window and beckoned to him to come in, and not keep her waiting forever.

Of course, Elaine had never loved him. She had not even been attracted to him. But if possession of her body was the price for rescuing herself and Freddie, she would have paid and thought nothing of it. She had been ready—and he had played Ritter Toggenburg. He found himself laughing again till the tears came.

Elaine had surely never loved anyone except Freddie. There were stories of her being passionately in love before her marriage (or even after it) with some romantic scamp, a dashing cavalry officer or, so the word sometimes went, a sloe-eyed, mustachioed Italian tenor.

Hinton had even heard whispered hints that Freddie was not Dennis Bancroft's son at all, but the child of that mysterious storybook lover.

But there was not the slightest doubt that Freddie was a Bancroft. His physical resemblance to the first viscount was so startling as to make Hinton take down the grandfather's portrait that hung in the Bancroft Brothers partners' room—it was too annoying to see Freddie every time he looked up from his desk. In personality and mind, too, Freddie was the first viscount all over again. The deals through which the grandfather had made Bancroft Brothers into a leading banking house were exactly like Freddie's counterfeiting scheme: brilliantly imaginative, planned in meticulous detail, then executed with lightning speed and daring.

In his other proclivities Freddie also took very much after the older man. "Why doesn't Frederick stick to respectable debauches?" old Mr. Eldridge had once wailed. What that meant one could guess by the size of the sums that used to be paid every quarter to Mr. Eldridge's firm under the heading of "The First Viscount's Charities." When Hinton took over Bancroft Brothers after Armistead's suicide, he had asked the first viscount's son what these "charities" were.

"All female," the son said dryly, and ordered the accounts shifted to his private ledger. Whether he had then continued to pay, renegotiated, or stopped payment, Hinton was never told and did not ask.

The only difference between grandfather and grandson was the direction of their activities: Freddie was out to destroy. As forces, grandfather and grandson had the same values, only one carried a plus sign and the other a minus sign. Their activities were very much the same, and so were the personalities and the temperaments behind them.

Just as the stories of Freddie's parentage were something Elaine had dreamed up and bruited about, so, Hinton thought, the mysterious lover could be dismissed as pure fabrication. Elaine Hinshaw, the only daughter of a widowed Admiralty judge who, late in life, had been given a baronetcy, had always known what she wanted—and it was not an impecunious lover and romance. It was power, wealth, position, and a title—but above all a child. There was indeed a man in Elaine's life: Freddie.

She barely tolerated her other children. The daughter—now for ten or more years married to the Earl of Cardiff, utterly domesticated and looking like a faded photograph of Elaine without her mother's fire or the animal energy that made Elaine dominate every room she entered—bored her. And Hinshaw, decent, bumbling, filial Hinshaw, who worshipped his mother, had always been patronized by her just as she had always patronized her equally worshipful, equally decent, equally ineffectual husband.

But she had loved Freddie possessively, passionately, totally, had done so even the first time Hinton saw Freddie as a little boy, only four and still in a smock rather than trousers, brought down from the nursery at Hinton's first dinner party there. For long minutes, mother and child had clung to each other completely oblivious of everyone else in the room.

A year or two ago, he remembered, there was that physician in Vienna—what was his name? Ferenczi, yes, that was it, Sandor Fe-renczi—one of those witty, clever Hungarians who provided the salt and pepper to Viennese society as the Irish provided it in London. Dr. Ferenczi had talked about a new psychological theory—he called it the "Oedipus Complex"—which had little boys desiring their mothers sexually and jealous of their fathers. The doctor had been quite surprised when Hinton said matter-of-factly: "I've known this ever since I was a small boy and lay awake nights hating my father and wanting to kill him so that I could get into my mother's bed."

And then Hinton had continued: "But tell me, Doctor, isn't there a complement to the Oedipus Complex—something I would call the Jocasta Complex? I've often felt that *Oedipus Rex* bowdlerizes the story. I never believed that the servant who spared Oedipus' life and had his wife bring up the baby rather than expose it did it out of pity; he did it, rather, because the mother, Jocasta, bribed him. I've never believed that a mother wouldn't know what had happened to her child, wouldn't know that he was alive and where he was, wouldn't visit him in secret. And then, I have thought, Jocasta arranged for her son, when grown up, to kill his father, both to revenge herself on Laertes for having taken away her child and to marry Oedipus, her son. I never believed that she was guilt-stricken when the story came out or even much bothered by having committed incest."

Ferenczi gave him a funny look—the same funny look Cantor had given him when he said that banking was applied mathematics, the same funny look most bankers gave him when he talked of "entrepreneurial mission"—and quickly moved away to another part of the room. But, of course, the doctor could not have known that he was talking of Elaine and Freddie.

And, he thought, Elaine is surely not the only one.

There's Melissa, who has never loved anyone, not even Anna, except the child who destroyed her, and who never wanted anything except to have a baby and be a mother.

And wasn't his own mother like that, too? How else could one explain her marrying his elderly father when she had come into the money that would have given her independence and enabled her to live somewhere in the South—on the Italian Riviera, perhaps, or in Madeira or southern Portugal around Lisbon, where one could live very well then on £100 a year—and where she might have recovered her health and overcome the fever that ravaged her lungs? She knew the man she married and could not have had any illusions. After all, she had lived in his house as his daughter's companion and as his housekeeper. That she did not love him, Hinton knew even as a small boy. And she must have known in advance that embracing her in bed he would not be embracing a woman but the income from £1,800. What other reason then to marry him, except for a passionate, desperate yearning to have a child?

"And perhaps the reason why I've fought shy of any woman's coming close to me is not just my fear of suffering again as I suffered when she died before I was eight, leaving me alone with a father who sold her belongings to the first peddler, never once kissed or hugged me but packed me immediately off to school, and who never wrote me a letter except to remind me that I was taking money away from him. Maybe I sensed even then that she had offered her body to have me. Maybe I was afraid even then of her passionate, possessive love for me, the love Elaine showed when she hugged that four-year-old Freddie as if embracing a lover.

"Elaine," Hinton mused, "is totally lawless, as lawless as Freddie. If it had helped Freddie, she would have given me her body without a moment's hesitation—and felt no more depraved than Jocasta did in committing incest with Oedipus. Only, it was not necessary—I was Ritter Toggenburg, already committed. Why else would I have married Melissa?"

Suddenly Hinton realized that he had married Melisssa to make sure that he would have to go to work for Bancroft Brothers and for Elaine and Freddie. It ensured that he could not join Mr. Morgan in New York—a colored wife was simply not conceivable there. And if he had taken on the International Industrial Bank, he would have had to entertain, keep a great house and have a wife who belonged, a wife who could represent. Being married to Melissa, even in utmost secrecy, thus made certain that he could work only for Bancroft Brothers, where he was expected not to compete socially but to leave society and entertaining to the "family" and to run the business for the Bancrofts' greater social glory.

Melissa had not wanted him to marry her; in fact, she had resisted. She never wanted to see him again, never wanted to be reminded of his existence, never wanted him to come between her and her grief, her pain, her remorse. He had to force her to go through with the ceremony. But he had wanted to be married to Melissa to make absolutely certain that he could not escape his commitment to Elaine and to Bancroft Brothers.

And then he realized that he had made that commitment nine months earlier. If Armistead had not looted the firm and then killed himself, the Bancrofts would not have called him back. But he had decided to wait for Melissa's baby so as to leave open the decision and to be available should the Bancrofts call him. Perhaps he had had an inkling of trouble at Bancrofts; or perhaps he had just indulged in wishful thinking. Before Melissa became pregnant, he had been ready to leave Vienna—both Mr. Morgan's partnership and the International Industrial Bank were all worked out, within his grasp, and not likely to improve if he waited. Melissa, for her part, had not wanted him to stay, had not wanted him around at all. All she wanted was to be alone with the child in her womb. She was probably even worried lest he might go back on his word and make her destroy the child, as all the other men had done earlier when they had made her pregnant.

Without Armistead, he would not have married Melissa. Without Armistead, he would not have gone back to the Bancrofts—but only because they would not have needed him. He was committed, had committed himself the moment he seized upon Melissa's pregnancy to procrastinate, to postpone, to keep open for another nine months the hope that the Bancrofts would summon him.

He realized now that the same forces had been at work at the first embezzlement of his life, the embezzlement of his mother's legacy. There, too, he had made the decision earlier; the embezzlement had only forced him, propelled him to carry out what he had decided months earlier. He had made the decision when he chose to do his dissertation on the history of mathematics rather than on mathematics itself and Hamilton's quaternions.

He had not known consciously that that meant abandoning a university career—though the kind old Goettingen professor, he remembered, had warned him. But he had known subconsciously, and had chosen. He had made the decision. The only thing the embezzlement then did was to enable him to go through with it as something he had no choice over.

Was he now caught up again in the same pattern? Had he again made a decision well before Freddie Bancroft's arrest and disgrace—and was now impelled by Freddie's crime to go through with something he had already subconsciously, unthinkingly, committed himself to?

The Decision

He knew at once. He had made the decision when he had said, three months ago, to the doctor: "The lady is my wife." Just as he had made the decision when he had shifted his dissertation topic from mathematics to history, and when he had postponed leaving Vienna to out-wait Melissa's pregnancy.

There had been no need to say anything to the doctor. Melissa had always been "Mrs. Pappas," had indeed insisted that the marriage certificate list them as "Mr. and Mrs. Pappas, Greek citizens." She had never talked of him or to him as "my husband," but always as "Mr. McGregor." No one except Anna and the Austrian doctor knew either of the dead child or the marriage. He had been just as silent as Melissa, both for her sake and for his own.

Why, then, had he blurted it out—to Montgomery Bramlett of all people? There was no greater gossip in all of London. Of course, he would not spread the story until his patient had died, and probably not until his bill had been paid. But then every dining room in London, after the ladies had withdrawn, would be treated to the juicy tale of the secret Mulatto wife of the famous banker, "so closely connected with one of our leading political families and always known to be a bachelor . . ."

Hinton had heard Bramlett often enough to know how he would spread the tale. He might as well have published his secret marriage in *The Times* agony column. He had spoken on the spur of the moment and had not planned the disclosure. But he had surely meant to make it, and to make it in a way that would guarantee its becoming public knowledge. No doubt: he had decided then and there. Freddie's crime, like his stepbrother's embezzlement and Armistead's suicide, had only been the forcing device.

The decision could have just one meaning: he had chosen to stop acting Ritter Toggenburg, to leave Bancroft, and to leave banking. As soon as he had said that to himself, he felt flooded with the euphoria, the warm well-being, the almost voluptuous sense of being right. So that was it. And that also explained the moment of panic earlier in the evening. It was then that the daimon in him had told him he had just changed his entire life, and had shaken him to the core of his being with the panic, the elemental fear, that an earthquake induces.

Swiftly there arose before his inner eye the vision of ten—maybe twelve—volumes of the *Monumenta Mathematica*, bound, he saw, in light blue, and bearing on their spines the names Bernoulli and Euler—he almost reached out to hold the books, to caress them. The seventeenth-century giants of mathematics—Descartes, Pascal, and Leibniz—were all but ready for the printer. Even Hinton's introductions, his major contribution and the hardest work, were finished.

Now he could start tackling the eighteenth century and the first generation of pure mathematicians. The seventeenth-century greats had still been philosophers, who spun systems out of words, with mathematics as a byproduct. But with the Swiss of the eighteenth century, with the seven or eight Bernoullis (father, uncles, sons, and cousins), and with Leonhard Euler, pure mathematics had begun its true reign. Philosophy would now be only an impediment to their vision of form and ratio, symbol and number.

The Bernoullis had moved the universe from cause and effect to probability, configuration, and mathematical statistics. They had put even Tyche, the Goddess of Chance, under the law, made her predictable and rational. In their mathematical statistics, the individual phenomenon, whether molecule or man, had freedom; but the universe was rigorously lawful and determined. And while before Euler all form and matter had existed in a space that itself had no properties, Euler's topology perceived space as having properties, space as having curve and edge, angle and dimensions. In topology, matter became an extension of space.

Ever since Hinton had first stumbled upon the eighteenth-century mathematicians while a student at Goettingen, he had loved them and thought them neglected and underrated. Now he could start looking for their papers in Basel, in St. Petersburg where they had spent so much of their lives, and in the archives of Europe. Now he could trace the unfolding of their thought and of their vision. Now he could make them accessible as mathematicians, as thinkers, as men.

Of course he was already sixty-three and might not live to finish the task. But his own father had only been a year or two younger when he sired him, and he had lived on for another twenty-five years, sickening only in the very last months. His mother had died young, but that was consumption. She came from healthy, long-lived stock; that great-uncle was almost ninety when he left her the £1,800. At least he could start, and he surely could train the young men who would then carry on if he did not live long enough to finish the task himself. Hinton almost felt his flanks quiver with eager anticipation as the flanks of a runner quiver when the starter cries "set."

But while he now knew that he had decided, he still knew just as little about the set, the configuration that was McGregor Hinton and his life. It surely seemed excessive for a major cataclysm—an embezzlement or a suicide—to be needed to trigger each of his humdrum decisions. His father, the vicar, would have spoken of Providence. Hinton had learned that this mysterious theological force, which the priests hypothesize the way the physicists hypothesize the equally unseen force of gravity in their universe, tends to operate through catastrophes—deformed babies and cataclysms that appear quite out of proportion to the occasion or the result. Anyhow, in mathematical statistics one does not talk causality; one talks statistical significance and correlation.

But no one, surely not Hinton, could write QED beneath his analysis. No one could either prove it or disprove it. Hinton knew it to be right. But was that feeling any more dependable than the firm conviction he encountered all the time, even among bankers, that 80 percent of 100 *must* be more than 12 percent of 1,000; wasn't 80 after all more than 12? One couldn't even say that Hinton's decision was right or that it had significant probability of being right. All one could say was that it seemed right for him. Surely, there was no predictive value to his configuration and no probability distribution.

In a rare moment of confidence, Mr. Morgan had once talked to him about leaving Goettingen and mathematics. "I felt mathematics to be empty," he had said. "It cannot account for what really matters"—and he gestured toward the Renaissance masterpieces that glowed on the wall behind him in their gilt frames.

Wasn't this also why Hinton in turn had left mathematics when he shifted his dissertation to its history? Mathematics, in any case, has no history; it existed before history and will exist after history has gone. Mathematicians have histories; his series, he thought, should really be called *Monumenta Mathematicorum*. He had left mathematics because it could not account for what really mattered: men and women and the way they behave and suffer and triumph, think and feel. But then, he said to himself, this defies any calculus, any system. The mantra of the swami dismisses it as delusion and Riemann's mantra dismisses it as irrelevant.

But at least he now knew what he had decided and was ready to act. With this he reached for the notepad and the pencil by his side and wrote down in big letters: ACTIONS.

First, at half past seven next morning—no, of course, it was already this morning—he would telephone Marburg, who was always in his study at that time thinking through the day to come.

"You have just bought," he'd say to him, "the eighteen and a half percent of the outstanding shares of the Bank of London & Austria which Bancroft Brothers owns, at yesterday's closing-bid price on the Vienna Bourse. The share certificate will be in your hands before noon. You will make payment in cash by the close of the business day today. You will also announce today—but not before four o'clock to keep it out of the evening papers—your purchase, the resignation of John McGregor Hinton, aged sixty-three, as chairman of the Bank of London & Austria, and your election to that position at an early meeting of the executive committee."

And Marburg would say: "Yes, Mr. Hinton," as he himself had countless times said: "Yes, Mr. Morgan," without ever regretting it.

Then he'd be at Bancroft Brothers at nine sharp, get the shares out of the vault and take them to Maimon & Marburg in Austin Friars. This would get him back to the West End in plenty of time for the ten o'clock meeting at Bancroft Terrace. He would wait until everybody had arrived—surely even Sheldon would be on time for once—before he took the floor.

"As chairman of Bancroft Brothers it is my duty," he'd start, "to shield old friends from the disgrace that has befallen the house of Bancroft. I have therefore sold against cash and delivered to the buyer the shares of the Bank of London & Austria owned by Bancroft Brothers, and will by tonight have ceased to be chairman of that Bank.

"But I also can no longer be associated myself with Bancroft Brothers.

"I am calling herewith an extraordinary meeting of the shareholders of the firm of Bancroft Brothers for nine o'clock this coming Monday, at the firm's registered offices in Leadenhall Street, with the first item on the agenda the acceptance of my resignation as chairman of the firm.

"Were I twenty years younger, I might carry on the banking business under my own name. But I am sixty-three and I have other things to do. I therefore intend to liquidate, and herewith offer to the members of the Bancroft family a sum equal to twenty-four and one half percent of Bancroft Brothers' net asset value as of last Wednesday, before Lord Frederick's arrest"—here Hinton jotted down the figure; he always knew the firm's net asset value to the last penny—

"This corresponds to the twenty-four and one half percent of the firm's stock held by the family. If you accept this offer, the sums due you will be paid in cash by next Friday, a week from today, and probably earlier. The same offer holds for the shares of the other minority shareholders, for Mr. Wyndham's seven and a half percent and Mr. Lovell's half percent. I would suggest that the family retain Mr. Lovell as its financial administrator; he is conscientious and conversant with your affairs.

"As for the rest of the small staff, all elderly, I suggest that we ask Mr. Eldridge to pension them off. We can trust him to be fair. The bank's office building, which stands in the books at one pound and which is easily salable, will net more than enough to buy retirement annuities.

"Should the family decide to continue the business, it will have to buy out at the same terms and for immediate cash the sixty-seven and one half percent of the stock I own—and, I should think, the seven and a half percent Mr. Wyndham owns as well.

"I expect to get your decision at nine o'clock Monday morning at the shareholders' meeting. Maybe Mr. Eldridge will convey it, as I imagine, you will not want to be in London where the newspapers can get hold of you. But if you neither accept my offer nor decide to buy me out on the same terms by nine-fifteen Monday morning, I shall move for the immediate liquidation of the firm. As you know, I have the votes to do so.

"The rest of the agenda of this meeting," he would continue, "is family business. In the past you have often honored me by including me in your family councils. I doubt that it is advisable for me to take part in this one today. I cannot think of anything to do in respect to Lord Frederick; and if I knew of anything, I'd be disinclined to do it. Our past attempts to save Lord Frederick from the consequences of his actions have done only harm to him and to us.

"I doubt," he'd conclude, "that we shall see each other again. But I do hope that the time will come when we can remember happier moments in our long association than the present one."

Then he'd go, even if Elaine were again to take his hands in hers. He was sure, however, that she would not try. She would never speak to him again, never acknowledge him again.

He'd go straight home to his dying wife. He would have to go out to dinner tonight, Friday, at Prince Sobieski's—fortunately Mosenthal would be there too, having just arrived in London. Thus he could formally submit his resignation as chairman of the Bank of London & Austria to Sobieski, the Bank's honorary chairman, and to Mosenthal, its director-general. He'd have to go out again on Monday morning to his last meeting at Bancroft Brothers. Otherwise he'd stay home until they carried Melissa out.

With this he got up, walked back into the house and up the stairs. Though it still lacked two hours until he could call Marburg, the full sun of a June morning was already streaming in through the fanlight over the front door.

In Melissa's room the curtains were tightly drawn and it was so dark that he could barely make out the nurse dozing on a loveseat in the corner. But when he sat down, there across the pulsing moan on

the bed glittered Anna's cat-green eyes, unblinking, sleepless, staring, as they had glittered, unblinking, sleepless, staring, that first
evening so very long ago, in the tawdry Vienna cabaret.

3. Mosenthal

The Banker
Sheila
Susie
The Homecoming

The Banker

They had supper served early, the banker Julius von Mosenthal and his guests: his brother Richard, the professor of anatomy; Richard's wife, Mariandl; and the Baron Paul Wald-Reifnitz, former Railway Minister and renowned authority on telegraph and telephone. The express to the West—to Paris and on to London via Calais—to which the banker's private railway carriage had been coupled had left Vienna a few minutes before noon. Six hours later, with the sun still high in the radiant blue of an early June evening, the steward was putting the evening meal on the table, just as the train began to slow down for the stop in Munich.

Nor did they tarry long over the meal, though the food was delicious: fresh salmon from Lake Constance with new asparagus, followed by the season's first strawberries in heavy cream.

Richard and Mariandl left first, while the train was still waiting in Munich's Central Station. "The English translation of the paper Richard's reading to the Congress next week only came in yesterday," Mariandl explained. "Of course he'll read it in German, but still we'd better go over the translation before it's distributed. And I need to run through my slides again. I've never operated the projector in front of so large an audience—and a foreign one, to boot—and I'm a little nervous."

Wald-Reifnitz also left as soon as he had finished the cigar he had lit after Mariandl was gone. He, too, he explained, had to work on the English translation of a paper for his congress: "Wireless Beyond Marconi." "And since, unlike my friend Richard, I promised in a moment of megalomania to read the paper in English, I'd better spend some time rehearsing."

The banker too had urgent work to do. He lingered just long enough after Wald-Reifnitz was gone not to give the impression that he was speeding his guests. Then he walked the few steps to his small office (originally the car's fourth bedroom) and closed the door firmly behind him.

It had been an early and a short meal, less like the dinner a great banker was supposed to serve, Julius Mosenthal thought; more like the "high teas" Sheila and he had had in small English country towns thirty years ago, in the New Forest, or in Sussex, around Hayward's Heath. Still, it was a festive, indeed, triumphant meal. For his guests were traveling with him to London to receive great honors—Wald-Reifnitz the Royal Society's Faraday Medal, Richard the equally distinguished Sydenham Medal of the Royal College of Physicians—and each of them the first Austrian scientist to be so honored. Yet the honor that awaited Mariandl was perhaps even more remarkable. As the first woman in the history of any of England's learned societies, she was to be presented with a special citation "in recognition of her photographs and drawings of the brain and the nervous system, which beautifully complement her distinguished husband's pioneering researches and greatly add to the pedagogic power of his famous books."

And so Julius had toasted all three of his guests, first Mariandl, then Wald-Reifnitz, Richard last. But after they had sat down again, Wald-Reifnitz (in his elegant "traveling suit" cut from gray knobbly silk) had risen once more, rapped on his glass, and said: "We must not forget the most important toast of the day—to our host. He won't tell us what he's working on; he never does. But I wager that the work our dear Julius settles down to after dinner is fully as important, for all its being done so quietly, as the work for which the three of us will be honored a few days hence. We three explore Nature. But you, my dear Julius, bring together the resources of Nature and the works of man, so that all of us, and our children and grandchildren, can live better and achieve more, and so that our Fatherland may become stronger and wealthier. I propose a toast to Julius von Mosenthal, who has done more than any other man of our generation to develop Austria's industry, her commerce, and her agriculture!"

They all clapped. And Mariandl, the shy aloof Mariandl, who rarely even shook hands, had thrown her arms around him and kissed him firmly on the mouth. Then they had eaten their meal in companionable silence.

"Wald-Reifnitz always exaggerates," thought Mosenthal, as he settled himself in his chair, unlocked his dispatch case, and took out his papers. "Yet however did he guess what I'm trying to do? I've never told anyone but Hinton, and that many years ago. Klauber might know, but he's worked with me for more than twenty years. And that extraordinary fellow Bienstock guessed it right away—but then he had good reason to study my record at the Bank carefully. But Wald-Reifnitz . . . he never pays attention to anyone or anything except his beloved electricity. How did he guess?

"At that," Mosenthal thought, "he may have been right about my work tonight. If I succeed on this trip, I should be able to finish the task glimpsed so faintly on my first trip to London, more than thirty years ago, when I couldn't sleep in that overcrowded third-class coach and began to speculate about my future, my goals in life. It was only a dream then and I was just twenty-four, little more than a clerk when I came to London to represent the obscure Viennese banking firm of Moritz Herzfeld & Company. But that dream never left me. It led me to Hinton in London and to founding the Bank of London & Austria with him five years later.

"If I succeed on this trip, and if the good Lord keeps me alive and healthy, fifteen years hence I should have turned Austria-Hungary into a major economic power, well ahead of France and not too far behind Germany. And then the various parts of the Empire will be so dependent on each other economically that it should no longer matter whether people speak Czech, German, Hungarian, or Croat. Their economic self-interest will be so much greater than the divisive forces of the nationalities or the 'classes' of which the Socialists always prattle. It can be done, I know; and I know how to do it.

"This trip to London," Mosenthal continued to himself, "should give me the one thing that's needed, the right team to lead the Bank. And then I'll be able to concentrate on really important tasks."

He knew very well what they were: to give Austria's poor mountain provinces the potential for industrial growth by developing cheap hydroelectric power; develop the chemical industry in northwest Bohemia until it could compete with the Germans; and develop the oil fields in Austrian Poland. There was work to be done and profit to be made in developing tourism—no reason why the Carinthian lakes, the Tyrolean Mountains, and the Adriatic beaches shouldn't rival both Switzerland and the Riviera as tourist resorts. And southern Hungary and the Adriatic coast were just waiting for the development of their wine and fruit-growing industries. The wines were at least as good as those of southern France and vastly cheaper.

"They say," reflected Mosenthal, "that to wage war three things are needed: 'Money, money, and again money.' What is needed for the tasks of peace is Time, time, and again time.' And I don't have it yet. With Klauber returned to Vienna, I'm almost there; at least I don't have to run the Bank any more day to day. But I really won't have time until Bienstock joins me and takes over the planning and thinking, as well as all those time-consuming relationships with the ministries, the other banks, and the companies who are our clients. With Bienstock, I'll finally have the team I need."

As soon as the bank Mosenthal had dreamed of on his first journey to London had become a reality as the Bank of London & Austria, with Hinton as chairman and himself as general manager, Mosenthal had started to build up his team. Jacob Klauber was his first candidate. Though only in his twenties, he was then old Moritz Herzfeld's chief clerk: the job Mosenthal himself had held before he was sent to London. Mosenthal hired Klauber away, and in succession put him into every executive job in the rapidly growing bank. Five years ago Mosenthal had made him the first Austrian to head the bank's London office. He had done a brilliant job. And then only five months ago, on New Year's Day, 1906, Klauber had returned from London to become the bank's second in command under Mosenthal, and its deputy director-general. It had taken twenty-five years, but it was well worth it.

Jacob Klauber, Mosenthal thought, was the best all-around banker in Europe today. People trusted him. And if you gave him a problem, he'd find the solution. There was nothing wrong with the younger men, either—Deutsch, who had succeeded Klauber in London, Gelb, Altmann, Breitner—there was no stronger team anywhere in Europe. And yet, Klauber will never be anything but Number Two. He couldn't and wouldn't think more than a year or two ahead, couldn't and wouldn't go beyond the specific problem, the individual deal, the next situation. He was a follower, with no wish to be a leader. Breitner had the vision, to be sure, but at thirty-three he was still ten years away from a top job. So Mosenthal had felt himself tied down until he had got Bienstock to agree to come in as his other deputy director-general.

Dr. Gottfried Bienstock had been a very long shot. A year earlier, at only forty-seven and almost ten years younger than any of his predecessors, Bienstock had been appointed Sektionschef in the Ministry of Finance, the highest civil-service rank. In his speech of introduction to the Bankers' Association, he had said things that were so unconventional and so similar to what Mosenthal himself had always believed that Mosenthal left the meeting thinking, "If only I could get him to join me."

It was a harebrained idea, or so it seemed. Senior Austrian civil servants who had made Sektionschef and "Excellency" looked down on business and businessmen, believing themselves far too grand even for the top job in a major bank. And Bienstock wouldn't be attracted by the money, either. His wife came from one of the oldest Jewish banking families, the Arnsteins, who had achieved their barony even before the Rothschilds.

Still, Mosenthal could not get Bienstock out of his mind. If approached, he was sure he'd be thrown out; the man might even be seriously offended. But one morning, about ten days after Bienstock's speech, he had his secretary call up the new Sektionschef, went to see him at the ministry, and, without preliminaries, asked him: "Is there any chance that you will join me in the management of the Bank of London & Austria?"

Bienstock sat stockstill for what seemed an eternity and was probably all of five minutes. Then he opened his eyes very wide, turned around in his swivel chair, and looking Mosenthal full in the face said: "May I ask you, Herr Generaldirektor, to come back a year from now, should you then still be interested in my answer to your question? At present I owe it to the Minister who has expressed such great confidence in me not even to listen to such a question."

A year later, to the day, Mosenthal had repeated the question. Bienstock had replied: "To everyone else, Herr Generaldirektor, I would immediately say 'No.' I am a public servant and I intend to remain one. But when I studied the records of your Bank, I realized that you are practicing what I have only been preaching. And I've gone as far in the government service as I can possibly go. If you were to offer me an assignment in which I can work constructively as a banker on Austria's economic and industrial development, I should consider it very seriously. And my wife, with whom I have discussed the matter—of course without mentioning your name or that of your Bank—agrees with me."

That had been just six weeks ago, and things had been moving fast since. The next step was to get Bienstock together with Klauber—for it was with Klauber that Bienstock would have to work most closely. Yet it seemed so very unlikely that the two would hit it off.

The Bienstocks had been cultured bourgeoisie for three generations, beginning with the grandfather who had become Austria's largest cotton importer and continuing with the father, only recently dead, who had been the lawyer for the largest textile companies. Gottfried Bienstock himself had graduated at the top of his class in law school, had had his doctor's thesis on banking law published by a prestigious publisher, and had managed, at the same time, to acquire on the side a second doctorate in art history. Both he and his wife were enthusiastic art lovers and generous patrons of young painters and architects.

Klauber, by contrast, had been born the son of a kosher butcher in the remote village of Mosenthal, high in the Hungarian mountains—the village from which the Mosenthals had taken their name. Thirty-five years ago, at fourteen, he had walked to Vienna with one pair of trousers, an old sheepskin jacket, one pair of boots—which he carried around his neck while he went barefoot—and a letter of introduction to Mosenthal's father, Dr. Joseph Mosenthal, the lawyer. The father had found him a place to sleep and a job of sorts as errand boy and general handyman with the same Moritz Herzfeld with whom his own son had started out as a trainee a few years earlier. Of course all this was a long time ago. But Klauber's German still had heavy traces of the hard Yiddish of his childhood. The Bienstocks entertained every distinguished artist who visited Vienna, whether writer, painter, or musician; Mrs. Klauber still kept a kosher home, never was seen in public, and never entertained anyone. Bienstock had two doctorates and lectured at the university on money and banking; Klauber was painfully, morbidly, conscious of his lack of formal education, indeed of any education at all. Bienstock had a dozen interests; Klauber knew and cared for one thing only: banking. Bienstock was suave, polished, articulate, Klauber so shy that he only came out of his shell after years of acquaintance.

But thanks to Bienstock, the dinner at which Mosenthal introduced the two to each other had been a complete success right from the start. No sooner had they sat down than Bienstock said: "I envy you, Direktor Klauber, your five years in London at the center of world banking and international finance. You must know so much more than we do in this backwater here about the latest trends in money and banking, and the latest theories."

And Klauber, the shy, diffident, taciturn Klauber, had at once begun to talk freely and fluently, indeed brilliantly. When he mentioned some new writers on monetary theory—some Swedes, a Frenchman, a couple of Germans—Bienstock interrupted: "I've heard of the works, but haven't been able to get hold of them yet."

"I have them at the Bank, Excellency," Klauber had said, beaming, "and should be honored to send them over to the Ministry tomorrow morning."

And then Bienstock had made a lifetime worshipper out of Klauber by saying, just as the meeting was breaking up, "I am the youngest here, and I know I'm grossly violating propriety. But if we are to work together, do we have to keep to our Austrian stiffness and call each other by our full titles all the time? The Bank, after all, is as much English as it is Austrian. Why don't we just do as the English do and call each other by our family names?"

But before Mosenthal could make a formal offer to Bienstock, he still had to get approval from the Prince Sobieski, Austro-Hungarian Ambassador to London, and from Hinton, the principal owner of the London banking firm of Bancroft Brothers. They were, respectively, the honorary chairman and chairman of the board of the Bank of London & Austria. More important, between them they owned almost 50 percent of the Bank's stock.

"Hinton," Mosenthal had told Klauber confidently, "will present little difficulty; he leaves the management of the Bank entirely to me. But the Prince always objects strenuously to paying anyone a decent salary. And the salary I have in mind for Bienstock is a good deal more than decent; it has to be generous"—and Klauber had agreed.

"Why, my dear Generaldirektor," Mosenthal could hear the Prince saying in his nicest, "reasonable" diplomat's voice, "pay your new colleague such an incredible sum? Why shouldn't what our government pays its senior civil servants with their enormous responsibilities be sufficient, with perhaps a little extra? I don't understand it at all."

It would take fifteen minutes of patient explaining: "Yes, the salaries of senior civil servants are adequate, indeed generous, for the average civil servant. But it is precisely the failure of the civil service to recognize anybody as far above average as Bienstock that makes such a man available at all," before the Prince conceded the point and fell back on his next—as he always thought, unanswerable—argument.

"My own Director-General, Birnbaum," he'd say, "surely has equal or greater responsibilities than a banker. I hope you don't take this personally, my dear Mosenthal, but the Sobieski estates are still a good deal larger than your bank. Yet I don't pay my Director-General a third of what you propose to pay Sektionschef Bienstock. And my Director-General seems perfectly content."

"One of these days," Mosenthal thought, "I won't be able to restrain myself and will give the Prince the right answer: 'Maybe you don't pay your Director-General more, but he costs you much more. He steals from you brazenly.'" It was common knowledge that the Sobieski Director-General stole openly, shamelessly, taking commissions from anyone who worked for the Sobieski estates, and demanding bribes from anybody who sold to the Sobieski estates or bought from them, and from the companies that insured the Sobieski palaces, factories, and office buildings.

Yet Mosenthal knew there was no point in saying this to the Prince. He simply would not hear it—or perhaps would treat it as a mild witticism. Yet the Prince was intelligent, level-headed, indeed superb in his understanding of business.

There was no point either, Mosenthal knew, in using the rational arguments for paying a man well and a good man extremely well. Years ago, by way of comment on Sobieski's aversion to paying decent salaries, Hinton had quoted a favorite saying of his American friend, the great banker J. P. Morgan: "If you employ someone to make you rich, you better make him wealthy."

He would quote Mr. Morgan to the Prince; Morgan, after all, was the century's greatest banker. But he knew in advance what the Prince's reply would be: "My dear Mosenthal," in his most charming, warmest, voice, "I am an incurable European. The only things American for which I have any use are the Havana cigar and the potato." People who heard this for the first time thought it terribly witty. Mosenthal had heard it too often to be greatly amused.

And so as his last resort he would have to force himself to use the only weapon to which the Prince yielded, gross flattery.

"Your Royal Highness," he'd say (strictly speaking, the Prince was not entitled to the "Royal," but he loved to hear it once in a while), "your Director-General has the honor and distinction of serving an ancient and exalted House and a great and gracious Prince. That is remuneration in itself, far beyond anything money can buy."

Then, he knew, the Prince would drop the matter and, after a little grumbling, move on to the next item on the agenda.

Yet the formal offer to Bienstock would still be useless unless Mosenthal succeeded in changing the ownership structure of the Bank. It had outgrown being dominated by two very rich men: Prince Sobieski and Hinton, neither of whom was or could be active in running it. But until there was a team at the top there had been no point moving on so difficult, even dangerous, an issue. Now that he had Klauber on board and Bienstock willing to join, he had to tackle it, and fast. Bienstock, in his blunt way, had said to him only three weeks ago, when they had settled the salary the Bank was to pay him, "Surely you realize that I would not give up being a servant of the state only to become a servant of Prince Sobieski." And the two ablest of his younger men, Gelb and Breitner—both of whom were rapidly becoming attractive "prospects" for top positions in the other Viennese banks—were also chafing under the Bank's structure.

When he and Hinton had conceived the Bank of London & Austria, way back in 1878, their first investor had not been Hinton's own bank, Bancroft Brothers. It had been Sir Solomon Maimon of Maimon & Company. The old man had not put much money in. "It has never been my policy," he said, "to put a lot of money into an untried venture." But the 5 percent of the initial capital that he pledged at once made the Bancrofts willing to come in for a big share: 37 percent. Sir Solomon was famed for his touch in picking winners, which counted for far more than even his wealth—other people had money too, after all.

It was also largely Sir Solomon's lead that had induced Prince Sobieski to become the third and largest stockholder. (Mosenthal himself had been the fourth, using all the money he had managed to lay aside in five years in London to subscribe to 1 percent of the stock.) He and Hinton got to see the Prince, then still in Berlin and not yet named ambassador to London, because Sir Solomon set up an appointment for them. The Prince had listened to them for a couple of hours, asked a few searching questions, and then said: "You are the first bankers who make sense to me. And if Solomon Maimon trusts you, you are also the first bankers I've met, other than he, who are honest men. How much do you need to get started?" The money was in their account forty-eight hours later.

When the Bank opened on New Year's Day of 1879, 37 percent of the stock was owned by Bancroft Brothers and 57 percent by Prince Sobieski. In the years since, the outstanding share capital had been doubled, with two issues of capital stock put on the market, one in London and one in Vienna. Both Mosenthal himself and Maimon & Company—or rather, its successor, Maimon & Marburg—had added steadily to their holdings, Mosenthal raising them to 5 percent, Maimon to around 10 percent. Bancroft Brothers and Sobieski had held on to their shares, so that now they owned respectively 18½ and 28½ percent of the total shares outstanding, or virtually 50 percent combined control.

Such a structure was of course wholly inappropriate for one of the continent's leading financial institutions. But what was merely a blemish now, a few years hence (when both Hinton and Sobieski should have left the scene) could stunt the Bank and might all too easily spell disaster.

Bancroft Brothers *was* Hinton; and Hinton was already sixty-three, with neither heirs nor real partners. What did he plan to do with his stock in the Bank of London & Austria? Would he leave it to those imbeciles, the Bancrofts, whom he seemed to worship? Why else had he not long ago pushed them out of a venture which they had bled dry, to which they had not made a single contribution in the quarter century since Hinton left Vienna to rescue the firm—when, as everybody knew, it had been ruined by the family's greed and incompetence. Or would Hinton leave his enormous wealth, including the Bank's shares, to his Oxford college, or some foundation to support the work in the history of mathematics to which he himself gave more and more of his time? The prospect of having one fifth of the Bank's shares in the hands of a stodgy college bursar, who probably could not even find Vienna on the map and thought all foreigners "dagos," was not much more appealing to Mosenthal than having its destiny dependent upon that frivolous lightweight, that eternal juvenile, Sheldon Bancroft.

But he could not ask Hinton—Hinton would not even acknowledge the question. He talked freely about banking and politics, about music and mathematics, about his days as a student in Goettingen and about his friend J. P. Morgan in New York. But he had never once in all the thirty years they had been friends spoken about himself or his family or childhood. When they first got to know each other (and they got along right away so well that, within weeks, they were calling each other "du" when they spoke German), Hinton had asked endless questions about Mosenthal's family, the mother whom Mosenthal adored, the father he greatly respected, and his younger twin brothers, who even then showed intellectual brilliance. But about his own background and family, Hinton had said nothing except that he had grown up in a village in the Fens, north of Cambridge, where his father had been the vicar, and that his mother had died when he was still a small boy.

Mosenthal had mentioned Hinton's reticence to his father-in-law, Dr. Augsburg, who had been Hinton's medical adviser in Vienna and on whom Hinton always called when he came to Austria. But

Papa had only said, with a sharpness that was quite unusual for him: "Leave Hinton alone; he has suffered much."

While Hinton worried Mosenthal because he had no heirs, Prince Sobieski worried him because he *had*—and with the Prince sixty-six years of age, the heirs might take over any day. The younger of the two did not really matter. At twenty-seven or twenty-eight, he still did little but chase women, and would apparently never do much else. It was the older one, the one in the army, who would be head of the house of Sobieski; and the more Mosenthal saw of him—and he had lately seen a good deal of him in connection with the Hungarian Lateral Railway project—the less comfortable he felt.

The young Prince and his father shared the facial characteristics that for generations had marked the male Sobieski: aquiline nose; pointed, triangular chin jutting sharply forward; small ears set so far back on the side of the head as to give the face a broad Slavonic cast; hooded eyes under bushy eyebrows; and a high forehead ending in a widow's peak. In the father, these features worked harmoniously together to form a face that, while far from handsome, was yet extraordinarily attractive, animated by a lively intelligence and warmed by a charming smile. But in the son there was hardly any "face" at all; the features seemed to have been stuck, helter-skelter, into heavy pastry dough, did not articulate or move together, indeed, did not even seem to belong together. It was a heavy, hard, indolent face, shuttered and with a touch of malice. What in the father was intelligence, in the son's face signaled meanness.

Father and son were both of medium height. The father stood, sat, walked, straight, his head erect on a slender neck. The son slouched, slumped, and shuffled. And the young Prince's General Staff uniform, though cut by a master tailor, could not hide a most unmilitary paunch. The father had all the arrogance of the great nobleman, of course; but it manifested itself above all in an exquisite courtesy to his social inferiors. The son always seemed to sense slights, always to be on the defensive, ready to assert that as a Prince Sobieski he was owed deference. And there was in the son a smoldering rage, a desire to lash out and hurt, a boundless but frustrated ambition, that all told made Mosenthal thoroughly ill at ease whenever he had to spend any time with the young man.

Ernest Marburg, with his caustic wit, had once said that the two Sobieskis exemplified Darwin in reverse: the descent of ape from man. But that, Mosenthal thought, maligned an innocent beast. The most apt simile for the young Prince was Caliban in Shakespeare's *Tempest*—a human being bred to the ultimate potential of man's basest traits, cunning, greed, and envy. And he knew—as everyone sensed who had any dealings with the man—that the young Prince could not be trusted, was unpredictable, and might betray or inflict pain for the sheer joy of doing so.

The young Prince would surely not be able to give direction and vision to the Sobieski Estates and Enterprises as his father was doing. He had neither his father's head for business nor his habit of hard work.

Yet Mosenthal knew that if he himself even attempted to interfere, he would do infinite harm. But if he didn't, it would be just as bad—or worse. If the young Prince left the management of his business affairs to his administrator, as most great nobles did (the present Prince Sobieski was an exception), Birnbaum would, in effect, become the Bank's master, unless the Sobieskis' holdings of the capital had first been reduced to a point where they represented merely an "investment" rather than ownership and control. And Birnbaum, Director-General of the Sobieski Estates and Enterprises, was a slimy toad, and pure greed, corruption, and concupiscence.

The real problem was his greed. Birnbaum was not without ability, Mosenthal had to concede. He was no Sobieski, to be sure; ideas and entrepreneurship came from the Prince, who made every major decision without even consulting his Director-General. But Birnbaum was a competent day-to-day manager, ran a tight office, and was good at executing orders. And whatever he did in the evenings, he was all business during the day.

But he could never get enough money, was always whining, begging, threatening to extort more for himself—a bigger commission, a bigger participation, an extra bonus. All the Sobieski managers, down to the foreman in the woodlands, had to put back a tenth of their salaries into Birnbaum's bottomless pockets. Every contract, whether of purchase or sale, included a "little something" for Birnbaum. Whenever he came to a board meeting of the Bank, he expected to find a check discreetly hidden in an unmarked envelope tucked into his director's notebook. And he always complained afterwards that it wasn't enough and tried (far too often successfully) to wheedle a second "bonus" out of Mosenthal.

"Do you think he'd try to take over the Bank's management if he were no longer on the old Prince's tight leash?" Bienstock had asked.

"No," Mosenthal had answered, "that's not the danger. Birnbaum is much too greedy to take a job where auditors and the Ministry's banking inspectors check the books and make reports. He'd become a bloodsucker—and he'd drive out any self-respecting banker. I would certainly leave rather than submit to Birnbaum's extortions.

"But," Mosenthal added, "if the Sobieski holdings are down to where they are an investment only, Mr. Birnbaum will be out on his ear the first time he tries to extort one penny."

The solution was clear: increase the Bank's capital through a substantial share issue to the public. The increase was long overdue anyhow. The Bank was grossly undercapitalized for its business and its liabilities. The stock market was ready. In both Vienna and London he could raise more capital than he needed, and at an excellent price: eight times the par value. And by issuing as many new shares as there were old ones outstanding, the proportion of the Bank's capital held by each existing shareholder would at once be halved. This would bring the Sobieski holdings below the 15 percent mark which, as Mosenthal knew from many conversations with him, the Prince considered the dividing line between "ownership" and "investment."

And then, as Mosenthal had confided in Bienstock—though of course Klauber also knew it—he would take step two within a year or eighteen months. He would give control to the top people as a group by providing that each of them—there would be seven at the outset—would buy enough shares to have the group overall hold 35 percent of the stock. The purchase would be financed by the Bank at prevailing rates of interest and paid for out of the Bank's dividends. The shares would then be repurchased by the Bank at the current stock market price whenever an executive left the Bank's employ for any reason, whether death, retirement, resignation, or dismissal. Ernest Marburg, the experienced financier, had urged this move on Mosenthal ever since he had joined the Bank's board when his father-in-law, Sir

Solomon Maimon, died twelve years ago. And Hinton, too, would see the logic of the move, however much he might resent it as the final cutting of the umbilical cord between him and his "firstborn." But then Hinton had long ago lost interest in the Bank, indeed, Mosenthal suspected, was rapidly losing interest in banking altogether.

Sobieski, however, would block the move unless the shift from owner to mere investor had already been made for him. As an investor he'd complain about "overpaying employes," but after two hours of grumbling would say, "What's the next item on the agenda?" As an owner, Sobieski would never accept sharing with other "co-owners" or "partners."

The Prince was certainly not anti-Semitic. Indeed, he had often been attacked as a "Jewish stooge" and a "Jew-lover" in Parliament and the Vienna City Council by the German Nationalists and the Anti-Semites among the Christian Socialists. He spoke constantly of the debt he owed to a Jew, his teacher and mentor Jeidels, the Sobieski administrator half a century ago, and the grandfather of Birnbaum's wife. And when he talked of Jeidels, there was unusual warmth and affection in his voice.

He was also more than willing to have Jews manage his companies and estates. "Of course," thought Mosenthal, "he has no choice. Capable non-Jews in Austria don't go into business; they go into the civil service, the army, and the professions."

And the Prince was perfectly content to have Jewish subordinates, whether they were named Birnbaum or Mosenthal. He had no compunction about sitting down with Jews at an "official" dinner, as he would do tomorrow night when the two Mosenthals and Ernest Marburg would be Sobieski's guests, together with Hinton and the famous doctor, Sir Montgomery Bramlett.

And yet, Mosenthal realized, Sobieski would never sit down with a Jew at a "social" occasion, though even the King of England now dined at the Marburgs' a dozen times a year, brought along his current mistress, and stayed half the night to play whist. And to be a "partner" with commoners, let alone with Jews, would be altogether unthinkable for "His Highness, Prince Sobieski, Duke of Przemysl," no matter how sincere his gratitude to and affection for a Jeidels.

Sobieski the investor would want to make money; Sobieski the owner had to be a Prince.

But once the Bank had doubled its capital and sold the new shares to the public, Sobieski would have no choice—and no qualms either.

This was the prospect Mosenthal presented to Bienstock, and this was indeed what he hoped to bring back from London in a few weeks. But what he did not mention—and Bienstock either did not see it or, more probably, did not think it politic to notice—was that all would be undone if either Sobieski or Hinton, or both, were to say: "Of course, the Bank needs more capital. But why go to strangers for it? I will put it up."

Either man could easily do so. For Hinton, the sum would be but a trifle. But Sobieski, too, could raise it right away. The public issue of his holdings in the Polonia Brewery alone, which the Bank had managed only yesterday, had produced enough net profit (and all in cash) for the Prince to pay for a big chunk of the Bank's new shares. Mosenthal was confident that he could dissuade Hinton from buying the new shares. "The Bank needs a much broader ownership base," was an argument Hinton would understand. But it would be lost on the Prince, who could not possibly understand that the Sobieski embrace might ever become too close for comfort, let alone that anyone could feel anything but honored to work for Prince Sobieski and wear his livery.

"I may be worrying about nothing," thought Mosenthal. "But I can't take the risk. And the only way to stop Sobieski if he wants to add to his holdings is to have both Hinton and Marburg agree beforehand to oppose him. He listens to them. Marburg can do it, and he will if he knows Hinton will back him. He's long forgotten his origins in Vienna's Jewish ghetto, is not in awe of any prince and duke, and probably considers himself—as an English baronet and the confidant of the King of England—several cuts above any Pole. He'd dare tell Sobieski that a bank has to have autonomy." Its clients have to be sure he'd say "that their interests will not be subordinated to those of any stockholder, and that their secrets will be safe." He could tell Sobieski plainly that his own industries were competing with most of the Bank's potential clients: "If you increase your hold-

ings, you'll endanger the Bank of London & Austria. And I'll leave
the board and tell the newspapers why."

But should he go first to Hinton and have him bring in Marburg?
Or should he talk first to Marburg, then let him work on Hinton? If
only it were Maimon & Marburg rather than Bancroft Brothers, and
Hinton who had the shares and the votes . . .

Finally, there was the Hungarian Lateral Railway. This, too, had to
be fitted into Mosenthal's strategy.

Seven or eight weeks ago, two officers from the General Staff had
called on him: Colonel Hellmann and his newly appointed assistant,
Lieutenant-Colonel Prince Sobieski. Hellmann, deputy head of the
Transportation Section, was the General Staff's rising star, expected
in just a year or two to become the first officer of Jewish birth (baptized, of course, somewhere along the line) to be made a general.
Hellmann was also known to be the brains behind Hoetzendorf, the
heir to the throne's candidate for Chief of Staff and the leader of the
"activist" party in the War Ministry. He had greatly increased his
power by persuading the young Prince Sobieski to leave his family's
prestigious cavalry regiment, the Sobieski Cuirassiers, and join the
General Staff's Transportation Section.

"We are coming to you, Herr Generaldirektor," Hellmann had
begun, "because we at the War Ministry are impressed by your record
of entrepreneurial vision and by your ability to grasp new ideas. The
General Staff, and especially His Excellency, Lieutenant-General von
Hoetzendorf"—here both he and young Sobieski slightly inclined
their heads—"have become convinced that Austria-Hungary needs a
new major railway. We have called it the Hungarian Lateral. It would
run from Bratislava in Slovakia southeast through Hungary to a ter-
minus in Zemlin across the river from Belgrade, the Serbian capital. We want you, Herr Generaldirektor, and your Bank of London &
Austria to lead in the financing of this important undertaking—the
first major new railway to be built in our country in twenty years."

"This new railway," Sobieski had taken over next, in what was
clearly a carefully rehearsed duet, "will open up enormous natural
resources and be of major economic benefit. Coal and timber, grain,

wine, cattle and sheep—all are there waiting and need only access to the markets."

"But," Hellmann had chimed in, "the Hungarian Lateral is also going to be of great military significance. It will make possible rapid troop movements should there be trouble in the Balkans, as is only too likely."

Every one of their arguments was spurious, as Mosenthal knew right away. The Hungarian Lateral was nothing but a gigantic bribe to the greatest and richest of Hungarian landowners, to make them join the heir to the throne's party. Yet Mosenthal was at first greatly attracted. As the leading Bank chosen by the War Ministry for so large a project, the Bank of London & Austria would at once be put on a par with the three "ranking" older Vienna banks. It would also make the increase in the Bank's capital a foregone conclusion.

Yet the more arguments for the project Hellmann presented, the more skeptical did Mosenthal become.

The project would be a waste of his time. Hellmann might get his promotion out of it; the archduke might get the support of the great Hungarian nobles. But no railway would ever be built. There would be far too much opposition—and not only in Parliament, where every other group and nationality, from the Czechs to the Social Democrats, would fight it. Wald-Reifnitz and the Railway Ministry he controlled had said again and again that the country already had more railways than it needed or could support. And the Ministry of Finance, considering the sorry state of Austria-Hungary's public finances, would be bound to oppose another military extravaganza.

"There will be studies, reports, commissions, ad infinitum," Mosenthal concluded; "but not one mile of track will ever be laid." And though it would be gratifying to be accepted as one of the "ranking" banks, it was not worth spending five or six years of his life in endless meetings and arduous negotiations which he knew all along could lead nowhere.

Still, he also knew that he had to put up a good fight for the project with Sobieski and Hinton, and be able to claim convincingly in the end that he had been overruled. Anything else would earn him the enmity of Hellmann, and of his patrons Hoetzendorf and the archduke. Of course, they would know; the young Prince surely had his spies in his father's household, either the valet or his private secretary, the pedantic Dr. Wegner. "I have to finesse it," Mosenthal decided, "so that I'm knocked down after a loud sham battle, but also so that my defeat advances my real objective—the conversion of Sobieski's and Hinton's 'ownership' stakes into 'investments.'"

As was his wont, Mosenthal worked through his plans and strategies systematically four or five times, until he had thought them through completely. He wrote out one memorandum to himself after another, carefully diagrammed every single move, checked and double-checked lest he had overlooked anything. Even the smallest detail forgotten, he had learned, could be fatal.

In the end, he decided how he would proceed. The Lateral Railway would come first. He would be turned down, planned to be turned down. Then he could argue that he had made an enormous sacrifice by giving up the chance of the Bank's becoming one of the "big four," and that he was owed something in exchange.

This would cut no ice with Hinton. Hinton never bargained. "But Sobieski is the professional diplomat to his fingertips," Mosenthal said to himself, "and believes that a concession by one side deserves a concession in return." So he could move in on the increase in the Bank's capital with Sobieski prepared.

Bienstock would come last. He needed another day to work out in his mind all the possible arguments any of the three men might advance, their words, their very gestures or intonations, and the right responses on his part—"Reading out the script," actors called it, except that he would also have to write the script. But that could wait till Sunday.

Now at last he was ready to celebrate the Homecoming.

It was well past midnight. Long ago they had passed Nancy, where the Calais-bound coaches had been uncoupled from the Paris train. It would be a long day tomorrow—or rather, today. He would have to get up very early, at six or so, for the morning ferry from Calais to Dover. And in the evening there was the dinner at Prince Sobieski's, which would last until all hours. Yet after he had shredded his working papers and flushed them down the toilet, he did not go to bed. Tired as he was, he went back to the salon where they had had their supper, poured himself another cognac, and lit another cigar. Both were part of the ritual of the Homecoming, the ritual that had begun more than a quarter of a century ago when he left London and Sheila to return to Vienna and the management of the newly founded Bank of London & Austria, the ritual which he observed every time he crossed the Channel on the way to or from England, even that sad time, eight years ago, when he had been called back to Vienna by the sudden death of his mother only a day after arriving in London.

Today, from the moment he woke up in Calais until he left the train at Victoria Station, he'd spend in his mind again with Sheila. Before he went to bed, therefore, he had to review their four years together to decide which of their days he would relive on the morrow. Then at last he could go to bed, to wake up in Calais to a day of memory and nostalgia.

Sheila

He still had the letter his mother had sent him in the late autumn of his first year away from home, the letter that had led to his meeting Sheila.

> *You are much too good to me, my beloved Julius [she had written] . . .*
>
> *There really is nothing I can think of for a Christmas present; you know how your dear Father spoils me. And I certainly will not allow you, my silly boy, to buy something expensive for me, even if you have been making such good money as you report. (Father tells me, by the way, that Mr. Herzfeld says glowing things about your work for him—I am so proud of you!)*
>
> *But, my dearest Julius, if you insist on sending a Christmas present to your old mother, there is one thing I would love to have from London: a few pairs of really fashionable elbow-length white opera gloves, the kind with three mother-of-pearl buttons that are all the rage here. Of course I can get them in Vienna; and your Father maintains that all such gloves, whatever the box they come in, are actually made in Bohemia, in Gablonz or some such place— you know how he loves to tease. Still, wherever they're made, it's so much more chic to have them in a London box. But don't buy them at Benson's in Bond Street, who have the most expensive millinery and gloves. Any decent shop will be more than adequate . . .*

And so he found himself at Benson's—his mother knew perfectly well that he would go there, of course—ill at ease as the only man amid a throng of fashionable ladies and surrounded by all kinds of female frippery. It was Sheila who had rescued him: "Is there anything I can do for you, sir?"

He could still hear her voice, the pleasant friendly voice with the smile in it, and only the slightest trace of Cockney. She seemed tall to him then but this, he later realized, was only because she carried herself so erect; actually, the top of her head barely came to his chin. And even in his bewilderment, he noticed her honey-colored hair, her gray eyes, and her long, tapering hands.

When she gave him his change, their fingers touched and he felt an electric jolt going up his arm. She too, it seemed, felt something; for he saw her color slightly and she quickly jerked back her hand.

In the days following, he found himself again and again, without conscious volition, taking the long detour past Benson's of Bond Street when walking from flat to office and back—even then he had loved walking in London, as he still did. One morning he found himself entering the store to buy another half-dozen pairs of opera gloves his mother surely did not need or want. Sheila immediately recognized him and even remembered his name. This time he willed his fingers to touch and press against hers when she handed him his package. She blushed but, instead of jerking her hand away, kept her fingers touching his and even, or so he thought, returned their pressure.

A tip of half a crown and the old ex-soldier who took care of the customers' carriages and horses showed him the Benson employes' entrance and told him at what hour the sales clerks would come off duty. When she came out of the shop that evening he was there, raised his hat, and asked whether he could see her home. And without saying one word, she put her arm in his.

They became lovers ten days later. And on Christmas Eve she moved into his flat, in time to help him trim the Christmas tree, the first one she had ever seen.

"There's no point in paying for a room I won't use any more; and we can also save the exorbitant wages you pay that slovenly manservant of yours."

A few months later he made her give up the job at Benson's. He had done very well out of a deal for Herzfeld, and used the money to give Sheila her heart's desire: a small millinery and accessory shop of her own, just off Baker Street, not far from Marylebone Station.

He had to teach her double-entry bookkeeping, though she learned fast enough. But otherwise she was superb. "She has a much better head for business than I have," Mosenthal had often said to himself; "a better one, in fact, than any man I know."

No one needed to teach her what to buy, how to price or to display. She put customers at their ease and made them feel comfortable the way she had immediately put the bashful Julius Mosenthal at ease when he ventured into a posh woman's shop for the first time in his life. Above all, she had an eye for fashion and was fascinated by it.

Within a year the shop was doing so well that Sheila—with a little help from him, to be sure—could buy the leasehold; and within another eighteen months she had opened a second shop, in Bloomsbury, close to Euston Station.

By now there were twenty-nine "Sheila's Notions" all over London! "The high-fashion store for the modest purse," exclaimed the posters in every Underground station.

She had never married. But she had become rich, and the darling of the popular press as "the first woman to build a business empire." Each of her manageresses was given a share in the profits of the store she ran. Half the remaining profits above a reasonable dividend were set aside for the employes, to be used for special needs—to pay for a wedding or an illness or a baby. In addition, she paid her clerks up to 50 percent more than what the famous stores like Benson's paid. "I don't want any of my girls," she had told a newspaperwoman, "to have to walk the streets to earn enough to live on. Many shopgirls had to when I was young, and far too many still have to." "Sheila Cunningham says: 'My girls need not be streetwalkers,'" the sensationalist Sunday paper had then headlined the interview on its front page. Mosenthal did not subscribe to the rag, of course, but his London clipping service had sent him the story.

It brought a smile to his lips and tears to his eyes. "So Sheila hasn't changed," he said to himself. She still had the same candor, the same unsentimental acceptance of reality, free alike of self-pity and false shame, that had both shocked and captivated him. She had been totally matter-of-fact about herself and totally frank, without apology or embellishment. The world of which she spoke, the London slums, was completely new to Mosenthal, raised in the secure, sheltered embrace of a well-to-do, close family. It was a world of greater horrors, it seemed to him, than Dante's Inferno, and he sometimes felt like putting his hands over his ears to shut it out. But the casual, simple way in which she dismissed experiences which, he knew, would have destroyed him, also touched him deeply. It drew her even closer to him, and made him want to hold her tight, to caress her, to reassure her as one reassures a child that there are no ghosts to be afraid of. Only Sheila's monsters were real, flesh and blood; and they seemed to Mosenthal far more terrible than "the things that go bump in the night."

Sheila's mother had been a barmaid, later a washerwoman. Sheila did not even remember her father, a porter at the vegetable market at Covent Garden who had abandoned her mother when the child was only two. Before she had turned thirteen, her mother forced her to submit to the man with whom she was then living and actually held her hand over the girl's mouth to stop her screaming.

"Poor Mum," Sheila had said; "it was her last desperate attempt to hold that man. Of course it didn't work. Soon after he'd had me, he left Mum and took up with a much younger woman."

Sheila was quite dispassionate about the brute who had violated her; she even felt some gratitude toward him for getting her an apprenticeship at a milliner's whose husband was a drinking companion of his. "Otherwise," she had said, "it would have been domestic service for me, as a scullery maid in a workmen's pub most likely, where you're on your feet sixteen hours a day and the landlord expects you to be 'nice' to any customer who orders a second pint."

The milliner's husband, too, considered his wife's female apprentices his by right and called them upstairs to his room whenever he felt like it. "They all do it," said Sheila, when Mosenthal expressed his shock and anger. "I was lucky, though—he preferred the plump and cuddly ones. And at least I learned a trade."

It was the milliner who got her the job at Benson's, where the management, only a few weeks before Julius's first visit, decided that she would be better employed selling to customers on the shop floor than trimming hats and bonnets in the back room.

Although she wrote a clear flowing hand, Sheila was quite uneducated. But she had a quick, enquiring mind and a burning desire for knowledge, and plied her lover constantly with questions about literature and history and the countries of the world. This soon made Mosenthal realize how little he himself knew, despite the "humanist education" on which his famous Viennese Gymnasium prided itself—or perhaps because of it. He had learned almost enough Latin to have made an adequate junior clerk in Cicero's law office in Republican Rome, not nearly enough Greek to do anything with, a modicum of the German classical poets, and enough Austrian history to rattle off in his sleep the names and dates of all the Habsburg emperors and their predecessors, the Babenberg dukes. But he knew just as little of English—or European—history and English literature as Sheila, who had never attended school uninterruptedly for more than four weeks at a time, and then for the first three or four years only.

The two began to read to each other in the evenings: novels and Shakespeare, ballads and Macaulay's *History of England*. Dickens, then only recently dead and England's most popular writer at the time, Sheila rejected. She knew his world and thought he sentimentalized it. But she adored Sir Walter Scott. And she fell in love with poetry, which opened to her enchanted gardens of delight. The copy of Palgrave's *Golden Treasury of English Poetry* from which they read aloud and in which she had underlined her favorite passages still stood on the office desk in his private railway car; on his business trips to Prague or Budapest or Berlin, he always dipped into it for fifteen minutes or so before going to sleep.

As the years with Sheila went on, he went out less and less in the evenings, whether to dinner parties or to the clubs to which he was invited or to the theater. He was happiest in the flat with Sheila, reading or working with her on her accounts, or perhaps talking to her about his plans. Most evenings they were alone: their only visitor had been Hinton. He came often—sometimes every other week—rarely said anything, but sat quietly, smoking his smelly German pipe, and listened. Hinton always treated Sheila as if she were a fragile China doll. Sheila, in turn, treated him with the friendly indifference one extends to a no-longer young bachelor-uncle, or to a good-natured but oversized St. Bernard puppy.

But their greatest happiness came from their days together in the English countryside.

Their first trip had been a disaster. She had never been out of London, let alone out of England. And so when she left the Benson job, he treated her to Paris. They had planned to stay a week, but Sheila was so miserable they came back after three days.

"In London they suspect, of course, that we aren't married," she had said; "but they pretend not to notice. In France everybody knows, and they smirk. I can't stand it. I won't go there again."

For weeks thereafter, she refused to set foot outside London. But in late summer, after she had worked day and night for two months to get her first store ready to open after the August Bank Holiday, he persuaded her to take a few days' break in the country. They went to Salisbury, and then on to Dorset: to Sherborne, Blandford, and Weymouth. The weather was dreadful—cold and rainy. But they fell in love with the English countryside, which was new to both of them. From then on, they went tramping in the country as often as they could get away from their work. They never again went as far as on that first trip. But they found beauty and happiness and unspoilt heaths and woods, close to London, in the Vale of Aylesbury, with its gentle gray hills and its lush river meadows; or around Bishop's Stortford and Great Dunmow to the north, where placid streams and ancient canals were bordered by the old trees of great estates and punctuated by busy locks and noisy mill races; or to the south, in Sussex, where they explored the gently rolling Downs around Haywards Heath, with their riot of wildflowers in early summer and their secretive lanes cut deeply between banks of honeysuckle and wild roses.

Best of all, Sheila had loved the New Forest—"How typical of the English," thought Mosenthal, "to call the oldest forest in Europe the 'New Forest'"—the splashes of speckled sunlight breaking through giant copper beeches on a clear day, the mist shrouding the trees on a rainy one, and the troops of wild ponies suddenly stampeding out of a copse to startle the human intruders, only to nuzzle them and beg to be petted a minute later. Three, sometimes four times a year, and in all seasons they would go to the New Forest, whenever they had more than one day to spend together.

It was to the New Forest that they had gone on their last outing—again before the Bank Holiday, in the late summer, just before he returned to Vienna to start the Bank of London & Austria.

For, of course, it could not last. Sheila, the fatalistic fact-facing Sheila, had known it from the beginning. Mosenthal himself had tried not to know it, not to accept it. But to no purpose.

It was probably after their first trip in the country, the trip to Salisbury and Dorset, that he talked to Sheila about marriage.

"You are a sweet darling," she said, "but I love you far too much to ruin you. And your marrying me *would* ruin you, as you well know. You're going to be a rich man, an important man and a great gentleman—you wouldn't be satisfied with anything else, anyhow. And then you'll need a lady for your wife and as the mother of your children, someone who can receive those grand gentlemen you're always talking about, and who won't be snubbed by their wives. I'll know when it's time for you to marry, and I'll tell you. And then I shall leave you, though I love you more than you will ever know. I won't allow you to ruin yourself over me. But I'm not going to be a married man's piece of fluff either, and spend my evenings waiting for you in a villa in St. John's Wood hoping you'll come in for a quick toss in the hay on your way home to your wife and children."

No matter how he cajoled and swore that he wouldn't marry anyone else, she would not budge.

Nor did she yield to his arguing that they could live in Vienna, where things were different and no one would know or care where she had come from.

"Oh, don't be so simple, my lamb," she would say. "That lovely lady your mother, whose photograph stands on your dresser [it was still standing there thirty years later] would know at one glance where I came from, that I was no virgin when we met, and that we lived together without being married—and she'd know at once that I'm not the woman she could accept as a wife for her Julius. Besides, I won't live anywhere except England. I don't belong anywhere else."

Had he been right to accept Sheila's protestations, Mosenthal had often wondered, or might taking her to Vienna as his wife have worked? His sister-in-law, Mariandl, had been a peasant girl, after all, and the poorest of the poor when Richard brought her to Vienna as his wife. And for all anyone knew, the two had been sleeping together for two or three summers before they married. In the remote Alpine village where Richard had spent several summers mountain climbing before he appeared with a wife no one had ever heard of before, it was not unusual for a young girl to act as "summer companion" to a tourist—there was no other way, as a rule, for her to amass the dowry she needed to get a local boy to marry her. And yet Mariandl was accepted—in the end, at least.

It had not been easy, though. And it might not have happened at all had not he himself, mindful of Sheila, pressed his own wife, Regina, to receive Mariandl as a sister, and if the old Baroness Wald-Reifnitz, the minister's mother, had not befriended her and taken her for a daughter because of her lovely voice and the folksongs she sang. Even now, some people still snubbed Mariandl: her other sister-in-law, for instance, the stuffy wife of Richard's twin brother, who was so conscious of the "good Jewish family" from which she came; not to mention the minister's wife, the younger Baroness Wald-Reifnitz, who as a former Countess Marchfelden looked down even on her own husband because he was not a prince or at least a count. Mariandl was an artist, furthermore—a musician and a painter—not a shopkeeper like Sheila; in Vienna at least artists were privileged, as were university professors like Richard. No, Sheila had been right; and she had been right also in sensing that she belonged in London and wouldn't thrive in any other soil.

But still, even when the Bank project was near completion and he was committing himself to an early return to Vienna as general manager, the separation from Sheila seemed somehow far away, in some hypothetical future. Of course, it was certain; but so is death. And when one says, "after my death," one feels very comfortably alive, as a rule. Even after he had actually fixed a mid-September date for his departure, he still did not really feel it, really believe it. He did not know that he had to give up Sheila, and had indeed already lost her, until that summer afternoon when Sir Solomon Maimon suddenly called him in.

Sir Solomon had been the first important financier in London to welcome him, to encourage him, and to do business with him. His home was the only one where Mosenthal still went regularly to dinner and where he felt very much at home—indeed, for all their being very grand and very English, the Maimons had some of the warm and relaxed cosiness of his own family in Vienna. Even the somewhat old-fashioned, pompous, and didactic speech in which Sir Solomon phrased the most ordinary observation—about the weather, for instance, or the stock market—was familiar. It reminded him of his father, who always spoke as if addressing judge and jury.

But he was totally unprepared for Sir Solomon's proposal.

"I want first to congratulate you, my dear Mosenthal," Sir Solomon had begun, "on your success in founding the Bank of London & Austria and in raising the money for it. I have rarely seen a difficult task so well done and never by one as young as you still are. You have every reason to be pleased and proud. You have accomplished all that you set out to do four years ago. I must admit that when you first talked to me about your plan, I did not think it practical, interesting though I found it even then.

"But, my dear Julius—I hope you'll allow me to call you that—are you sure you want to return to Vienna and run the Bank? Your friend Hinton, I understand, has agreed to act as chairman for a few years. Are you sure you are needed, too? There are plenty of experienced bankers who could take the role of general manager and Mr. Hinton's second-in-command.

"To put it bluntly, I very much hope that you'll consider an alternative: to stay in London where you so clearly feel at home, and join me as my associate at Maimon & Company—perhaps to take over in a few years when I'm gone. You know that the Lord has blessed me with five lovely daughters but denied me a son. If you were to join me, I would have a successor—and I should hope soon a son as well. I think you know that your attentions would not be spurned in a certain quarter, should you be inclined to link your future to my family."

Mosenthal had been overwhelmed, touched to the point of tears. A partnership in Maimon & Company, England's—if not Europe's—oldest banking house and one of its wealthiest, and that before he was thirty! And he greatly respected Sir Solomon personally for his shrewdness, his absolute integrity, and his genuine kindness. He could see himself revering him as a son should revere a father. His own family in Vienna would be overawed. The Maimons were as great as the Rothschilds, and perhaps more aristocratic for being so modest and self-effacing. And Sir Solomon was right: the Bank of London & Austria could get along without him. It would be a little awkward to bow out at such a late date; but, he thought, Sir Solomon could easily handle this with the Bancrofts and with Hinton.

And yet he knew at once that he would say "No"—and Sheila was the reason. Accepting Sir Solomon's offer meant that Sheila would leave. She would not wait around while he got ready to marry Becky Maimon (exactly the kind of wife, by the way, that Sheila had often told him he would have to marry). But to live in London, to know that she was nearby and yet to have to be without her—he could not, he knew, go through with it. However much parting from Sheila would hurt, in Vienna he could accept it as inevitable. In London, where every street corner and every park would remind him of the walks with her, meetings with her, secrets with her . . . no, he couldn't do it. But also, could he be so cruel to her? As Sir Solomon's partner and son-in-law he would be in the papers, sit on company boards, be always nearby. In Vienna, at least, he would be out of sight, even if not for a long time out of mind.

"Don't rush your answer, my dear Julius," Sir Solomon had said when he noticed his perturbation. "I know this came as a surprise to you, but I hope a pleasant one. Only do call on me soon. I'll be in for you whenever it's convenient."

He had not called. A few days later he wrote a guarded letter expressing his profound gratitude, but pleading that he had pledged himself to launch the new Bank in Vienna and could not go back on his word. He knew he was not fooling the old man. Of course, Solomon Maimon knew about Sheila; he did not make a move without reconnaissance and probably knew more about Mosenthal than Mosenthal did himself. Years later, long after Ernest Marburg had taken on the partnership originally offered to "my dear Julius" and had married Becky Maimon, Sir Solomon had said—in a jesting tone but clearly with serious intent—"London is a bigger place, my dear Julius, than I believe you once thought."

He did not tell Sheila. He knew that she would press him to take the glittering offer. But from the moment on the long walk home from the Maimon Bank in the City when he decided to keep Sir Solomon's offer a secret (the first he had not shared with Sheila since their love began), he knew that they had parted.

They went once more to the New Forest, had one more Bank Holiday together over a hot, cloudless August weekend. They walked hand-in-hand along their favorite paths, not daring to talk to each other. When they were in bed together in the small, airless room under the eaves of their favorite inn in Lyndhurst, the shadow of parting lay between them like a ghost or a corpse. They tried hard to cheer each other up, to point out beloved glades or pretty spots. But they returned to London already strangers.

He left for Vienna a few weeks later. He had asked her not to see him off at Victoria Station, so they said goodbye in the flat that had been their home for four years. Already it had the lifeless, empty air of "Premises to Let."

"Sheila," he had said, after he had held her hands for an eternity, "promise you'll let me know when you need anything, when you are in any trouble."

Only then did she break down, flinging herself into his arms and sobbing wildly. But she pulled herself together almost at once and moved roughly away from him.

"I promise, Julius," she had said. "But now it's time for you to go. I'll make sure the furniture gets stored."

She had never written; neither had he. But on that long, lonely trip to Vienna he had lived through in his mind the days and weeks and months of his time with Sheila. Gradually it had become the ritual of the Homecoming. He relived his life with Sheila the night before the London-bound train reached the Channel port where he would take the ferry the following morning, and then again, on the return trip, on the last evening in London before his departure from Victoria Station in the morning. And before going to bed, he decided which of the happinesses of those years (their first meeting, perhaps, or their first holiday trip to Salisbury and Dorset) he would live through again on the morrow during that suspended interval between the continent and London—the interval that belonged to neither of his two worlds. Afterwards he would wake up to spend a day with Sheila, a day of memory and nostalgia.

"What should it be tomorrow—or rather today?" asked Julius von Mosenthal as he stubbed out his cigar and drank the last drop of cognac. The answer came right away: the last trip, the farewell trip to the New Forest. He had often thought of this before, but always pulled back—it was still too painful. But now he knew that it was the choice for this Homecoming. Tomorrow—or rather, today—he would set out again from Lyndhurst hand-in-hand with Sheila for the copper beeches, the wild ponies, the hidden, secretive glades and copses of the New Forest she had loved so much.

Susie

"It's after eight, but no need to hurry," said the valet as he brought Mosenthal his morning cup of tea. "It was so foggy over Dover last night the evening ferry couldn't get out. And it's so foggy here that the ferry can't make it in yet." And when the man raised the blind, the fog outside was indeed so thick that the powerful arc light under which Mosenthal's private railway carriage was parked showed only as a diffuse halo.

"The word is that the ferry boat will leave Dover within the hour and arrive here around eleven to start by noon on the return trip," the valet concluded.

Mosenthal was tempted to go back to sleep—it had been a short night and he felt tired. But then he remembered: this was the day of the Homecoming. He had already wasted in sleep hours he could have spent with Sheila!

He dressed hurriedly and went outside into the fog with its familiar smells of a French Channel port: the brine from the sea, the sweet, slightly sickly stink of the coal the French railways burned, and an unidentifiable but unmistakable odor which said "France" and always brought to Mosenthal's mind the peculiar blue of French workingmen's smocks. There in the fog, he knew, Sheila would be waiting, invisible to everyone but him, would put her hand in his and whisk him away at once to Lyndhurst and a cloudless August day, to relive their last rambles together.

"Wouldn't it be nice, though," he thought suddenly, "to show off Susie to Sheila, to share with her my love for Susie? And how Susie would enjoy meeting Sheila. How I'd love to tell her about Sheila and my life with her long before Susie was born."

And rather than the New Forest in the hot August sun, he was instead suddenly in the cheerful office of Dr. Moll, the Viennese doctor who specialized in the emotional aspects of adolescence, with its brightly upholstered easy chairs and its lithographs of Baroque churches on the walls. And the hand he felt in his wasn't Sheila's; it was Susie's.

Mosenthal had of course married as Sheila had known all along he would, and he had married the kind of wife Sheila had expected him to marry. He had known Regina Augsburg all her life—her father had been their family physician since the Mosenthal parents first got married. Regina was ten years younger than he, still a child barely out of the nursery when he left for London. Five years later, when he returned, she had grown into an attractive young woman of whom his mother approved highly. Two and a half years after that he had proposed to her and been accepted. He was never in love with her; but she was good-looking, good-natured, a good housekeeper, a perfect hostess, well educated and mildly musical. And he felt very much at home with her, with her father (by then the most distinguished diagnostician in Vienna) and her older brother, already a rising star among the younger doctors. Regina, in turn, felt equally at home with his family, and especially close to his mother—she had lost her own mother while quite young. It had been a good marriage and he, he thought, had been a good husband, better than most.

He had also been a good father to their children: Hans-Ludwig, named after his maternal uncle and his maternal grandfather; Josephine, named after her Mosenthal grandfather and always called "Fifi" in the Viennese fashion; and Susie, the youngest, now not quite fourteen. They could be proud of all three, Mosenthal thought. They were turning out well. Of course, Hans-Ludwig's pompous Socialist talk about "come the Revolution" was irritating. And whenever he spouted his romantic twaddle of the "noble exploited proletarian," his father felt tempted to tell him about the real proletarians of Sheila's London slums. But Hans-Ludwig worked at his studies—he had known that he would go into medicine since he had been ten or so—and according to his uncle Hans would make an excellent surgeon.

"They're all flaming revolutionaries at this stage," Hans had said. "He'll soon discover that the Revolution neither prevents nor cures syphilis."

Hans-Ludwig was as close to his mother as he, the father, had been close to his—"and," thought Mosenthal, "he's nicer to his mother than I was to mine at his age."

But Fifi was even closer to her mother. Indeed, the two were more like sisters than mother and daughter, especially now that Fifi had a baby boy on whom her mother doted. She would always be very much like her mother—good-looking, good-natured, placid, and fond of creature comforts.

She had made the perfect marriage, at least for her. The fact that Mosenthal found Oskar Pollack von Paltitz a bore was irrelevant. "I'm not the one, after all, who is married to him. He's the right husband for her, adores her, and is as crazy about the baby as she is. He works hard at the Pollack-Paltitz companies, though he has more money than he'll ever know what to do with. How proud his father was, a few months ago at the board meeting, when he told us that his son, not yet thirty, had developed and put into production three new synthetic dyes, every one as good as anything the Germans have! And Fifi loves all those servants and the big house his parents built for them as their wedding present, not to mention the summer villa in Gastein and those huge parties she throws. What does it matter that there's not one book in the house other than Oskar's chemical-engineering texts?

"But," mused Mosenthal, "Susie is the child who is closest to me, and has been all along. Perhaps it's because she came so long after the others, when Regina and I had given up on having more children. Or perhaps it's because she looks so much like my mother—that dark-brown, luxuriant hair, the brown eyes, the perfect oval of the face—and moves so much like her, with her quick energetic movements and the walk that's almost a dance, that it's quite uncanny. But perhaps Susie is so much closer to me than the other two because of that sunny, loving temperament of hers." And Mosenthal remembered and savored again the moment when at seventeen months Susie had climbed into his lap, hugged him, and spoken her first word: "Kiss."

But all of a sudden, eight, nine months ago, Susie had changed. She had begun to pout, to scream at her parents and even at the servants, to refuse to do things she had loved to do before—going on a Sunday morning walk with her father in the Vienna Woods, for instance—and to have temper tantrums in which she threw herself on the floor and kicked like a two-year-old. At first Regina and he had shrugged off these episodes, and so had Dr. Gottesmann, the family physician. Adolescent girls go through a few difficult years, after all; even the placid, easygoing Fifi had had her moments when she was fourteen and fifteen. But Susie grew steadily worse. She refused to eat, sometimes for days. She had sudden fits of uncontrollable sobbing and weeping, sometimes lasting for hours. Or she would be found at two in the morning reading in the library, complaining that she couldn't sleep.

It was then that Hans, her uncle, had suggested they consult Dr. Moll, a former assistant of his father, Dr. Ludwig Augsburg, and now head of the Neurological Department at the children's hospital. "Moll," Hans had said, "has remarkable results with the emotional problems of adolescents. They trust him and talk to him." And Susie was willing to be treated—she herself was frightened by the changes that were happening to her.

Three weeks ago, after he had seen Susie a dozen times, Dr. Moll had called in all three of them: Regina, Susie, and Julius.

"Miss Susanna," he had begun, "you know what I am going to tell your parents. But I want you to listen closely all the same, and stop me if I say anything with which you don't agree."

Mosenthal had been startled to hear him call her "Miss Susanna." No one had ever called her that, even though it was the name on her baptismal certificate. But above all, the "Miss" had stabbed him with an almost physical pain. Was he going to lose her so soon to adulthood and womanhood?

"I don't think you need to worry overmuch about your daughter," Dr. Moll had started gently. "Her problems are those of health rather than of sickness. Her biggest one, she and I agree, is that she is dreadfully bored in school. Am I right," the doctor asked, "in thinking that her unhappiness began shortly after the present school year started in September?" All three of them nodded.

"Miss Susanna," Dr. Moll continued, "is a very intelligent young lady—no wonder, considering her ancestry. But her school treats her as an infant and an idiot. She is quite gifted in mathematics, indeed she already knows far more than I do. But when she wants to do trigonometry or conic sections or logarithms, the school says: 'No, no, that's not ladylike.' Am I right, Miss Susanna?"

Susie had laughed out loud—for the first time in months—and nodded vehemently.

"She speaks fluent English," the doctor went on, "since you have English visitors practically every weekend. But the school demands that she do English grammar for beginners rather than read the English poets and novelists. Altogether," said Dr. Moll, "your daughter wants to prepare for the university. I know not many women in Austria do this yet—and I imagine that you, my dear lady, may be a little shocked at the idea of your daughter as a university student. But, believe me, it's coming, and the young women who do reach the university are doing well. She doesn't know yet what she might want to study. With her ability in mathematics and her languages, she might well go into economics; I hear that there are a few very good women students in the field already. Or it could be history—it's much too early to say. And, of course, in four or five years she might have different plans.

"But she needs a tough school that will make demands on that good mind of hers and impose mental discipline, and she needs to know that she will be prepared for the university, should she choose to go there. I strongly recommend that you put Miss Susanna into the toughest college preparatory course for girls we have in Vienna—and we do have a few good ones.

"Then, too," Dr. Moll continued, "Miss Susanna feels that you, her parents, haven't quite accepted that she isn't a child any longer. She knows how much her parents love her. But I suspect—am I right, Miss Susanna?—that she feels you're keeping her in the nursery when she is ready for the drawing room. She feels, I think, that you don't let her come close. I am a little envious of her, I must admit, with nothing but Tyrolean peasants in my own background. Miss Susanna, on her mother's side, has for her grandfather my revered teacher, Professor Augsburg, with his sixty years of leadership in building the

Vienna School of Medicine, and, before him, his father—I've heard enough about that old doctor in Frankfurt to know that he was a great man, and an interesting one to boot—and my friend, Susanna's Uncle Hans, is as eminent in his own field of urology as her grandfather is in his. Yet she knows nothing about any of these people.

"And then, Herr Generaldirektor, there's your side of her ancestry. First you yourself, with your interesting years in England and your great achievements since, then your twin brothers, each a great scholar, and your father, the eminent jurist. Miss Susanna has heard of them all her life, but feels she isn't allowed near any of them. Perhaps you could ask her to write a family history—they are becoming quite the fashion now. That might give her the challenge she needs; and her uncle, the historian, can surely help her.

"And now," Dr. Moll continued after a short pause, "I come to something much more delicate. Miss Susanna has asked me not to bring it up, but she is wrong—and I think she knows it."

Mosenthal suddenly felt Susie's hand in his, saw that she grasped Regina's hand too, felt her go quite tense and saw her first blush then pale.

"I've told Miss Susanna," the doctor said firmly, "that she is a little goose. But she is still afraid that she will be pushed by her parents into marriage and family responsibilities before she is ready.

"She has seen her sister, Fifi" ("Josephine," Susie corrected under her breath) "get married when not yet nineteen and have a baby before she was twenty. She knows that was what Josephine wanted and that it was right for her. But she is very much afraid lest you might think it right for her too. And just now the prospect of a husband and of married life and having children frightens her.

"I've told her that her parents are much too intelligent not to know that different people mature in different ways, and that what was right for Josephine may not be right for Susanna. But particularly since Josephine had her baby and she saw how delighted you were with your grandchild, my dear lady, she worries that she'll be pressured into marriage and a husband and a relationship she isn't ready for."

Susie, sobbing wildly, had buried her face against his shoulder. But Mosenthal saw the flush on his wife's face, whether of anger or embarrassment. "So," he thought, "Susie is right in her fears. Regina is already thinking of pushing her into a man's arms and a man's bed."

"My last point," said Dr. Moll, after a few moments of silence to allow Susie to wipe her face, "is the only one I haven't told Susie about, but I am sure she won't object. You, Susie"—and suddenly it was "Susie" and "du"—"like your given name; and you think your parents should use it. And it's 'Susanna,' not 'Susie,' isn't it? In a few years, I think, you may well be old enough to want to be Susie again. But for now, let's make it 'our grownup Miss Susanna.'"

With this the doctor affectionately took both of Susanna's hands, pulled her close to him, and smiled at her. And Susie through her tears smiled back, then, blushing furiously, gave him a kiss.

On the way home she sat between the two of them in the car, crying softly and, he thought, happily, and holding hands with both. And that night Regina had come to his bed for the first time since they had begun to sleep in separate rooms all those years ago—three or four months after she had conceived Susie.

Regina had not been convinced, but he insisted. The following week Susie was enrolled in the school Dr. Moll recommended. And he had promised her to work with her on the "family history" upon his return from London as soon as her summer vacation began.

"But why wait so long?" he suddenly asked himself, as he paced up and down alongside his private railway car in a fog that was slowly thinning. "Susie has always been Papa Augsburg's favorite and he'll be delighted to talk to her. She can read up on his professional career. There's the Festschrift the Vienna Medical society put out four months ago when Papa was eighty-five, *Sixty Years of Internal Medicine in Vienna*. And Papa loves to talk about his early days, when his father sent him with his new medical doctorate to Vienna to become the family physician to the Rothschilds, and how he talked the Rothschilds into putting up the money for the Jewish Hospital, of which he became chief physician, and of which his own son Hans is now chief physician. And Papa has long wanted a listener for his stories about his own father, Susie's great-grandfather, how as a poor Jewish boy from some Hessian hamlet he walked all the way to Paris during the Napoleonic Wars because Jews were not admitted into medical school in Germany; how he became the first Jewish physician in Frankfurt and the first to use a stethoscope; and finally, already an old man, had been the first physician in Germany to use the clinical thermometer in his practice."

Papa, Mosenthal knew, had kept his father's papers and letters, and would be delighted to have Susie go through them with him.

And his own aunt, Aunt Judith, would be even more delighted to tell Susie all about the Mosenthals. She had always wanted to tell him; but he had never stood still for her endless tales. He saw her, of course, a few times a year and always called on her on her birthday. But she had long since given up trying to talk to him. Now she'd have an audience for the stories he had resisted in his youth, the stories he had actually rejected.

Mosenthal tried to remember what the old woman had talked about when he was a boy. There was, for instance, her tale of the first Mosenthal, the ancestor and founder—like something out of a romantic novel, Sir Walter Scott or, more likely, *The Three Musketeers*, rather than sober history. But Aunt Judith had sworn it was all true.

She had told him the tale many times, but he had listened only once—when he came back from London and announced his plans for the Bank of London & Austria. "So you are going to be partners with Prince Sobieski," she had said. "Does he know that we are related to his House?"

"Oh, don't tell fairy tales, Aunt Judith," he had said; "the Royal House of Poland and poor Jews from a Godforsaken Hungarian mountain village?"

"You are the silly one," she had retorted sharply. "You'd know what I'm talking about had you but listened earlier. And your father knows, don't you, Joseph?"

To his surprise, his totally unromantic father, who usually had no more patience with his sister's stories than he did, had nodded and said: "Yes, I know, and it's all quite well documented and may even be true." So Aunt Judith proceeded to tell him the story:

"The first Mosenthal lived in the mid-seventeenth century. His mother's family had settled in Venice after being driven out of Spain or Portugal, and had become bankers and fiscal agents for some eastern European noble families, including the Polish Sobieskis. The father of the first Mosenthal, however, was a young Sobieski—later to become the father of the Soldier-King—who stayed in Venice on the Grand Tour and there seduced his fiscal agent's daughter. In Jewish law, the child of a Jewish mother is a Jew, and so the boy grew up as a Jew.

"As a young man, he joined the false Messiah, Sabbatai Zevi, in his crusade to the Holy Land, and became one of his chief lieutenants. And when Sabbatai Zevi betrayed the Jewish cause and turned Moslem, the Mosenthal ancestor led a band of Zevi's former followers on a perilous trek out of Turkey, through Hungary to a secluded mountain valley below the passes into Poland—a Sobieski fief, which he called the 'Mosenthal,' the Valley of Moses. There he settled his flock, with himself as their rabbi and hereditary chief."

Then there were Aunt Judith's stories about his grandfather and his wife's father, his great-grandfather.

"Mendel Schachtmann, your great-grandfather—your father and I still knew him when he was a very old man—was the Rabbi of Leipzig during and after the Napoleonic Wars, and a distinguished historian of the Enlightenment, whose *History of the Jews of Germany and Austria* is still the standard text. He was also the first Jew to teach at a German university: he lectured at Leipzig on the Old Testament and the Talmud. His aim in life was to reconcile the Jewish religion and the rationalism of the Enlightenment. But he failed. Both his son and his son-in-law lost their faith. The son turned Protestant and became a professor of church history. He married his predecessor's daughter; and his son, my and your father's first cousin, Eduard, is now a famous professor of family law in Berlin and a Geheimrat. Our father, your grandfather, was sent to Rabbi Mendel Schachtmann to study the Talmud. He married the rabbi's daughter Ruth, my mother and your grandmother. He, too, lost his faith and became a rationalist. But he did not dare tell his father, so he returned to become Rabbi of Mosenthal. There he stayed for forty years, depressed, ashamed of himself, and unable either to give up his office or to perform it."

His own father, Susie's grandfather—Susie was too young to remember him—had rarely talked about himself. But Aunt Judith told him that the grandfather, the rabbi who had lost his faith, had sent his son to Vienna to study law and had all but ordered him to become baptized. The rest of his father's history Mosenthal himself knew: how he had become Austria's first railway lawyer, and successful by allying himself with the two early railroad entrepreneurs, Baron Wald-Reifnitz, father of the minister, and Wald-Reifnitz's brother-in-law, Baron Perkacz; how he had become the first lawyer of Jewish extraction to be elected head of the Vienna Bar Association for three terms in a row; how he had authored the Austrian laws on railways, their liabilities, their tariffs, and so on; and how, finally, on his sixtieth birthday—a year after his oldest son had returned from London—he had been ennobled and they had all become "von Mosenthal."

"I doubt that Susie will find all this terribly interesting," Mosenthal mused. "It's hardly what she probably thinks history should be— no kings or battles, no 'march of progress,' and no great discoveries. None of us will get even a footnote in her history books, or deserve one. But it would be nice to have it all written down before it's forgotten, and neither Papa Augsburg nor Aunt Judith will be around much longer. I'll write Susie a letter from London, perhaps tomorrow, and tell her to go and see Papa and Aunt Judith."

The fog, he suddenly realized, was lifting fast. And to his surprise, his watch said 10:55. The morning was almost gone, and he had not yet started on the Homecoming, had not yet spent any time with Sheila! Well, there were still a few hours left before London.

At that moment his private secretary came up the path from the station. "Herr Generaldirektor," he said, "the ferry is just coming in." And indeed through the mist Mosenthal could see a gray shape moving slowly toward the pier. "It will sail in an hour," the private secretary said. "I've already told your brother, the Professor, and His Excellency the Minister to get ready, and I shall send porters for the luggage."

"I'll be coming right away," Mosenthal responded. Then, to his own surprise, he added: "But first I have to send off a telegram. Please wait here a minute."

He went back into the train, to his office compartment, picked up a telegram blank, and wrote:

Frau von Mosenthal
Opernring 3B
Vienna I, Austria

Would be most happy if you and Susie could join me in London soonest possible STOP Business finished in few days STOP We could take leisurely holiday together STOP Would love show London and England to you Susie STOP With Susie changing schools, missing semester's last weeks should not matter STOP Please ask Holzmann at Bank to arrange private car to Calais and transportation thence to London STOP Very much hope to see you Susie before end of coming week
    Love
    Julius

"Please send this off immediately the fastest way," he said to the secretary. But as the man turned toward the station, he added: "One moment please," took the telegram, and changed every "Susie" in it to "Susanna." "Now it's ready to go," he said, and watched his secretary walk off briskly toward station and post office before starting himself in the opposite direction, for the pier.

"And now I really have to begin the Homecoming," he thought. But before he had taken the first few steps, he was asking himself instead: "Should I make an appointment with Marburg when I see him tonight at Prince Sobieski's dinner? Or should I wait until I've had a quiet hour with Hinton?"

The Homecoming

A note waiting for Mosenthal at his London flat summoned him to a pre-dinner meeting at Sobieski's house in Atherton Square. When he got there, after barely enough time to change, he found Hinton and Marburg already closeted with Sobieski in the Prince's private study.

"Mr. Hinton," Sobieski began immediately, "has something urgent to tell us." Then Hinton reported Frederick Bancroft's arrest as a counterfeiter, his almost certain conviction and deportation to Devil's Island, the sale of the Bancroft shares in the Bank of London & Austria to Maimon & Marburg, his resignation as the Bank's chairman, and his nomination of Sir Ernest Marburg to succeed him. All of which, he added, would be in the papers either the following morning or on Monday.

He concluded: "And on Monday evening or, at the latest, Tuesday morning, the papers will announce that Bancroft Brothers is being liquidated. I expect the liquidation to be finished a week from today, except for the sale of the firm's office building."

They were stunned but, thought Mosenthal, not really surprised. That Freddie Bancroft would end up destroying himself, they had known all along. "What a shame that he cannot even commit suicide like a gentleman," Marburg muttered, half to himself. "And that," thought Mosenthal, "is probably all the epitaph Freddie Bancroft will ever get or deserve."

"How dreadful for you, my dear Hinton," said Sobieski, "what a terrible blow it must be."

"Your Highness is kind," Hinton replied—could there be a touch of gaiety in his voice?—"but, for me, it is really a blessing in disguise. It forces me to do what I should have done much earlier. I am returning to my first love, mathematics and its history. Of course it has been a blow, I won't deny it. But mainly for the terrible pain it inflicts on people I hold dear, especially that wretched Frederick's mother, Elaine Bancroft."

There was a tone in Hinton's voice when he spoke that name that Mosenthal had never heard, a tone that made him look up sharply. As he did so, he met Marburg's eye—so Ernest had noticed it, too! Could it possibly be? But what other explanation was there for the tone in Hinton's voice than that he and that frozen-faced, arrogant, domineering Elaine Bancroft had been secret lovers all along? At once it fell into place in Mosenthal's mind—and as he again looked at Marburg, he was sure the same thoughts were going through his mind, too.

"That—and nothing else," Mosenthal thought, "really explains Hinton's secretiveness about his private life, his return from Vienna to Bancroft Brothers despite the shabby way the firm had been treating him, and his willingness to suffer those supercilious incompetents, the young Bancrofts, in a firm he controls and totally runs. But how have they managed, those two, without anyone's guessing—and in London, where the rumor mill works harder and grinds more finely than in any other place I know?"

His thoughts were interrupted by Sobieski's voice.

"Mr. Hinton isn't the only one with news, although mine is somewhat more prosaic. In August when I see His Apostolic Majesty, the Emperor, I shall ask to be relieved of my duties as Austro-Hungarian Ambassador to the Court of St. James's. I will then have served twenty-seven years in the post. And I, too, like our friend Hinton, have other things to do, which I should not postpone any longer. I plan a thorough tour of inspection of the Sobieski estates and industries over the next two years, beginning with our Polish properties, which I haven't visited since I entered diplomatic service forty years ago. The Princess and I will continue to make our headquarters in England at Horne Abbey; we're both at home here. But this coming winter, at least, we'll spend in a milder climate, probably in the villa I built for my late mother on Lake Garda.

"Of course," the Prince concluded, "the news will not be made public until I have called on the Emperor in two months' time. But I know I can count on your discretion, gentlemen."

There was silence at first, then animated small talk. Hinton was asked to stay on the Bank's board until his term expired, two years hence—and finally agreed. The Prince then agreed—with alacrity, it seemed to Mosenthal—to stay on as honorary chairman until age seventy. "Of course," Mosenthal thought—and again Marburg, he sensed, was thinking the same—"he likes the stipend we pay him for doing nothing."

Marburg also clearly understood what Mosenthal was up to when he said to the Prince: "I trust Your Highness will not think me presumptuous if I use this occasion to declare on behalf of the Bank's management that the position of honorary chairman must not be filled when Your Highness vacates it—though we hope that you'll reconsider and not leave until well beyond your seventieth year. For a position that has been filled by Prince Sobieski, whose vision made the Bank possible, there can be no successor."

The Prince was greatly pleased. "And this," Mosenthal thought, "eliminates the young Prince as a threat once and for all."

But Mosenthal was not really listening to what was being said. What he heard was the almost festive tone, one of celebration, in everybody's voice. That Marburg was elated was understandable; he had wanted to be the Bank's chairman for a long time. But he was struck by the note of relief—yes, even happiness—in the voices of both Hinton and Sobieski.

As for himself, he could barely refrain from shouting out loud. All his troubles were over at once—he needn't have prepared himself for combat and hard negotiations. The only task left was for him to persuade Marburg to hold his shares in the Bank until after Sobieski had agreed to reduce his holdings. The two men now actually held the same percentage—28½ each. This meant that unless Marburg immediately sold the shares he had bought from Hinton, the Prince would insist on selling enough of his to become an investor. Otherwise he'd have to be a partner with Marburg; and not even the senior partner, at that, but an equal partner. Ernest Marburg—for all his baronetcy, his two titled sons-in-law, his money, and his friendship with the King of England—could never be anything to Prince Sobieski but the Orthodox cantor's son from the Jewish ghetto—not someone surely to be equal partners with.

"Do I have to be tactful when discussing this with Marburg, or can I be blunt?" Mosenthal wondered. But then he looked at Marburg and saw that, once again, their thoughts ran parallel.

The dinner party lasted for hours. Mosenthal thought he had never seen the Prince a more gracious host, more charming or more entertaining, relaxed and relaxing. But all he remembered was that he and Marburg made an appointment to meet for dinner next evening, Saturday, at Marburg's club. Otherwise he suddenly felt drained, spent—and not just with the physical fatigue of travel, of a short night and a long day.

It was midnight when he got back to his flat and found a telegram waiting for him. It was from Regina in Vienna:

Wonderful idea. Susanna can hardly wait till we join you London STOP Susanna bought Baedeker and started packing STOP Leaving private car Thursday morning, arriving London Friday noon STOP Till then all love, Susanna, Regina.

"If the weather holds," thought Mosenthal, "we'll go down on Sunday to the New Forest for a few days. There's no place in England that will make Susie feel more welcome!"

4. "An die Musik"

Renata

The Perkaczes

Arthur

Paul

Maria

"An die Musik"

Renata

The *Portrait of a Young Woman in Love*, painted by Ferdinand Waldmueller and hanging in a Viennese museum, may not be the best but is surely the best-known work of the nineteenth-century Austrian master. It shows a young woman, hardly more than a girl, in a light blue, loose dress, one arm resting on the corner of a rosewood piano, with the face looking left toward the beholder's right. It is an arresting, hauntingly beautiful face—a perfect oval, skin the color of fresh cream, shoulder-length hair so deeply black that it sparkles with steely tints, and big eyes the color of mountain gentian and several shades darker than the dress. Like most of Waldmueller's works—and like most Austrian art of those Biedermeier years of the 1840s—the painting is somewhat sweet for modern tastes. But it is saved from being sugary by the radiance of the young woman's face, a radiance of such trusting bliss that it has earned for the work the popular sobriquet of "Die Verliebte" or "Young Woman in Love," although the legend on the painting itself says simply "Unknown Young Woman." There is always an answering smile on the face of the viewers, who, whatever their age or sex, tend to move to the right until they stand where her beloved must have stood while Waldmueller sketched his sitter.

Whereas Waldmueller's *Young Woman* is well known, Gustav Klimt's *An die Musik* has never been published and has been seen only by a few carefully screened art historians and museum curators. Not many people have even heard of the great collection of modern European art which a secretive Swiss has built up since the 1920s, with the Klimt painting his first acquisition, bought while still a junior in his family's banking house. *An die Musik* is also a woman's portrait, is indeed a portrait of the same woman who, fifty years earlier, sat for Ferdinand Waldmueller—the same perfect oval of a face, the same creamy-white skin, the same deep blue eyes and blue dress. Only the hair has turned into a lustrous white, though, piled on top of the head, it is still abundant. And the face reposes in serene calm rather than glowing in the radiance of love. Painted when Klimt was turning from the Impressionism of his youth to the Expressionism of his mature years, the woman is bathed in shimmering light streaming through a window behind her. She sits at a rosewood piano—perhaps the same Waldmueller sketched in *Young Woman in Love*—with both hands resting lightly on the keyboard, while the face and body are turned toward the beholder. There is no title on the painting itself, only Klimt's signature. But on the back of the canvas in a woman's hand is written in India ink "An die Musik" and a date: 14 June 1896.

No one since the years of the First World War has seen the two paintings side by side, and no one knows that they portray the same person, though half a century apart. Nor does anyone today know—or care—who that unknown woman with the big dark blue eyes was or might have been. The last person to know made very sure that no one would ask, let alone find out.

When Renata Kohout, in the terrible hunger years of inflation-ridden Austria after the First World War, found herself forced to sell the two portraits of her grandmother, the Baroness Rafaela Wald-Reifnitz, she stipulated that each must be sold separately and to a different buyer, and that neither buyer was to be told who the woman in the painting had been. Even the Zurich art dealer to whom she entrusted the sale was not told, though he had been a fellow student of Renata and her dead husband, the painter Erich Kohout, at the Art Academy in Vienna, and had long been a close friend. The dealer demurred—such secrecy, he pointed out, could only depress the price. But Renata would not be budged.

Despite the secrecy, the dealer did, however, get a good deal of money for the paintings—far more than he had expected, and many times what Renata had dared to hope for. He did so well that Mrs. Kohout could move with her two small sons from starving and freezing Vienna to a small house on the Lake of Zurich and live for a few years in modest comfort until she had reestablished herself as an illustrator of children's books and a book and fabric designer. A few years later, of course, the world discovered Erich Kohout as a painter of genius and one of the pioneers of Expressionism. The fifteen or twenty paintings that were all the possessions he left behind when he died of the Spanish influenza after coming home unscathed by four years of wartime service in the trenches sold so well that his widow finally became quite affluent again.

But when the letter from Zurich had arrived with the news that, suddenly, her money worries were over, Renata was dejected rather than elated. She read the letter over and over, again and again converted the amount of Swiss Francs in her mind into the all-but-worthless Austrian Kronen with their endless rows of zeroes at the end, again and again fingered the three tickets to Zurich which the art dealer had bought for her and enclosed in the letter. For the first time since Erich had died two years earlier, for the first time since she had realized that inflation had eaten up all the war bonds into which she (like everyone else in Austria) had invested the substantial fortunes her grandmother and father had left her, she was free of corrosive money fear, nagging financial worry. Yet she felt dirty, despicable, degraded.

"One pities a whore who sells her body to get bread for her children," she said to herself, "but she's still a whore."

She had been at her wits' end, with no one to turn to. Her only brother had been killed early in the war; and since the Wald-Reifnitz estates had been entailed, they had passed into the hands of strangers, distant relatives who had probably never even heard of Renata. Maybe the younger of her two sisters might have taken her in; the older one, she knew, would blithely let her starve rather than talk to her or take any notice of her and the Kohout sons. But even at her younger sister's she would never be allowed to forget that she, a Baroness Wald-Reifnitz, had dishonored the family by marrying an impecunious art student, the son of a proletarian upholsterer, raised in a slum tenement.

And her two sons, Erich's sons, would grow up despised, treated as beggars who did not deserve better, made to feel every day that they were a "disgrace to the family." She knew that selling the paintings was the right thing to do, was indeed what Grandmother herself would have wanted her to do—and in her place would have done without heartbreak or dithering. And yet she felt that she had betrayed a trust, cheapened herself, forsaken the integrity that was at the core of her inner being. Even the dealer's assurance that he had followed her instructions and made it impossible for the buyers ever to discover whose portrait the paintings were did little to assuage the guilt, the depression, the self-loathing, that lasted well beyond the stages of packing her meager belongings, taking the long train ride to Zurich with her sons, and settling into fresh, carefree surroundings and a new life.

Of all her family, her grandmother had been the only one to whom Renata was attracted while growing up. Her grandfather, Grandmother's husband, had died while she was still a small child. Father was courteous to her as he was courteous to everyone. But he was far too busy, far too important, too famous, to bother with a child's trivial concerns. That Mother had always resented her, she knew, if only because she looked so much like the grandmother whom Mother hated. Her sisters were too old—they were already betrothed and society ladies before Renata was old enough to come down from the nursery and join the "grownups." And while her brother was closer in age (being only three years her senior), he was a boy, after all, with little time for a baby sister.

But Grandmother always treated her with respect and always had time and attention for her. Whereas the other grownups had smiled indulgently at her childish drawings, Grandmother would look at them, discuss them, ask what Renata was trying to do—and, greatest bliss, criticize them as if they mattered. Or she would herself take pencil in hand and show Renata how to change this or produce that effect. And she could laugh, laugh like a child, laugh the way the *Young Woman in Love* laughed, with her whole being.

Renata worshipped her grandmother; but she was not allowed to see much of her while she grew up. Her mother frowned on any contact and kept relations on the level of formal, icy politeness—and not even too much of that. Of course, Grandmother did not perform in public; still, she was a "musician," and her house was always full of young women who studied music and who were performers or intended to be performers—"Bohemians or worse," as her mother sniffed. Grandmother had for many years worked closely with her late husband, and accompanied him on trips to remote, out of the way places, wherever he had gone to design or build a bridge, which was definitely not ladylike. Grandmother's watercolors and drawings of Grandfather's bridges had then been published in Grandfather's great book on bridge design; furthermore, they had been exhibited and finally donated to the Museum of Technology, where now every lout could look at them. "No lady of breeding would ever have done that," Mother asserted, though only when Father was not around.

Above all, as Renata understood early—though it was never said—Grandmother was an "upstart" to be ashamed of.

The Wald-Reifnitzes were, of course, well below the level of the Marchfeldens, whose daughter Mother was, imperial counts with a title going back to the first Habsburg Emperor, Rudolf, in the thirteenth century. Mother made it abundantly clear that she would never have married a mere Wald-Reifnitz had her own august family not become so totally impoverished that she had to "sacrifice herself." Still, the Wald-Reifnitzes, though barons for less than one hundred fifty years and hardly "true aristocracy," had been respectable landed gentry for a long time. And Grandfather's own father had been a distinguished soldier in the Napoleonic Wars, who had risen to lieutenant field marshal and chief of ordnance, first for the Austrian Army, and then for the Allied Armies, all the way to Waterloo.

But Grandmother's father had been a commoner when Grandmother was born, a real estate speculator and building contractor who had been made a baron when Grandmother was already in her teens. Worst of all—though it was never even alluded to—the Perkaczes, Grandmother's parents, despite their baronial title and their pew in St. Peter's Church were, of course, Jews. And whenever Mother mentioned Grandmother, one could hear her think (if not actually mutter under her breath) "despicable, pushy, nouveau-riche Jewess."

Mother was particularly incensed by Grandmother's annual memorial concert in her home on Grandfather's birthday, June 14. "Vulgar," "ostentatious," and "heathenish," Mother called it. And so Renata had never been allowed to attend, though Grandmother sent her an invitation every year.

But even Mother, however much she frowned, could not forbid her to attend the concert on the ninetieth anniversary of Grandfather's birth—after all, Renata was almost eighteen and no longer a child. And when she found herself warmly greeted by Grandmother, then seated next to the old woman at the tea that preceded the music and asked whether there was anything Grandmother could do for her, she heard herself, to her own amazement, burst out: "Grandmother, if only you could help me get permission to go to the Art Academy!"

"What about the entrance examination?" Grandmother had asked matter-of-factly.

Renata found herself confessing that she had secretly taken the examination, had passed with flying colors, but had not dared tell her mother of such an outlandish, such an undignified, unladylike ambition.

"Don't you worry, child," was all her grandmother had said.

Three weeks later came a letter of acceptance, and three months after that, at the end of September when the Art Academy opened, Renata found herself going to the classes—even though Mother for a whole year insisted on humiliating her in front of her fellow students by sending a maid along as a chaperone.

In another few years, Grandmother had come to the rescue again. Mother had already picked as Renata's husband a young count of impeccable lineage, ineffable arrogance, and abysmal stupidity—just like the husbands she had earlier picked for her two older sisters. But Renata had fallen in love with her penniless, proletarian, uncouth fellow student, Erich Kohout, whose upholsterer-father, the illegitimate son of a Czech servant girl, did not even know who his own father had been. And when, after a long struggle, Mother conceded defeat if only because Renata had come of age, but refused to have anything to do with her depraved daughter's wedding, it was Grandmother who married her off, and Grandmother who gave her a lovely wedding present: a charming apartment in Grandmother's eighteenth-century townhouse, big enough for her, for Erich, with space for children and with two airy studios with skylights, one for him and one for her.

"Of course, these were originally servants' quarters," said Grandmother; "but they are under the roof and have the right light for a painter."

Grandmother gave her a sparkling wedding reception. Neither her mother nor her sisters came, of course—indeed, not one of them would ever speak to her again or acknowledge her existence in any way. Her father, always kind, came to the church and gave her away, but found his usual excuse, "Too much work at the Ministry," to escape the reception. Her brother, then serving his military term with the Sobieski Cuirassiers, should, of course, have asked for leave to attend his sister's wedding; at least he had sent a telegram.

But while she was without immediate family, though those simple, good people, the Kohout parents, had taken her into their hearts and into their love as if she had been their own daughter, she was cosseted by Grandmother's friends.

"You'll have to find your own painter friends," Grandmother had said at the wedding; "we are mostly musicians, but we, too, are artists." And there they all were—above all, the gorgeous Mariandl, wife of a famous anatomist, and so beautiful, so gifted!

Her mother disapproved of Mariandl. "Who is she, after all," she said, "but peasant baggage that professor picked up in some hovel in the mountains and now foists on decent society?"

The fact that Mariandl had become famous in her own right as the author of the illustrations to her husband's books made her all the more suspect. "Text by Professor Richard von Mosenthal; Drawings, Photographs, and Diagrams by Marianne von Mosenthal," said the frontispiece of each of the volumes of the *Pathology of the Sense Organs*. The professor always sent a copy to her father, though her mother considered them much too indecent and indelicate for her daughters to look at. But even her mother had to admit that Mariandl had a lovely soprano voice, though she would not concede that the folksongs Mariandl sang were "serious music" fit for the drawing room.

And there were others, most of them young people not much older than Renata herself, yet already established as performers. They sang the Bach "Wedding Cantata" for her. Then a tall young woman with a long nose and a beautiful alto voice—later Renata would learn that her name was Emmy Heim, and much later she would become one of Renata's closest friends—sang Hugo Wolf and then imitated a French *Diseuse* doing some very funny and quite risqué cabaret ditties.

Another young woman, whose name was Alice Ehlers, played on an instrument Renata had not even heard of called a harpsichord; it had been out of fashion for more than a hundred years, she was told, but sounded enchanting.

And when the party was breaking up and she and Erich were ready to leave for their new apartment, Grandmother had said: "I have given you *my* wedding present. Now let me give you your grandfather's." And she had taken them up a hidden staircase Renata had never known existed, unlocked a door—and there were the two paintings hanging opposite a piano.

"My husband, your grandfather, loved these paintings more than any other thing, except for a little bridge high up in the mountains," Grandmother had said. "He never showed them to anybody. But he would have wanted you to have them, now that we have a daughter once again."

The Perkaczes

Renata had been the last guest to leave the concert on her grandfather's ninetieth anniversary. When she had finally gone, after hugging and kissing her grandmother and telling her over and over again how grateful she was and how much she adored her, only Mariandl stayed behind, as she always did, to oversee the cleaning up. The Baroness Rafaela Wald-Reifnitz then slowly made her way upstairs to her dead husband's private apartment to sit there quietly for an hour or two, as she and Arthur had always done after each of their concerts and parties, and as she still did now that he no longer attended these functions. For in the apartment which she had furnished for him as office and working quarters when they had first, twenty-five years or more ago, bought the dilapidated "Palais" of a long-forgotten eighteenth-century nobleman and restored it for their own use, Arthur was still very much alive, still present, still with her. There was the square rosewood piano, totally out of style by now, of course, and made obsolete by the sonorities of the concert grand, but endowed with a mellowness and sweetness of tone which the modern monster could not equal. It was the same piano on which she had accompanied Arthur when he sang for them on his first visit to her parents' house. And it was the same piano on which he, later that evening, had in turn accompanied her when she sang for him, and when they both suddenly and at the same moment realized that they were deeply, totally in love with one another. Whenever he sang for her—and he never afterwards sang for anyone else—he had insisted on her accompanying him on the rosewood piano.

Next to the piano hung the only possession that was "his" rather than "theirs": the engraving of the Duke of Wellington, which the Duke had autographed and sent when Arthur's father had reported

to him the birth of a son named after the old chief. And the way
the Duke had spelled "Arthur" in the inscription was the reason that
her husband, throughout his life, put a British "h" after the "t" in
his name.

On the opposite wall, where the sun of the June evening was just
reaching them with golden fingers, hung the two portraits of her,
each chosen by Arthur. The first was her wedding present to him
exactly sixty years ago—for they were married on his thirtieth birthday; the second her present to him on their golden wedding anniversary, his eightieth birthday, ten years ago today.

A few steps up—the music room of Arthur's apartment had originally been a servants' antechamber in the old Palais—there was the
studio with its northern window cut into the mansard roof, Arthur's
drafting table running almost the entire length of the big room, with
his rolltop desk in one corner for his papers, and an easel for her
drawings and watercolors. Arthur had died in this room, seven years
ago, falling asleep at the drafting table never to wake up. But if his
body had left, his spirit, his personality, had stayed on. She could still
smell his personal fragrance, part the *Cuir de Russe* eau de Cologne
he used after shaving, part after-dinner cigar, part his own aggres-
sively masculine odor. Arthur was there for her, waiting for her,
with her, whenever she sat down at the piano bench on which he
had wanted her to sit whenever he had anything of importance to
talk over.

After their birthday parties—at least in the later years, when they
had found their way back to each other and had lived through what
Arthur had called "our second honeymoon"—they had always reminisced in this room, about how they had first met, fallen in love, first
lived together. And she had kept up the habit after Arthur's death.
But as she settled herself on the piano bench this time, she found she
was not ready yet for reminiscing. Before she could go back to the
beginning, to the first time she had sung for him Schubert's "An die
Musik" more than sixty years ago, she needed to recover from the
shock of the last time she had sung it for him—today, only a few minutes ago, at his ninetieth birthday party.

"An die Musik" had always been the final number at his birthday
concerts, just as it had been the final number at their first meeting.

After that first meeting she had never sung it except for Arthur—but many times for him. However, during the last ten or fifteen years, even well before Arthur's death, she had not really sung it. Rather, she had spoken it in a parlando recitative that hinted at the music more than voiced it. She still had breath control; one did not lose that as long as one could practice every day. But her voice was long gone—she was eighty-one, after all.

Tonight, however, something had happened. After the first rest, when the music turns somber on the words "wo mich des Lebens wilder Kreis umstrickt," she suddenly found her voice again. Or rather a voice found *her*, took possession of her, sang through her. It was not, of course, a big voice—she had never had a big one. It was also still the mezzo soprano she had been for fifty years. But it was a voice, purer than she had ever produced, carrying better even though a mere whisper, with a pianissimo that echoed back from the furthest corner of the fair-sized hall the long-dead nobleman had built for his dances. She had never before sung as she had sung just now.

This, she knew, must be how Franz Schubert himself had heard the song when he first set his friend Schober's trite words to music. And the others, too, had sensed something out of the ordinary. When she finished on the words "du holde Kunst, ich danke dir dafür!"— breathing them rather than voicing them—Mariandl on the piano had tears running down her cheeks and could barely get through the last five bars. Even those thorough professionals, Emmy Heim and Alice Ehlers, were sobbing aloud. Had Arthur sent her a sign? Was he telling her to come and join him?

"Don't be a superstitious old woman," she heard his voice in her ears—so he was still there in this room. "You are still learning, still growing. You couldn't have sung like that when you were younger. It takes old age to ripen to Schubert's level."

How old was Schubert when he wrote "An die Musik" in 1815 or so—all of eighteen? But then this is perhaps what we mean by "genius," the ability to transcend age, to transcend experience, to leap over learning and suffering and surviving. For she surely could not have sung like this when she was young and in full voice, acclaimed as the best *Lieder* singer in all Vienna. Nor could that young Emmy

Heim do it, even though she was a much better singer than she, Rafaela, had ever been, with the purest of alto voices and a musical sensibility like no singer Rafaela had ever known. Was that what being old meant?

Only a few months earlier these young women musicians, her students and friends and confidantes, had sung for her at her own eightieth birthday. Mariandl, dear Mariandl, had sung a popular Viennese hit tune. But instead of the words, "Du bist nur einmal jung" (You're only young once), she had sung, "Du bist doch ewig jung" (You're young forever), and had brought the house down. It was sweet of Mariandl—but nonsense. Of course she was old; and she would far rather not be "young forever."

But it was also not true that "You're only young once." You are young many, many times, each time differently. That child, Renata, her granddaughter, was young, very young, one way; she herself, only a few years older when she first met Arthur, had been young in a very different way—but still young. That intensely gifted, intensely funny, and intensely bitter Emmy Heim—bitter because God had given her the loveliest small alto instead of a heroic Wagnerian soprano, and that long funny nose and high intelligence instead of the insipid, simpering, pretty-pretty beauty her sister had—was young, very young, in a different way. Mariandl when she had met her, then barely twenty, had been young in yet another way, and Mariandl today at forty was still young, but in a quite different way. Arthur had been young many times, until he was quite an old man, and young each time a different way.

"Du bist doch vielmals jung" (You are young many times), Rafaela hummed; "but you are old only once and only one way."

"What to the young are hopes to the old are memories," Arthur had once said. He claimed to have read it, but like so many of Arthur's epigrams he had probably made it up and was too modest to claim the credit. Hopes change, and change fast, yet memories remain. "You're old only once—it's the last of all possible worlds," Rafaela mused. But perhaps there is more to be said for being old than another of her husband's *mots*—which he had indeed probably read someplace as, thank God, he was not in the habit of being witty—"It beats the alternative." Maybe being old does enable you at eighty-one and without being a genius yourself to sing "An die Musik" the way Schubert, the genius, had written it at eighteen.

But had she herself ever been young the way that child, Renata, her granddaughter, had been young today? She could not remember—it was so long since she was eighteen herself, and the world had changed so much. She doubted it, though.

People always remarked how much Renata resembled her. But then no one, of course, remembered her own, Rafaela's, mother any more, let alone how she had looked and acted as a young woman. And that was whom Renata looked and acted like. There was a strong family resemblance—all three of them shared the same coloring. But whereas Ferdinand Waldmueller had remarked when he painted her sixty years ago that hers were "bold" colors—her mother, she remembered, had been quite upset by the word—Renata, like Mother, was soft, muted, a little blurry, and in her colors very "tame" indeed. Whereas she, Rafaela, was tall, well above average, Renata, like her mother, was petite and lithe, with the quick movements of the lizard and the same darting motions of the small, well-proportioned head. And Renata who had, of course, never known her great-grandmother, had the same seemingly naive cunning, the same innocent ability to outmaneuver the "grown-up" world that Mother had had—whereas she, Rafaela, could never meet anything or anybody except head-on. How cunning that little vixen had been to go on the sly and take the entrance examination at the Art Academy without telling anyone! She must know that she had already won that battle. Her father, Rafaela's son Paul, would have to capitulate, what with his pedantic respect for academic rules and regulations and his pride in a daughter who could pass the notoriously difficult examination, made doubly so for a woman whom the professors at the Art Academy did not exactly welcome with enthusiasm. Now that the little sly-boots had passed the exam, she, Grandmother, could easily do the rest.

Of course, she knew the director of the Academy. As a young architect he had been Arthur's draftsman on that big suspension bridge over the Norwegian fjord. Tomorrow she would call on him, pay her granddaughter's tuition for the first year, and have him write a letter of acceptance. Then she would talk to her son. Her daughter-in-law, that frozen dish towel, would not make much trouble. She was, Rafaela knew, afraid of her mother-in-law, and did not really care for her youngest daughter, so clearly not a Marchfelden, and not even a Wald-Reifnitz, but one of the despised Perkaczes.

Yes, the young woman's trick was exactly how her own mother would have handled it. And Rafaela began to chuckle as she did whenever she remembered how Mother had outflanked her parents to marry Michael Perkacz.

Her parents had not, of course, told her the story—in her childhood, parents did not talk about themselves to their children, and anyhow Mother rarely talked about her family. It was her brother, many years later, when both parents were dead, who had reluctantly told it to her—and been amazed when she roared with laughter rather than being shocked by what he clearly thought a raffish tale.

Father—this much Rafaela had known—had been born in some small Jewish town in Bohemia or Moravia, and his name had originally been a good Jewish one too, Baer-Katz. He must have converted to Catholicism at a very early age. For when he left home, barely fourteen or fifteen, he went straight to Vienna where in those years, around 1805, Jews were still not allowed access unless they had a special permit which a penniless fifteen-year-old could hardly have procured. And then Father had gone into building and real estate—and Jews were then still forbidden to buy, sell, or own property in the city. Anyhow, he soon did very well.

At an early age he also gained the confidence of Vienna's most clannish, most exclusive, most self-contained community, the few extremely rich families of Sephardic Jews who had been allowed to settle under an old treaty with Turkey, who enjoyed tremendous privileges such as perpetual tax exemption and freedom from military service, but were forbidden to own any property except in Vienna's Judengasse behind St. Mary's Church. Even now, in the twentieth century, these Sephardic Jews still lived by themselves, still spoke medieval Spanish at home, still married only among themselves, never visiting outside their own community—at least Rafaela knew of no Sephardic Jew who had ever visited other people, nor of any non-Sephardic, either Jew or Gentile, who had ever been invited behind the doors of a Sephardic home. And they guarded their women more jealously than even the Turks or the Spaniards did.

Somehow her father earned their confidence, for he became the front man through whom the Sephardics began to buy property after the Napoleonic Wars, when they were still forbidden to do so but realized, being shrewd merchants, that the city was growing by leaps and bounds. And somehow her mother must have seen the handsome young stranger when he came to discuss his real estate deals—maybe they had, like the Moslems in their harems, little windows through which the women could see without being seen themselves. Anyhow, as in an Arabian Nights tale, her mother had fallen in love with the exotic visitor from the outside, had somehow managed to meet him—"She probably bribed her maid," her brother had speculated—and decided to marry him. But that was, of course, impossible. Sephardics married only Sephardics, never a Gentile, and certainly never, never that low-class abomination, a non-Sephardic, Ashkenazi Jew! And so Mother—at all of eighteen or nineteen, Renata's age—had contrived to slip out to the priest at the nearby Catholic church and started taking instruction in the Catholic faith, undoubtedly with the same innocent, "butter-won't-melt-in-my-mouth" mien with which little Renata had slipped out to take the Art Academy examination.

And then her family was foiled. A young woman in those days could not marry without her parents' consent, certainly not at eighteen. But for religious conversion the age of consent was fourteen, and a Jew who interfered with a mature person's rational desire to be saved by becoming a Catholic risked a heavy fine, imprisonment, perhaps even deportation in the rigidly Catholic Austria of the time (perhaps, thought Rafaela, even today). But a Sephardic family could also not accept having a daughter turn Catholic, but had to expel her. And so, as her brother had put it, a little crudely, "The little cheat had her parents over a barrel." Of course she was read out of the Sephardic synagogue and her name struck off the family rolls as if she had never been born. But she got her man. The family did not even completely break with her. At least her mother's father, her own grandfather, still came every Saturday for a visit during Rafaela's childhood, though he never touched food in his daughter's house.

And apparently her own father somehow managed to retain the lucrative Sephardic business for a good many years, just as her mother, at least in the privacy of her house, kept her lovely Sephardic name, Shulamit, using the Catholic "Mary" only outside. And yet curiously, like Renata, her mother had always appeared to Rafaela to dither, to be timid, panicky, and in need of help.

"It was really Mother," mused Rafaela, "who was the brains behind Father's business success. Surely it must have been Mother who had the ideas, Mother who realized how Vienna would be growing, Mother who got Father to start building apartment houses and workers' tenements in the suburbs when the city still had walls, Mother who got him to start a mortgage bank to get cheap money for his projects." Indeed, Rafaela knew for sure that twenty-five years later, in the 1840s and 1850s, it was her mother (already aging) who had pushed her brother into railway construction when everybody else thought railways far too much of a gamble. It was her mother who had thus laid the foundation both of her brother's and of her own husband's fortunes.

"Perhaps," thought Rafaela, "it was also Mother who got the barony." The story, or what Rafaela knew of it, did not sound like her careful, self-effacing father. What had happened—again, her brother was the source of information—was that the Prime Minister's wife, the Countess Kolowrat, had speculated in real estate without her husband's knowledge. Panic hit in 1837 and the countess was in deep trouble, over-extended beyond hope of extricating herself. The count's political enemies—above all, Metternich, whom Kolowrat had pushed aside as First Minister and confined to the Foreign Office—were closing in for the kill when her father called on Kolowrat and offered to have the Perkacz mortgage bank take over the countess's holdings and her debts against a baronial patent. "And," her brother concluded, "when Papa sold these holdings four years later at a nice profit, Mother made him go back to Kolowrat and turn over the profit. And another two years later we got our most profitable business, the government concession to build and run the first horse-drawn streetcar line in the city!"

Well, if that child, Renata, really meant to go into painting as a profession, she would need all the cunning and commercial sense her great-grandmother had possessed. Whoever thought up the idea that artists were impractical and unworldly, not concerned with sales and fees and commissions? It was hard enough to be a musician, but at least one could be an ensemble player. But every painter was a soloist—and there weren't many engagements for soloists in any profession. Renata might still give up; most art or music students did, after all. "But I doubt it," thought Rafaela. "No one who could play that entrance examination trick gives up easily. Of course her mother will push hard to get her to 'marry well.' But once they've gone to the Art Academy, they somehow lose their taste for eternally juvenile counts whose only accomplishments are a few card tricks and the ability to recite their family tree in their sleep."

Arthur

That was unfair. Arthur, too, had known his family tree for a few hundred years back; and so, she was quite sure, had those super-snobs, their mother's great Sephardic family, the Ephrussi, who, as Father once had told her, could trace their ancestry back all the way to the philosopher Maimonides, and who still, she had once read, had hanging in their family's main home in Salonika the key to their former house in Moslem Spain. No, to be prejudiced against old families and aristocrats as those modern intellectuals and so-called liberals were was just as bigoted, just as narrow-minded, as her daughter-in-law's creed that nothing else counted. What had made Arthur so unusual was exactly that he was openly proud of his name and lineage and yet never measured anybody by name or rank, title or descent.

Otherwise he would hardly have come to her home that Satur-day afternoon, in 1845, when her brother had first brought him to sing Schubert songs with her. He and her brother were colleagues then, both instructors at the Technical University, Arthur as cap-tain of engineers, her brother as a young architect. But while they were equals at work, there was a world of social difference between a Wald-Reifnitz, the son of a field marshal, and the Perkaczes, children of a real estate developer and mortgage banker. Yet when he heard that his colleague had a sister who sang Schubert—then almost for-gotten by the fickle Viennese—he asked to be introduced to her, since he too loved Schubert and sang his songs.

He had a pleasant light baritone and was easy to accompany; and she had enjoyed his singing of *Die Winterreise*—though she realized even then that he would always remain an amateur, a lover of music, and never become a student, let alone a genuine musician.

But then something happened when, after supper, they changed places and he began to accompany her while she sang. The occasion was suddenly no longer "social." She had already finished the songs she had wanted to sing when he asked her for one more. That was when she chose "An die Musik," always one of her favorites but quite unknown then, as were most of Schubert's early songs, and unknown to Arthur too. When she finished, he had said softly: "Thank you, Rafaela."

And she knew immediately. Until then he had called her "Baroness" or "*Gnaediges Fräulein.*" Still, it was only a little forward of him to call her "Rafaela." She was very young, not yet twenty, and almost ten years younger than he. Indeed, she still wore her hair hanging loose and long, instead of putting it on top of her head as a woman did. Thus she declared herself to be more child than woman.

But by the way he said "Rafaela," she knew that he had said: "I love you, will you marry me?" and she needed all her self-control not to cry out: "Yes, many times yes!" though he saw her blush and did not have to be told.

She was not surprised when next day her father called her in around noontime and said: "Rafaela, Baron Wald-Reifnitz has just been here with a most astonishing story."

"I expected it, Father, and I think I know what he told you," she had replied.

Her father was clearly taken aback. "I thought you and the gentleman met only yesterday," he exclaimed.

"We did."

"Then how do you know? Has he talked to you?"

"Father," she had said then, quite indignant, "you yourself called him a gentleman. But I do know that he came to ask you for my hand, and I can tell you that I know he loves me, and that I love him and will marry him."

Her father, whose great favorite she was, took her into his arms as if she were a child and said: "But, Rafaela, such a thing happens only in books, not in real life!"

"This time, Father," she had answered firmly, "it did happen in real life."

Arthur did not have to ask anybody for permission. He was old enough. His father had died when he was a boy, and his mother, while only in her fifties, had retired to live in genteel melancholia on one of the Reifnitz estates on a Carinthian lake. She did come to the wedding, but would otherwise take no further interest in either her son or his wife.

But Rafaela needed permission from her parents. A Baron Wald-Reifnitz was of course eminently eligible, indeed, so grand as to frighten her father—her mother, Rafaela realized even then, knew herself to be every bit as good as any baron. Still, her parents consented, but imposed a year's wait—which they waived a few months later, when they saw the radiant look on their daughter's face in Ferdinand Waldmueller's first sketches.

She conceived almost at once. Paul was born within ten months of their wedding. Altogether these first two years they lived the typical life of the young married upper-class couple. Arthur taught at the Technical University—he was still an officer in the army, promoted to major, but on permanent assignment to teach, and inordinately proud of being the youngest full professor in any Austrian university. And he then began the study of bridges and bridge building that would later make him famous. She nursed the baby—they both rejected the fashionable idea of a wet nurse; she had enough milk and loved the feel of the baby's cheek against her breasts. She managed the household and supervised the servants, most of them old family retainers of her parents who indulged and spoiled her.

She still took music lessons and Arthur continued to pore over civil-engineering texts from antiquity on. Their life together centered on their evenings, and especially on the musicales they attended two or three times a week, either in their own house or at friends'. This was well before going to concerts was the fashionable thing to do for people who could afford to have the musicians come to them. But these were also the years in which Vienna was first inundated by the waltz, and both she and Arthur found themselves swept away by the tide.

They thought themselves happy, of course, very happy. Later, in retrospect, they knew that they had only been young, busy, content, and conventional. Had they continued that way—and there was really no reason why they should not have—they would have soon drifted into the routine "good marriage" in which the partners stay together only because they are too bored with one another to do anything else.

What changed their lives was the 1848 Revolution. Her brother immediately—to his own surprise—became one of the leaders and one of the Liberals' most effective orators. But for the fact that he was a "baron" and thus suspect to the "Radicals," he might have gotten what he wanted: election as Vienna's representative to the Frankfurt Parliament. But he sat in the Revolutionary councils for Vienna and for Austria, and was nominated to be a minister in the cabinet the Revolution tried to impose on the Emperor.

Arthur as a serving officer could not, of course, take part in politics. Anyhow, politics did not suit his temperament; he hated crowds. But like all the young men of his generation, he was a romantic liberal to whom the old absolutism was a despised anachronism and the Revolution the dawn of a new day of freedom and justice. When the army was ordered to march on Vienna and suppress the Revolution, he therefore resigned his commission. Shortly thereafter, he joined her brother, whose political career had come to an abrupt end when the troops marched into the city. Together they founded the construction company in which Arthur became a partner and the consulting engineer for railways.

The company, as her mother had predicted, was immediately successful beyond the founders' wildest dreams. The one thing the government had learned from the uprising of 1848 was the need for railways to move troops fast. And so the era of government-financed railway construction began, whereas formerly the government had left railway building to the ultra-conservative and greedy Rothschilds.

This then meant that Arthur had to start traveling all over the country: to lay out routes, supervise survey crews, work out estimates and, above all, design the bridges and viaducts, trestles and culverts which, in mountainous Austria, were what railway building was all about. From the beginning, he insisted that she come along, despite the fears of her parents and the tut-tutting of respectable folk at his dragging a delicately nurtured lady into the wilds of construction camps and the dirt of Alpine inns.

They both immediately became aware of how much the baby had come between them at home. She had had a glowing pregnancy—she was one of those high-breasted, long-legged women who carry well and are at their peak when expecting. But Arthur had treated her from the first moment of the pregnancy as if she were made of spun sugar, and only "imposed" on her, as he apologetically put it, when his desire overwhelmed him and then only to the point where his most urgent needs were stilled. And when she breast-fed Paul, Arthur hardly ever came near her, staying away for weeks. The baby slept in her room, not he. Of course that was only proper, what well-bred men and women were then supposed to be doing. "I wonder," thought Rafaela, "whether the young today are more intelligent than we were then?"

Altogether in Vienna Arthur always treated her as a "lady."

But the moment they were on a journey together, he treated her as his woman. The change was almost too much for her, too abrupt, too complete, too demanding. All of a sudden Arthur was an animal—rampant, aggressive, demanding, insatiable, rough to the point of hurting her. She was at first shocked, then frightened, then repelled—but also totally overwhelmed. How often had she been too embarrassed next morning even to think of what they had been doing together during the night—and enjoying it, which was even more embarrassing. For she was perhaps more frightened by her response than by Arthur's open sensuality, more disturbed to find that there was a dimension to her that was totally sensuous, totally carnal. And Arthur on those trips wanted her and took her in the oddest places and at the oddest moments: when they were walking together in a quiet forest, or if there was a rock by a roadside behind which one could hide, or in the tents of the construction camp when the workmen left for their midday meal.

Once in a high Alpine meadow—it must have been late in June, for the first hay had just been mowed—he pulled her behind a hayrick at ten in the morning, only an hour or so after breakfast, and began to wrestle her to the ground.

"But, Arthur," she had cried out, genuinely upset, "I'm not a peasant girl!"

"Then what are you doing behind a hayrick?" he had returned. "Behind a hayrick every woman is a peasant girl," and had proceeded to prove it methodically, in great detail.

When they were both exhausted and fumbling for their clothes, he had said: "This is our real honeymoon."

To their great joy, she became pregnant again. And this time they knew better. Her mother scolded, nagged, predicted terrible catastrophes. But Rafaela kept on traveling with Arthur until a few weeks before the baby's birth, and started traveling with him again a few weeks afterwards with Maria on her breast. And whereas Paul had come between them and had divided them, Maria from the beginning traveled as one of them, joining them and pulling them ever closer to each other. Arthur was totally enthralled by his daughter from the first, and she felt closer to the child than she had ever felt to anyone, including even Arthur. Maria, in turn, almost from the moment of her birth, reached out for them, took their hearts into her little hands, and gave back joy in boundless measure.

Paul

"Could we have built a similar relationship with Paul if we had taken him along on our trips and treated him as a love child?" Rafaela and Arthur had asked that question of themselves hundreds of times. "Would it have made any difference to Paul either? Would his relationship to us have been different?" The answer was always "No."

Paul was Paul, and would have been Paul whatever they could or would have done differently. Perhaps it might have made a difference to their relationship, Arthur's and Rafaela's, those first two years, if Arthur instead of Paul had shared her bedroom then. But as for Paul—no, it would not have changed him nor his relationship to his parents nor his personality. Of course, he never lacked attention and love. In fact, he seemed to like it better when they began to travel and leave him behind. For then he and his nurse and his governess— and later his tutor—would move to the apartment her parents always kept ready for him. And there he was smothered in the love of a doting grandmother and enjoyed the company of the one person who, in Paul's life, was a close friend, her by then semi-retired father, who never wearied of the company of his clever grandson.

Arthur had seen Paul's abilities early and was proud of him all along. He was proud when the boy finished the Gymnasium at four-teen, four years ahead of his class, and when he published his first scientific paper at seventeen. He was even prouder of him when he was appointed a professor at the Technical University at an even ear-lier age than Arthur himself had attained this distinction. He glo-ried in the knowledge that Paul's inventions and patents in telegraph and telephone made his son a richer man than he himself had ever been—and a more famous one as well. And the only time she had seen Arthur be positively arrogant was when Paul, still barely forty, was appointed Minister of Railways and friends and acquaintances descended on them with their congratulations. Arthur was even pleased when Paul, three years later, when the ministry fell, did not return to academic life—"A scientist's best years are over by the time he's forty," he said—but stayed on in the ministry as the first Sektion-schef and principal civil servant, although he still kept his laboratory at the Technical University and spent many of his evenings there, aside from constant travel to scientific congresses to read a paper or receive a medal.

The only action of Paul's that Arthur had found hard to accept—and even harder to understand—was his marrying Isabella March-felden. Of course, as a grown man in his thirties, he had every right to choose the woman he wanted to be his wife. He had not acted impetuously—Paul never acted impetuously. He had courted Isabella for a good two years. In worldly terms, it was an excellent match. A countess of the Holy Roman Empire who was entitled to call the Emperor "Cousin" was a *"grande partie"* for a Wald-Reifnitz whose mother was a Jewish Perkacz. As for her having no money; well, the Wald-Reifnitzes and the Perkaczes had enough for a dozen impover-ished countesses.

But how could he have married so disagreeable, so unhappy, so negative and disapproving a person, one who never had anything good to say about anybody, was always disappointed or offended, read nothing, absolutely nothing, except the *Court Circular*, and who talked only, but forever, of titles and lineages, who had precedence over whom, and who had received a higher Imperial order?

Arthur could never see that his daughter-in-law was pitiful; to him, she was only offensive. Rafaela at least learned to have compas-sion for the woman, obnoxious though she was.

Not long after Paul's marriage to Isabella Marchfelden—a huge society event with no end of princes, margraves, and even an arch-duke, and three bishops officiating—she found herself sitting at an official dinner next to that grand personage, the Prince Sobieski, Duke of Przemysl, the Austrian Ambassador in London. The Prince, as she remembered, was honorary patron and she was on the ladies' committee for the Austrian tour of some English choral society—she still shuddered as she recalled how the rafters shook when those five hundred earnest, bearded choristers had roared out a Mendelssohn Pianissimo, slightly off-key.

At that dinner the Prince had leaned across and said to her: "Baroness, it's true, isn't it, that the Countess Isabella Marchfelden has married your son and become a member of your family? My congratulations; there is no better blood in Austria.

"I did meet your daughter-in-law a few years back, by the way. As you may know, I am Commander-in-Chief of the Sobieski Cuirassiers, of which Count Marchfelden was the commanding officer for so long. And so when I paid one of my quinquennial visits to the regiment, your new daughter-in-law was my official hostess, the colonel being a widower. That was six or seven years ago, and she was still a child, not quite fifteen. The burden of entertaining me for those three weeks was a little heavy for those young shoulders, so perhaps you had better not remind her of me. What I remember vividly is how ashamed and crushed the young lady was by the dreadful poverty into which the House of Marchfelden had fallen. She came down to dinner every night for three weeks in the same old gown her mother had left, the only one I imagine the family possessed. It was twenty years out of fashion and at least three sizes too big for the child, so that the sleeves had been tucked in, the hem taken up with basting thread, and the back pinched with safety pins.

"The poor young lady sat there for three weeks every evening at the head of the table, unable to speak or swallow a bite, with big tears rolling slowly down her cheeks. I'm delighted that she can now afford as many new gowns as she can possibly want—and I hope she enjoys them!"

The Prince had meant to be amusing. But Rafaela was not amused, liking neither the story nor its teller. Everybody always sang the Prince's praises. Her husband had thought him the most polished nobleman he had ever met, and the most charming. Even today, at the party, Mosenthal, Mariandl's husband, had told her the same thing—the Mosenthals had just been to London and had only returned that morning on the Orient Express to join her for Arthur's ninetieth anniversary party. Mosenthal had raved about the small private dinner party to which Prince Sobieski had invited him and his banker-brother just a few days earlier. Paul, her son, was still

at this moment in London, on one of his congresses to receive another medal, and as a former minister was staying at the embassy
as the Prince's guest. In the letter she had received from him only
this morning (a letter of apology for his absence and of best wishes
for the day) he too had spoken with unusual enthusiasm—Paul was
rarely enthusiastic—about the Prince, his charm, and the enjoyable
dinner party.

Well, charming or not charming, she, Rafaela, had not liked either
the Prince Sobieski or his story. She did not mind that he was being
condescending—he would probably have called it being "affable." It
was very hard, she imagined, for a Prince Sobieski to be anything
else with the likes of a Wald-Reifnitz, who were not their servants
and were not peasants and yet somehow could not be accepted as
equals. And she did not mind too much his saying so clearly: "If
the girl had not been so beggarly-poor, she would never have had to
marry so far below her station."

It was crude but it was true, and Rafaela always was willing to
face the truth.

What she could not stand was that he had enjoyed seeing the
child suffer. He had had the same expression on his face that she had
seen on the faces of people watching a cat playing with a mouse—
and she could not abide it.

But ironically he had done her a service: for she had been immediately flooded with compassion and pity for her disagreeable, deplor-
able daughter-in-law. Whenever Isabella thereafter tried to provoke
her mother-in-law—and that was every time they met—she pictured
her at that dinner table in the shabby, tawdry old woman's taffeta,
sitting next to that bejeweled and beperfumed, supercilious Prince,
money oozing out of his every pore, and probably feeling thrice
humiliated because she had been brought up to believe that as a
German-Austrian countess of the Holy Roman Empire she was infinitely superior in rank, breeding, and importance to any slovenly
Pole from a barbarous country where princes were a dime a dozen
and not much better than swineherds.

Arthur had called Rafaela "sentimental" when she tried to say
something like this about their daughter-in-law. But he had to admit that it did not really matter whether they approved of her nor

whether she got along with them. They were not married to her, Paul was. The only thing that really mattered was what kind of wife she made Paul, and what kind of husband he made her—and to both questions the answer was an eminently satisfactory one.

Paul was clearly proud of Isabella's formal, cold, haughty hand-someness. He clearly did not want a wife who shared his work, but one who took pride in his titles, honors, and medals. Arthur proba-bly had received as many medals as Paul; he had always tossed them into the bottom drawer of the rolltop desk and never looked at them again. In Paul's big apartment across from the Opera, all the medals were displayed in a large, lighted display case a visitor could not pos-sibly miss—and they were taken out and polished once a week.

What Paul wanted—and what he got—was a punctilious house-keeper and a reliable, conscientious governess for his children. And Isabella, in turn, in addition to the economic security she had so badly lacked as a child and so desperately needed, wanted a man, who even if not the prince of the blood her name and lineage might have entitled her to if only she had had a little money, was "famous" and an ex-minister, called "Your Excellency" and entitled to imme-diate access to the Emperor as if he were of the first rank of nobility.

As for the rest, what mattered to her was that the Princess Wot-tawa, Prince Sobieski's married daughter, left her calling card, and that the Countess-Dowager Schwechat-Schwadron—the mother of the Princess Wottawa's reputed lover—invited her to the christening of a grandchild. The two cards to that effect had been prominently displayed on a silver tray in the foyer of her house the last time Rafa-ela dined there just before Paul left for London. That this suited the two of them mattered; not the relationship to parents-in-law.

But even though Arthur had to concede that she was right, and even though he was so proud of his son and of his achievements and his standing in the world of science, there was a fundamental incom-patibility between father and son that had been there ever since Paul as a precociously bright boy had begun to ask "Why." The two simply did not see the same world, did not share the same values.

Once, in discussing Paul, Mariandl's husband, Mosenthal, the anatomist—who in his own field was as great and famous a savant as Paul was in his—had called her son a "modern technical man" and "a

man of the twentieth century," with his "scientific truth," his "objectivity," and his habit of dismissing all except "facts."

But Paul was really a replica of his paternal grandfather, the field
marshal who had been very much an eighteenth-century man, not a
bit "modern," and as much a success in the age of Napoleon as Paul
was in that of electricity and telephones. A few years earlier a historian had published a biography of the field marshal; and in every
line Rafaela had recognized her own son: in the field marshal's total
absorption with his gun-casting techniques, for instance, but also in
the fact that once he had left home, at thirteen, to enter the Cadet
Academy, he had never again visited his home or his parents at Castle Reifnitz (though dutifully writing a letter every ninety days) until
he retired, more than forty years later, after which he had never left
Castle Reifnitz again until the day he died there.

"Lieutenant Field Marshal Baron Wald-Reifnitz," the historian
had concluded, "left behind two lasting achievements: the standardization of cannons, which enabled the Imperial Army Foundry to
cast one hundred gun barrels in a month where formerly it could
barely turn out that many in a year; and the standardization of gun-
nery training, which made it possible to turn out a fully qualified ar-
tilleryman in nine months where formerly it had taken five years."

If Paul's biography ever came to be written, the conclusions might
not read too differently, his mother thought.

This, as it always did, set Rafaela to musing about the three men
she had known well in her life, all three of high achievement and
each so very different.

Paul, of course, was the simplest and, she suspected, the most enduring type. He was a superbly gifted craftsman, for all his scientific
training, his mathematics, and his systematic research. The world
was always in need of craftsmen, and, she hoped, there would always
be an adequate supply. They were, she thought, the bread of civilization and by themselves give enough sustenance for survival—but
they do not give much more, do not give any spice or diversity, nor
much joy.

Arthur too, she thought, represented a basic and enduring type,
the artist. When he had finally finished his great book on bridges
and bridge building, after working on it for twenty years, he had put

at the end: "AD MAJOREM DEI GLORIAM," and people raised their eye-brows since Arthur was known to be anticlerical. But the deity to whose glory the book was dedicated was not Jehovah, it was Nature. And the first paragraph of the book read:

> The matters with which builders of bridges concern themselves the most, the matters which therefore will constitute the main top-ics of this book: materials, suspension, support, stress and strain, wind shear and water flow, load factors and economics, while cru-cially important, are primarily restraints on bridge design. They tell us what we cannot do. What we can and should do is dictated by that great master-builder Nature, without whom all our work is as nought. The ultimate test of a bridge or a viaduct is its effect on landscape or citiscape. The hallmark of a well-designed bridge is its bringing out the best features of its natural surroundings.

Arthur had never once asked her: "Do you like this bridge?" He had always asked her: "How does the valley look to you with the bridge in it?"

And that, of course, was what artists asked. She remembered the first time that the young—then extremely young—Gustav Mahler, still a Conservatory student, came to one of her musical evenings with his very early songs. He was only willing to play them after a lot of coaxing. But then he had not asked: "Do you like them?" He had asked: "Will they sing well?", and she had known at once that she was in the presence of an artist and a musician, though the songs them-selves were still those of a beginner and quite derivative.

The one of these three men who baffled her, although he had never baffled Arthur, was her brother. There was no one except per-haps Maria, her daughter, with whom her relationship had been easier, more harmonious, less friction-laden, or beset with fewer mis-understandings and doubts.

After 1848, her brother had forsworn politics. When ten years later the Liberals came into power in the Habsburg monarchy and had offered him a post in their cabinet, he had turned it down with-out a moment's hesitation. He had become a businessman with a vengeance. After the first major push in railway building that had made him—and Arthur—rich, he had returned to the urban real estate with which his father had started. He soon became the leading developer and builder of the city's large structures: apartment houses, museums, ministries, office buildings, and hotels. Whenever she walked or drove down the Ringstrasse, she saw one building after another that had been put up by his First Austrian Construction Company, on land developed by his First Austrian Property Company, and financed by his Perkacz Mortgage Bank. All the top architects had been under contract to the architectural firm of Perkacz & Associates. And in his very last years, her brother had turned with the same energy and enthusiasm to developing resorts for tourists and to building hotels—in the mountains, on the lakes and the seashore, in the Dolomites and the Bohemian spas and on the Adriatic. In all these ventures he had been eminently successful and had made more money than she ever knew existed—she had been quite stunned when the lawyers read his will.

But, as he had said himself, he never had been truly a "businessman." When he lay dying, he had begun to write his memoirs. He did not live to finish them, but his son, her nephew, had had the fragment privately printed. It began:

> In my younger days I believed in constitutions and was ready to lay down my life for constitutional government, for manhood franchise, for parliamentary elections and for freedom of the press. My aim throughout life has remained the same: to build the free and just society of which we dreamed as young men on the barricades of 1848. But I learned long ago that one does not reach this goal through constitutions. The way lies in developing citizens rather than in writing laws. Citizens develop at home. They are formed by the dignity, the self-respect, the responsibility which enter their souls from the environment of their formative years.
>
> I am still a revolutionary—every one of the buildings I have put up for the last forty years is a manifesto. I still dream of the virtuous Roman Republic to which we, as schoolboys, first swore allegiance during the dreary years of reaction in the 1830s. But now I know that only another tyranny can be created by Brutus' dagger.

The right tools are the tools of the builder, not those of the killer. My aim has been to build a human environment in which citizens can stand straight.

Further on in the book her brother did indeed claim that his way to build was the most profitable, in fact, the only profitable way. He had poured scorn on the cheap builders who ran up horrible workers' tenements or airless middle-class barracks. They were, he claimed, incompetent businessmen. To be sure, their original costs seemed lower. But ten years later their buildings and the entire neighborhood were deteriorating. "As the rats take over," he wrote, "property values go down, the costs of upkeep soar, and rents decline steadily." His buildings, by contrast, he declared—and he cited enough figures to prove it—steadily increased in value, while their maintenance costs remained low or even went down.

But Rafaela suspected that this was a secondary point with her brother; he would have built the way he did even if it had meant less profit. He insisted on perfection in every detail, even on the roofs, where only the crows would ever see it. He paid the architects the highest fees, hired only the best and most expensive Italian stonemasons. And he kept the ceilings of the apartments high, even though the building code would have permitted him to lower them enough to squeeze another rent-paying floor into the houses and office blocks he put up.

"In my buildings," he boasted, "people stand up straight."

But was this persona—in her own mind Rafaela called it the "Patrician"—as basic a type and as enduring as the craftsman or the artist? Or was it, as her husband thought, strictly a type of that last, that optimistic, nineteenth century?

There did not seem to be any Patricians any more, a scant ten years after her brother's death. The businessmen she now encountered (not that she knew many, or had ever known many outside her own father's family) were interested only in money or, in a few rare cases, in being "clever."

There was, for instance, the brother of Mariandl's Mosenthal, the banker who was reputed to have the best financial mind in Austria and perhaps Europe, and to be in a class with that financial magician, the Banker-Prince J. P. Morgan in far-away America, or at least with Mosenthal's English friend, Mr. Hinton.

Rafaela knew both Mosenthal and Hinton quite well—and she respected Hinton's musical ear and his intelligence as a listener. Neither Mosenthal nor Hinton (she could not vouch for the legendary Mr. Morgan, nor for anything so exotic as an American altogether) was particularly interested in making money, although both surely made plenty of it. But they were also not interested in what their work did or could do. They were interested in the cleverness—what they called the "concept"—of their ideas, of their eternal "deals," their complicated transactions. They were craftsmen like Paul and Paul's field marshal grandfather.

The heirs to her brother's dream of making over the world were however once more believers in "constitution"—only now they were Socialists like her brother's grandson and his close friend, the banker Mosenthal's son, both medical students, both at bottom very conventional young people, even though they chain-smoked cigarettes, despised their fathers and grandfathers as "hopelessly bourgeois," and were as ready to lay down their lives on the barricades for "the Revolution" or "the Proletariat" as her brother, at their age, had been ready to lay down his for manhood franchise. They were terribly earnest but, she thought, quite ineffectual. Mosenthal, the banker, and his friend Hinton were terribly effective. But were they serious or only playing games with their own cleverness?

"Stop worrying about the twentieth century," Arthur would always say when she reached this point in their talks. "The twentieth century will have to take care of itself without the two of us, and probably without even Paul. Anyhow, you are just trying to avoid thinking and talking about Maria."

Maria

Arthur was right. Even after half a century it hurt to think and talk about Maria, and even more to think and talk about the years afterwards.

It was the first time since Maria's birth almost five years earlier that they had been separated for any length of time. All winter long Arthur had been working on the drawings of bridges and viaducts for the new railway line in the westernmost part of the country, the bridges and viaducts across the Arlberg Pass between Innsbruck and the Swiss border that were later to become his most famous works and surely his most original ones. The final measurements had, of course, to be done on the spot, and they had to be done before excavation and building could begin. That meant he had to be in the High Tyrol while it was still deep winter in the mountains, when the roads, such as they were, were impassable, with avalanches, heavy falls of wet spring snow, and flooding rivers. Reluctantly, they had decided that he would go alone, and that she and Maria would follow six weeks later, after the snows had melted.

Maria had never been more enchanting than in the weeks just before Arthur left, more feminine, more flirtatious. One moment she would roll on the floor in gales of laughter after sneaking up on her father from behind and tickling him with a feather. The next she would be completely serious and startle her parents by the thoughtfulness of a question about one of Arthur's drawings or her mother's songs. She could romp for hours without getting tired. But she could also sit motionless for hours, watching the goldfish in the aquarium which had been her favorite present the preceding Christmas. Much as Arthur would miss Rafaela, he would miss Maria even more, they both knew. But it would only be for six weeks.

Then, ten days after Arthur had left—just when he should have reached his remote destination—Maria, one evening, began to complain of pains in her head and shoulders, and to grow feverish. By the time Dr. Augsburg came, an hour later, she was in convulsions, screaming in agony. The doctor worked on her all night and he summoned all the medical help Vienna could offer. But by sunrise Maria was dead.

"Galloping brain fever," Augsburg said—he was almost as shaken as she was. But when she wanted to pray for the child to live, he had said: "Don't Baroness; be thankful she is dying. If she lived, she would be an idiot for the rest of her life, or paralyzed."

And when she had then screamed at herself: "Why didn't I take Maria along with Arthur and out of danger?" he had said quietly: "You can't outrun the Angel of Death. From what we know about this disease, the incubation period is weeks, if not months. The child would have died wherever you might have taken her."

Her brother left his own young family (his wife had just given birth to a child) to move in with her until Arthur's return; and the doctor, too, almost never left her until Arthur finally arrived. The weeks Arthur spent alone, trying frantically to get home after he got word that his daughter had died—this was before railways and the telegraph—must have been even worse for him.

Rationally, both of them knew of course that no one was to blame. But neither could help thinking constantly "if only," and both blamed themselves, tore themselves apart. Neither could help being bitter. Alive, Maria had been the strongest bond between them; dead, the child all but destroyed their marriage, all but destroyed the two of them.

Arthur still, during those dreadful years (two, almost three years) came to her bed once in a while. But she knew he did it as a duty, not out of desire or joy. She knew (how, she was not sure, but she knew) that he had an affair with another woman during that time, maybe several, though, thank God, he never then or later told her. But when she lay alone in her bed during those endless sleepless nights, she was not jealous. She blamed herself: "What have I done to cease being attractive to him. What have I done to offend him?"

But when he came to her bed, she was so petrified by fear that she all but pushed him away. She could not bear the thought of being pregnant again. Her dreams were dreams of giving birth to a monster, to the idiot the doctor said Maria would have become had she survived the attack, or, worst of all, of bearing Maria again and having her die again. Every time after Arthur had been with her at night she waited in terror until her next period. Many years later, when they could talk about this time to one another, Arthur confessed that he had been as afraid of begetting a child as she had been of conceiving one.

And yet these years of living hell were also the years during which both Arthur and she became professionals, became tempered, matured as performers and artists. Both threw themselves into their work, drugged themselves with it. These were the years in which Arthur began to write his big book, but also the years during which he bid on every design on the continent for a bridge or a viaduct, so that he became known as the master builder.

She in turn changed herself from a gifted amateur into a true musician. It began, she thought, with her disappointment with Schumann's song cycle, *Frauenliebe und Leben*, then at the peak of its popularity. She had hoped that it would speak to her woman's grief, but found it instead shallow and sentimental—she still felt that way about it. And so she began to search for music that would respond to her and to which she could respond, music she then found far beyond Vienna's narrow horizons, in the lovely, serene, transcendental Berlioz songs, then still virtually unknown even in France. But she did not have the technical equipment to sing them. So she went back to school and to hard work on breath control and placement. To her immeasurable surprise, she then found that she who had all her life been singing as a high soprano, really had a mezzo voice of such range as to be almost a true alto.

Gradually, she acquired a reputation as a musical pioneer, the reputation she still had. Of course she could no longer sing, as she did then, the music the parochial Viennese found so strange, the *Lieder* of the eighteenth-century German forerunners of Schubert, for instance, or the nineteenth-century French from Berlioz through

Fauré to Debussy, or, her latest finds, the strange and beautiful folksongs those two very young men in Budapest, Bartók and Kodály,
had lately collected in eastern Hungary and Romania. But she could
have them performed and thus made accessible. And she also acquired a reputation for musicianship and technique, which was what
got her into the teaching she had found the most satisfying of all her
musical activities, and the one she could keep up long after her own
voice had given out.

Indeed, for many years (but that came later, after Maria's Bridge)
she was a professor at the Conservatory, teaching both a course in
the *Lied* and the techniques of breath control and voice placement,
though of course she never took a penny in salary and was discreetly
listed in the catalogue as "Fräulein Wald" only.

Finally she and Arthur found their way back to each other.

In her journeys with him during their earlier, happier days before Maria's death, she had always taken along sketch pad, easel,
and watercolors, and had painted Arthur's bridges and viaducts as
they grew from the rock and emerged ultimately like living beings
from their scaffolding—Arthur had loved her paintings and kept
them carefully. But this was amateur work to entertain herself and
to please him, no substitute for the careful drawings with their precise measurements on which he based his bridges. But when she had
all but given up on their marriage, he came to her and said: "I cannot
visualize how a finished viaduct will look in its valley. Would you be
willing to come with me to paint the site and sketch out how the various alternatives might look and where they might best be placed?"

From then on, she traveled with him once more. It became their
custom to have her sketch out his tentative designs in her paintings before he finally committed himself. Indeed, from there on she
became Arthur's partner, a junior partner only, but junior partner in
all his work.

As soon as they began again to travel together, they also again
became man and wife, or rather man and woman. Only now it was
she who led, she who took the initiative, she who explored, probed,
and pushed for new experiences. Not that she pulled Arthur behind
hayricks. Such episodes as there were—and there were some—she
left to him to initiate; hayricks, she thought, were strictly a male pre-

rogative. But otherwise she became the initiator, and he the respondent. Perhaps after those long lonely nights she had become so hungry as to forget the proprieties. "Or else," she thought, "our roles have changed altogether." Before Maria's death there had been "his" world, the world of his work, and "their" world, the world of baby and home. Now there was "their" world, the world of his bridges and viaducts in which she was a full participant, and "her" world, the world of music in which Arthur was just a listener, though an admiring one.

But whatever the reason, the new relationship became steadily stronger and as joyous as the old one had been. And just as Maria's birth had been a capstone of the old relationship, so Maria's Bridge became the capstone and fulfillment of the new one.

Normally Arthur would not have bothered by that time—in the late 1850s—with a little rustic bridge for a narrow-gauge branch railway. He was far too busy by then for minor commissions. But the valley in which the little railway was to be built to give access from the main line to an old pilgrimage church on the other side of the mountain had a special meaning for both of them. It had been there that they had stayed on their first journey together, there that what Arthur then called "our real honeymoon" had begun. Both of them were fond of the little valley with its lovely mountain flowers and its secretive beauty, and they did not want to see it spoilt.

Of all Arthur's bridges, Maria's Bridge came closest to being their joint design. It was Arthur, of course, who found the technical solution: a rustic wooden trestle looking deceptively simple and fragile, high above the waterfall. But then she had the happy idea of placing the little bridge at a gentle angle, parallel to the crest line of the ridge behind it, which made the critics acclaim it as the most perfect of all Arthur's works. And it was Arthur, in turn, who stunned her at the dedication ceremony when he named the little span "Marien-Bruecke" (Maria's Bridge) and years later chose her watercolor of the bridge for the frontispiece of his book.

That evening, after she had finished the sketch of the completed bridge in the evening sun, they sat for a long time, silent, holding hands as if they had been teenagers at their first shy meeting. And then, when it had grown completely dark, Arthur said: "Thank you,

Rafaela," in the same voice in which he had said the words to her ten years or more ago, when she had first sung "An die Musik" for him. Then they both knew that they had reached the *rosa mystica*, the mystery of married love, that enduring bond woven out of shared sorrow and shared joy.

"And so we lived happily ever after," thought the Baroness Rafaela Wald-Reifnitz. Indeed, when they reminisced together, she and Arthur always stopped here, at what Arthur called "our second honeymoon."

"An die Musik"

But for her there was still one more unfolding, still one more ripening: Mariandl.

They had known the anatomist Mosenthal since he was a boy—his father, Austria's leading railway lawyer, had been a friend of her brother's from student days and then for years her brother's and Arthur's legal adviser. And since the anatomist loved music, he had become a regular visitor in their house quite early. Indeed, it was Rafaela who had advised him when he was thirteen or so to take up the viola rather than violin or piano, the instruments which everybody played. Mosenthal never became more than an amateur on the instrument. But even mediocre viola players are scarce, so that he was always welcome at the Wald-Reifnitz musical evenings. Neither Rafaela nor Arthur were mountaineers; but they shared the young man's love for the country and knew that he had become a dedicated climber, long before rock climbing had grown popular.

They had, of course, heard the news that, one fine September day, he had returned to Vienna from the Dolomites with a wife—a girl from a remote village high up in the Groednertal, the daughter, it was said, of a woodcarver and the sister of the climbing guide who had led Mosenthal on many of his first ascents. The girl, Rafaela was told, was very good-looking but also uneducated, a peasant, a barbarian, uncouth, unmannered, probably illiterate.

"Mosenthal has ruined himself," her daughter-in-law had said with considerable *Schadenfreude*; "there is no decent house in Vienna that will receive such trash."

Thus she was unsurprised when Mosenthal called on her to introduce his young wife. But she was quite unprepared for the young woman's beauty: a Perugino or a Rafael *Madonna*, with the Madonna's serious tenderness but also just the hint of a dimple in the cheek. And when the young woman curtseyed and called her "Gracious Baroness," she was struck by the charming voice and asked on a hunch: "Do you sing?"

The young woman blushed to the roots of her hair and could not speak. But her husband answered eagerly for her: "She knows the loveliest folksongs, Baroness, and sings them well."

"Will you sing one for me?"

After much persuasion the young woman sang—then kept on singing, folksong after folksong, most of them never heard before (for this was well before it became fashionable to collect them) in a bell-like soprano voice, and with perfect pitch and intonation.

Rafaela was sixty and had given up teaching. But Mariandl became her student, by far the best she had ever had, and soon a better singer and a better musician than Rafaela had ever been. And when Mariandl discovered Rafaela's drawings and sketches of her husband's bridges, she begged the older woman to teach her drawing, too—and soon began to work with her husband, sketching and painting the beautiful, astonishing things he uncovered in human cranium and brain under scalpel and microscope. And Mariandl surpassed her teacher in drawing and painting, just as she had surpassed her as a musician.

Rafaela knew very well that as a painter she had never been more than an amateur; she knew that at best she had illustrated while the work was her husband's. "But," Rafaela thought, "if Mosenthal's *Atlas of the Sense Organs* is becoming a standard work, in a class with *Gray's Anatomy*, if not with Vesalius, it is as much because of Mariandl's art as her husband's science. I have never been more than a junior partner with Arthur, never could have been more. Mariandl is an equal.

"Of course I am not 'young forever,' as Mariandl pretended on my birthday a few months ago. I'm an old woman. But I owe it to Mariandl that I have not given in, that I did not retire and retreat into old age. Mariandl has postponed old age for me by twenty years or more. She brought young people into the house just as Arthur and I were beginning to settle into our past achievements. Without Mariandl, to be sure, I could not cope with these youngsters, their love affairs and their feuds, their noise and their youth. But without Mariandl, they would not come here at all."

Mariandl then got both Arthur and Rafaela to work again, on something new and different. Arthur had long given up designing all over Europe—he was past seventy, after all, and only did a big consulting job once in a while. As a result, she too had stopped drawing and painting, for she only drew and painted for him. It was Mariandl who talked them into their closest and most successful venture together, the three-summer-long, leisurely trip through the Alps from the Riviera to the Adriatic, to select fifty examples for their joint book, *Alpine Viaducts and Bridges from Roman Times to Today*, for which he wrote the historical and technical text while she did the illustrations—for the first time as a full partner. The book was published in time for Arthur's eightieth birthday, and nothing he ever did made him happier or gained him more recognition.

But the biggest gift Mariandl had brought Rafaela was to make her confide, make her talk.

Rafaela had been brought up never to talk about herself. "Ladies listen" had been the motto of her childhood—and she had become a good listener. The tendency not to talk was surely strengthened, too, by the secretiveness she had inherited with her Sephardic blood, the secretiveness of a race that managed for hundreds of years to live among enemies as outwardly Christian while maintaining its Jewishness inside the home, the secretiveness of a race that for centuries managed to keep intact and alive the medieval Spanish language of its remote forebears, a race in which everyone knew which house in the alley in Granada or Toledo would open to the key hanging on the ornamental hook in a secluded corner and taken from one place of exile to another.

But with Mariandl she began to talk, to confide, to become the subject of her own thoughts and a person, rather than her brother's sister, or Arthur's wife, or Maria's mother.

"It is a curious relationship," Rafaela thought. "I am the older by forty years, after all, and we acknowledge that in the way we address each other. Of course it was 'Mariandl' from the beginning—and soon it was 'du' as well. But Mariandl still calls me 'Baroness' or in rare moments of intimacy 'Baroness Rafaela,' although she has gradually learned to say 'du' to her so much older friend.

"But otherwise," thought Rafaela, "she is the sure-footed, the secure, the confident one, and I talk to her for advice, for reassurance, for strength and support. But above all I *talk* to her. Above all, I have a friend."

It had taken some time, of course, several years of patient, exquisite courting by Mariandl, before Rafaela could talk—first about her marriage and her early years with Arthur, and then, though still with pain, about Maria and the dreadful years after her death.

And finally she even confided to Mariandl what "An Die Musik" had come to mean to her and Arthur.

It was the morning of Arthur's eightieth birthday and the Klimt portrait of her was already standing on an easel next to the table with his other gifts. On an impulse she had taken a draftsman's pen and written "An die Musik" and the date on the back of the canvas.

Mariandl had given her the most quizzical look with that impish smile of hers: Rafaela found herself blushing as if she were a schoolgirl instead of an old woman past seventy with four grandchildren, and had told her of that evening after Arthur had dedicated Maria's Bridge for her, when they sat together side by side in their bedroom at the inn.

After it became pitch-dark and the maid had brought in a candle, he had taken down a book from his traveling library—Jean-Paul Richter perhaps, or Novalis, or *Tristram Shandy*, his perennial favorites—and had read: "Making love is like making music; the more you practice it, the better it gets."

She had laughed, a little embarrassed. Poor Franz Schubert, whose only experience of love and women had probably been that one encounter with a prostitute and the syphilis that then caused his early death, surely had never meant that.

But whenever afterward she had sung the song, she and Arthur had heard it as a call to a tryst, and had understood what the "holde Kunst," the gentle art, means to which at the end the *Lied* sings, "Ich danke dir dafür!"

"Even today? And at our age?" she heard Arthur's voice in her inner ear, with the half-teasing, half-loving tone he used whenever she took off on what he called her "romantic wings."

"Especially today," she answered, in the same firm no-nonsense voice in which, sixty years ago, she had told her father, "This time it did happen in real life."

And as if to make an end to the silly argument, she opened the cover of the rosewood piano keyboard and began softly to play the *Lied* and hum the words. After a few bars she slowed down and, still with her hands on the keyboard, drifted off into the light sleep of the very old. Thus, still asleep, with the bodice of her blue dress rising and falling with her shallow breathing, Mariandl found her a few minutes later when she came to take her leave. And the younger woman was deeply moved when she perceived how closely that wrinkled, worn face resembled Waldmueller's *Young Woman* in the radiance of youth's first love.

THE TEMPTATION
TO DO GOOD

Part One

That something was very wrong she knew the moment she saw the mail, still neatly bundled, lying on the floor outside the unopened office door.

She had the key, of course; often she was the first to get to the office, but only when Father President was either sick or out of town. And he had been perfectly well and hadn't said a word about a trip or an early-morning appointment yesterday, Sunday, when she had taken him the folders on several potential donors to the university he wanted to work on, and he asked her to stay and have lunch with him, Father Ritter, and Dr. Meyeroff, the new Law School dean.

No, Father Heinz was not out of town and not sick—and yet he wasn't there ahead of her. Nothing like this had ever happened before. She found herself trembling with anxiety as she stooped to pick up the mail and then fumbled for the key to the door.

She half expected to hear, as on every normal morning, his light baritone singing out: "Agnes, good morning, come in and help me sort the mail." But everything was emptiness and silence in the president's office.

She was so shaky that she had to sit down at her desk, still in her coat and the heavy gloves and fur hat she had put on to protect herself against the icy winds of a January cold wave during the walk from her little house, just outside the campus gates, first to hear Mass at the chapel of St. Mary in the Plains, and then across the sprawling campus to her own office.

She knew she was silly and superstitious. Surely nothing whatever could be the matter. Father Heinz had overslept, or had been delayed by an early telephone call—in the East, in New York and Washington, the business day, after all, was already in full swing—or a dean

or department head had waylaid him on the way from saying Mass at
the university church.

But while she knew in her mind that there was nothing to worry
about, she was filled with a dread she could not shake off. She had not
been so frightened since the day they had phoned her and told her:
"Jake has had an accident"—and she had known at once that her husband was dead.

In the secretarial course at St. Mary in the Plains Girls' High School,
from which she had graduated first in her class, she had been taught
that the proper secretary always arrives at the office ahead of her
boss. And Sister Hildegard, the assistant principal of the school, who
had hired her before she even graduated, had made it very clear that
she expected her secretary to be at her desk and ready for the day's
work when she herself showed up at eight. So when, twenty years
ago now, she first began to work for Father Zimmerman (even then,
of course, everybody else was calling him Father Heinz, if not simply Heinz), she had made carefully sure of getting to the office fifteen
minutes earlier than he. Yet she soon sensed that this irritated him—
he wanted to be alone with the mail. He never said a word; but three
or four weeks into the job, when she had asked him, "Would you
rather have me come in a little later?" a smile of total relief lit up his
face and he happily nodded assent. So she scheduled herself to arrive
exactly twenty minutes later than he did.

It took them only a few months more to develop the daily routine
for working together—the routine that had not been changed or broken once until today.

He was a creature of habits, as men who live alone so often are.
And she knew his habits, knew them as well as if she had shared a
bed with him. He was up every morning at six-thirty, did ten minutes of vigorous exercising, shaved, showered and, at seven sharp,
walked over to the university church to say Mass. He liked to lin-
ger over Mass—"I abhor priests who apply time and motion study to
make the Mass efficient," he had said once, to the great annoyance
of that man of efficiency, Bishop O'Malley. But still he was through
by 7:45 and, after disrobing, got to his office always a minute or two
after 8.

She, too, got up at 6:30. But then she had to make breakfast—for years for the children, now only for her old mother who still lived with her. This delayed her leaving the house until 7:15, just in time for the 7:30 Mass at the Chapel of St. Mary in the Plains and for an 8:20 or 8:25 arrival at the office. And there the door with its frosted glass marked: FATHER HENRY ZIMMERMAN: PH.D.; CSH; PRESIDENT, and below it, in smaller letters: "Mrs. Agnes Muller, Assistant to the President," would already be open and the lights turned on in all four rooms of the president's suite, Father's big corner office, her own outer office, his conference room and her own (much smaller) conference room, one corner of which she had converted into a kitchen and pantry with a gas burner, a cabinet, a small refrigerator, and sink.

Father Heinz would be standing at his big desk, with his back to the window, opening the mail. But before she reached the door, he'd sense her coming and would sing out: "Good morning, Agnes, come in and help me sort the mail." And before she could even hang up her coat, he'd say something flattering or pleasant: "How nice you look this morning," or, "That's a very becoming dress you're wearing today," or, "Come quick—we got a really nice donation in the mail. It's all because you wrote such a skillful begging letter."

Father loved mail—was obsessed by mail. As soon as it came in he threw himself at it, sorted it, and opened every letter, even the sandwich menu from the local deli down the road. "It's a legacy of the war years," he explained once when she told him he'd missed his vocation and should have become a postal clerk. "Whether you're in combat or not, nothing is more boring than to be a soldier—and I had to be one for three long years during World War II. It was almost a relief when I got shot up at Anzio; at least something had finally happened. The one break in that mindless, endless monotony was the mail call: the suspense as to whether your name would be called, the ecstasy when there was a letter for you, no matter who from or what was inside it. They say," he added, "that people who have suffered through a long famine will always wolf down their food no matter how much is on the table. Well, soldiering to me was worse than any famine I can imagine, and lasted longer—and mail was what food is to a starving man. We dreamed of it when we didn't get it and wolfed it down when we did. And I still do."

Then she'd go and get breakfast: strong black coffee and two soft-boiled eggs for Father, with a few slices of the dark heavy German bread she baked for him as she had earlier baked it for Jake, and ample servings of the jams and jellies she put up every summer. They would eat breakfast sitting together at the table in her conference room. During those ten minutes, talk of business was strictly forbidden.

Then they'd move to his office, where they sat across from each other at his big desk, and the day's work would begin. First they'd dispose of the mail. Then they'd tackle the day's agenda, first his appointments and meetings, on which he'd ask her advice; then her work and projects, particularly those where she needed a decision from him. If Father Heinz had to give a speech, especially on something that was a little offbeat, or if he had to make a presentation for funds to a government agency or a foundation, or write an article or one of his annual reports (to Regents, faculty, alumni, or students), she would have roughed out the first draft, which they would then polish together. They also discussed in these morning sessions the approach to donors, after she had first done the research on them and drawn up what Father called a "donor profile."

Then, usually around ten or eleven, they would each start separately on their own working day. Today, for instance, Father had an eleven o'clock appointment in town with a potential donor, a local oil millionaire, whose donor's profile she had done Saturday night at home and brought to his house yesterday before lunch. At 3:30 he had a session with the dean of faculties and the Tenure Committee on the final decisions for next year's tenure appointments. She herself had a 10:30 session—it would last through lunch—in her conference room with the heads of the eleven departments who reported to her: all the university's noninstructional and nonfinancial functions. It was the first round on the budget for the next academic year, 1980–81, and together her departments accounted for half the university's total expenditures.

That had been the routine five or six days every week, for more often than not they would both come to the office on Saturdays, too. And it had remained unchanged, even though both her work and her title had changed. When they first began to work together, Father had only recently been appointed assistant to an ailing president and she, recently widowed, had been hired as a stenotypist and to answer his phone. But just a few months later Father turned over to her two important departments: Personnel and Building and Grounds. "And since then," Agnes Muller said to herself, "I've been in on every one of the big ones: the start-up of the Engineering School, the merger with St. Mary in the Plains Women's College, setting up the Graduate School of Arts and Sciences and the Graduate School of Management, the health-care schools, Dentistry, Pharmacy, and Nursing, and the Advanced Institute of Theoretical Physics, and only last year the expansion of the Law School—all the moves that have converted a cow college in the sticks, known only for its basketball team, the Jerome Lions, into a national university.

"And now Father Heinz is a famous university president. And even though I never went to college and only have a high-school degree in secretarial studies, I sit on the Executive Committee and Father wanted to make me a vice president when he reorganized the university's top management three years ago.

"I was passionately in love with Jake," she thought, "in all the years of our marriage before he was killed. Yet I don't think I was ever as happy with him those six years as I've been every day in this drab office. It's only two days since I sat across from Father and worked with him at his desk. Is it all over now?

"It's not even nine," the more rational half of her countered. "Why the hysterics? He'll be here any minute now and there'll be a perfectly rational explanation." He came only minutes later, but there was no rational explanation; only worse nightmare.

When he came in, he did indeed say, "Good morning, Agnes," but he didn't stop at her desk, just kept on walking. She proffered him the mail; he pushed it aside, saying "Later." Then he went through the door and closed it behind him—the very first time in twenty years that the door between their offices had been shut. After a minute or two she timidly got up, knocked at his door—something she had never had to do before—and asked, "Shall I make breakfast?"

"No need to," he answered. "I slept poorly and am not hungry. Perhaps a cup of coffee, that would be nice. Can you bring it in to me, please?" And when she had brought it in, he did not ask her to sit down and join him but said instead: "Please close my door and hold all calls. I have some thinking to do." Not even a "Thank you," let alone a question about her, a comment, or any explanation.

She was so overcome that she buried her face in her hands. Something made her look up, however, so that she caught sight of the red light flashing on her switchboard: Father Heinz was making a call. This, too, had never happened before—he had always asked her to put calls through for him and usually wanted her to listen in and make notes. Now he sat behind a closed door and dialed a call, shutting her out entirely.

She was racked by slow, painful sobs. To keep them soundless cost so much effort that she didn't even notice, twenty minutes later, that the light on the switchboard was going on again. Father Heinz was making a second call behind the closed door, without telling her.

Father Heinz Zimmerman, president of St. Jerome University, had turned his chair sideways so that he faced what Agnes Muller called the "trophy wall." In its center hung his proudest possession, the honorary doctorate, its citation in sonorous Latin, awarded him by Freiburg University in Germany where he had gone for his advanced degree, on the twenty-fifth anniversary of what the Germans call "Promotion," his receiving the Doctor of Philosophy degree. Ranged around it like an oval frame were his six honorary doctorates from American universities, with the most prestigious, the one from Columbia in New York City, at the top. And arranged around those in a square were his main civic honors. They consisted of two *Time* magazine covers with his portrait, one from 1965 honoring him as the university president who had increased endowment by the largest proportion in the preceding five years, the other from 1970 featuring him as the university president who had most skillfully handled the student unrest of the late sixties; a presidential citation from Lyndon Johnson for serving on the Civil Rights Commission; the Brotherhood Award from the National Conference of Christians and Jews; and the Certificates of Election to their respective boards from the Medieval Academy of America, the American Association of University Presidents, the Boy Scouts, and the American Red Cross.

On either side of these hung photographs of the winning basketball teams on which he had played in his high school and college days.

"Of course, it's pure vanity, and in spades," he'd say to any visitor who looked at the display, as a visitor was supposed to do. "But it reminds me of the good friends and colleagues I have in so many places, who are working in their own way for the same things I believe in and am working for."

Father Heinz (for he rarely thought of himself simply as Heinz and never as Henry) loved to look at the trophy wall. It always reassured him and cheered him up whenever he was upset or angry.

But today the trophy wall was invisible to him; he sat staring sightlessly into space.

"I've been rude to Agnes," he said to himself; "I should have apologized. But I need to be alone and not have anyone around till I've calmed down."

Today, for the first time since his ordination as a priest more than a quarter century ago, he had been unable to concentrate at Mass, and unable to concentrate when he knelt afterwards and tried to find serenity and inner strength in a long prayer. Somehow the memory of the Holloways intruded even when he raised the Cup to his lips.

He had never been a mystic or much interested in the mystic's experiences. His theology professor in Freiburg had made him read the German mystics, Roswitha von Gandersheim, Meister Eckhart, and Jakob Boehme. And on his own he had tackled St. John of the Cross, the great Spaniard. But he had never felt as they felt, shared in their experiences, or even glimpsed the visions that filled them with such exquisite pain and the fire of love. It was surely no accident that he chose for his doctoral dissertation the most rationalist of the Schoolmen, the superb logician and anti-mystic Peter Abélard—sentimental, to be sure, and a teen-age romantic in that celebrated love affair with Héloïse, but icily cold and systematic in his thought, and hostile to anything not susceptible to logical proof. The concluding sentence of his thesis had read: "If Abélard had had Arabic numerals and the tools of algebra at his disposal in the early twelfth century, quantification in logic would have begun then instead of having to wait eight hundred years for Russell and Whitehead in 1900 Cambridge and the Logical Positivists in 1920 Vienna."

But during Mass Heinz Zimmerman did experience for a few minutes each day a taste of that ecstasy in which mystics spend their lives. He savored anew every word each day, willed every gesture, lived the Mass with his whole being: with mind and body, reason and emotions. Today, however, the Mass had failed him—or rather, he had failed the Mass. Today, it had been exercise rather than experience, obligation rather than ecstasy.

"But what is it," Heinz Zimmerman asked himself, "that upsets me so dreadfully? What happened yesterday was nothing out of the ordinary. An incompetent faculty member and his aggressive wife came to see me to appeal a unanimous decision on the part of the faculty in the field, the chairman of the department, and the dean of faculties not to renew the man's contract. They surely knew that I have no control over such a decision. What's more, the decision was fully justified, indeed, the only possible one on the record.

"That the Holloways are upset and angry I can understand, even though we warned him when we hired him three years ago that it was a probationary appointment, not on the tenure track, and that the probability of his being reappointed wasn't great. But why am *I* so upset? Things like this have happened countless times before without causing me more than five minutes of concern."

Sunday had started out pleasant and relaxed. In the morning, after Mass, he had played tennis for two hours on the university's new indoor courts, and had beaten the faculty's best player, a man twenty years his junior. Dick Meyeroff of the Law School had come for lunch and greatly impressed them all—himself and Erwin Ritter, and Agnes, who had brought some work and stayed for the meal—with his first report since he had taken over as dean the preceding fall.

"I've analyzed the Bar examination records of our graduates," Meyeroff had started, "and found that the decline in their scores to where fewer than seventy-five percent now pass the first time around—the decline that rightly concerned you so much, Father Heinz, when you made me dean of the Law School five months ago— is concentrated in two fields. They are the fields which ironically, but not perhaps surprisingly, are being taught by the two most eminent legal scholars on our faculty. I am arranging for our best assistant professors to take the cram sessions in these two subjects, and have instructed them to stress practice rather than history or theory. I think you'll see a decided change in the Bar examination results as early as this summer.

"And then I've appointed a competent placement officer to help our graduates get a decent first job with a good law firm or a good clerkship in the courts. Our top graduates place themselves; the others need help. And I'm proposing to the Law School faculty that twice a year we run a Practicing Law Institute of three weeks' duration, for which our third-year students will serve as staff. This way they'll see what the practice of law is all about, and also get to be known by prospective employers."

Meyeroff's appointment as dean of the Law School had been a break with tradition, opposed by the old-timers, and especially by Erwin Ritter, dean of faculties and Heinz Zimmerman's oldest friend at St. Jerome. The Law School dean had always before been a priest, a St. Jerome graduate, and a canon lawyer. Meyeroff was a tax expert, a product of Chicago who had come to St. Jerome only six years earlier, and, of course, no Catholic. But when he left after lunch, Ritter said: "I've got to admit it, Heinz. I was wrong and you were right. He's exactly what the Law School needs."

Then Heinz Zimmerman had settled down to a few hours' work on the donor profiles Agnes had brought over.

But it was only three, though quite dark—for it was a midwinter day with snow falling steadily since morning—when Erwin Ritter had come into his study. "Sorry to interrupt you, Father President," and the formal salutation gave warning of something both official and unpleasant, "but Professor and Mrs. Holloway would like a few minutes of your time."

He would not, of course, have recognized them, even though Professor Holloway's appearance was eye-catching: a tall, cadaverous scarecrow with eyes set deep in the long bony face, an untidy shock of bright red hair, and clothes that seemed to have been made for a man two sizes heavier. But there were now almost a thousand faculty members at St. Jerome, eight times what the faculty had been in his own student days thirty-five years ago. And he surely had never met the wife, a dumpy woman dressed in crumpled tweeds.

But he recognized the name immediately and knew at once why they had come, and also why they had done so without telephoning ahead for an appointment.

He had first heard of Holloway three years earlier when Erwin Ritter and Clem Boglund, the chairman of chemistry, had come to consult him. "We wouldn't have bothered you, Heinz," Ritter had said, "but for the memo you sent to all of us a few weeks ago warning against discrimination by age in faculty appointments. Among the applicants for a starting position in Chemistry is a Martin Holloway, a doctoral candidate at Purdue. His adviser there—Clem's known him for years and trusts him—tells us that he'll have his thesis finished this term and recommends him as conscientious. He had fifteen years' experience working in industry before he went back for his Ph.D.—and that's a plus Clem thinks, as the students need a whiff of the practical. But he's almost forty-four. If we hire him now for his first probationary appointment and he doesn't work out (and two out of three don't, as you know), he'll be forty-seven and way too old to get another teaching job. Personally," Ritter had finished, "I wouldn't hire anyone that old for the entrance job. But in view of your memo, Clem and I thought we should consult you."

"Is his age the main reason you wouldn't hire him?" Zimmerman had asked; and when Ritter nodded, he said: "Then I have no choice but to order you to hire him. Anything else is a clear violation of the law. But make sure you spell out in your letter to him that the odds for reappointment three years hence are quite poor and that it will depend on his publications and on the semi-annual appraisals of his teaching performance. And Clem," he had added, "the appraisals better be very thorough. I suggest you do them yourself and make sure they are read and signed by Holloway and are clearly recorded."

And now, only three weeks ago, right after the New Year, Ritter and Boglund had come into his office with a unanimous recommendation from the tenured Chemistry faculty not to reappoint Holloway, in which the chairman of the department had fully concurred.

"We have no alternative," Boglund had said. "Holloway hasn't published anything, not even a book review. And his classroom performance is not acceptable either, as I've had to point out to him at every one of his performance reviews. He's conscientious, all right; weak students rate him quite high and comment on his willingness to help them. But even average students—let alone the good ones— flatly refuse to enroll in his sections of the introductory courses, and we'd never let him teach anything else. Those of his students who do go on to more advanced work find themselves hopelessly behind and usually drop out discouraged. Altogether in the final exams his students score twenty or more points below those in the other sections. If he belongs in teaching at all—and I've told him bluntly several times that he doesn't and should go back to industry and testing work—he belongs in high school."

So here were the Holloways to appeal against a decision they must know to be final and irrevocable. Under the university's bylaws, no different from those of any other respectable institution, the president could propose appointment after the probationary period only upon recommendation of the faculty in the field and of its chairman. Still he had no choice but to see them and to be as pleasant as he could.

To his surprise it was not the husband but the wife who spoke up. "Father President," she began, "a monstrous injustice is being done to my poor husband, whose only crime is that he is a true Christian in a university that calls itself Catholic but is dominated by heretics and Jews, and unbelievers. They deny reappointment to my husband, who goes to Mass every morning and works harder than any of them to help the weak students, and then they give tenure to three men whose names are Herzfeld, Abercrombie, and Yamanaka, and who have no time for undergraduates but remain closeted in their labs doing what they call research."

"You are unfair, Lisa," Holloway broke in; "those three men do good work."

"Oh, be quiet, Martin," she almost screamed, and two big red patches appeared on her cheeks. "He's just too simple, Father," she said, turning to Zimmerman, "and sees nothing but good in everybody, even when it's as obvious as the nose on my face what they're up to.

"You are a priest of Holy Church and President of this university. It's your sacred duty to stop these evildoers and their machinations.

You'd expect such treachery in a secular university. But we chose St. Jerome when Martin got his doctorate precisely because we thought that in a Catholic university there's still some authority left, some decency and respect for religion and dedication."

"I am afraid," Heinz Zimmerman replied gently, "that you over-rate both my power and my position. I am bound by the recommen-dation of the faculty. And I can assure you that the Regents, who make the final decision, would never appoint anyone who lacks fac-ulty recommendation—even if I proposed him. You surely know that your husband's performance from the beginning did not satisfy our standards, whether in research or in teaching."

For a moment he thought she might attack him physically. Her face, which had been mottled before, turned a deep purple, her hands shook violently, and her eyes stared at him like those of a feral ani-mal. He saw her husband cringe as if he himself expected a blow. But she controlled herself—barely, he thought—and hissed in a hoarse whisper:

"So you're in bed with them! Do you really think you can fool me with that pious cant about your power and your position? That the appraisals of Martin were negative only proves it. Your lot were out to get him from the beginning—the moment you discovered that we aren't apostates and hypocrites but take our religion seriously. You call this a Catholic university. But the girl students are shameless and sleep around openly, are painted like whores and smoke pot. And the faculty is worse. You have men who are divorced and have remar-ried, with their wives in the eyes of God still living. No wonder you can't abide God-fearing people like us and conspire to drive them out; we're a living reproof to you. You didn't dare refuse appointment to my husband three years ago—it would have been too obvious. But ever since, you, all of you, have plotted to get rid of him.

"But it won't be so easy—you haven't heard the last of it yet. I'll write to the bishop, and I'll write to the chairman of the Regents, and I'll write to the General of the Order—I'll do so today."

With that she yanked her husband out of the chair in which he had huddled in dejection, pushed him out of the room, and slammed the door.

A few seconds later Ritter came in with a wry half-smile on his face. "So, you too have joined the great anti-Catholic conspiracy of the priests of St. Jerome," he said.

"Of course," Heinz Zimmerman thought to himself when Erwin Ritter had again left his study, "the anti-Catholic conspiracy at St. Jerome is plain ludicrous. Four fifths of the faculty are Catholics except maybe in the Law School, and an even larger proportion of the students—a percentage that won't change as far as I can see ahead. And then the wretched woman got her facts wrong. I can well believe that Herzfeld and Yamanaka aren't Catholics; but Abercrombie is, despite his Scots Calvinist name. He was an altar boy in high school and assists me regularly at Sunday Mass before we play tennis.

"But that's not really the point. In her demented, distorted harangue, that woman has raised a key question: What is a Catholic university and what should it be?

"I know the answer," Zimmerman went on to himself, "and have known it for more than twenty-five years. It's because I have known it that I became President of St. Jerome and have been able to transform this university from a parochial backwater with no more students than hundreds of other small denominational colleges, and a faculty not much different from what you'd find in a high school, into a national university with three or four potential Nobel Prize-winners on the faculty.

"But I also know that this Mrs. Holloway isn't the only one who refuses to accept the answer. Even Erwin Ritter doesn't, at least not wholeheartedly. And yet it was really my having the answer that made him push me all the way into the presidency of St. Jerome."

And Zimmerman's mind flashed back twenty-seven years to one of his first faculty meetings as a very young assistant professor, a few months after he had returned to St. Jerome from Germany, only recently ordained a priest and with a brand-new doctor's degree. Erwin Ritter had presided—he had just been appointed dean. As his first official act, he asked all faculty members to submit in writing their ideas for the future of St. Jerome. The university was then still quite small, only 2,400 students, all male, with a faculty of 120 or so, most of them priests. But Ritter had clearly foreseen the coming explosion of American higher education, "although even Erwin," thought Zimmerman, "could hardly have imagined that only twenty-five years later we would have more than twelve thousand students, two fifths of them women, and a faculty that will reach a thousand by next fall—all but a handful not priests but lay men and lay women."

A month or six weeks afterwards, at the next faculty meeting, Ritter had warmly thanked the faculty for its cooperation and praised the "many thoughtful memos I've received and will study carefully." But he had called in only one faculty member for further discussion: Heinz Zimmerman. "Heinz," he had said, "you wrote only two pages; most of the others wrote at least twenty. But your memo is the only one that says anything and really addresses St. Jerome's future.

"Yet what you say upsets me greatly, not because I disagree but because I have had to agree, despite misgivings and a great deal of internal resistance and discomfort."

And then Ritter, in that careful, precise, pedantic voice of his, had read out slowly the two-page memo Zimmerman had sent in:

November 15, 1952

Dear Father Dean:

For St. Jerome to survive, let alone to prosper, it must cease aiming at being a first-rate *Catholic* university and must instead aim at becoming a first-rate Catholic *university*.

Only a dozen years ago, before this country had entered World War II, to be a first-rate Catholic university in America meant being a first-rate Catholic institution and no worse than average as a center of teaching and learning, of scholarship and research, that is, as a university. When I first came to St. Jerome as a freshman just before Pearl Harbor, and when you, Dean Ritter, taught me in your first philosophy class as a newly appointed instructor and the youngest member of the faculty, Catholics, at least American-born ones, had to teach at a Catholic college or university; there were very few teaching jobs for them in other places. And even where Catholic students were being admitted freely, they were not exactly welcome.

All this, of course, had begun to change by the thirties, though slowly. But by now it's gone—only we refuse to accept it. Neither Catholic scholars nor Catholic students any longer *have* to go to a Catholic school to teach or to learn. Indeed, more and more of the younger prominent Catholics have not attended Catholic schools but nondenominational ones; that rising political star, John F. Kennedy, who just got elected to the Senate from Massachusetts is but one example.

To be able to attract first-rate faculty and first-rate students, St. Jerome will therefore have to be a first-rate university first and a Catholic one second.

There is no alternative. To continue on the traditional course would condemn us—and fast—to becoming a game preserve for the third-rate among both Catholic scholars and Catholic students. Only if St. Jerome is accepted by the intellectual and scholarly communities in this country, and by American—and that means non-Catholic—public opinion, as one of the country's leading universities, will we of the Brotherhood of St. Jerome have remained true to the mission that our founder, Father Aloysius Schneider, the immigrant German priest, gave us almost exactly a century ago: "To be the spiritual and intellectual leaders of the Catholics in America."

"You frighten me, Heinz," Erwin Ritter had said, "and upset me. I've always regarded myself as a priest first and a scholar second. You demand me to change my whole life. But I have to admit that you're right."

From that day on, Erwin Ritter had been Zimmerman's sponsor, pushing him up the ladder step by step. Only four years later, Ritter had gotten Zimmerman promoted to assistant dean and moved into his own office. Two years after that, when Father Hasselmeier, the old president, became ill, Ritter had talked the Regents into naming Heinz Zimmerman assistant to the ailing man. Two more years and Father Hasselmeier had become so weak that he had to take a leave of absence. The Regents wanted to appoint Ritter acting president, but he turned them down, proposing Zimmerman instead. Another two years later, when Father Hasselmeier died, Ritter had declined once more and had again nominated Zimmerman for president of the university established by the *Confraternitas Sancti Hieronymi*, the Brotherhood of St. Jerome, as a small college in 1892. "I know what needs to be done, but Heinz Zimmerman knows how to do it," he had said firmly.

Yet even Erwin Ritter was only persuaded and not truly convinced, to use the fine Socratic distinction he had tried so hard in his "Introductory Philosophy 101" to drill into eighteen-year-old Heinz Zimmerman, who until then had given little thought to anything except basketball and girls.

Only six weeks ago, recalled Zimmerman, Ritter at the annual meeting of the Catholic universities just after Christmas had come to him one evening and asked for a few minutes of his time.

"As you know," he began, "I'll be sixty-four by the end of this year and I've been dean for twenty-seven years, which is twenty years longer than anyone should hold the job. If the Good Lord gives me life and health, I'd like to stay on another six years—but not as dean. I'd like to go back into the classroom, that's where I was happiest. I intend to announce my resignation at Commencement in June to become effective at year end, on December 31. So you'd better spend a little time thinking through the specifications for my successor."

"That's easy," Zimmerman had responded immediately. "I'll delegate the assignment to the most qualified person, you."

"I thought you'd pull something like that," Erwin Ritter had said with his half-smile, "and I know the specs. The first two are not too hard to satisfy, especially if you move Sister Mary Annunciata of the Women's College into the job of budget director, which I'd recommend anyhow. First, you need someone the faculty and the deans of the schools can trust, accept, and respect. And secondly, the next dean of faculties needs to know how to balance educational and scholarly values and financial realities. It's the third qualification that bothers me.

"St. Jerome needs as its dean of faculties and its number two executive under our structure—and the most likely candidate eventually to succeed you as chief executive—someone who believes in the first-rate Catholic university with both heart and head. You know that I fully accept it in my head, but I think you also know that I never quite got to fully believing it in my heart. That's not good enough for my successor. There are, of course, quite a few people at St. Jerome who believe in the first-rate university, without its necessarily being more than nominally Catholic—the very way perhaps that Princeton is still 'Calvinist' And there are quite a few, if only among the older ones, who believe in the first-rate Catholic institution without its necessarily being any great shakes as a university. But I'm not sure there is anyone who believes with both head and heart in a St. Jerome that is first-rate both as a Catholic institution and as a university."

"I know Erwin is right," Heinz Zimmerman said to himself. "And I know that the St. Jerome faculty is not alone in its doubts. Anti-Catholics deny that it's possible at all. Three months ago I was raked over the coals in *The Voice of Reason* for my speech on 'The Great Catholic University in America,' and the writer trotted out all the old clichés, the Inquisition, the Index of Forbidden Books, the doctrine of papal infallibility, to argue that a Catholic university is a contradiction in terms. But even our own bishop here in Capital City feels much the same way, I have a hunch. Last year at Commencement when he spent an hour resting in my office, he spotted the trophy wall and saw that I'd put my honorary doctorate from Columbia up at the top rather than the one from Notre Dame. He shook his head and said, 'Does this mean, Heinz, that being a great university requires being secular, if not Godless and atheist?'

"But I know I'm right. And if it doesn't work, there won't be a St. Jerome twenty years hence. If it doesn't work there won't be intellectual excellence and leadership in this country at all except from what the bishop calls the Godless and the atheists. And I know it can work. I know it isn't true that a first-rate scientist can't be both a Christian and a Catholic. And I also know it isn't true, as that dreadful woman, Mrs. Holloway, wants us to believe, that being a good Catholic excuses being an incompetent scientist.

"Then why did the Holloways upset me so much?

"It's not the Holloway *woman* who upsets me," he suddenly realized. "It's the husband." The moment he said it to himself, he knew it to be true. At once he saw again in his mind's eye that tall scarecrow of a man huddling in despair in the chair, his face buried in his hands, ashamed to the very core of his being, of himself and even more of that harridan, frightened of her but completely dominated by her—defeated by life, by his sense of incompetence, and by the open contempt of his own wife.

"What really upsets me," Heinz Zimmerman said out loud, aimlessly swishing the spoon around in the cup of coffee Agnes had brought in twenty minutes earlier but from which he had not yet drunk, "is my own attitude toward Martin Holloway. I feel guilty. Not because I can't renew his contract or change the poor devil's marriage. I feel guilty because I have not one shred of pity or compassion for him, his suffering or his degradation. All I feel is infinite contempt.

"No human being should have to look the way he did yesterday. And instead of feeling sorry for him, I despised him, hated him for his incompetence, his abject failure, his weakness and cowardice. *She* only bothered me; but he offended, humiliated, and hurt me."

That despicable woman had invoked his "sacred duty" as president of the university and as a priest. Well, he had a duty as president, sacred or profane, to prevent Holloway's continuing at St. Jerome. But didn't he also have some kind of duty as a priest, or perhaps even only as a Christian? A duty to relieve that poor creature, Martin Holloway's, self-loathing—the self-loathing from which he had shrunk as from the stench of an oozing plague boil. "It is my bounden duty," Heinz Zimmerman, Christian and priest, said to himself, almost as in prayer, "to succor the sick and to wash and bind up the wounds of the flesh. Isn't it my duty as well to wash and bind up the wounds of the spirit?

"I know that it's not a matter of money or of a job. Clem told me that Holloway can easily get back the kind of job in industry he had before he left to get his Ph.D. And in industry he'll make far more than what we can pay an assistant professor."

Holloway must know this, if only, thought Zimmerman, because Boglund, who looked after his Chemistry faculty like a mother hen, had surely told him. "It must be his failure as an academic, as a teacher and scholar, rather than any material threat that has destroyed his self-respect and earned him the scathing contempt of his wife. And yet, if Holloway can be a teacher at all, Boglund said, it could only be at the high-school level.

"But where just recently have I heard someone talk of needing conscientious high-school-level science teachers in college jobs? I know. It was Louise McCollough."

At once Zimmerman saw before him the tall, raw-boned Mrs. McCollough, only recently arrived from a deanship at Smith, or Wellesley, or some such Eastern women's school to assume the presidency of Harriet Beecher Stowe, the women's college on the other, northern side of Capital City. She was sitting bolt upright in the chair across from him with her New England boarding school posture and saying in her clear New England boarding school voice:

"Your agreeing to let our upper-class women who need advanced work in the sciences attend classes and get grades at St. Jerome is more of a help to us than you can realize, Father Zimmerman. It solves half of my problem—the easier half, I'm afraid."

"And what is the tougher half?" Zimmerman had asked.

"Oh, you know the answer, Father," Mrs. McCollough responded with a shrug of her shoulders. "It's the perennial problem of a women's college: how to attract and hold science faculty who have the credentials for college teaching and then have to do what is really high-school work, year in and year out, and do so conscientiously.

"The introductory-level courses in the sciences for the first- and second-year students we cannot subcontract but have to provide ourselves, if only because the numbers are so large: between six and seven hundred as against the sixty or seventy each year who intend to major in a science or go to medical school and need advanced work. And the instructors must have a Ph. D. and must have taught for a few years in a major university, or else we risk losing accreditation and not getting our graduates into medical or graduate schools. Yet no one with those kind of qualifications is likely to be willing to teach kids who mostly have no science background and no science interest, and are only taking the courses because we require two semesters of science for the degree . . . and fully intend, I can assure you, to continue to do so.

"No, pay isn't the problem. We are able to pay quite well. But qualified people consider this work demeaning. 'If I had wanted to teach high school, I wouldn't have spent six years of my life getting my Ph.D. in physics,' my best young science teacher said to me a few weeks ago when she came in to tell me that she's taking a job as a researcher at Bell Lab. And I am afraid I'd have to agree with her."

Louise McCollough wasn't the type of woman Zimmerman particularly liked; not enough of a sense of humor and too much of a sense of superiority, he thought. But she had a mind he respected—cool, crisp, facing realities, and not afraid of saying or doing unconventional things like contracting out her advanced science courses.

And so now, without further thought, he took the phone, dialed her number, and said to her:

"Remember our talk in my office just before Christmas about your difficulty in getting qualified people to teach the introductory science courses at Harriet Beecher Stowe? Maybe I can help a little. I may have a man who has the qualifications to satisfy accrediting boards and medical school deans and yet is willing to teach chemistry at the high-school level to students without much background, and to do so conscientiously."

When he had hung up, he felt at first greatly relieved. "I really should call in Agnes and tell her," he thought, almost getting out of his chair to open the door and speak to her. Then he hesitated. Agnes would not approve. Indeed, he knew that she'd call him "Father President," as she only did when she was strongly opposed to something he wanted to do.

"Father President," she'd say, "you are always so wonderfully kind and considerate, but in this case your kindness strikes me as somewhat unwarranted. Should the President of St. Jerome really go job-hunting for an incompetent assistant professor? And can you truly recommend this Professor Holloway in light of what Dean Ritter and Professor Boglund have told you about him? May I suggest"—Agnes was strong on suggesting—"that you tell Professor Boglund of the possible interest at Harriet Beecher Stowe and then leave it to him to advise Professor Holloway to apply there, provided of course he feels he can support Holloway?"

Was Agnes right? Had he acted rashly and let his heart overrule his head? Or had he simply acted in self-indulgence to make himself feel better? Or—and the thought made Heinz Zimmerman blanch—had he in fact been intimidated by that dreadful woman, the wife, and acted to appease that she-devil rather than out of any Christian duty to help the poor husband?

The more Heinz Zimmerman thought about his phone call to Louise McCollough, the less sure he became that it had been the right thing to do. "It's trivial," he thought, "but it bothers me. I need to tell someone, someone I know and trust, if only to be told 'Don't worry.'

"I can't tell Agnes, and I rather think I don't want to discuss it with Erwin. He dislikes my concerning myself with faculty matters he thinks are his concern; he'd call it meddling. What about Seymour Bercovitz?"

Unlike Erwin Ritter, whom he had known for forty years, and Agnes Muller, whom he had known for twenty, Seymour Bercovitz, M.D., Professor of Psychiatry, chairman of the Department of Community Medicine at the state university's Medical School, and State Commissioner of Mental Health, had only recently become Heinz Zimmerman's friend.

They had met six years earlier when serving together on a State Commission on Mental Health. From the first they had found each other *simpatico*. Eventually they wrote the Commission's report together, which led to the appointment of a State Commissioner of Mental Health as a member of the governor's cabinet. They had, Heinz Zimmerman felt, very much the same kind of mind and the same sense of humor. And he enjoyed the salty Jewish stories Bercovitz told with tongue-in-cheek seriousness in a rasping Brooklyn accent. But there was also something faintly clerical about the short yet dignified doctor, with his carefully trimmed, slightly graying beard and his controlled, precise gestures—"very much like those of a priest saying Mass," Zimmerman had once thought. He was not surprised when he learned later that Bercovitz's father had been a rabbi and that Bercovitz himself had started out to study for the rabbinate before switching to medicine.

Over the years Heinz Zimmerman and Dr. Bercovitz had come to see more and more of each other. Both were enthusiastic though thoroughly mediocre chess players, and their chess evening had become a weekly event, with Bercovitz cooking a simple but exquisite meal and Zimmerman providing a bottle of wine. But it had taken a long time before Bercovitz began to talk about himself, though he was intensely lonely and needed a friend. About five years younger than Zimmerman, he had been a widower for almost a decade. His wife, whom he had loved deeply, had been killed in an automobile accident shortly after he moved to Capital City as Professor of Psychiatry from his native New York, and had left him alone with two children, a boy and a girl, both now teenagers. He was totally wrapped up in them: "They are my trust from Lillian," he had once said in a rare outburst of confidence. "I know I need to remarry, and there'd be no lack of candidates; but Lillian's children would feel betrayed."

Gradually Bercovitz had also begun to talk about other problems, and especially the ones he faced in so political a job as State Commissioner of Mental Health—first to Heinz Zimmerman, and then increasingly also to Agnes Muller, who had come to approve highly of the quiet, reserved man with his courtly, almost Old World manners.

But Bercovitz had only become a real friend a few months ago when he had said "No" to Heinz Zimmerman. For several years Zimmerman had planned to enlarge his board and include a few prominent non-Catholics. "After all," he had said to Bercovitz, "St. Jerome is the leading private and nongovernmental institution of higher learning in the state." He knew that his Regents would not swallow a Protestant yet, but what about a prominent Jew? And if a Jew, who better qualified than a leading physician, chairman of a department in the Medical School, and a high state official? Yet when he broached the idea to Bercovitz, he met with a flat refusal.

"I am touched and honored, Father Heinz," Bercovitz had said. "And I am greatly tempted. But you'd damage the university, and I can't let you do that. You'd only offend the prominent Jews in Capital City, the very people whose support and money you need.

"You don't understand? Then I'm afraid I have to bore you with a piece of personal history. I told you, didn't I, that I started out to become a rabbi like my father? But I dropped out of the seminary in my second year. It was in the late forties and Israel had just become an independent state. And I don't think, Father Heinz, you can imagine what that meant to us American Jews. Every one of us suddenly felt three feet taller.

"Have you ever heard of an Englishman named Victor Gollancz? No reason why you should, of course. He was an English publisher, a very well-known and successful one, a prominent figure in world Jewry and an ardent Zionist from way back. But when the Israelis drove out the Arabs, Gollancz broke with them. The Jews, he wrote in books and articles and pamphlets, had just suffered the worst persecution of any people in history for no other crime than that of being Jews. And immediately upon getting themselves a little power, they persecuted the Arabs and drove them out of lands they had peacefully farmed for more than a thousand years, making them homeless for no other crime than their not being Jews.

"Gollancz was considered a traitor by Jews everywhere, and especially, of course, by Zionists—and I was an ardent one. But he shook me profoundly. I prayed and I prayed but I got no answer. What almost destroyed me was not that I had to agree with Gollancz. It was that I saw no alternative for the Israelis. What the Jews did to the Palestinians, I had to agree with Gollancz, was a sin and not too different from what Hitler had done to the Jews. But what alternative did the Israelis have? What way out was there other than to heap persecution upon persecution, injustice upon injustice, sin upon sin?

"And then I lost my faith in God. It had been hard enough for a Jew, believe me, to accept His allowing the fate that had been meted out to us in the Holocaust. But if even God could not find any other solution for saving the Children of Israel than for them to become like their persecutors, then where was His wisdom, His mercy, His power? He was no better than any of us; indeed, there was no God in whom I could have faith. What could I have said to my congregation about this God? How could I have promised them that God would reward virtue and righteousness and punish vice? How could I have solaced the afflicted?

"And so," Seymour Bercovitz continued, "I decided to give up becoming a minister to the afflicted and a healer of souls and switched instead to healing the sicknesses of the mind.

"But this also means that I am not much of a Zionist anymore. Of course I haven't told anyone this story. You're only the third person after my father, who was greatly hurt when I dropped out of the seminary, and my wife. But where other Jews are concerned, Jews have good noses. The Jews in Capital City whose support and money you need at St. Jerome, the Kesslers and the Fynemans and Judge Rosenbaum, all know that I don't buy State of Israel bonds or appear when the Israeli ambassador comes to town. They don't say it to my face; but in their eyes, I am a kind of traitor. So I could only harm you if I joined your board."

"But can't I bring you in at all?" Zimmerman had pleaded.

"You can always count on me as a member of your kitchen cabinet," Bercovitz had said with a smile and a firm handshake. And from that moment Zimmerman had considered Bercovitz a friend. So why not talk to him about that Holloway business? He could almost hear Bercovitz saying as he had said so many times in the past, "It's nothing, Father Heinz. Just a small pebble in the shoe."

But when he reached Bercovitz on the telephone at his office, the doctor, after listening for a few moments, said with quite unusual sharpness: "Go back to the beginning and tell me everything, every little detail, every word you can remember. When and how did you first come into contact with these people? Begin there, and leave nothing out."

After the whole story had been told, there was such a long silence at the other end that Heinz Zimmerman asked twice: "Seymour, are you still there?" until Bercovitz finally spoke.

"In all likelihood this is the end of the affair and there is nothing to worry about. But, Heinz"—and Zimmerman realized with a start that Bercovitz had called him Heinz for the first time instead of Father Heinz—"you shouldn't have made that phone call to Harriet Beecher Stowe. We all do it, of course, it's almost impossible to resist the temptation to appease a paranoid. And I've no business making such a diagnosis without even having seen the woman. But the fact that they create guilt feelings in normal people is the hallmark of paranoids and what makes them so dangerous. Appeasement only confirms them in their delusion, that's the very nature of their sickness. Well, in all probability it's only a small pebble in the shoe. But I still wish you hadn't made that phone call."

And when he hung up, Bercovitz murmured to himself, "A nasty business. I don't like it at all."

Part Two

"Are there any more letters or reports, Tom?" asked Bishop O'Malley.

"One more, Bishop," Father Martini, the bishop's secretary, replied. "It was delivered by hand last night, in a St. Jerome University envelope marked 'Personal.' I don't think I should open it."

The bishop tore open the envelope and extracted six handwritten sheets. He took one look at the signature, muttered, "I don't think I know this person or have ever heard of her," and handed the letter back to Tom. "Read it and tell me what's it all about."

"It's from a Mrs. Lisa Holloway," Martini began, after quickly scanning the six pages. "Her husband, his first name is Martin, is an assistant professor of chemistry at St. Jerome University, has been there three years. He is apparently an older man.

"'When I first met him,' she writes, 'he lived a life without God and served Mammon. With the help of the Holy Spirit I was able to lead him into the True Catholic Church and to make him dedicate himself to educating the young.'"

The bishop made a sound—whether chuckle or groan was hard to tell. But when Martini looked up, he only said, "Go on, Tom."

"'And now, the Chemistry faculty and the department chairman have unanimously recommended that his contract not be renewed. And Father Zimmerman, the President, refuses to intervene.'"

"Of course," said the bishop.

"But," continued Martini, "she writes that her husband's only fault—I am quoting, sir—is that they are good Catholics and he is the victim of a rampant anti-Catholic conspiracy at St. Jerome University. 'It isn't only,' she writes, 'that my husband is being fired when three men who are much younger, Herzfeld, Abercrombie, and Yamanaka—hardly good Catholic names—are being reappointed to tenure-track positions. A few months ago, to the great shock and pain of all good Catholics on the St. Jerome faculty, the associate dean of the Law School, Father Breuner'" ("That old windbag," interjected the bishop), "'a distinguished canonist, an experienced administrator, and a pillar of the true faith, was pointedly passed over, and a Jewish tax lawyer who is only interested in saving the rich money was appointed Law School dean.'

"And then," said Martini, "she goes on to say that the university is being given over to domination by heretics and unbelievers and Jews with the full connivance of its President, and that the students who come to St. Jerome because their parents expect them to be nurtured there in Christian values and the Catholic tradition are instead led into lives of vice, debauchery, and Godlessness—and so on and so on."

"You know what to do, I'm sure," said the bishop.

"Yes, sir. I'll send her a note telling her that the university and the Brotherhood of St. Jerome are autonomous and not under your control."

"Right. And send Father Zimmerman a Xerox copy of the woman's letter and a copy of your note to her, with my compliments."

"Is that necessary?" asked Martini.

"Of course. Why do you ask?"

"There is one paragraph in the letter, Bishop," said Martini, blushing a little, "that might offend Father Zimmerman."

"Read it to me," said the bishop, "and don't pussyfoot."

"'And in a university that calls itself Catholic,'" Martini read out, "'and is supposed to set an example of Christian virtue and moral living, the President, an ordained priest of Holy Church, gives grave offense by sharing an office with a woman much younger than he, who is constantly in his company and who openly without even attempting discretion visits him at the President's residence most Sundays under the pretext of taking work to him. Much as it pains me, I have to submit to Your Excellency that such conduct on the part of an ordained priest calls for a most shameful interpretation.' Bitch," added Tom Martini, half under his breath.

"Now, Father, that's no language for a priest to use." But while the words were a formal reprimand, there was no reproach in the bishop's voice, and he immediately added: "A vile woman, all right, and a slanderer to boot. I don't think you know Father Zimmerman well, Tom, do you? Believe me, there's no better priest in the diocese, whatever one might think of some of his educational ideas. And the lady in question is about as decent a woman as you could hope to find anywhere, and a crackerjack at her job. Have you met Agnes Muller, Father Zimmerman's assistant at St. Jerome? If Canon Law allowed putting a lay person, let alone a woman, in the position, I'd have tried long ago to lure her away from St. Jerome and put her in here as Vicar General—I don't know an abler executive.

"To be sure," the bishop went on, "this piece of garbage makes it all the more necessary to send the letter and a copy of your note to Father Zimmerman. But I'd better add a personal word to him.

"Write: 'Dear Heinz: We all get letters like this once in a while and have learned to disregard them. But should you decide to take disciplinary action against the writer, I'd understand it and would support you.

"'Yours Faithfully in Christ,' and bring it to me for my signature.

"And now, Tom, I want you to go to Monsignor Murtagh's office. I asked him two weeks ago to get me the figures and projections for total population and Catholic population for the state and each county in it, and he phoned me Friday afternoon that they're ready. Go over the figures with Bernie Murtagh till you're absolutely sure they are correct; you know Bernie can be a little slipshod. And I want you to know those figures by heart, forward and backward.

"Why, you ask? I'll tell you—but please don't tell anyone else, least of all Murtagh.

"I've decided to appoint a Senior Vice Chancellor or a Deputy Vicar General—I'll let Rome worry about the title—as my deputy and representative in Palmer, and have the Western counties work directly with him. No other state of the Union has a Catholic population growing at a faster rate; and the forecast is for even speedier growth, especially in the West, with the steady influx of immigrants from Mexico. The diocese already has a larger Catholic population than any other in the country except Brooklyn—and that's a special case, right next to the New York Archdiocese and really part of it. It violates every principle of organization to centralize everything here in Capital City. That's why all the vice chancellors are bogged down in paperwork and no one can get a decision out of this office.

"But I don't have to tell you," the bishop continued, "that what I propose is against tradition and convention, though there is nothing in Canon Law that forbids it, and a few precedents. I'll have to make out a strong case with the Nuncio when I see him in Washington on Friday. I don't expect any major problems. Allessandri, the Nuncio's counselor, is all for it. Still, you'd better have the figures at your fingertips and know how to present them if there are questions."

"Whom would you put into Palmer?" Martini asked.

"Whom would *you* put in, Tom?" was the bishop's rejoinder.

"Probably Monsignor Sullivan," Martini said, after a moment's thought. "He's the senior vice chancellor and he is sixty-six."

The bishop laughed with pleasure. "Right on the button, Tom. Of course I plan to appoint Sullivan. His age will ensure that he and everybody else knows it's his terminal job. He'll reach retirement age before I do, being three years older. By then Rome will have had enough time to pick their own man."

"And," said Martini, "to pick the first Bishop of Palmer."

"Precisely," said the bishop, "and high time too. I plan—but please, Tom, this is for your ears only—to ask the Nuncio that he recommend to Rome that Palmer be made a diocese (it has more than enough Catholics already) and that Capital City be raised to an archdiocese. I strongly suspect that Rome intended to do this fifteen years ago when my predecessor died. But he left behind such a financial mess that the plan had to be shelved. Mind you, Tom, Bishop Byrne was a wonderful man, a first-rate theologian and a fine teacher. I owe him a lot—he was rector of the Diocesan Seminary when I was a student there and couldn't have been kinder or more generous to me. But he was no administrator and the diocese was on the brink of financial disaster. That's when the Nuncio called me in—an auxiliary bishop in northern California—and said, 'You'll be the first diocesan ever chosen by the Holy Father because he has an MBA degree.' But you've heard all this before."

Tom nodded, with a smile.

"You know, Tom," the bishop went on, "that I'm far from satisfied with the financial condition of the diocese. It's still quite precarious. But at least we aren't bankrupt and we're in better shape than most of the other dioceses in North America. And now I think I can revive the archdiocesan idea. Of course, Rome likes to do such things when there is a change anyhow. But if my successor is to be consecrated Archbishop of Capital City, we'd better start now. The longest I have is twelve years and Rome likes to take its time. And I *do* want to have been the last bishop of Capital City, so make sure of those figures and projections."

As Tom Martini was about to leave the room, the bishop added:

"Come back in an hour, please. That should give me time to go over these budget figures of yours on our hospitals. And make an appointment with Monsignor Duffy to discuss the budgets either tomorrow afternoon or Wednesday first thing in the morning. I want to run through the hospital budgets before you and I leave for Washington on Wednesday afternoon."

Then the bishop reached across and picked up a blue folder marked "Hospitals—1980/81" that had been lying on Father Martini's side of the desk. But instead of reading it, he leaned back in his chair and murmured to himself: "I wonder whether even Tom guesses the most important item on the Washington agenda: Thomas Martini himself, and his future."

Bishop O'Malley never kept a secretary for more than four years. He was convinced that staying on longer in the job did permanent damage to a young priest. Either he'd become a "subordinate" and thus forever remain a clerk, unable to make a decision of his own; or, worse, he'd become a wirepuller who abused the close personal relationship to the "boss" to lord it over the diocesan clergy. And Tom Martini had been O'Malley's secretary—his fourth since he had come to Capital City as its bishop fifteen years ago—for a little over three and a half years now.

"Of course," said Patrick O'Malley to himself, "I could do with Tom what I did with his predecessors, make him a vice chancellor. But it's not the right job for Tom. He needs greater exposure than the little world of Capital City—and he needs to be known in a greater world, too. What he really needs is the kind of experience I was lucky to have at his age, as an associate secretary, say, at the National Conference of Catholic Bishops in Washington, or an attaché in the Nuncio's office."

Tom Martini had not been O'Malley's first choice when Father Duffy had neared the end of his four years as the bishop's secretary. O'Malley did not even think of choosing any but an Irishman for the job—someone like himself and his three earlier secretaries, who had grown up in the same Irish-American working-class world, with a staunch trade unionist for a father, someone who spoke the same language and looked the same.

But a few weeks before Father Duffy was to move out, O'Malley had been invited to Washington together with a handful of fellow bishops as dinner guests of the newly arrived counselor to the Nuncio, Monsignor Allessandri. And Allessandri had said in that near-perfect "English" English he had acquired at Oxford, and in the half-joking tone he always affected when he wanted to say something especially serious: "In the few months I've been in the United States, I've learned what extraordinary people you Irish-Americans are"— his guests, all being Irish, chuckled. "But the Irish, I take it, are a small minority among American Catholics, and a small minority even among American Catholic priests. Yet every one of your secretaries I've met today for the first time, and an impressive group they are, has an Irish name. Are there no young able priests around who aren't Irish?"

The others had laughed it off. But O'Malley was thunderstruck. If there was one thing he believed in, one thing he'd learned in the evening classes in management he'd attended at George Washington after obtaining his doctorate in Canon Law at Georgetown, one thing he then taught in his own classes in management and organization as a young adjunct professor, it was that an executive must consider *all* the people in his organization for training, development, and promotion. And yet in his own practice he had totally disregarded this elementary rule.

There was an explanation, of course. In his formative years, from the time when, as a very young priest, he had been sent to Washington a few months after Pearl Harbor to help organize the Chaplain Corps for the armed services until, twenty years later, he was appointed auxiliary bishop to a near-bankrupt diocese in northern California and given the job of straightening out its finances, he had worked directly under Cardinal Spellman of New York, had been taught by him, formed by him, and had come to admire Spellman profoundly. And for Spellman, despite (or perhaps, because of) all his years in Rome before becoming Cardinal-Archbishop of New York, the Catholic Church in America was an Irish Church and ordained to remain an Irish Church.

But that was clearly no excuse. And so, as soon as he returned from that trip to Washington, O'Malley began to look for a non-Irish successor to Gerald Duffy.

Tom Martini emerged almost immediately as the leading candidate. He was the right age, thirty-one, and had been a priest for five years. He had graduated at the top of his class in the joint five-year college-seminary program which Bishop O'Malley had worked out with Father Heinz Zimmerman of St. Jerome University for the diocesan seminarians. He had then spent four years at the Gregorian University in Rome, earning a doctorate with honors in medieval history and medieval philosophy, and steeping himself in Dante. Then, after returning to his native Capital City, he had become an assistant pastor at St. Anne's, where he handled administration and finance for the diocese's largest parish.

From his first day as the bishop's secretary, Martini had performed better than any of his predecessors, sure-footed, with tact, exquisite courtesy, and just the right mixture of deference and independence. Above all, from the first day he had displayed great ability with both people and numbers.

"Tom Martini," the bishop had once told Allessandri, "is better with numbers than I am, despite my MBA in finance and accounting. Yet people don't think him cold and don't resent him. I know that I'm not loved by my clergy and the young priests call me 'His Efficiency' instead of 'His Excellency' behind my back. Martini is far more budget-conscious than I am. But they like him even when he kills off their pet projects and cuts their appropriations by seventy percent."

And yet O'Malley was at first not at all comfortable with his new secretary. He used to ask himself whether he'd have felt the same if the name had been Martin instead of Martini; but, no, it went much deeper than that. The young priest was just too different from anything an O'Malley was used to.

"All his four grandparents," the bishop said to himself, "were dirt-poor like mine, and like the grandparents of all the rest of us; landless farm laborers as far back as anyone could trace their ancestry. It shouldn't really make a difference that his came from Calabria and Apulia and mine from County Mayo—peasants are peasants everywhere. I'll never look like anything else, nor will Murtagh or Duffy or Corrigan, no matter how many doctorates or titles we earn. All right, I'm the gaunt peasant with the pot belly, and Murtagh is the roly-poly one, but no one will ever mistake either of us for anything but the shanty Irish we are.

"But this young priest, this Italian peasant boy, looks to the purple born—he really looks like a Prince of the Church. And he walks and talks and sits like one, and wears his well-worn clothes like a cardinal's robes. He's like a figure in an early Italian painting, a Duccio perhaps, or one of the other early Sienese, a youthful St. John the Baptist or a St. Sebastian in his martyrdom, with that radiant smile and manly beauty but also with a saint's asceticism and other-worldliness."

O'Malley had felt so uncomfortable with his new secretary that he thought it his duty to mention it to the young man and to apologize for his parochial prejudices. Tom Martini had laughed good-humoredly and said: "I hope you'll not think me presumptuous, sir, if I say that I know exactly how you must feel with a Martini instead of a Martin. It's how we Martinis and Calabreses and Antonellis and all of us in Little Italy felt when we heard that a Pole had been elected Pope. My grandfather was still alive then—his name was Buonsegni—and he said, 'Thank God, it could have been worse; it could have been an Irish.'" They had both roared with laughter. And from then on there was no more uneasiness.

"Tom is an extraordinary person"—thought O'Malley—"a far abler man than I am or ever could have been, a far abler man than a good many of my colleagues among the American bishops." And now the time had come to think of Tom's next assignment, which would be crucial to his career.

The door opened and Martini was back.

"Here are the population figures, all checked out," he said; "and the letter to Father Zimmerman for you to sign. And I've arranged for the conference on the hospital budgets to be held in this office at three tomorrow afternoon."

"Good work, Tom," said the bishop, as he signed the Zimmerman letter. "And now we really must go to work on those hospital budgets—I need you to tell me where all the corpses are buried."

But instead, O'Malley found himself talking again of St. Jerome University and of Heinz Zimmerman.

"I respect Father Zimmerman, and admire his achievements at St. Jerome. I have absolute trust in his integrity as a man and as a priest. But I fear he's headed for real trouble. I don't think his 'Great Catholic University' can possibly work. And he's so completely wrapped up in it that even a slight setback might shatter him."

"I don't follow you, sir," said Martini. "Every book or magazine article about American higher education, whether by a Catholic or a non-Catholic, holds up St. Jerome as the very model of success."

"But that's the surface," said the bishop. "Enrollment and endowment and the number of prizes and awards the faculty gets. But the core is hollow.

"Tell me, Tom, have you read Father Zimmerman's paper on the Catholic University in America?"

"Of course, sir, you distributed it to all the clergy in the diocese."

"It's a brilliant piece of work. It gave me an entirely new perspective, but not, I'm afraid, the one Zimmerman wanted his readers to get. It explained to me for the first time why we have Catholic colleges and Catholic universities in this country. All of us in the American Catholic Church always thought that we have them to teach Catholic students Catholic values—I bet you think so, too?"

Martini nodded.

"But Zimmerman proves that that was not the real reason. We have Catholic colleges and universities in America because the United States has been so Protestant and anti-Catholic that otherwise Catholics would have had no access to secular learning. Catholic teachers would have been denied jobs in non-Catholic universities and Catholic students would have had a hard time getting admitted. We needed our own schools, not to preserve Catholic values, but to acquire the secular skills of a modern society. Zimmerman didn't say it—and I doubt whether he even sees it. But the way he presents it, the Catholic college in America isn't that much different from the Negro colleges in the South which came into being because black teachers and black students couldn't otherwise gain access to the learning and the skills of the white society around them.

"Father Zimmerman," the bishop continued, "likes to quote that great Franciscan saint and philosopher St. Bonaventure, who, as you once told me, Tom, influenced Dante so greatly, and who wrote that lovely little pamphlet *How All Knowledge Leads Back to the Knowledge of God*. It's true enough, of course, for a Christian, but it's not true in the way Zimmerman interprets it. In the twentieth century, knowledge has become thoroughly secular and leads nowhere except to more secular knowledge."

"Yes," commented Martini, "if the dean of the St. Jerome Law School were a Catholic priest and indeed a 'pillar of the true faith,' to quote that horrible woman's letter, tax law would still not lead anywhere near the Knowledge of God."

"Nor," said the bishop dryly, "would the course in Chemical Analysis, even if taught by the most devoutly Catholic Professor Holloway.

"You know, Tom, after I'd read Zimmerman's paper I sent to the library for the catalogues of all the St. Jerome colleges and schools— quite a collection, running to several thousand pages of course offerings. And I couldn't find more than a mere handful of courses that might have anything to do with the Knowledge of God or leading a student there. In fact, I could find very little difference between what St. Jerome and the most un-Catholic university would offer."

"But, Bishop," protested Martini, "in that case why do you stress learning as much as you do and demand that all priests in the diocese get an advanced degree in some academic or professional discipline?"

"A priest is a generalist, Tom, and generalists need to have one area in which they are experts and can be held to standards of craftsmanship. Otherwise they become dilettantes. That's a sound principle of management. But also the priest is no longer the only literate person in an illiterate society. He has to be equal in learning and skill to the educated laity in order to command their respect, and should really be their superior." ("Here he goes again," thought Martini to himself with a groan. "Whenever I'm in here, I feel like a character in a platonic dialogue. All they do is say every five pages, 'It would indeed seem so, Socrates.' Well, they learned—and I certainly do.")

The bishop meanwhile had been silent for a minute, but now he began again.

"Zimmerman is quite right. The discrimination against Catholics as teachers and students on the part of non-Catholic institutions is gone, or going fast. And then the traditional Catholic university cannot survive in America if it stays second-rate. But if his premise is correct—and he has completely convinced me—and the purpose of the Catholic universities in this country was to give Catholics access to secular learning, then his conclusion is a logical fallacy. In fact, I'm surprised that he didn't see this—after all, he was a Professor of Logic and, so I'm told, a good one. From his premise there follows only one conclusion, and an inescapable one, I'd say. The more a university succeeds in becoming a 'great university,' the more completely secular it must become. It cannot be both a 'great university' and a 'Catholic university.' The only logical conclusion from Father Zimmerman's premise is to do what the Protestants, Harvard and Yale and Princeton and Columbia, did a hundred years ago: becoming nonsectarian and nondenominational and cut all ties to organized religion. It hasn't done them any harm; but it also didn't do the Protestant denominations any harm, as far as I can judge.

"I know my fellow bishops think this heresy, and I haven't even dared mention it to Heinz Zimmerman. But do you see any other conclusion that makes logical sense?"

"Isn't there," Martini asked, "another possible conclusion: to go 'fundamentalist,' as so many of the small Protestant colleges have been doing quite successfully?"

"In theory, yes," said the bishop, "but only in theory. In practice it's seven hundred years too late. That was, of course, what the fundamentalists of the thirteenth century wanted, those anti-intellectual Franciscan *Illuminati* against whom St. Bonaventure wrote his little book. You know, Tom, of all the philosophy I had to read in the seminary I enjoyed that pamphlet the most, though otherwise I didn't ever understand one sentence St. Bonaventure wrote. Maybe fundamentalism would have worked at that point. But since then there has been too much scholarship and learning in the Church, and too much humanism and painting and music. A Catholic, I realize, should not be a rationalist, as so much of modern learning is. But he can even less afford to be anti-intellectual, as fundamentalists have to be. Whenever we try, we immediately come to look like those horrible, eroded, intellectually bankrupt small schools I have to visit and make polite noises about—St. Joseph's in Palmer, for instance, or St. Roche in Buffalo Junction where I was born—self-styled 'colleges' which are really just second-rate kindergartens with a football team and fraudulent pretensions. They always seem to me to be outrageous caricatures of those obscurantist Jesuit schools in Dublin that James Joyce described in *Portrait of the Artist as a Young Man*. Maybe they can survive in Ireland—it's amazing how many things can survive there. But Zimmerman is right, in our competitive climate here they're doomed."

"This bishop of mine," Tom Martini said to himself with an inward smile, "is as full of goodies as a plum pudding. My friends call him 'His Efficiency' and wince when he talks of management principles and cost/efficiency ratios—the very things we went into the Church to get away from. And he's amazingly good at it. I've learned more about management and organization, finance and marketing, from him than I would have learned at the Harvard Business School where my dad hoped I'd go. Then he talks about St. Bonaventure and alludes to an obscure episode in Church history. And now he's trotting out *Portrait of the Artist as a Young Man*, which I always thought a good Irish Catholic wasn't supposed to have heard of, let alone to have read."

The bishop was still pursuing the same train of thought. "In Roman Law there is a proverb: 'What is flawed from the beginning can never be made whole.' That, I am quite sure, applies to Father Zimmerman's university. Okay, St. Jerome may be able to retain a few outward vestiges of a religious past—no unisex dorms, for instance, and no free abortions for women students."

"But if those things become general in the outside world, Bishop," said Martini, "then I'd say even St. Jerome would have to accept them in the end."

"I don't intend to be around that long, Tom," the bishop said. "But you're right. Sooner or later—and I'd say sooner—Zimmerman's very success will force St. Jerome into choosing between being a 'great university,' as he phrases it, on a par with the leaders, or remaining a Catholic institution in any sense whatever. I don't think Zimmerman can face up to this decision—I'm very much afraid it would destroy him. But I do respect him, Tom, and think him the finest priest in my diocese."

"He isn't particularly popular, sir," said Martini. "I've heard him called vain and stuck-up more than once."

The bishop chuckled. "Oh, yes, the famous trophy wall. But believe me, Tom, that's no more serious than a ten-year-old girl putting a ribbon in her hair and admiring herself in the mirror.

"No, Heinz Zimmerman's real problem is a great deal more serious than a little childish vanity. He's one of those who don't know that they are intensely ambitious."

"I don't think I understand, Bishop."

"'Blessed are the Meek,' it says in the Beatitudes. But you know, Tom, I've never seen the meek make a contribution or achieve anything. The achievers are all people who think enough of themselves to make high demands on themselves, people who are highly ambitious. It's a theological riddle I've long ago given up on.

"But some of them, and often the highest achievers, don't realize that they are ambitious—and Heinz Zimmerman is one such. He is convinced, I'm sure, that in all he does he is motivated solely by his desire to serve his Order, his university, and the Church. The rest of us know very well that our motives are mixed; the Heinz Zimmermans don't. Then, when someone attacks their motives, they can get terribly hurt. They suddenly realize that they are flawed like the rest of us—ordinary human beings, and not totally admirable. And then I've seen the likes of Zimmerman lose all self-confidence. You ever heard of Venetian tears, Tom?"

"I don't think so, sir."

"They were popular toys in my childhood, globs of molten glass that had been dropped into ice-cold water. They hardened into a little hollow ball with a long, hairlike tail. They were so hard you could throw them against a wall or stomp on them or hit them with a hammer, and they wouldn't break. But snap off that little tail, and they'd shatter into dust so fine you couldn't even see the particles. That's what I've seen happen to the likes of Heinz Zimmerman when they suddenly discover that they're no different from the rest of us."

The bishop paused, and looked at his note to Zimmerman and the Xerox of Mrs. Holloway's letter which Martini had stapled onto it.

"This vile woman," he said, "doesn't give a damn for St. Jerome, of course. She only wants revenge for her husband's failure. But she managed to touch an exposed nerve. A nasty business. I don't like it one bit."

When he saw the letter addressed in a woman's hand and marked "<u>PERSONAL!</u>" in the corner—underlined, and with an exclamation mark—Jack Mulcahey almost panicked. Such letters had made his life a nightmare some years earlier.

Mulcahey had considered secretaries and shopgirls fair game, from the time he had gone to work in the Depression as manager of one of the four small shops his father owned in Capital City until, a generation later, in 1969, he had sold Mulcahey's Value Stores with its five hundred supermarkets and discount centers for a fancy price to a New York conglomerate. He had always kept these affairs casual, had never pretended to "love" any of the women or even to have much interest in them. And yet, after the sale of his company, when *Fortune* ran a story on him and called him "one of America's twenty-five richest men," he found himself inundated with letters, all in a feminine hand, all marked "<u>PERSONAL</u>" in the corner, all demanding money, threatening exposure, paternity suit, or scandal. Most of the writers withdrew hastily when his attorney pointed out that the law has an ugly word for people who demand money under threats. Altogether the episode had cost him more in lawyers' fees than in money to buy the women off.

But all his life Jack Mulcahey had been morbidly afraid of scandal, of exposure, and of derision, whether to his face or behind his back. His father had delighted in humiliating and shaming him in public when he was a little boy and wet his bed or, some years later, when he had gotten slapped in public by a girl at a junior-high-school party as he clumsily tried to put his hand down the front of her dress.

Those letters made the worst of his fears come true and upset him for months.

"But," he reassured himself, "that was ten years ago." He had not abandoned the pursuit of casual sex, and had no intention of doing so. Only now he satisfied his needs by entertaining call girls several times a week in the suite he maintained as "Mr. Gray" in Capital City's leading hotel—a different woman each time, procured for him by the doorman.

Still his hands shook slightly as he opened the envelope. One glance at the signature reassured him; there was no "Lisa Holloway" in his life and never had been. A second glance at the opening sentence, and he knew what kind of letter this was: a perfectly harmless one, the truculent whine of a fired employee, or rather, the employee's wife. Such a letter called for only one response, the wastepaper basket.

But as he began to shred the six pages into small pieces (that much at least he had learned ten years ago), his eye was caught by the one word "woman." And so he read:

> . . . the President gives grave offense by sharing an office with a woman much younger than he, who is constantly in his company and who openly without even attempting discretion visits him at the President's residence most Sundays under the pretext of taking work to him. Much as it pains me, I have to submit to you, Mr. Chairman, that such conduct on the part of an ordained priest calls for a most shameful interpretation.

Mulcahey collapsed into his chair and groaned so loudly that Mrs. Gould, his old secretary, looked up sharply and almost spoke to him without first being spoken to. This was worse, far worse, than a threat to publish indiscreet letters, to sue for money allegedly promised a former girlfriend, to bring a paternity suit, or even to pillory him for having debauched a fifteen-year-old virgin after luring her into his apartment and plying her with liquor—all the themes of earlier letters. Such things might have gotten him into the papers or perhaps even into court. But the charge that Father Heinz Zimmerman and his administrative assistant had a clandestine affair, if ever it became public, was all his daughters needed to try to get control of him and, above all, of his money.

Jack Mulcahey's wife—he had married her when he graduated
from college forty-four years ago—would be totally indifferent to any
scandal about St. Jerome University, just as she had become totally
indifferent to her husband's flagrant infidelities which began as soon
as they were married: he seduced their newly hired maid, a young
Irish girl, ten days after returning to Capital City from their brief
honeymoon. But his three daughters would make a Roman circus
out of it. They resented nothing as much as his gifts to St. Jerome,
feared nothing as much as that he would leave something in his will
away from them and to the university. "You have no right," Jackie,
the oldest, had shouted at him years ago, "to give our money to those
no-good priests!"

Even without the trust funds he had set up for them, his daughters were very well off, each having made an excellent marriage.
And yet they always wanted more. They wanted money, of course;
but they even more wanted control of the money. And his gifts to
St. Jerome were a constant reminder that he, not they, was in control, a constant reminder of their dependence on him, of his offense
in being still alive and even active, when there was nothing he could
contribute to them except his speedy demise.

Any scandal about St. Jerome, and especially a scandal involving Heinz Zimmerman, whom none of his daughters had ever met
but whom all three had come to hate as the symbol of their frustra-
tion and impotence, would give them the handle they needed. Maybe
they could not have their father declared legally incompetent and put
under guardianship, though if they tried their mother would surely
cheer them on. But they would do everything they possibly could
to humiliate, deride, and ridicule him. If they ever found out that
a hypocrite, an imposter, a false priest, had diddled him—no, not
him, *them*—out of millions of dollars, they would hound him until
he gave in and handed over the money to them, or until he left the St.
Jerome board, and with it the activity he had come to enjoy the most.

Mulcahey had been hesitant when, fifteen years earlier, he had
been asked to become the first layman to serve on the St. Jerome
Board of Regents. Of course, it was a great honor. But though he was
an alumnus of St. Jerome (he had received a Bachelor of Commerce
degree in the depth of the Great Depression in the first class of the

new undergraduate Business School), he had never felt at ease with professors, deans, and priests. Fifteen years later, he still much preferred the company of businessmen, such as Walter Fyneman of the department store or the Kessler brothers, Bobbie of the bank and Dannie of the insurance company, with whom he played golf on weekends and traveled during the winter to Palm Springs and Boca Raton. Jews though they were, they spoke his language and shared his interests. He could swap stories with them, and they laughed at his jokes.

Much to his surprise—"and I've no doubt the priests were equally surprised," Mulcahey had said to himself more than once—he soon found that he contributed far more to St. Jerome than his money. Obviously, the eleven million he had given over fifteen years were most welcome. But indirectly he had made even more money for the university through real-estate deals without which it would hardly have been able to expand; through successful management of endowment funds; and, perhaps most valuably by supervising architects, building plans, and contractors, and the financing of the university's building projects.

Then, after he had sold his own company and in the same year accepted election as the university's board chairman, St. Jerome had begun to repay him. It hadn't taken him long to find out that at fifty-three he was not ready for retirement and that managing his own investments, while fun, did not keep him busy more than a day a week. The two days he gradually came to spend each week at his St. Jerome office, working closely with the university's financial and business people, came to be his real life. Once again he was doing what he did best: building rapid growth.

And now all this was in jeopardy because a fool woman was spreading slander. But was the woman (what was her name . . . Holloway?) really the problem? Or was she just hitting out in blind rage to defend the incompetent she had married? Wasn't it Heinz Zimmerman who was to blame? Not for fornication, which in any case was his own business, and that of his confessor. No, for something far more serious: imprudence.

Once in the horrible months when all those former women employees had been hounding him with their claims for money and

their threats of scandal and exposure, Mulcahey had complained to
his lawyer that he hadn't been doing anything hundreds of other employers weren't doing every day without any aftereffects. "Yes, Jack,"
the lawyer had said, "and when you did it, you were just like them.
But now you are somebody highly visible. To behave like other men
is worse than a crime; it's imprudent. It doesn't even matter," the lawyer had concluded, "whether you actually do the things that make
you vulnerable or not. If you appear to do them, you're imprudent."

Prudence—that much Jack Mulcahey remembered from the Philosophy course he had been forced to sit through as a freshman at St.
Jerome—was a cardinal virtue and Imprudence a deadly sin.

Heinz Zimmerman was surely "somebody," and highly visible.
He was thus clearly guilty of gross imprudence. What did it matter
that he had probably never noticed that Agnes Muller was a beautiful
woman, or even that she was a woman at all? He had no business putting himself in a compromising situation by being alone all day with
a sexy-looking gal and having her come to his apartment in full view
of everybody every Sunday so that a disgruntled employee could
slander him and thereby endanger the university and Jack Mulcahey's peace of mind and happiness at St. Jerome.

"God only knows," thought Mulcahey to himself in horror, "how
many other people she sent a similar letter to. I'm afraid it's too late
to stop her, all we can do is contain the damage. I can't do much—
Zimmerman isn't my subordinate. But Heinz Zimmerman is a monk;
he does have a superior. It's Willy Huber's responsibility to put a stop
to such imprudence. After all, it's a threat to his Order."

Of all the men on the St. Jerome Board, Mulcahey respected
Willy Huber least. Huber was the very personification of the schoolmaster; though fifteen years out of the classroom (he had been principal of one of the Order's junior high schools before being elected
General), Huber always looked and moved and smelled as if envel-
oped in a cloud of chalk dust. And he spoke with a schoolmaster's
nasal falsetto, and in the measured, bored monotone of a schoolmaster dictating to the slow spellers in the class.

And then Mulcahey, the self-made man, despised Willy Huber
as an also-ran. What made this so delicate in the present predica-
ment was that it was Heinz Zimmerman who had beaten Huber in

every race. The two, Mulcahey had learned long ago, were born and grew up in the same German blue-collar precinct in Milwaukee and had entered the same parochial school together. But whereas Heinz Zimmerman had become the star of his high school's championship basketball team and the toast of the neighborhood, Huber had finished as business manager of the school paper. Zimmerman had returned from World War II a captain and a much-decorated combat hero; Huber had served throughout the war as a chaplain's assistant and had come back a PFC. The Order had sent Zimmerman upon graduation from St. Jerome to a prestigious German university to get a doctorate. Huber went to the state's Aggie college to get a master of arts in teaching. Zimmerman had become, first, a university professor, then university president; Huber had started as a language teacher in one of the Order's junior highs and then became a junior-high principal. Willy Huber even owed his election as General of the Brotherhood of St. Jerome to Heinz Zimmerman, who had thrown it to him as one throws a dog a bone when Dean Ritter, the Brothers' first and unanimous choice, had declined. "How do you at St. Jerome select your General?" Mulcahey had asked in the faculty dining room shortly after the election. "By proven incompetence, it seems," one of the older priests at the table had answered, and everyone chuckled.

Yet Willy Huber *was* Brother General and Heinz Zimmerman *was* a member of the Order. And so, with a wry grimace, Jack Mulcahey dialed Father Huber's number.

"So you, too, have received that scurrilous letter," Willy Huber said immediately. "I was just debating with myself whether I should throw it straight in the wastepaper basket or send it on to Heinz Zimmerman."

"Don't do either," Jack Mulcahey said. "Let's first think through what we should do about the allegations."

"You can't possibly take this nonsense about the anti-Catholic conspiracy at St. Jerome seriously?" asked Willy Huber incredulously.

"That's not what I mean, Father Willy," said Mulcahey, totally mystified. "It's the insinuation about Heinz Zimmerman and Agnes Muller that's bothering me."

Now it was Willy Huber's turn to be mystified, and he had to be told where to find the paragraph about Zimmerman's imprudence in his relations with Agnes Muller. "Oh that," he said; "pay no attention to it. They say that about every priest" (except those, he added to himself, whom they suspect of misconduct with boys); "no one who knows either Heinz or Mrs. Muller will believe a word of it."

"But," Mulcahey answered, quite irritated and quite sharp, "how many people *know* Heinz Zimmerman or Agnes Muller? You and I and the others on the board and the senior men in St. Jerome's administration, that's all. The rest will be only too willing to believe it. And Zimmerman's conduct almost asks to be questioned. It's been the height of imprudence. I could kick myself for not blowing the whistle sooner—and you should have done so, too. Now I think we must demand of these two that they make sure they cannot be suspected or accused. There must be no further occasion at which they are alone together and appear to have an opportunity to be intimate. Both of us have the duty to make sure of that, you as Superior of the Order, I as chairman of the Regents."

There was a long silence at the other end. "He believes," thought Mulcahey to himself, "that an accusation of sexual misconduct at this time and age isn't so very serious anymore, but being a priest doesn't dare say so. And of course, he's wrong. He doesn't know my daughters." But all Mulcahey said to break the silence was: "And what, Father Willy, do you as General of the Order propose to *do*? The least I can think of is to command Zimmerman to take the proper steps so that he isn't seen alone with Mrs. Muller at the office anymore—and she must stop coming to his home, whether there's somebody else there or not." And with that he hung up firmly.

Willy Huber sat quietly for a long time before, with a look of utter disgust at the receiver, he put it back into its cradle. "He believes this preposterous story. But maybe I shouldn't be too surprised. If one tenth of what I've heard about Jack Mulcahey is fact, he probably can't imagine that a man can be alone with a woman for more than ten minutes without bedding her. And if he believes something so utterly absurd when he's known Heinz Zimmerman for fifteen years, what won't a stranger believe? Mulcahey is coarse and vulgar, but he's shrewd and knows the world. What if he was right and there is genuine danger to the Order and the university?"

With this Huber felt anger rising in him, anger at that wretched woman, anger at Mulcahey, but above all anger at Heinz Zimmerman. "Jack Mulcahey is correct," he thought. "Heinz has been grossly imprudent. I've got to act. If there is a scandal and it hurts St. Jerome, I must be able to show that I did something."

Willy Huber had no great desire to lock horns with Heinz Zimmerman. Whenever he had done so in the past, ever since their first fight as little boys in elementary school, he had come out second-best.

Huber also had no desire to be reminded once again that all he had achieved on his own until Zimmerman had nominated him for election as General had been to teach junior high. But for all his arrogance, Heinz Zimmerman was still a St. Jerome Brother. And Willy Huber, for all that he had never gotten a Ph.D. or made the cover of *Time* magazine, was still his superior as General of the Brotherhood. So Willy Huber, sternly reminding himself of his duty, put in a call to Heinz Zimmerman.

He should have felt elated when, ten minutes later, he hung up. He had never before won against Heinz Zimmerman; at the very least he had expected a hard fight. But Heinz had given in—fast and completely.

Thank God, he had already known of the woman's letter; the Bishop, it seemed, had sent him a copy, so Huber did not have to explain why he was calling. Heinz had, of course, tried to argue: "What you want me to do, Willy," he had said when told to put a secretary from the typists' pool into one of the office rooms he shared with Agnes Muller, "is an insult to a good and decent woman."

"Your responsibility and mine," Huber had replied stiffly, "is to the Order of which Mrs. Muller is a paid employee."

Heinz had shown fight only when Huber, adding that he also spoke for Jack Mulcahey, had demanded that he not let Agnes call anymore at his residence and had overruled as irrelevant the argument that Father Ritter lived there too and was always present. "Any psychiatrist will tell you, Willy," Heinz had argued, "that you must not appease a paranoid." Then Huber had found himself saying, with great satisfaction, "You leave me no choice but to call a convocation of the Order and submit our dispute to the entire Brotherhood. If you have any regard for the good name and feelings of the

lady, you wouldn't want that, I am sure." And Heinz Zimmerman
had caved in.

But instead of being elated, Willy Huber was uneasy and scared.
It was almost as if Zimmerman had felt guilty. Yet this was preposterous. It was not that Heinz was incapable of being attracted by a
woman or of having sexual relations with her. On the contrary, the
young Heinz Zimmerman had had quite a reputation as a ladykiller,
so much so that at first his friends had refused to believe he had
decided to enter the priesthood at the end of his first year back from
the war and again at the university. What Heinz Zimmerman *was*
incapable of, however, was concealment. Willy Huber had known
many of Zimmerman's moods in the fifty years since they had first
met in parochial kindergarten. He had known him arrogant and
contentious, bullheaded and aggressive, and overbearing—but secretive, never. And it would take a master of intrigue and dissimulation
to carry on an affair with Agnes Muller in full view of the entire university and living in the same house with that paragon of priestly virtue, Erwin Ritter.

What, then, was the explanation for Zimmerman's meekness
when he should have charged like a wounded bull?

Heinz Zimmerman asked himself the same question after Willy
Huber finally hung up. But he knew the answer. His concern was not
Huber, or Jack Mulcahey; it was Agnes.

Tuesday morning had begun with a return to normality and
routine. When Agnes arrived at the office at twenty minutes past
eight, the door was open, the lights were on, and Father President
was standing at his desk and singing out: "Good morning, Agnes, do
come in and help me sort the mail." And as she took off her coat, he
looked up and said: "I hope you didn't freeze; it's beastly cold outside.
But I must say the red the wind puts in your cheeks becomes you."

Then she had made breakfast for both of them and they had eaten
it at the conference room table. Afterwards they had sat down across
from each other at his desk and begun the day's work.

But just before she came in—he had already heard her footsteps
in the hall—Heinz Zimmerman had espied a letter with the bish-

op's crest and address, marked "Personal" in the corner, and had, on a hunch, hastily slipped it into his pocket. He opened it an hour later when Agnes had gone off to Dean Ritter's office down the hall to fetch a potential donor's file. Inside he found Lisa Holloway's letter and the bishop's note of encouragement and support.

The Holloway letter Heinz Zimmerman shrugged off; it wasn't the first time that he had wasted his pity. But the bishop's brief words set off alarm bells in his mind.

The bishop must have known that the university could not take any action against Mrs. Holloway. She was not even an employee, and had carefully refrained from making an accusation, instead piously expressing her fear lest others might do so.

No, the note was surely meant as a warning. And the only part of the Holloway letter in which O'Malley could have detected any sort of danger was that passage about him and Agnes.

In his high-school and early college days Heinz Zimmerman, the glamorous basketball hero, had been chased by the girls and seen no reason to run away from them. He had forsworn carnal love, of course, when he entered the novitiate. But while he stayed faithful to his obligation, the recollection of his earlier sexual activities had increasingly come to make him doubt his fitness for the priesthood. Toward the end of his first year as a novice, he felt he had to make a clean breast of his sinful past to the Father Novice-Master.

"Why do you tell me all this filth?" Father Riem had asked, quite harshly.

"I thought you and the Order ought to know."

"You are a simpleton," the priest had said. "Don't you realize that we checked you out pretty carefully before we accepted you as a novice? We may not know of every girl you slept with, but we know of more than you probably remember yourself, and enough to tell us you were as much of an athlete off the field as on it.

"But, Heinz," Father Riem had continued in a warmer tone, "it's not such a bad idea for a young man who aspires to the priesthood to have known the temptations of the flesh. Then he understands what sacrifice he has to bring to become a servant of Holy Church. If he gets through the novitiate without unbearable suffering and without succumbing, he can take the vow of chastity with confidence and a good conscience."

"And that," thought Zimmerman, "is precisely how it did work out. Which is why Agnes and I can have the relationship we do.

"Of course," he mused, "I've always known that Agnes Muller is a very beautiful woman. And if I weren't a priest, it wouldn't be at all hard for me to fall in love with her. But I *am* a priest; and I learned years ago not to fall into that kind of love with a woman. I know it and Agnes knows it, and everyone else who knows either of us, even superficially, knows it too. Anyway, it would be easier to hide an elephant in my desk drawer than for Agnes and me to conceal an affair in this office where the door is always open, a hundred people troop in and out each day, and there's less privacy than at the baggage counter at Kennedy Airport with eight jumbo jets arriving at the same time."

But still the bishop must have seen a threat to Agnes to send so strong, so atypical a signal. "No one who knows us will believe the ravings of this sick woman," he thought. "Yet even in this age of women's lib, it's always the woman to whom the mud sticks."

What should he do? What could he do? He wondered whether he should tell Agnes, but knew at once that his relationship with her would never be the same were he to show her the Holloway letter. Could it be the same if he were to conceal it from her? He had never hidden anything from her, certainly not when it concerned her. What would she think if she ever found out that he had kept secret from her a letter like this, with its vile insinuations against her decency, her honesty, and her honor as a woman?

All these thoughts went through Zimmerman's head again and again as he half-mechanically sorted the papers of a proposed fundraising drive for the Engineering School. He had almost decided to keep the letter to himself, at least until he could discuss it with Erwin Ritter after dinner in the evening, when the phone rang and Agnes said: "It's Father Willy Huber. He wants to talk to you in private."

Whatever else it did, that telephone call settled the issue of whether to tell Agnes or not. As soon as he had hung up, Zimmerman walked over to Agnes's desk, sat down on the chair beside it, and told her, first, of the Holloways' visit on Sunday and his call on Monday to Harriet Beecher Stowe. Then he gave her the two letters to read, Lisa Holloway's and the bishop's. And finally he repeated to her the orders—for they were orders—that Willy Huber and Jack Mulcahey had given them.

His mind was completely calm; he was not conscious of any emotion, not even of rage. It was also completely made up. Agnes, he was sure, would start crying—any woman would. And he would then put his arms around her and console her. For thirty-three years, since that hour with Father Riem when he was still a novice, he had avoided physical contact with a woman. But surely the time had come for him to remember that the world called him "Father" and to start acting like one.

Of course, if anyone should see him holding Agnes sobbing in his arms there would be no need for Lisa Holloway's letter; all of St. Jerome would put the same interpretation on their relationship. "But," he thought, "I'd rather be guilty of a lack of prudence than a lack of compassion. Anyhow, it's unlikely. The desk in her corner can't be seen from the hall or until one has come right inside the door.

"I'm already infected by that horrible letter," he thought with that detachment and tendency to look at himself as if from the outside that had set him aside from his friends and playmates even as a little boy. "That's why I chose to sit at Agnes's desk rather than have her come in and sit at mine where we normally sit together, and where everyone can see us from the hall through the open door. Never mind. What matters now is Agnes, and being at her own desk might make it a little easier for her."

But Agnes had totally spoilt his script, had, indeed, totally confounded him. She listened in silence. When he told her of Willy Huber's call, she turned so pale that he was afraid she would faint. But then, just as he thought, "She's starting to cry," he saw to his utter amazement a deep blush begin at her throat and spread upward until her whole face up to the hairline glowed crimson. "Please, Father Heinz," she said, very softly but quite distinctly, "please go away and let me think for a few minutes." And when he had walked back to his

own desk, quite bewildered, she got up and quietly closed the door
between their offices behind him.

As soon as Father Heinz began to speak, Agnes Muller knew that
her worst forebodings of yesterday had come true. It was the tone
of his voice rather than what he said that told her something very
serious, something irreparable, had happened to their relationship.
And when he gave her the two letters, something inside her snapped.
Never again, she knew, would she be unself-conscious in his presence. That woman's touch—and equally the bishop's letter, a letter
she found hamhanded, patronizing, and almost contemptuous—had
forever defiled what had been a pure, childlike trust, a love of brother
and sister, a partnership in a common venture. Both of them, but she
especially, from now on would always have to emphasize, to accent
the innocence of their relations. They would forever have to stress
that there was nothing between them, which could only render every
word spoken between them, every gesture, every moment together
rancid with suppressed sensuality.

Then, when she heard the preposterous story of Willy Huber's call
and his "rules" for their future conduct, she almost died of guilt. She
had a low opinion of Huber, shared, she knew, by Father Heinz; he
was a fussy bureaucrat. She had an even lower opinion of Jack Mulcahey, a haberdasher's clerk for all his money, who every time they
met at a board meeting or a conference tried to undress her with his
eyes. That these two apes dared humiliate Father Heinz, dared gloat
over him, treat him like a schoolboy caught cheating at an exam, was
her fault, entirely her fault. She had exposed him, had made him vulnerable, had brought him low. And it was for her sake, she knew,
that Heinz Zimmerman had submitted, had not at once called their
bluff, and chased them with their tails between their legs back into
the fetid holes out of which they had crawled.

"I'm old enough," she thought, "not to mind what people say
about me and my morals. If I had loved a man I would not, as a
widow, have had much compunction about an affair with him, even
if he had been married—though I know I would never have been a
priest's mistress. But that I have been the means to wound, to com-

promise the one person I worship, that I have failed to protect him, have endangered his mission . . . no, I can't stand it."

At that moment she had felt herself going under, and it needed all her strength not to reach out and grasp Heinz Zimmerman's arm to steady herself.

But then she suddenly felt a totally different sensation, felt herself almost overwhelmed by passion and desire. "Heinz, Heinz," she wanted to cry out aloud, "why don't you take me in your arms and say, 'Let's run away together'? Why don't you at least say, 'I wish it could have been true'?" She had not felt such fierce, raw emotion since that summer's night, ages ago, when, still a few months before their wedding (indeed, even before their engagement had been officially announced), she had given herself to Jake. Suddenly she was back again behind the bushes in the park, and felt again the ecstasy and joyous pride, the guilt and even the pain—for Jake had been almost as inexperienced as she was and quite clumsy.

She was so ashamed of herself that she didn't dare look at Heinz Zimmerman. "So this horrible woman is right," she said to herself. "I am not chaste, and my relationship with Heinz Zimmerman is not what I've pretended it to be all these years."

And Marietta, her daughter, had been right too, when at sixteen in her teen-age need to hurt her mother, she had screamed: "You don't love me, you don't care one hoot about me. The only one you care for is that lover-boy of yours, that wonderful Father President!" And Sister Renée, the university's public-relations V. P., had been right too when she had called Agnes in three years ago and tried to talk her into accepting the vice presidency Heinz had offered her. "But, Renée," Agnes had argued, "I don't even have a college degree and all of you have Ph.Ds."

"Nonsense, Aggie," Renée had replied, "degrees have nothing to do with it and you know it: VP-Administration isn't an academic job. The only reason you don't want to take it is that you don't want to move out of Heinz's office, where you can see him all day long, sit next to him every working hour, and know everything he's doing or planning." She'd been so mad at Renée that she had stormed out of her office, slammed the door, and hadn't spoken to her for weeks. Yet Renée had been her closest friend since they were schoolgirls together.

Both Marietta and Renée had been right—and everybody else must have known it too, everybody but the shameless fool she'd been.

It was then she felt hot all over with a blush that was both shame and desire. "Heinz *must* see it," she thought, "and will forever fear and loathe and despise me."

But with an effort that seemed to take a whole eternity, she forced herself to speak in a quiet voice and ask him to leave her alone for a few minutes. Only after she had closed the door behind him and crept back to her corner did the tears come, hot, angry tears that gave no relief.

Fifteen minutes later she had herself under control again and went back to Heinz Zimmerman's office.

"Father Huber and Mr. Mulcahey," she said, "might have been a little more tactful; but they have a point. I should have seen it myself, and long ago. You and your work are much too important to be exposed to gossip, however groundless it is. I'll have a desk moved into the other corner of my office tomorrow and ask Mrs. Lopez—the woman in the typing pool who has been doing both your work and mine—to move in and do her typing here and answer the phone. And I'll get one of the men from Maintenance to take the work to you at the President's residence on Sundays. Maybe," and she forced a wan smile, "I can have you and Father Ritter once in a while come to my place for Sunday dinner. I daresay my cooking is better than that of the lay brothers at the residence hall."

Willy Huber woke up Wednesday morning with a throbbing headache. He had spent a miserable night tossing in his bed, until at three he had knocked himself out for a few hours of nightmare dreams with a double dose of sleeping pills.

After reporting his Tuesday morning conversation with Zimmerman to Jack Mulcahey, Willy Huber had put St. Jerome University out of his mind and gone to work on his own urgent problem: the upcoming negotiations with the lay teachers at the Order's high schools, who were threatening to join a labor union unless they received raises way beyond the Order's ability to pay.

It was only after dinner that Huber again thought of Heinz Zimmerman and the morning's conversation with him. Then near-panic seized him. All of a sudden he saw a possible, indeed a highly probable, explanation for both Zimmerman's meekness and Mulcahey's alarm: that odious woman in her letter had only repeated what all of St. Jerome was already talking about. There *was* a scandal—and both Zimmerman and Mulcahey knew it. The only person who had not heard it, apparently, was he himself, the Brotherhood's General and the man responsible both to the Brothers and the hierarchy of the Church for the Order's conduct and good name. What an incompetent they must all think him!

Willy Huber knew himself to be fully qualified, perhaps even overqualified, as the Order's administrator. But even during the moment of triumph when he accepted the election to an office he had never dared aspire to, he had suffered agonies of self-doubt about his ability to give leadership in a genuine crisis. Here now was a crisis—and he didn't even know whether it really was one, or only a spiteful letter by a hysterical female that belonged in the wastepaper basket. If scandal genuinely threatened the Order's most prominent member and proudest possession, the university, what should he do?

One thing was clear to Huber. It was his duty to find out what was really going on; or rather, whether anything was really going on. But how? He had spent a sleepless night without finding an answer.

Then, as he was preparing his simple breakfast, it came to him suddenly: "Ask Foxy!" He almost shouted with relief.

Father Foxy Frantzen still had the long pointed fox's nose, but he had long ago lost most of the bushy red hair that had earned him the nickname in his student days; and what was left of it, as well as of the bristly red mustache, had long turned iron-gray. What explained the persistence of the nickname was his constant sniffing for gossip: Foxy attracted gossip as a magnet attracts steel filings. He was not malicious. He was not salacious, though he seemed to know what went on in every faculty bedroom. He did not make up tales, nor deal in gossip to make himself important. He was simply as "'satiably curious" as Kipling's Elephant Child.

Surely, Willy Huber thought, Foxy would have heard if there were even the slightest whiff of a rumor, even the slightest snicker about two such prominent and visible members of the university community as its president and his chief assistant.

"No, Willy, there's no such rumor, I am positive. I would have heard it, believe me," Foxy had responded, totally surprised.

Then Willy Huber made his great mistake—the mistake for which he was to atone three months later when, after a long session with Erwin Ritter, he announced his resignation as General of the Brotherhood "for personal reasons." Huber said: "Foxy, believe me, I'm not asking out of idle curiosity. I have a good reason, even though I can't tell you what it is. I do need to know whether there is any such gossip anywhere on campus and who is spreading it. I know you'll be discreet. Keep your ears open and let me know if you hear anything."

Willy Huber's question about Heinz Zimmerman and Agnes Muller had amused Foxy. How could anyone believe such a tale when the two were always in full view of the whole administrative staff, in an office with an open door just off the building's main entrance? But Huber's request upset Foxy. He had never seen any harm in repeating gossip. Starting it was another matter. And wasn't this what Huber had asked him to do?

Still, Huber was the General, and apparently something was going on, something dark and secret, affecting the Order's welfare. He could not simply disregard Huber's request as he had at first meant to do. But he had to be extraordinarily careful and discreet. And it was precisely Foxy's attempts to be discreet that caused the damage.

Had Foxy gone out about the job in his normal way, had he for instance button-holed colleagues and asked point-blank: "Have you heard the latest, the silly rumor about Heinz Zimmerman and Agnes Muller?", he might have done damage to his own reputation but very little else.

But by making a big to-do, by telling everybody that he couldn't tell them why he asked, swearing them to secrecy, checking whether anyone else was listening, and, above all, by hinting rather than speaking plainly, he produced the greatest possible disturbance. "I know it isn't true," he would say to a colleague and fellow priest, "but have you heard anyone tell an odd story about an unusual relationship between a man and a woman very high up in the university? Anything of this sort?" And he asked the questions in a whisper, in a corner, or after having made carefully sure that the door was closed. He created an atmosphere of intrigue, of mystery—and the tale spread like wildfire through the small community of St. Jerome priests on campus.

Foxy himself was at first totally unaware of what he had done. On Thursday evening, thirty-six hours after Willy Huber had talked to him, he left for a conference in the East on the teaching of mathematics to undergraduates. When he returned to the priests' residence hall just in time for the Sunday evening meal, he found himself immediately surrounded and besieged, mainly of course by the younger men. "Is it true, Foxy, that you have a choice story to tell?" an assistant professor of classics greeted him. "Foxy," another asked, "what is this I hear about a scandal in the Administration Building?" And, "Have you heard, Foxy, that the Brother General has ordered an investigation very high up?"

Foxy fled, leaving his dinner uneaten. He ran straight to Erwin Ritter, caught him just as he was going to bed, and poured out the story. Ritter knew about Lisa Holloway's letter, Willy Huber's telephone call, and Agnes's decision to accede to Huber's request; Heinz Zimmerman had gone to him shortly after his talk with Agnes. But he had no inkling of Huber's subsequent call to Foxy, nor of the uproar among the faculty. His closest friend would never have dared repeat gossip to Erwin Ritter.

Ritter sternly ordered Foxy to keep his mouth shut. "If anyone asks you anything about the rumor, you tell him to come to me." But that only heightened the mystery, ensuring that all the priests became convinced something momentous was going on. Anyone who did go to Ritter—and many of the older men who had known him for years did so—got a stern lecture about spreading slander and the wickedness of even mentioning something so palpably absurd and cruelly vicious, with strict instructions to discipline any junior who might indulge in loose talk. And, as he hadn't done for years, Erwin Ritter took to having his supper in the refectory of the priests' residence instead of in his own rooms in the house next door he shared with Heinz Zimmerman. There, his silence and his grim looks dared anyone to as much as mention the subject.

But making it taboo only convinced his colleagues, and especially the younger men, to whom both Heinz Zimmerman and Agnes

Muller were remote names rather than flesh-and-blood people with whom they had worked closely, that there must be something going on. What, no one quite knew—few believed in an illicit love affair; it was obviously quite impossible for those two ever to have been together where they wouldn't be seen and observed by countless eyes. Yet surely something terribly important, terribly serious, must be happening. Why otherwise these attempts to hush things up? Where at first a good many of the priests had shouted, they now began to whisper. Where they had talked openly, they now began to argue in corners, often heatedly, only to break off and turn silent the moment someone else approached. Where they had at first treated the whole thing as a joke, albeit one in very dubious taste (but then Foxy wasn't much noted for his taste, anyhow), they now began to be afraid.

Erwin Ritter soon realized that he had done the worst thing. But there was no one with whom he could discuss the matter. He surely could not mention it to Heinz with whom, for almost thirty years, he had talked out every problem at St. Jerome. He could not discuss it with the chairman of the Regents or the General of the Order, even if he had had greater respect for either Mulcahey or Huber.

Then he thought of Seymour Bercovitz and decided to pay him a visit.

Bercovitz was Heinz Zimmerman's friend rather than Ritter's. But Ritter had seen enough of the doctor to have come to like him and have confidence in his judgment. And what was going on at St. Jerome seemed to Ritter to call for a psychiatrist's knowledge and advice.

"You are quite right, Father Dean," said Dr. Bercovitz. "What you are faced with at the university falls within our province. It sounds to me suspiciously like an attack of mass hysteria, though a fairly mild one. I know laymen think that's an affliction of women, and mainly adolescent ones. But that's a misunderstanding. Hysteria is equally common to both sexes and has nothing to do with age. It's a kind of emotional epidemic—and highly contagious. It typically occurs in small, self-contained, rather isolated communities where there is considerable emotional tension, with conflicts being suppressed in the subconscious" ("And what greater tension," Bercovitz added to himself, "could there be among today's young Catholic priests than worry about sex and celibacy? They must hear every day of one of their colleagues leaving the priesthood to get married.")

"There is no known treatment and no known cure," he went on. "In the old days one called in the priest, who tried exorcism. It rarely worked. Now you call in the psychiatrist, who talks learnedly about suppression and sublimation and psychic dynamics and drives. That doesn't work, either. Fortunately, mass hysteria usually takes care of itself, and pretty fast. I won't pretend that it's no worse than the common cold; it can do a lot of damage. And it's very painful, as you've found out, but so is a pebble in the shoe. Usually it burns itself out within a few weeks. There is only one thing that must be avoided, one thing that can make it dangerous. It's really the oldest media event around and feeds on attention, publicity, and speechmaking. Just treat it with neglect and amused tolerance. Laughter, believe me, and being made light of, are the two things mass hysteria cannot survive.

"The important point to make sure of for you at the university," Bercovitz concluded, "is that your senior men, the department chairmen and deans and distinguished older faculty, keep cool heads and go about their normal business as if nothing out of the ordinary were happening. That shouldn't be too difficult, I trust."

Erwin Ritter assured the psychiatrist that, indeed, it shouldn't be difficult at all. But he left Bercovitz's office with considerable forebodings. In his own heart he was by no means sure that the senior men at St. Jerome would have the self-discipline to go about their business as usual and give Heinz Zimmerman and the university their unquestioning support. Some of them, he was very much afraid, were busy blowing up a storm of their own. And once again the Holloways were at the center of this second turbulence.

Part Three

When Clem Boglund returned to his office on Monday afternoon from a luncheon meeting with his senior chemistry professors, he found Philip Oberhumer, the chairman of Earth Sciences, waiting for him. "Can I see you for a few minutes in private?" Oberhumer asked.

Oberhumer had been one of Heinz Zimmerman's "coups." Highly distinguished among the country's oil geologists and the holder of an endowed chair at a famous Eastern university, he had become available to St. Jerome only because his wife, Patricia Dunn, then a psychology teacher at a college near Boston, would not accept deanship at Harriet Beecher Stowe unless a first-rate job in Capital City could be found for her husband. Zimmerman had seen his opportunity and seized it. Oberhumer could not resist the offer St. Jerome had made him: no teaching duties except for the supervision of a few doctoral candidates, a substantially higher salary, and full freedom to do all the consulting work he wanted.

Oberhumer for his part had done very well by St. Jerome. He had built a strong department, which attracted first-rate young faculty. He got the cream of the country's doctoral students in his own field—and they got top jobs in industry and teaching immediately upon graduation. He also brought St. Jerome a good deal of oil money. Indeed, the oil millionaire with whom Heinz Zimmerman was having lunch that very same Monday and from whom he hoped to get enough money for a new Earth Sciences building and for three endowed professorships in geology, geophysics, and petroleum engineering, respectively, was one of Oberhumer's satisfied clients and had been brought by him to St. Jerome.

But Oberhumer was also the faculty's leading troublemaker. At every meeting of the Chairman's Council—the university's most powerful committee and the final arbiter in most matters of academic policy and curriculum—he would bore one half to death with his impassioned tirades on "University constitution" and against "tyrannical administrators." In particular, he railed against what he called "administrative arrogance in the American university." "Instead of a president, vice presidents, and deans in battalion strength," he would declaim, "all a university needs is one clerk to make sure that the paperwork gets done and the salary checks go out on time. The rest should be run by the senior faculty, the full professors, who elect rectors and deans for short periods (three years maximum) and who alone make all decisions. Anything else is usurpation of faculty authority and results in control of science and scholarship by the vested interests, and especially the moneybags."

Oberhumer was not particularly popular with his colleagues, least of all with Boglund, whom he had once openly sneered at as "Zimmerman's tame poodle." Boglund was therefore quite surprised to find Oberhumer at his doorstep, but could hardly refuse to give him a few minutes.

"Tell me, Clem," Oberhumer began. "Who is Martin Holloway?"

"An incompetent assistant professor in my department," Boglund replied, much surprised; "an older man whom Heinz Zimmerman ordered us to hire three years ago. Otherwise, Heinz said, we'd be guilty of discrimination by age. I never thought he'd work out. And now my faculty has voted unanimously not to reappoint him."

"That's what I thought," said Oberhumer, "and that's what I told my wife."

"Why should Pat be interested?" asked Boglund, mystified.

"It's a weird story, and the only thing I can figure out is that our sneaky administration is once again trying to whittle down faculty rights. Pat called just before lunch. Her president—you've met Louise McCollough, I think—apparently got a phone call from Zimmerman this morning suggesting she hire Holloway."

"You must be making it up," said Boglund. "I can't believe it. Zimmerman knows nothing about the man except that we unanimously recommended not to reappoint him and consider him totally unfit for college teaching."

"You better believe it, Clem," said Oberhumer. "That's exactly the kind of game administrators will play unless the faculty clips their wings. Anyhow, Mrs. McCollough asked Pat to find out who this Holloway is and what goes on. After all, university presidents don't as a rule try to find jobs for fired assistant professors."

"I still can't understand it," said Boglund. "If Heinz Zimmerman sees any problem in letting Holloway go, why doesn't he bring it up with me? After all, I would have to recommend the fellow before any college hires him—and I sure couldn't do it. You can tell that to Pat. Actually, I've lined up a few industry offers for Holloway. That's where he belongs."

"You take much too relaxed a view of this, Clem," said Oberhumer. "It's a slap in your face. You and your faculty unanimously declare the man unfit, and then the President, who knows nothing about him, disavows you behind your back and recommends him for a teaching job. If that's not a declaration of nonconfidence in you and your faculty—and in all of us chairmen—I don't know what it is."

"Phil," protested Boglund, "you exaggerate. I admit that I'm stunned. Nothing like this has happened to me in my whole academic career. But I know Heinz Zimmerman. There must be some explanation, though I'm damned if I can figure it out."

"Don't be naive, Clem. There's an explanation all right. Our precious President doesn't give a fig for the rights of the faculty and never will if we let him get away with his little games. Maybe you don't want to make an issue out of it, but I shall. I'll bring it up at the next Chairmen's Council meeting two weeks from today. I think it's an outrage and an open attack on all of us chairmen and the senior faculty we represent."

Boglund didn't wait two weeks. As soon as Oberhumer had left, he phoned Erwin Ritter. And when Ritter said that he knew nothing about a telephone call about Holloway to Harriet Beecher Stowe, Boglund called Zimmerman and made an appointment to see him Wednesday morning.

Clement Boglund was not a very observant person, and he had not been in the president's office often enough to know its routine. But even he sensed immediately on Wednesday morning that something was amiss. Agnes Muller, instead of greeting him with her usual warm smile, barely nodded to him. She seemed distracted, and Boglund thought her face and eyes were swollen as if she had been crying. In one corner of the office a sour-looking middle-aged woman was exchanging angry words with a crew from Maintenance who were pushing furniture around. And Zimmerman himself seemed very different from his usual courteous and genial self. He didn't inquire after Boglund's health or his wife and children, nor about affairs in the Chemistry Department. He didn't even offer Boglund a seat.

"What's the matter, Clem?" he asked curtly. "Try to make it brief. I'm busy."

"Yes," he said, after Boglund had put his question. "I did call Louise McCollough on Monday and mentioned Holloway to her. Did Erwin Ritter tell you that he and his wife came to see me Sunday afternoon—uninvited, to be sure—and asked me to overrule you and your faculty and renew his contract? Of course I said no. But I felt sorry for the fellow, he was so totally crushed. And then I remembered that Louise McCollough had told me some weeks ago that she needs science teachers who have the full academic credentials but are willing to teach—and teach conscientiously—at the high-school level. I'm sorry if you feel I by-passed you; I didn't intend to. I just thought I might help a poor devil and a neighboring school as well."

"I don't understand, Heinz," Boglund said with considerable heat. "The entire faculty in Chemistry declares this man unfit to teach college courses and you, who know nothing about him or about chemistry, overrule us and recommend him for a teaching position. Don't you have any respect for our judgment or confidence in me? You know I consider it my duty as chairman to look after my faculty. If you don't trust my doing so, you better tell me so and get yourself another chairman."

"Clem," said Heinz Zimmerman in an angry voice that Boglund had never heard before, "you are making a mountain out of a molehill. If I hurt you, I'm sorry and I apologize. But I won't apologize for my phoning. It was nothing but an attempt in ordinary charity to help a fellow man in distress, and I'd do it again."

And Zimmerman all but turned his back on Boglund, staring at the wall on which his honorary doctorates were hanging. Always before he had been friendly, courteous, and had given Boglund his full attention. Now he didn't even listen.

So Boglund left, baffled. What had gotten into the man? But he was also hurt, upset, and very, very angry. "Is Oberhumer right, after all?" he asked himself as he walked across the campus. He had always scoffed at Oberhumer's rantings. Now all of a sudden he made sense to Boglund in his distrust of "Administration" and his hostility toward it.

Hiring Clem Boglund as the first department chairman who was not a priest had been one of Heinz Zimmerman's early moves upon his appointment as acting president and a giant step toward his "first-rate Catholic university."

Boglund had been barely thirty then, an associate professor at Minnesota and a newly appointed one at that. But he was already known as a "comer." He had never heard of Heinz Zimmerman, of course, and St. Jerome was barely even a name to him. If he thought of moving at all, he thought of Stanford, where his former teacher had recently gone. But he himself had been an undergraduate, and a deeply dissatisfied one, at a Catholic university. And so when, by sheer accident, he had come across a speech this Father Zimmerman had made about the American Catholic University of the Future, he felt moved to sit down and pour out his own thoughts in a long letter. At most, he expected a polite acknowledgment. Instead, a telephone call came ten days later. "I am Heinz Zimmerman. I'll be in Minneapolis the week after next and would like to discuss your exciting letter." And at the end of their dinner Zimmerman had said, "I want you to come to St. Jerome and start doing the things your letter talks about."

Boglund had no regrets about choosing St. Jerome over Stanford. Professionally, he could not have done better. St. Jerome had been generous with lab equipment and research assistants and even with time. Boglund had managed to publish fourteen major research papers in his seventeen years at St. Jerome; and the big text on organic metallic compounds on which he had already been working in Minnesota was published five years after his move to St. Jerome, immediately became the standard work in the field, and had recently been reissued in a new and much-enlarged third edition. Meanwhile he had, indeed, built up a strong and nationally recognized Chemistry Department.

But, as Boglund knew well, his strength at St. Jerome rested less on his achievements in his own field and department than on his being the "bridge"—trusted, accepted, and followed in both camps—between the "new breed" of lay chairmen and that of the "cliff dwellers," the priests and nuns in departmental chairs. There was no open enmity between the two groups; but still they saw themselves as different, as competing, and as representing opposed, if not mutually incompatible, values and aspirations. Both, however, accepted and trusted Boglund; the one because Oberhumer tended to follow his lead, the other one because of his close friendship with Father Dennis Levecque.

Oberhumer's values, or rather, the man's total lack of values, Boglund could not abide. Boglund himself, although he had not realized it at the time, had chosen St. Jerome in preference to the prestige and glamour of Stanford in large part because, as a Catholic school, he expected it to be less corrupted by commercialism and less compromised by the embrace of industry. He passionately believed in academia's total divorce from mammon and in the scholar's single-minded dedication to the pursuit of knowledge rather than the pursuit of profit. "There is pure science and applied science," he was fond of saying, "and both are needed. But there is also pure science and impure science—and impure science no more belongs in academe than the money changers belonged in the Temple at Jerusalem." Or, "I have nothing against business and businessmen; but I am a scientist. And business and science are like eating and sleeping. You need both, but they don't mix."

And here was this Oberhumer, who freely admitted that he had chosen St. Jerome largely because it put no restrictions on his consulting work for industry, who boasted openly that his research was paid for by industry and was directed toward its needs, that, indeed, he aligned it deliberately with the research programs of the most bloated of fat cats, the oil companies. What irked Boglund the most was that Oberhumer was not a bit apologetic. On the contrary, he asserted loudly that sound theory and pure knowledge in science were most likely to result from wrestling with the problems of industry, and he had his own research achievements and those of his students to point to as proof of this detestable doctrine.

Yet in everything that really mattered—curriculum or educational policies or standards, even staffing and organization—Oberhumer always followed Boglund's lead. He made his silly speech attacking administration in general and St. Jerome's administration in particular, then voted the way Boglund had indicated he'd vote, which practically always was the straight administration ticket. And the other lay chairmen would duly fall into line behind Oberhumer.

Boglund found no such agreement on policy matters with the "cliff dwellers," nor did he expect it. They were nostalgic for the days when all chairmen were St. Jerome priests, and tended to resent him as the symbol of that new order in which St. Jerome was no longer "their" university. All of them—the two nuns who headed departments as well as the priests holding chairmanships—had serious reservations about a good many of Heinz Zimmerman's ideas, policies, and appointments, even though they could not find cogent rational arguments against them. Yet they accepted Clement Boglund as a person, trusted him, worked with him. And the main reason was his close friendship with one of them, Father Dennis Levecque, the chairman of Economics.

The friendship had begun on Boglund's first trip to St. Jerome, well before he had accepted the appointment, when Dennis and he discovered, sitting by accident at the same table at lunch, that they both came from the iron-mining country of northern Michigan and that their fathers, though at different times, had actually been working for the same mining company, one as electrician, the other in truck maintenance. The two of them, having grown up in the North Woods and as outdoorsmen, began to go cross-country skiing together in the winter and fishing in the summer on a remote island close to the Canadian border which could be reached only by canoe and on which Levecque owned a primitive shack.

But what kept them friends were their common values. For all their policy differences—and these were sharp—they were as one in what they thought essential. Boglund was a moderate, Levecque an extremist; but that was a matter of temperament rather than of conviction. Levecque was as firmly committed as Boglund to "keeping the money changers out of the Temple," that is, to the total divorce of academia and business, and indeed of academia and the false values and vanities of a secular, profit-seeking possession-loving society altogether. Levecque saw himself first as a priest of the Church. Boglund saw himself as a secular scientist. But both believed in the motto, *Ad majorem Dei gloriam*, which the first president of St. Jerome almost a century ago had had chiseled over the mock-Gothic portal of the Administration Building.

And they were both being defeated.

Every day Boglund saw new evidence of the enemy's advance. One after another the science departments of St. Jerome—first Biology, then Physics, finally the mathematicians—joined Oberhumer in the worship of the golden calf and the brazen pursuit of consulting assignments in industry, research contracts from business and corporation fellowships. But Boglund at least had some control over his own Chemistry Department. Control of Economics had already passed to commercialism and big business.

Dennis Levecque was a labor economist and an acknowledged expert on white-collar unions. He was active as adviser and counselor to labor leaders, most of them of the "progressive" persuasion. When the legislature had passed a law drafted by Levecque, which permitted state employees to unionize and to bargain collectively, Levecque had become Labor's appointee on the State Labor Commission. Levecque was a colorful speaker who loved the limelight and courted the press. At a time when even supposedly "radical" labor leaders had come to talk about such bloodless things as "cost/benefit ratios," "cost of living," and "productivity," Levecque's fiery, old-fashioned, "give 'em hell" rhetoric was in high demand and made excellent copy.

Needless to say, the business leaders of Capital City were not exactly enchanted by headlines such as: ST. JEROME ECONOMICS CHAIRMAN CALLS FOR NATIONALIZATION OF BIG COMPANIES. But their opposition to Levecque got nowhere until the Graduate School of Management was founded and had begun to grow fast. As the dean of the new school soon found out, Dennis Levecque as chairman of Economics and in control of the economics taught throughout the university, including the School of Management, was a major liability in recruiting students, placing graduates, and soliciting money.

"Economics," Levecque maintained, "is a moral discipline. Its goal is a better, a more just, a more Christian society. The 'moderns,' the quantifiers with their wonderful techniques, prostitute economics. Since the only thing that can be quantified is a model of the stock market, the stock market becomes their ideal of a just economy and they become servants of corporate capitalism at its worst." And so Levecque, as chairman of Economics, pushed the old-fashioned courses: Labor Economics, Government Control of Business, Economic History, and History of Economic Thought.

"But this isn't Economics," said the Management people. "If St. Jerome wants to teach these things, put them into Philosophy or Social Science or History—but we do need real Economics." And when Levecque wouldn't budge, they played their trump card: they got the Association of Collegiate Schools of Business to suspend St. Jerome's full accreditation "pending the establishment of an adequate program in Economics."

Of course, Levecque could not be deprived of the chairmanship. The St. Jerome priests on the faculty would have revolted. What the Management people proposed was even more humiliating: to have two departments of Economics, with the new one, headquartered in Management, in control of everything except the introductory freshman courses and the seminars in Economic Policy (by which was meant only one course, the seminar in Labor Economics Levecque himself taught to a handful of students). All Boglund could accomplish—and even that almost foundered on the last-ditch resistance of the Management School—was a lame compromise: the department remained officially unsplit, with Levecque the only "Economics Chairman" at St. Jerome. But a "subdepartment" of "Managerial Economics and Statistics" was set up in the Management School with responsibility for Economics in all professional schools: Undergraduate Business, Law School, Graduate Management, and Engineering, and for quantitative and analytical courses throughout the university.

It wasn't much of a compromise, but it saved Levecque's face and that of the "cliff dwellers." Dennis was almost pathetically grateful.

And the senior "cliff dweller," Father Carstens, chairman of Religion and, after Erwin Ritter, the most respected St. Jerome priest, had come in person to Boglund's office to tell him how much he appreciated what Clem had done.

All this went through Clement Boglund's mind as he fought his way against a bitter wind toward his own office at the other end of the campus. Heinz Zimmerman had hurt him deeply. And yet he couldn't see himself accepting Oberhumer's position. "I need to talk this out with someone. Why not Dennis? He usually laughs at the things that bother me, especially administrative worries. But he knows how much my responsibility for my faculty means to me and he shares my concern."

To Boglund's amazement, Dennis Levecque did not laugh. "Of course, Clem," he said, "the incident in itself is trivial. But it's far from trivial as a symptom of what's wrong with St. Jerome. It shows you how far we have gone toward the 'imperial presidency.' Forget his being rough; that's unimportant. Heinz isn't, usually, we both know that. But his going over your head and disavowing you in respect to that incompetent you're letting go—that's something else again. It shows that Zimmerman wants to have it both ways. If St. Jerome is indeed the 'first-rate university' he is forever talking about, the President has no business interfering with faculty. But the moment it pleases him, he's running St. Jerome with the personal authority of an old-fashioned religious superior. He can't have it both ways.

"Are you going to bring it up at the Chairmen's Council meeting in two weeks, Clem?"

Boglund shook his head. "I don't know yet, though I doubt it. But Oberhumer surely will."

"And Phil will make the most of it," said Levecque. "I think I'd better discuss this on Friday with the Twelve Apostles."

In its pre-Zimmerman days, St. Jerome had had twelve academic departments, all chaired by St. Jerome Fathers. By now the number of departments had almost doubled—to twenty-three—and only eight of them were chaired by religious, and two of those (Modern Languages and Journalism) by a "chairperson," one of the Sisters of St. Mary in the Plains rather than a priest. Still, the nickname of "the Twelve Apostles" hung on, as did the custom of the remaining eight lunching together at the Faculty Club every Friday at a table of their own.

On the Friday after his talk with Clem Boglund, Father Dennis Levecque carried his tray toward the table where the Twelve Apostles seemed to be having a heated argument, everybody leaning forward and whispering. But when he slid into the seat he always occupied, between Fred Carstens, chairman of Religion, and Piet Boerhave, chairman of Philosophy, everyone immediately stopped talking.

"So you, too, are gossiping about Heinz Zimmerman and Agnes Muller," he said in a bantering voice to Father Carstens.

Carstens was not amused. "You know better than that, Dennis," he said in a tone of irritation that was quite unusual for that serene man. "I leave gossiping to Foxy; he does enough of it for all of us. I am appalled though by the way everybody else is gossiping, and especially the younger priests. Twenty years ago we wouldn't have dignified such a mean little piece of dirt with a moment's attention. Now all the young priests are chattering about it like a bunch of hysterical schoolgirls discussing the sex life of a movie starlet. If that's what being a first-rate university means, give me a kindergarten any time.

"Last night I heard two of our younger priests telling each other that this absurd rumor shows how ill-advised it is of Rome not to permit priests to marry."

"You're quite right, Fred," said the chairman of classics, who as the youngest of the group both in years and seniority always felt called upon to defend the younger generation. "It's been a miserable week. But Foxy's rumor, it seems to me, has only uncovered how low morale is among the St. Jerome priests here. It hasn't been the cause. And frankly I do think that those young priests you overheard have a point. After all, there are married priests in perfectly respectable rites within the church—the Ukrainians with their Greek-Catholic Rite, for instance. Why can't Rome accept an American Rite and give us the freedom to choose our own observances in matters that do not concern Faith or Doctrine but purely discipline?"

As the Classics chairman had intended, both Carstens and Boerhave, champions of tradition and guardians of orthodoxy at St. Jerome, immediately rose to the bait. To stop them before they could launch into the set speeches everybody at the table had heard a dozen times before, Dennis Levecque intervened hastily: "Hold it. I came here with something important, something that we ought to think about"—and he told them of his talk with Clem Boglund two days earlier. "When Oberhumer makes an issue out of Heinz Zimmerman's running around Boglund—and mind you, I'm saying 'when' not 'if'; I'm sure he'll bring it up and make it sound like the crime of the century—are we going to support the administration?"

"Isn't this purely a matter between the lay faculty and the administration of which we should stay clear?" asked Sister Malvina, chairperson of Journalism, who was known to consider the Council meetings a waste of time anyway and who used very un-nunlike terms—"intellectual masturbation," for example—to express what she thought of most of the issues and problems that engaged the Council's time and attention. But Sister Malvina made far too much sense for anyone to pay attention to her.

Tall and angular, Sister Malvina was not noted for flights of fancy; totally unsentimental and without imagination, she was known as "Madam Facts" among Journalism faculty and students. But when a few weeks later she talked of the luncheon meeting of the Twelve Apostles to Tom Martini, whom the bishop had sent to find out what was going on at St. Jerome, she broke down and sobbed. "It was hateful, hateful," she said. "I felt like part of a lynch mob."

"Oh, it began quietly enough," she continued. "'I hope, Dennis,' Father Carstens said, 'that you told Clem Boglund not to pay attention to Heinz Zimmerman's rudeness. We all know—and Boglund must know it too by now—that Zimmerman was terribly upset that morning. What really goes on there, I don't know, but it must have something to do with that malicious rumor Foxy has been spreading.'

"Father Levecque assured Father Carstens that that was precisely what he had said to Professor Boglund. 'But,' he went on, 'I also told Clem Boglund that the incident and Father Zimmerman's interference on behalf of that incompetent chemist were a serious matter, if only as a symptom of the confusion St. Jerome suffers from in respect to its role and that of faculty and administration.'

"And that's when the shit hit the fan. The first one to scream—and I do mean scream—was Father Wydling, the chairman of Classics.

'That's just the way all of us have been treated,' he shouted, hammering the table with his fist. 'When Beatrice [that, said Sister Malvina, is Sister Beatrice, who chairs Modern Languages] and I went to Ritter and Zimmerman to protest against the abolition of the language requirement, they didn't even listen to us. Mind you, we didn't ask them to restore the old rule under which a student had to have both one year of Latin and one year of a modern language although both of us believe that that's a minimum. All we asked them was to keep some language requirement—and they wouldn't even listen! Zimmerman said, 'We have a hard enough time getting good students to apply to St. Jerome and have to be competitive in our requirements. No respect at all for what's right, for educational values and tradition, nothing but commercial considerations.'

"Then Sister Beatrice chimed in: 'I call it meretricious, and then Felix Wydling and I get criticized because enrollments in our departments are dropping. We have a right, I'd say, to expect the President of a Catholic university to stand up for a true liberal education and not throw us to the wolves just to be trendy.'

"'And he doesn't treat Economics any differently,' Father Levecque said, and I noticed his hands were trembling with rage. Then Father Boerhave, who is usually so quiet, broke in and bellowed: 'But things are even worse in appointments and the administration is even more highhanded. It's a shame and a disgrace how in a Catholic university, one that belongs to and is run by an Order, priests are discriminated against and told we aren't good enough and don't measure up. They put a dean in at the Law School who isn't even a Catholic and pass over the priest who's been associate dean for eight years. And they put a layman into the chair of the biggest department, English, though there are eleven qualified priests and sisters among the department's faculty. And I don't know,' he went on, turning to Father Boninger, 'why we stood still when they closed down your School of Education, making it a mere department and demoting you from dean to department chairman. I know they pleaded falling enrollments, but we shouldn't have let them bamboozle us!'"

"I know, Father Martini," Sister Malvina finished up, "it all sounds petty—and it was. But I make it sound orderly and rational and at worst peevish. In fact, it was wild and vicious. They were screaming, really screaming—the whole faculty dining room stared at our table as though we'd gone mad, and, of course, we had. I tried to remind them that every one of these measures—the abolition of the language requirements, the reorganization of the Economics Department, and the change in Education from a separate school to a department—had been discussed endlessly in the Council and carried by an overwhelming majority. Dropping the language requirement was recommended unanimously by a faculty committee. As I recall, the only ones voting to keep it were Father Wydling and Sister Beatrice. But they didn't want to hear me, they wanted to hate. They glared at me, and for a moment I thought one of them might strike me, they were so full of hatred and meanness and self-pity.

"I don't know what would have happened if Father Carstens, who was more shaken than I've ever seen him, and he's usually so unflappable, hadn't said: 'It's one-thirty and our rule is to adjourn now. Some of us have classes or appointments.' But it took him quite some time to get them to stop shouting at each other and cursing the administration.

"I know one table," Sister Malvina concluded, "where I shan't eat lunch anymore, Friday or any other day of the week."

It had been known as the "Academic Council" for a full ten years now, but it was still the "Chairmen's Council" for everyone but Erwin Ritter. The monthly meetings were indeed attended as a rule only by the chairmen and chairwomen of the twenty-three university-wide academic departments.

But when Phil Oberhumer rose on a blustery February afternoon to make an issue out of Heinz Zimmerman's telephone call to Harriet Beecher Stowe on behalf of Martin Holloway, he faced a full house. In addition to the "chairs," all seven professional-school deans were in attendance; even the three deans of the Health Care schools were there, who rarely set foot on the main St. Jerome Campus as their offices were downtown in St. Clare Hospital, nine miles away. The dean of the undergraduate liberal arts college was there, of course. But so too was the director of the Advanced Institute of Theoretical Physics, the distinguished scientist Jerry Ashenbach, who had never before in his eight years at St. Jerome shown up at a Council meeting.

There was only one absentee: the president. Heinz Zimmerman had refused to come, despite Erwin Ritter's repeated urgings. "If I show up," he had said, "everyone will know that I've come because of Oberhumer's attack—and it isn't even on the agenda. They'll expect me to apologize or to defend myself. I won't do either." And when Ritter, a few days later, tried again, Heinz Zimmerman grew petulant, said, "I'm busy," and walked out.

But what bothered Ritter most was not Zimmerman's words. It was the way they were said: listlessly, and in a tone of resignation, almost defeat.

Outwardly, there seemed to be no change in Heinz Zimmerman, and he kept to his daily routine. He had not lost his golden touch, had, for instance, without apparent effort, gotten Oberhumer's oil millionaire to pledge himself to a huge matching grant for half the cost of both a new earth sciences building and three new earth sciences professorships—far more than the donor had ever dreamed of giving, and almost twice what Zimmerman himself had expected to get when he first started courting the oilman. When he chaired meetings, Zimmerman was as courteous and considerate as ever, though, Ritter thought, one saw very little these days of the famous Zimmerman smile with its infectious warmth.

Yet to Erwin Ritter's eyes and ears there was something terribly wrong here, something terribly contrived. Zimmerman's heart simply wasn't in what he was doing, no matter how well he did it.

Ritter had known Zimmerman for forty years, since his own first week as a college teacher and Heinz Zimmerman's first week as a college freshman. During one of the very first discussion sessions of "Philosophy 101: Introduction to Logic and Philosophy," Ritter had realized that this huge, handsome, outgoing basketball player was a brilliant intellect with a searching mind, but also that this mind had never been challenged, never been disciplined, never been taught. When the young philosophy instructor returned to his room that evening, totally exhausted but also exhilarated as never before, he had gone down on his knees to thank the Lord for making him a teacher, and to pray for the strength to meet the challenge of the likes of Heinz Zimmerman. And when he got up from his prayer, he thought he heard a voice within him speak the words with which Our Lord on the Cross commended his favorite disciple to his Mother: "This is Your Son."

Fifteen years later, when he had wanted to make Zimmerman assistant dean, he had to convince an elderly and very conservative president who thought the young professor of logic "far too radical" and "full of half-baked notions."

"But Zimmerman," Ritter had argued, "is himself the best proof of his thesis that Catholic colleges in the United States must change radically. In all my years of teaching I've never encountered a more brilliant student, one more eager to learn and one who so fully exemplifies St. Augustine's dictum: *Anima est naturaliter Christiana* (The soul is Christian by nature). Yet when he arrived here, after twelve years of the best education American Catholic schools can supposedly provide, his mind had never been put to work, challenged, permitted to ask a question, touched, or inspired. All he had been allowed to learn were a few phrases of the Catechism, any number of vulgar terms for the private parts of men and women, and how to throw a basketball."

Erwin Ritter had been under Zimmerman's spell from the first day they met; but he had always had one serious reservation. Heinz Zimmerman, he thought, far too much loved a fight. He was what Ritter's Austrian-born grandmother used to call a "*Raufhansl*," a tavern brawler. Again and again in the years when Ritter was carefully grooming the younger man for higher office, he'd find himself saying: "Why can't you learn, Heinz, that one catches flies with honey?" Zimmerman's instinctive reaction was to hit out at whoever opposed him or stood in his way.

Now, it seemed, all the *Raufhansl* had gone out of him. Ritter would have expected him to be fighting mad. Instead, Heinz had become mulish, stubborn, and passive.

Ritter once more sought out Seymour Bercovitz. But the psychiatrist had no explanation. "I've noticed it, too," he said, "and so did my children when he came to the house the other evening for our weekly chess game. My daughter, she's very fond of Father Heinz, spotted it and asked me after he left whether I thought he was sick or in pain. In fact, Dean Ritter, I was tempted to call up and ask what ails Father Heinz."

"You know, doctor," Ritter replied, choosing his words carefully, "I cannot see anything that would explain Heinz being frightened or ashamed—and yet that's the way he acts. He is used to fights in the faculty; in fact, he enjoys them. To be sure, he must be annoyed at that stupid story about him and Agnes Muller, and in his shoes, I'd be so angry with those two heroes, the chairman of the Regents and the Brother General, that I'd have told them what they can do with my job. But he acts as if there were some shameful secret, some hidden wound. Yet all that's happened is a spiteful letter."

"And, as I told him," Bercovitz added, "a letter from a very sick woman who is hardly rational."

The evening before the Council meeting, Ritter had tried once more. He had gotten Heinz to promise to reconsider. But when the meeting opened, Zimmerman wasn't there.

Oberhumer, Erwin Ritter thought, was beginning to lose his audience.

He had started out with full-blown Ciceronian oratory.

"It is my duty, Father Dean," he had begun, "to bring before the Academic Council an incident which, while perhaps none too important in itself, raises profound and disturbing questions of academic freedom and university constitution; an incident which threatens to undermine the confidence faculty must have in the university's administration. Yes, I know, the Holloway incident is only that, an incident. But it constitutes a gross violation of the rights of department chairpersons and bespeaks a dangerous lack of trust in the integrity and judgment of the department chairman—and, above all, a lack of clarity regarding the role and functions of both administration and faculty and its chairpersons, which augurs ill for the future of this great university."

This was far too dramatic for the prosaic Academic Council at St. Jerome. But it made everyone sit up. Jerry Ashenbach, for instance, had been slumped in his chair half asleep. But when Oberhumer began, he jerked upright as if stabbed with a cattle prod. And one of the health-care deans who had been equally somnolent was heard to whisper to the other two: "Now I know why Ritter insisted we come."

But as soon as he had everyone's attention, Oberhumer turned icy calm.

"As an isolated incident, the Holloway episode wouldn't matter, but it isn't an isolated incident. Unfortunately, it's but the latest in a long series of similar events, each showing that the administration is confused about its role—and about our role as well. Whether this results from a lack of clarity or whether it bespeaks a refusal on the administration's part to honor and respect the constitutional limitations on its power is, I submit, quite irrelevant. The result is the same: interference with the rights of the faculty, and usurpation of power."

And then Oberhumer had rehashed eight or nine such "incidents": the downgrading of Education from a separate school to a department; the handling of the language requirements ("Hypocrite," Ritter said to himself, for Oberhumer had been the prime mover in abolishing Latin as a required subject); the restructuring of Economics; and several others. Each time he would add, "I don't question the decision itself, only the way in which the administration acted, the same way, pretty much, in which it has acted now in the Holloway matter in the Chemistry Department. I don't accuse the administration of intent to undermine the departmental chairs or to encroach on the autonomy of faculty. But that's the result. I don't consider this a matter of personalities. It's the absence of clear ground rules that makes for confusion."

Oberhumer was clever and effective, Ritter thought; but would he know when to stop? For his audience was becoming bored. Chairs began to scrape; there was coughing; in the back there was even some whispering; and Jerry Ashenbach was slumping back into near-somnolence. Oberhumer sensed this failing attention just in time. He stopped in mid-sentence and said: "All of us know that I could go on reciting similar incidents for a couple of hours—there have been far too many. I submit, Father Dean, that I have proven our need for constitutional clarification. I therefore move that the Academic Council adopt the following amendments to our bylaws: let me read them." And he whipped out a typewritten page while his sidekick Dr.

Shoemacher, chairman of Life Sciences, produced a sheaf of copies and began to hand them out. Oberhumer read:

(1) The Chairpersons of the all-university academic departments of St. Jerome University shall elect by secret ballot three of their colleagues to form an Executive Committee of the Faculty, each member to serve for three years and be eligible to be reelected once.

(2) In all matters affecting either curriculum or faculty, including appointment and termination, promotion, tenure, salary, and disciplinary action, the Executive Committee of the Faculty shall be the final decision-making organ of St. Jerome University, subject only to the powers of the Board of Regents. In particular, the Executive Committee of the Faculty shall be the only body empowered to make recommendations to the Board of Regents regarding faculty personnel, curriculum, and academic organization.

(3) Grievances, complaints, or disputes regarding promotion, tenure, teaching assignments, termination, or salary of a member of the faculty which cannot be settled within the appropriate academic department can be appealed only to the Executive Committee of the Faculty, whose decisions shall be considered final and binding.

"That," Oberhumer said softly, "should clarify matters." He sat down amid a stunned silence.

Ritter waited a minute, then asked dryly: "Anyone seconding?"

To everyone's surprise, including clearly Oberhumer's, it was not Dr. Shoemacher who first said: "I second the motion." It was a priest, Father Dennis Levecque, chairman of Economics.

Before Ritter could open the discussion, the dean of engineering was on his feet. "I have a question of clarification, Professor Oberhumer," he began. "As I read this, you propose to restrict administration to one main role: getting the money, with the faculty, or rather, the chairmen and chairwomen, deciding how and where to spend it, and how much. Am I right?"

"That's a pretty broad interpretation, Dean Grommet," Oberhumer responded, "a bit broader than I'd make it. But, yes, you're right, that's the general intention. I've never made any bones about my conviction that administration in a properly run university should be restricted to raising money, recruiting qualified students, and keeping house, and should leave all policy and personnel matters to the faculty."

After that it was a free-for-all. Ritter soon gave up keeping order or holding the discussion to any one topic. "Now I know," he said later to Bercovitz, describing the meeting, "how the Tower of Babel sounded. I've suffered through forty years of faculty meetings. But I've never sat through one as confused, undisciplined, or emotional as that, nor as nasty underneath."

"I told you, Father Dean, we are dealing with an attack of hysteria," was Bercovitz's only comment.

Very slowly the sense of the meeting began to swing against Oberhumer and his proposal. The chairmen and chairwomen were in a sullen mood all right; but they were not ready for revolution. "Another five minutes," Ritter said to himself, "and I'll call for the vote."

Then Father Boerhave, the chairman of Religion, who had so far stayed silent, bailed out Oberhumer—clearly without realizing what he was doing. "Father Dean," he said, "I believe that most of us would agree that we shouldn't vote on the spur of the moment on so difficult and serious a matter as constitutional reform. It deserves a lot of study and thought. I therefore hope that Professor Oberhumer will be willing to let me offer a substitute for his motion and withdraw his own for the time being. I would like to propose and to move: The Academic Council of St. Jerome University, conscious of the need to clarify the respective powers and responsibilities of administration and chairpersons in matters of faculty personnel and academic curriculum, and in order to clarify the relations between the two groups, hearby resolves that all communications to an individual faculty member from the university administration be henceforth channeled exclusively through the appropriate chairperson, and that no action with respect to an individual faculty member be taken by the administration either inside or outside the university except with the knowledge and concurrence of the appropriate academic chairperson.

"I submit, Father Dean," he added, "that this motion essentially represents the policy we thought we had all along. Apparently, it needs to be spelled out. And it does, I submit, accomplish Professor Oberhumer's main objective—to prevent what he calls 'incidents.' I only hope he'll be willing to withdraw his motion for the time being. We need to study it a little more carefully than we can in this meeting."

"Oh, sure," said Oberhumer, with a broad grin.

Five minutes later they voted. Boerhave's motion was roundly defeated—17 votes against 8 for, 7 abstentions. But it was a Pyrrhic victory for the administration. No sooner had Ritter announced the tally than Oberhumer got up and asked for a recount. Then he turned triumphantly to Ritter and said: "I hope you realize, Father Dean, that we only lost because of the votes of the eight deans. If you disregard their votes, and that of Dr. Ashenbach, who is also administration, and count only departmental chairpersons, that is, faculty, it's eight to eight with seven abstentions. And what may be more important in a Catholic university, out of the religious, the priests and nuns in departmental chairs, only one, Sister Malvina of Journalism, voted with the administration and against Father Boerhave's motion. One abstained, and six voted for the motion. That's hardly a resounding declaration of confidence in the administration by the university's faculty."

"I must correct you, Professor Oberhumer," said Erwin Ritter through clenched teeth. "Department chairpersons are as much 'administration' as a dean or the President. What's been defeated here today was an attempted power grab."

But Ritter knew that this was a half-truth. It was mutiny, and it had attained its main objective: to kick Heinz Zimmerman in the teeth.

Jerry Ashenbach, the physicist, and Dick Meyeroff, the Law School dean, walked together out of the meeting and down Campus Drive.

"What a disgusting farce," Meyeroff said bitterly. "I wonder how Erin Ritter kept his temper."

"Don't those idiots realize there'd *be* no St. Jerome without Zimmerman, no big jobs for them, no research grants or prestigious chairmanships," said Ashenbach, equally bitter. "I know what St. Jerome was like before Heinz took charge. I came here as an undergraduate on the G.I. Bill after World War II when the only decent job in the whole university was football coach. Of course, the lay faculty, some of them, at least, might have found good jobs elsewhere. But without Heinz Zimmerman, the St. Jerome priests would be teaching junior-high school with twenty-five hours of classroom work a week, instead of chairing a big, rich university department. And then they desert him at the very first vote and stab him in the back."

The two walked on in silence for five minutes until they came to the fork where one path led toward the Mulcahey Law Center and the other to the Advanced Physics Institute. There Ashenbach stopped again and said: "We've got to do something, and fast. I'm quite sure that no one, except Oberhumer perhaps, wants to see Zimmerman destroyed or damaged. But that's the way we're going. Maybe we ought to organize a meeting of senior faculty to affirm our support of Heinz, or get up a petition. It shouldn't be too difficult to get most of the senior faculty behind it."

"That's exactly what I've been thinking, Jerry," replied Meyeroff eagerly. "And you're right; it needs to be done swiftly. It shouldn't be too difficult. Let's you and me think about it for a day or two, then we'll decide what to do and do it fast."

And Meyeroff swung off toward his Law School with the stride of a man who has had a heavy burden lifted off his shoulders.

But in the end, neither Ashenbach nor Meyeroff would do anything.

Back at his office, Jerry Ashenbach tried to concentrate on the job he had been working on before he left for the Council meeting: the final proofs of a communication to *Physics Letters*, reporting important work done by one of his research fellows and himself. But his mind was still on Heinz Zimmerman.

"I'll finish the proofs at home," he said to his secretary, and left to talk to his wife, Gene.

It was because of Gene that the Ashenbachs were in Capital City. Gerhart Ashenbach, the son of a Capital City obstetrician, had become a full professor of physics at Princeton soon after he had published the Ashenbach equations for super-cooled magnets, when not quite thirty. He would have been content to stay in Princeton the rest of his life. But Gene was becoming increasingly unhappy there. A first-rate viola player—she was the daughter of his boyhood cello teacher at Capital City—she felt frustrated by the lack of professional opportunities for a musician in Princeton, with both New York City and Philadelphia much too far for commuting.

He had mentioned this to Zimmerman when Heinz—his roommate in his freshman year at St. Jerome right after both had returned from wartime service—had come to stay with them in Princeton one weekend nine years ago. "That's wonderful," Heinz had said. "We can help each other, I'm sure. If I raise the money, would you be willing to move to St. Jerome and head a new Advanced Physics Institute? You'd have no teaching to do except what you yourself chose, enough money to bring in five or six outstanding young physicists as research fellows each year, and all the freedom you want for your own research and travel. And there's work aplenty in Capital City for a professional musician."

Less than a year later they had moved. It had worked out well for him—he actually got more work done than in Princeton where he had had a heavy load of doctoral students. And for Gene, Capital City was sheer bliss. She was the first viola on the Capital City Symphony, "one of the best American orchestras of the second rank, and on a par with Louisville, Kansas City, and Oklahoma," according to the music critic of the *New York Times*, and taught chamber music spring semesters at St. Mary in the Plains as her father had done before her.

Gene knew that she owed this happiness to Heinz Zimmerman. She would be outraged when he told her of the Council meeting. And with her quick, practical mind, she'd know right away what to do.

But to his surprise, Gene vetoed doing anything.

"Gerhart," she had protested immediately, "you must be out of your mind! You've practically got the Nobel Prize at last after being a finalist three times in a row. You know you should have gotten it years ago and would have if you'd stayed on at Princeton. But now that you've finally overcome the prejudice of those Swedes and the big-shot Eastern physicists against anything Catholic, you want to jeopardize it by taking the side of a 'reactionary' and opposing such 'liberal causes' as academic freedom and faculty autonomy. I could kick myself for letting you go to St. Jerome before you got the prize, but I didn't realize then how political this wretched Nobel business is. Now that it's within your reach again, I just won't let you throw it away!"

Dick Meyeroff, too, was stopped by his wife from taking any action on Heinz Zimmerman's behalf.

"No wonder you're upset," Sandra had said when he told her of the meeting. "I've known for a long time that academia is Peyton Place with Ph.D.'s. But this is going too far. I agree there's a need to do something. But you, Dick Meyeroff, are absolutely the last person to start it or even to take part in it. You stay out of it. That's an order, Counselor, not just a legal opinion.

"I know they're nice to you here, and Zimmerman and Ritter support you. But you're still an outsider—and a Jew. We Kesslers have been in this country and in Capital City for five generations, the Meyeroffs for only two. We've learned not to get in the middle when the Gentiles fight each other: they at once drop their fight and unite against the pushy Jew. And this is a fight among the priests. You have no more business taking part in it than a Nice Jewish Girl like me has in joining the Altar Guild. They'd cut you into little pieces and feed them to the ducks."

"I had no idea, Sandra," said Meyeroff, taken aback by her vehemence, "that you were so unhappy here."

"Oh you ninny," she cried, getting up from the sofa and coming over to his chair, where she sat on his lap and put her arms around his neck. "It's precisely because I *am* so happy here that I don't want you to do anything that would endanger us. I'm happy because you love the job and enjoy what you are doing. You'd never have gotten the opportunity any other place, surely not in Chicago, where a law school dean can only live up to a great past and mustn't make waves. And I'm back home where I grew up, in the city I love, where the Kesslers have been important for over a century as business leaders and pioneers. The children are happy here. They love going out to Grandfather's farm on weekends, riding the ponies and going fishing and being spoilt by our old servants. And soon I'll even be able to get a payoff from my law school degree—though I don't think I'll ever get a bigger payoff than I've gotten already: the handsomest law school prof as a husband and three lovely kids. But when Susan is in third grade I'll go to work as a lawyer in one of the family businesses, the insurance company maybe or the bank. Both Dannie and Bobbie want me.

"No, it's precisely because I'm so happy here that I don't want you to do anything to endanger our life. And believe me, if you get mixed up in that fight, whoever wins, you'll lose. Anyhow, why should *you* lead with your chin? What's Erwin Ritter doing?"

"What's Erwin Ritter doing?" Sandra Myeroff was not the only one asking the question. Even Ritter himself was asking it. And the answer was, As little as possible.

Not that he did not want to act—he itched for action. But whenever he felt like taking the initiative, Bercovitz dissuaded him:

"That's just what they want, Father Dean; hysterical people need publicity, they need to be taken seriously, they need to be important. The less attention you pay them, the sooner they'll tire of the game. Minimize it, don't play it up. As far as you're concerned, the faculty has reaffirmed what has been standard policy all along—that's how Father Boerhave introduced his resolution, isn't it? In due course, when the Regents meet here at the end of March, you'll report it to them with all the other unimportant resolutions the faculty has passed since the last Regents meeting before Christmas. You know how one treats a child in a tantrum, don't you? Well, hysteria is a grown-up tantrum."

It was not easy for Ritter to follow the advice. Things got rough right after the Council meeting and the silliest rumors began to sweep the campus. Suddenly there were stories that Heinz Zimmerman and Agnes Muller had been seen together coming out of, or checking into, a hotel in New York or Washington or Chicago. It was total fantasy, or course. Agnes Muller had never taken one day's vacation and always stayed behind to keep the office running when the president was away. But although this was common knowledge, it didn't seem to stop the rumors.

"Do you think, Dr. Bercovitz," Ritter asked, "that someone is deliberately plotting a smear campaign?"

"Possible, but unlikely," was the doctor's answer. "Anyone trying to spread poison deliberately would think up a better story. Such wild ones are precisely the ones hysteria breeds spontaneously."

But there were also rumors that the Regents had met in extraordinary and stormy session and had asked Heinz Zimmerman to resign; that he had refused, and that the Regents thereupon had secretly appointed a search committee to look for a successor.

Again, the story was patently absurd. There had been no Regents meeting at St. Jerome since before Christmas, well before the Holloway incident that had started all the trouble. And if there had been one off campus, neither Zimmerman nor Ritter could have attended since neither man had been away from St. Jerome for a single day in the last two months.

"Shall I point this out to a few of the senior faculty members, Dr. Bercovitz?" Ritter asked.

"I'd rather you didn't," was the answer. "Of course, you give them the facts should they ask. Otherwise you pretend you haven't heard anything deserving serious attention. And you haven't really, have you?"

Which was what Erwin Ritter then said to everybody who urged him to do something: to Dean Grommet of the Engineering School; to Father Hausman, dean of the undergraduate school of arts and sciences; to Ashenbach and Meyeroff; and to many others. Not everyone was happy with the answer, though Ashenbach and Meyeroff seemed relieved, Ritter thought; but they all accepted it.

Harder, much harder, to deal with were the "volunteers," as Bercovitz called them.

The first was Clement Boglund, chairman of Chemistry.

Boglund had begun to feel uneasy the moment Oberhumer started his speech. Although he had long come to understand why Zimmerman had been so gruff and upset when he called on him to talk about the Holloway phone call, Boglund still felt that he had been treated roughly. But Oberhumer, he thought, was turning a moment of rudeness into a court-martial offense. And as Oberhumer kept on talking, Boglund became progressively more wretched. Were Heinz Zimmerman and the university he had helped him to build going to be destroyed just because his, Boglund's, vanity had been piqued?

Was he guilty of such gross self-indulgence, like a child spoilt rotten? If Oberhumer had gone on talking five minutes longer, Boglund would have voted against whatever motion he made or supported. He wavered, then caught Dennis Levecque's eye on him and abstained so as not to offend his closest friend.

But as soon as the vote was over, he began to curse himself for a fool and a coward. He spent a sleepless night becoming more and more upset by his own self-indulgence and irresponsibility. He had a class, his doctoral seminar, until eleven. Then he walked over to the Administration Building and into the dean's office and said:

"Erwin, I am here to offer my resignation as chairman of Chemistry and, if you think it'll help you or Heinz or St. Jerome, my resignation from the faculty altogether. I have allowed pride and vanity to overrule my judgment and have made a mountain out of a trivial slight. And I've done what I cannot forgive myself for: I've harmed the university and you and Heinz Zimmerman, just because my feelings were hurt."

"You're dead wrong, and I won't let you resign," Ritter said immediately. "In the first place you had reason to be hurt. Heinz was thoughtless and impetuous. We both know he rarely is; but he was that morning. We know that it was a trying time for him and why; but that's an explanation, not an excuse. So forget it."

"But look at what Oberhumer did with it yesterday," protested Boglund.

"That's Oberhumer, not you. Anyhow, he'd have found something else to beat us with. You were simply the stick nearest to his hand. Not a very dignified role, I grant you, but hardly something to make speeches about."

But Boglund would not budge until Ritter had pointed out that his resigning would do real harm, indeed, far more harm than Oberhumer had been able to do so far.

"If you resign now, Clem," he had said, "everyone will be convinced that Zimmerman and I forced you to and did it to punish you. They'll be absolutely certain that you were fired. Then that little tiff you had with Heinz, the kind of thing that happens in a big organization every day, will assume monstrous proportions. You couldn't do anything that would help Oberhumer or discredit the administration and Heinz Zimmerman more. Don't you see that, Clem?"

The only thing Ritter achieved—and that took an hour's patient talking—was Boglund's promise to postpone any action until June and the end of the academic year.

"You'll have more 'volunteers,'" Bercovitz warned, when Ritter called him as soon as Boglund had left. "The belief in self-immolation to appease angry gods is strong in our hearts."

The next to offer herself up as a human sacrifice three days later was Agnes Muller.

◆ ◆ ◆

"I have decided, Father Dean," she began, "that it is my duty to leave St. Jerome. It's the only home I have, and I've been happier here than I ever thought I could be. I don't know where I'm going to go or what I'm going to do the rest of my life. But I have no right to do more harm than I've already done. It was my selfishness that led to this vicious attack on Father President, which threatens his life's work. If I hadn't enjoyed working with him and serving him so much, I would have seen long ago that I was putting him in a false position and would have moved out of his office. I don't think he can ever trust me again."

She said all this with an appearance of utter calm and sweet reasonableness, as if she had carefully rehearsed it (as indeed she had). It was this rigid mask, this fiendish self-discipline, that infuriated Ritter. As he told Bercovitz later: "I felt like shaking her or choking her—anything to get her out of that martyr pose."

He didn't lay hands on her. But he did something as unprecedented, something no one in living memory had ever heard him do: he shouted at her so loudly that the secretaries in the adjoining offices came running out in near-panic:

"Stop feeling sorry for yourself, Agnes Muller, and wipe that self-righteous virgin smirk off your face! You aren't that important. So stop grandstanding."

Agnes's self-composure immediately crumpled. She began to sob wildly. "Father Dean," she said, when she could finally speak between her sobs. "I'm so ashamed. Not that people would say such things about me—I have been a married woman for a long time, after all, and have grown children. But that they can say such things about Father Heinz, and all because of me. And I'm afraid, too. Father Heinz is so changed. I hardly know him anymore. Oh, he's as polite and considerate to me as ever, and he lets me do even more of the work than before. But when he's alone and thinks himself unobserved, he just sits and stares into space or pretends to be busy without doing anything. He has to make a tremendous effort to be the Father Heinz we all know."

"Agnes," said Erwin Ritter, "that's more like you. Now you're making some sense.

"I sympathize with you; it must be very hard. But don't you see you mustn't desert Heinz now? Don't you see that now is the time when he needs everyone who loves him as you and I do? Forget that stupid rumor—you know that no one takes it seriously. You know how people love to gossip; it titillates. Is it the first time they've said things about you and another man? I bet is isn't. ("But I bet it is," said Erwin Ritter silently to himself). "Believe me, it isn't the first time they've said something about Father Heinz and women. That happens to every priest, and especially one like Heinz who takes his vows seriously. You'd only confirm the worst if you cut and run. It would be desertion in the face of the enemy.

"Yes, I realize Heinz is depressed," Ritter went on. "It's a rough time for him, and for all of us. But you know the university well enough to understand that the Holloway letter was only the match. Twenty years of rapid growth and success such as we've had create a lot of tension, a lot of friction. There are a number of people whose jobs have outgrown them and whose feelings of inadequacy make them bitter, suspicious, and hostile."

("I sound like Bercovitz," Erwin Ritter thought; and indeed he was repeating almost word for word arguments the psychiatrist had put forth just a day or two earlier. But they made sense to Agnes, who even raised a wan smile as if to say "I know exactly whom you have in mind.")

"Perhaps," Ritter continued, still paraphrasing Bercovitz, "it's a good thing that these tensions and problems are coming out, and that the occasion is nothing more serious than a poison-pen letter by a very sick woman. At least the boil is lanced.

"Believe me, Agnes, Heinz will bounce back. Just give him a few weeks. Right now he needs you, he needs everyone who cares for him and believes in him."

All this took endless time. But in the end Agnes Muller had wiped the tears off her face, calmed down, promised not to do anything rash or foolish, and had left. But as she went out the door, Erwin Ritter for the first time noticed that she did not walk like a girl or a young woman; there was no spring to her step and no sway to her hips. For the first time she looked and moved middle-aged.

"But also," he said later to Bercovitz, "for the first time I really liked her."

It had taken Ritter many years to accept Agnes Muller. He could have accepted a nun. But a lay woman, in the inner circles of a university run by an Order of Brothers, and a married one to boot, he had found hard to swallow. Gradually, however, Agnes's performance, her quiet efficiency, her devotion to St. Jerome and to Heinz Zimmerman had won him over. Yet the very qualities he had come to admire in Agnes Muller, the assistant to the president, had made him feel quite uncomfortable about Agnes Muller, the woman.

"I'm an old existentialist," he told Bercovitz when he reported his conversation with Agnes. "I know that there is a dark, emotional side to us, a soul and passions and existential despair. And I had never even glimpsed those in Agnes; nothing but self-control, composure, evenness, rationality. I just didn't know or see anything but a mask. Now I feel I know a person and one, I am confident, I can trust."

In fact, Ritter had been badly shaken by Agnes's visit. As a teenager he had been feared for his violent outbursts; he had mastered his temper by the time he was twenty. But when Agnes Muller talked about quitting, a wave of rage rose up in him such as he had not known for more than forty years. It took all his strength to make himself keep his hands off her. He was still trembling when she left, ashamed of himself but also quite frightened. "So the distemper that's turning St. Jerome into a madhouse has gotten to me, too," he thought.

Even worse, he had lied to Agnes Muller, or, at least, he had withheld the truth. To be sure, what he had said about Zimmerman was exactly what Dr. Bercovitz had told him; and Bercovitz, the trained psychiatrist, was the expert in emotional problems, after all. But Ritter himself did not share the doctor's optimism, nor his certainty that Zimmerman would bounce back completely very soon. He could not figure out what ailed Heinz; but it was serious, and he was worried.

Erwin Ritter had always relied on prayer, and he prayed more and longer these days than he had ever done before. Yet when he got up from his knees, again and again he found himself quoting the despairing words of Claudius in *Hamlet*:

Words without thoughts never to heaven go.

He had the words. But he did not have the thoughts. He did not really know what he was praying for. He could not figure out what ailed Heinz Zimmerman.

"Have I pushed him too fast," Ritter asked himself; "have I made it so easy for him that he has no immunity at all, no antibodies against the common afflictions of life?" Bercovitz, to whom he submitted this question, thought it most unlikely. "After all, Heinz has had troubles and problems and fights enough in all these years. And many of them, I'd guess, were far more serious than this Holloway affair, which isn't even a tempest in a tea cup; more like a tempest in a demitasse. Have any of them ever bothered him before?"

Ritter had to admit that not one of them ever did. "On the contrary," he said, "every one brought out the *Raufhansl* in Heinz."

Now it was as if all the energy had been drained out of the man. When Ritter went past the president's office and looked through the open door, he saw Heinz sitting at his desk staring at his trophy wall. Later he asked Bercovitz, "Have you heard of *accidie*?" The doctor shook his head.

"It was the occupational disease of medieval monks," Ritter said. "The torpor of the soul from which few ever recovered. That's what Heinz's condition reminds me of. Is taking a part of his workload off his shoulders really the only thing I can do, doctor?"

"Yes," said Bercovitz. "A wound has to heal by itself."

But it was not the answer Ritter wanted to hear, and surely not enough help to give the man of whom his inner voice years ago had said, "This is your son."

"Can't I at least ask him what ails him, doctor?" he had persisted.

"That's the last thing you should do, Dean Ritter," Bercovitz replied firmly. "You must wait till he comes to you to talk."

But when Ritter one morning again passed by the president's office and saw Heinz sitting at his desk idly shuffling papers, he went in on impulse and asked: "What *is* the matter with you, Heinz? I can't understand you letting Oberhumer get under your skin like this."

"Oberhumer?" Zimmerman responded in a voice of amazement. "I don't even think of Oberhumer. Actually, Erwin"—and suddenly the old Heinz Zimmerman was back—"St. Jerome could do worse than elect Oberhumer President after I am gone."

"Are you joking, Heinz?" asked Ritter, quite startled.

"No, I'm not. Oberhumer is a great scholar with a worldwide reputation. He has standards. He has proven himself a first-rate administrator; look at the way he's built up his department in no time at all. He is excellent at raising money, better perhaps than I am. And no one else in the entire faculty really cares about the university and thinks about it. The others think only of their own fields and concerns."

"But what about all that drivel he's forever talking about, 'faculty democracy' and 'administrative tyranny'?"

Heinz Zimmerman chuckled. "I didn't think he'd take you in, Erwin. The day he becomes President, Oberhumer will forget every word he ever said on that subject, I guarantee you. Anyhow, he may have a point, you know. St. Jerome may be getting too big for the way you and I are running it. Our successors surely will have to manage it quite differently.

"All told, Erwin," Zimmerman continued, "it's not the faculty that's bothering me. Sure, it would be nice to get a little support. And it does hurt, I admit, that no one these last weeks has come forward to say 'Thank you' to you and me. But I didn't expect it. It's only a few weeks since you warned me, when you told me you want to step down as dean by the end of the year, that there really isn't anyone on the faculty who is committed head and heart to the first-rate Catholic university."

Zimmerman fell silent and began to play around with the papers on his desk. But just as Ritter thought he should get up and leave, he began again.

"What really bothers me," he said, "is that I can't figure out anymore why I am doing all this, and for whom. You know, Erwin, the inscription over the door to this building: *Ad majorem Dei gloriam*? Every morning when I come to work it's given me a lift all these years and made me say to myself: 'To the greater glory of God.'"

"Me, too," said Ritter.

"It doesn't any longer, not since this Holloway business started. It mocks me now, taunts me, says: *Ad majorem Mei gloriam*. It all seems nothing but vanity and personal ambition, aggrandizement and self-interest, and the desire to prove to myself that I'm a great man."

"Heinz," said Ritter, thoroughly alarmed, "stop at once. You're talking like a spoilt teenager. Have you forgotten all you ever learned in philosophy and logic and theology? Have you forgotten the definition of a saint as someone who knows where his true self-interest lies? That the work matters, and not the workman? Believe me, *not* to know what you've achieved would be worse than stupidity; it would be a sin."

"Erwin, I know you're trying to help and mean well," Zimmerman said with a wan smile. "I'm grateful, believe me. But what you're saying is pure sophistry, and you know it."

"I've been called worse names," Ritter responded, and there was suddenly deep anger beneath his bantering tone. "Being a sophist is, after all, part of a dean's job description. But, don't you see, you are letting all of us down—the Order and the university, me and all the faculty who look to you for leadership, and yourself worst of all. You can't just run away from responsibility to indulge yourself in hurt and self-pity."

But Heinz Zimmerman did not reply. He sat staring silently in front of him. When Ritter a few minutes later got up to leave, he nodded and let him go without another word.

Seymour Bercovitz also had a talk with Heinz Zimmerman.

It was after the weekly dinner at Bercovitz's place, when the two men sat down for their game of chess. They had already set up the board and chosen sides. Zimmerman had drawn white and the right to open; but instead of making the first move, he leaned back in his chair and said:

"Remember, Seymour, how you told me last fall why you dropped out of the seminary and didn't become a rabbi? I'd like to tell you now why I did become a priest.

"Of course, I'd given quite a bit of thought to my future career all those years in the army during World War II. But I knew then that I was much too fond of women to belong in the priesthood; I thought I'd probably become a teacher, though 1 had no idea of what. And then I came back to St. Jerome as a student on the G.I. Bill, determined to get a good education but also to have a good time after all those boring years in the service. I did well in my studies—it was easy enough. But that first year back at school I spent far more time sleeping around than with my books.

"And then I got a girl pregnant. She wanted to marry, of course. But I didn't want to give up my freedom and I really didn't care that much for her, so I persuaded her to have an abortion. It wasn't easy then, you know. We neither of us had any money. And being Catholics—she was a sophomore at St. Mary in the Plains—we didn't know our way around and had no one we could ask for help. We finally found a woman who did abortions for the servant girls of Capital City. And she botched it. The girl got infected. She was in horrible pain and almost died. And all that week while I sat by her bedside in a mean little room downtown where the landlady extorted money from me with the threat of going to the police, I couldn't make myself even feel pity for that poor girl. All I could think about was that I would go to jail if she died. And then I realized that I hadn't ever cared for any of the girls I'd had affairs with, hadn't ever thought of them, but had just used them for my pleasure as if they were whores.

"As soon as that girl was out of danger and I had received absolution, I applied to become a priest."

"Why are you telling me all this, Heinz?" Bercovitz asked.

"Because I've realized in these last few weeks that I was quite mistaken about myself. I know now that I could have been as good a husband as any and as good a father."

"Do you regret that you went into the priesthood?"

"Oh, no, far from it. It was absolutely the right thing for me, absolutely my true vocation. Anything else would have been wrong for me. And that I did the right thing for the wrong reason, isn't that what we call Providence?

"You mean, Seymour, don't you, do I regret that I can't make love to Agnes and marry her? But it's a silly question. Agnes has made it clear, abundantly clear, that all she's interested in is her work and her working relationship with me.

"No, Seymour, what bothers me—upsets and confuses me—is that I realize I haven't changed. I am using people just exactly the way I used those girls before I went into the priesthood. Of course, I don't use them carnally. But I use them—and above all I use Agnes, for my purposes, to achieve what I want to achieve, and for my own satisfaction and self-glorification."

Long after Zimmerman had left, Bercovitz remained seated at the table looking at the chessboard. "Poor Heinz," he murmured to himself when, near midnight, he finally got up to put the set away. "He won't ever get back into the cocoon that has shielded him for thirty years. It'll be hard for him to have to learn to live with guilt and shame, self-doubt and ambiguity like all the rest of us."

Part Four

February turned into March—and early March was the meanest time of the year in Capital City, bringing the "Capital City specials": ice storms and freezing rains. Whoever could do so fled in early March. Jack Mulcahey, for instance, was in Palm Springs, and planning to stay there until the Regents' meeting at the end of the month. Phil Oberhumer, too, had escaped. He was in Ecuador or some such warm place on a geological survey for the World Bank.

What made early March particularly mean and depressing to the spirit were the first rare tantalizing glimpses of spring: a few days when the sky suddenly turned brilliantly blue, with small, fleecy white clouds sailing across it before a warm Southern breeze; when the first pussy willows were spotted on the banks of the still-frozen brook that meandered through the St. Jerome campus; and when a few hardy co-eds, like exotic butterflies, emerged from their winter cocoons of thermal underwear, longjohns, fur-lined boots and anoraks to sunbathe on the balconies of their dormitories in T-shirts and shorts. But these precious moments of spring were treacherous and deceptive. They actually signaled the next ice storm, or the next three-day freezing rain.

And yet—or so at least the optimists maintained—every one of these glimpses of spring lasted a little longer and every one brought a few more co-eds in T-shirts and shorts flaunting bare skin at the sun's rays and youthful laughter at middle-aged professors.

The emotional climate at St. Jerome that early March faithfully mirrored the weather outside. It was very mean indeed.

Everybody knew, of course, that the story of an affair between Heinz Zimmerman and Agnes Muller was pure fabrication. But increasingly heads nodded when someone sagely observed: "Where there's smoke, there's fire." Ritter was tried almost beyond endurance when three of the elderly St. Jerome priests on the faculty—total nonentities each but old-timers still—cornered him after Sunday Mass one day and said: "We know there isn't anything to that story; it's a vicious lie. But the President of St. Jerome? Shouldn't he be like Caesar's wife and above suspicion? It surely can't be good for the university to have a President of whom such stories are being told, however unfounded."

When Ritter finished telling the three what he thought of them, they looked very small and apologized like children who know they have been naughty. But what those three had said to him, Ritter realized, others were saying among themselves, only knowing better than to mention it in his presence.

The faculty mutiny also had not come to an end with the Boerhave resolution, but smoldered on after the Council meeting. Twice within one week Oberhumer's sidekick, the Life Sciences chairman, stormed into Ritter's office to "lodge a formal protest" against some perfectly normal and harmless administrative action: first it was a circular letter to all faculty members on the tenure track, advising them of the changes in tenure policy the Council had voted on; then it was a letter to all faculty reminding them that the dean's office had to sanction the use of a nonfaculty member as a substitute instructor for an absent professor. "I know that the Boerhave resolution didn't pass," Dr. Shoemacher said glibly. "But it was defeated because we were assured that it only codified already existing policy and was redundant. And now you are violating it both in letter and in spirit. Clearly, the administration has no intention of respecting the rights of chairpersons or of the faculty altogether, no intention of playing by the rules it officially endorses. We'll have something to say about this at the next Council meeting; and Phil Oberhumer will be back then."

What made this a genuine threat was that the Life Sciences chairman both times was accompanied by Dennis Levecque of Economics. Apparently the unholy alliance between "Great Research University" and "Great Catholic University"—the alliance to tear down Heinz Zimmerman and the university's administration—still held together.

Then, just like the weather outside, March began to bring the first signs of spring to the emotional climate. Or, rather, there were signs of a return to more normal, more conventional, more traditional turbulences. And as in the weather outside, the optimists could discern in the emotional climate that these intervals of normality were becoming more frequent and were lasting longer, and that they increasingly diverted the faculty from Heinz Zimmerman and the "Holloway Affair"—as it was now called by everyone, including the majority who had no idea who or what Holloway was—to more normal follies and idiocies, and especially to the deeply cherished traditional feuds of academia.

First there came an outbreak of the perennial wrangle between chairpersons of the university-wide departments and the deans of the individual schools over the assignment of teaching faculty. Did the schools, Business, say, or Engineering, have a veto power over which English or Physics instructor was assigned to teach in them? Was it perhaps even *their* job to decide which instructor should teach their students? Or did this power rest with the department and its chairperson?

Normally these silly disputes both disgusted and bored Erwin Ritter, and he settled them by banging heads together. They annoyed him just as much this March, but he almost welcomed them as the first sign that St. Jerome was moving back from a singularly mean to a normally silly season.

And then, right on schedule in the second week of March arrived the Annual Athletic Feud. In the twenty-seven years during which Ritter had been dean, there had been six or seven different athletic directors at St. Jerome. And each, the second week of March, had called a press conference of the state's sportswriters and started a public, raucous fight with one of the coaches. It would have been as funny as a Punch and Judy show if it had not been so drearily vulgar.

This year, Father Bernardi, the athletic director and the only St. Jerome football player ever to make All-American, called for the dismissal of the football coach, who had just concluded his fourth victorious season and was the hero of students and alumni alike. "He pads his expense account," he proclaimed; "and what's worse, his entertainment charges are not for high-school football coaches and prospective players. His guests are all female!"

Students took sides with gusto, and so did alumni. During one morning Erwin Ritter answered twenty-four phone calls from alumni, half demanding the coach's immediate discharge, the other half threatening to cancel their annual donation unless the athletic director was fired. But football was important also to the faculty, and especially to the priests on the faculty. In a stormy meeting in Ritter's office, Father Carstens, the senior priest on the faculty, chairman of Religion and of the Faculty Athletics Committee, and a football fan, screamed at Father Bernardi: "The coach is a layman and you have no goddamn business poking into his sex life!"

"I don't give a shit for his sex life," Bernardi screamed back; "he's a crook and steals from the university!"

Ritter had always dreaded the Annual Athletic Feud. But this year he reveled in it, even mischievously encouraged it. It was a nagging toothache; but at least it wasn't cancer.

And then at last Heinz Zimmerman was beginning to have sunny intervals, though for most of the time he was still as unfriendly, as gray and cloud-shrouded, as the March sky.

The first Sunday in March, Heinz even accepted an invitation, tendered him at Ritter's insistence, to have lunch with Erwin at Agnes Muller's house. As Agnes had predicted, her food was infinitely better than what the lay brothers provided at the president's residence, and all three greatly enjoyed the meal.

In the office, too, the old harmony seemed to reestablish itself. An extra desk still stood in Agnes's office. But it was unoccupied, Mrs. Lopez long ago having fled to the cozier atmosphere of the typists' pool with its coffee breaks and its companionable chats. Heinz Zimmerman and Agnes Muller were back at their old routine and the door between their offices was kept open again. If there was a change, it was that the president delegated far more to Agnes than he had ever done before and kept her working until late at night most days. But she didn't complain; at least Heinz hadn't lost his trust in her.

When the check for the first installment on the oil millionaire's pledge came in, Zimmerman threw a victory party in his office for his entire Executive Committee. And to everyone's surprise he proposed a formal vote of thanks to Philip Oberhumer, "who has done so much to bring to St. Jerome first-rate science and the means to sustain it."

In mid-March, almost five weeks after the Holloways had called on him that disastrous Sunday afternoon, the old Heinz Zimmerman, the forceful executive, finally reappeared, if only for an instant. All deans and chairpersons found in their mail a Letter from the President, which read:

> As you probably know, we intend to introduce during the next two academic years, that is between now and Spring Semester 1982, a required non-credit computer course in all professional schools— similar to the one already being taught in the Engineering and Management Schools. Within another twelve months we should then begin to introduce the same required non-credit course for undergraduates majoring in a science or social science or enrolled in the premedical program. We ourselves therefore had better make sure that we know what the computer is all about. I have arranged for computer courses for deans and chairpersons to be given on six consecutive Saturday evenings, the first to start on April 15. I myself have enrolled—please let me know when you intend to take it.

Erwin Ritter had tears in his eyes as he phoned Dr. Bercovitz to read him the letter. "Yes," said Seymour (they were beginning to be on a first-name basis), "that's the light at the end of the tunnel. I am a little bit superstitious. Accidents do happen, so I don't want to shout 'Hallelujah' yet. But barring an accident, this nasty affair should be behind us by the time your Regents meet for their next session at the end of the month. And then I'll invite you and Heinz and Agnes Muller to the best dinner I can serve—I'll cook and you can bring the champagne."

The Voice of Reason had had substantial circulation and considerable influence in the twenties, and even more so in the thirties when, faithfully following every twist and turn in the Stalinist line and nicknamed *The Voice of Treason*, it had been the house organ of fellow travelers in academia, journalism, and Hollywood.

It had died long before 1980, however. And the only reason the corpse had not been buried was that the founder, heiress to a Chicago meat-packing fortune, had made all the payments from her estate to her only son dependent on his continuing weekly publication of the magazine. Circulation had shrunk to 8,000, most of which went to libraries where no one read the copies. Advertising had disappeared except for a few pathetic "Personals": "Intelligent woman, college degree, still young, seeks correspondence with mature male professional who shares her interests in chamber music and progressive causes." And the magazine itself, both in its Art Nouveau layout and in the references to Sacco and Vanzetti and the Scottsboro Boys that studded its editorial pages, looked and smelled as musty as a bachelor's laundry hamper left unemptied the entire summer.

As far as anyone could discover, *The Voice of Reason* had only one subscriber in Capital City: the library of St. Jerome University. The librarian there had already decided not to renew; for quite a few years now she had not seen anybody take it up from the shelves, let alone read it. But within two days after she put the newly arrived issue, dated March 22, 1980, in the Periodicals Room, every one of the 970 members of the St. Jerome faculty, down to the lowliest graduate assistant, had seen and read a copy of the editorial that was advertised on the magazine's bright red cover in big black letters:

EDITORIAL: THE CASE OF ST. JEROME U.

When several months ago we discussed the remarkable address on the "Great Catholic University" by Heinz Zimmerman, monk and president of a Catholic university calling itself St. Jerome University, we were sharply criticized. We had pointed out the incompatibility of the beliefs and practices of the Roman Church: the Inquisition; the Index of Forbidden Books; Papal Infallibility; and the Roman Church's claim to have the duty to control the minds, morals, and beliefs of its members, with the very values—freedom of inquiry, thought, and expression, and the supremacy of reason as against revelation and dogma—on which any institution deserving the name "university" must be based.

This, we were told by several correspondents, is anachronistic. Today's Catholic Church, they asserted, has changed its spots.

It has embraced the beliefs of an open democratic society. Some of the letters even called us "old-fashioned" and "bigoted."

Now hear this! A most distinguished scientist on the St. Jerome University faculty, a geologist of world renown, felt it necessary recently to put forth a motion of censure against the apostle of the "Great Catholic University," Heinz Zimmerman, monk and president, for grossly violating the rights of the faculty and interfering willfully with faculty autonomy. When it came to the vote, only eight of the twenty-three departmental chairpersons—a bare one third—sided with the president and the university's administration over this issue. The majority even of the Catholic monks and priests in departmental chairs did not support the president in this vote, which surely argues that there is not, at St. Jerome University, enough respect for faculty rights and faculty autonomy to satisfy even the (presumably fairly modest) expectations of monks and nuns as to what a "university" has to be. And not one of the distinguished scholars and scientists whom Dr. Zimmerman has recruited for the faculty of St. Jerome University has seen fit since to speak out in defense of the university's administration.

We are further informed that there is a move afoot, especially among the monks and priests, to oust Dr. Zimmerman as president of St. Jerome University because of an alleged romantic involvement with a lady on his staff—both of them adults, of course, and, incidentally, unmarried. To consider the private life and behavior of a member of the academic community a public concern and relevant to the individual's fitness for office is as incompatible with what a "university" is all about as is thought control and administrative interference with faculty autonomy and academic freedom. Yet it is inherent in the creed, laws, and practices of the Roman Church.

Can there really be a "Catholic University," let alone a "Great Catholic University"? Has the Roman Church changed its spots—or is it still the Church of the Inquisition, of the Index of Forbidden Books, of Papal Infallibility, and of obscurantism and thought control?

And who deserves to be called "bigoted"?

"The Great Stone Face," Heinz Zimmerman had once, at a staff party, called Dean Ritter's long-time secretary; she had been so pleased with the compliment that she almost smiled. But when she brought back a Xerox copy of the editorial from her morning coffee break, "The Great Stone Face" was so upset that her voice broke. Her hands shook violently as she thrust the sheet across his desk at her boss.

"You ought to know by now," Ritter said mildly after he had read the page slowly twice, "that some people don't much like Catholics. Otherwise I see nothing in here that deserves getting excited about."

But few members of the faculty shared Erwin Ritter's opinion. No event in the whole history of St. Jerome—not even the merger with a woman's college, St. Mary in the Plains, which the priests on the faculty and the alumni had fought bitterly for three long years—had ever set off a firestorm comparable to the one unleashed by *The Voice of Reason*.

Ten or fifteen minutes after Ritter had read the editorial, Dennis Levecque burst into his office waving a copy of the sheet, almost blue in the face with rage and shouting at the top of his lungs: "Erwin, we'll sue the bastards for libel and get the last penny in damages out of them. This is an outrage!"

"Now wait a minute, Dennis," Ritter said with a touch of self-righteousness in his voice. "Of course the piece distorts. But everything it says is factual. What did you think Oberhumer's motion was if not a declaration of nonconfidence in Heinz Zimmerman and the St. Jerome administration? And who was the first to second it? You, Dennis."

"But you know, and so did everybody else in the meeting, that that wasn't my intention. You know I'd never attack St. Jerome."

"That time you did, Dennis," said Ritter dryly. "How do you think you'd look on the witness stand admitting that you immediately seconded the Oberhumer motion, but claiming that you never intended to do what you did?"

Dennis Levecque would not abandon his demand that St. Jerome should sue *The Voice of Reason* for libel, or, he said, "for defamation of character or invasion of privacy or slander or whatever else the lawyers can think up," until both Sister Renée, the public-relations vice president, and the university's outside lawyers had confirmed that there were no possible grounds for a suit. Even then, he wanted the university to demand a public retraction; and he actually drafted a Letter to the Editor protesting that he had never meant what the editorial imputed to him.

When Levecque finally had to admit that ignoring the editorial was the only possible course, he turned on Ritter: "Why didn't you warn me, Erwin, that I would be totally misunderstood? You saw it, yet you didn't do anything to stop me or protect me. You and Heinz Zimmerman let me down. I'll never forgive the two of you!"

No sooner had Erwin Ritter disposed of Levecque than he had to deal with Jim Schenk, a professor of classics and one of the oldest of the St. Jerome priests on the faculty. It was Schenk whom Ritter had taken to task a few days earlier for worrying about the damage which the rumor of an affair between Heinz Zimmerman and Agnes Muller might do to the university and the Order. "Now you see, Erwin," Jim Schenk said, "that we were right to worry. Zimmerman is endangering St. Jerome and all of us by his imprudence. The sooner he quits as President, the sooner this will be forgotten."

"You know there's nothing to the story, don't you, Jim?" Ritter asked. Father Schenk nodded. "Now, how would you feel if there were such a story about you, which all of us knew to be totally groundless and pure fabrication, and we asked you to resign?"

"But, Erwin," Schenk retorted, "I'm a nobody, not the university's President, a national figure and on the cover of *Time*. What I do and what they say about me cannot possibly harm anyone but myself. But a man in Zimmerman's position has failed in his duty if he gets attacked like this, even if it's totally groundless. He has given aid and comfort to the enemy"—and Schenk rambled off into a long quotation from Horace or Virgil.

Then there were the deans and chairpersons and professors who earlier had wanted "to do something" or had wanted Ritter "to do something." Each of them now came and blamed Ritter for putting them in a position where *The Voice of Reason* could point to their inaction as proof of their joining in the attack on Zimmerman. Even Zimmerman himself, showing normal emotions for the first time in weeks, came to Ritter to complain about being attacked and vilified and wanting to know what the university could and should do about it.

And Agnes Muller came back to offer her resignation once more and to blame herself again for having betrayed Heinz Zimmerman and St. Jerome. "At least," thought Ritter, "she blames herself. All the others blame Zimmerman or me."

But whereas St. Jerome was erupting like a volcanic park with geysers and foul-smelling gases, mudslides and minor earthquakes, no one on the outside, it seemed, paid the slightest attention to *The Voice of Reason* and its editorial. Apparently nobody had seen the piece, let alone read it.

"You insult me, Sister Renée," the editor of the *Capital City Gazette*, the state's leading morning paper, said when she called him to make sure he wouldn't run the story. "I'd be ashamed to take note of anything that appears in that rag."

The much younger editor of the smaller but friskier afternoon paper, the *News* (a newcomer to Capital City, where he had moved only three years earlier) had never even heard of *The Voice of Reason*. "Sounds like something that was published during the American Revolution," he said. "Hold on, that was *The Age of Reason*, wasn't it?" And when he was read the editorial over the phone, he chortled and said: "Sister Renée, any news about St. Jerome University is news in Capital City. But don't tell me this is *news*. Maybe the fact that a faculty and its president *aren't* squabbling might be news these days. But who cares for faculty motions? And even though I'm a practicing Catholic myself, I couldn't get excited these days about a story of a priest having a girl friend, whether it's true or not."

Nor did Seymour Bercovitz seem perturbed when Ritter phoned him. "What," he said, "*The Voice of Reason* still exists? My father used to subscribe to it some forty years ago when I was a youngster. He dropped his subscription when it endorsed the Stalin-Hitler Pact in 1939. Since then I haven't even heard of the sheet—and I daresay nobody else has, either. No one reads it. No one pays any attention to it. I bet you nobody under fifty today has even heard of it. You wouldn't pay much attention to a story about St. Jerome in the *Arkansas Beekeeper* or the *Idaho Turnip Grower*, would you? Then why pay attention to *The Voice of Reason*?"

Which was what Erwin Ritter then told everyone on his own faculty, as well as Heinz Zimmerman and Agnes Muller.

"No one reads the sheet or even knows about it," Ritter also said to Father Tom Martini, when the young priest called to enquire what he should tell his bishop.

Martini himself had never heard of *The Voice of Reason*. But when one of the young priests on the St. Jerome faculty—a former classmate in the seminary—told him of the editorial, he thought it his duty to show it to Bishop O'Malley; after all, St. Jerome was in the bishop's diocese. He could not, however, find a single copy anywhere in Capital City. The magazine was not in the public library nor in the state house nor in the legislative reference library of the state legislature. Indeed, the three librarians of these institutions assured him that it had long ceased to exist. He had to drive out to St. Jerome and its library to find a copy to Xerox, and then called on Dean Ritter to find out what he should tell Bishop O'Malley and, indeed, what all the fuss was about.

And so when, the following morning, Monsignor Allesandri called from Washington and asked the bishop about the editorial, O'Malley answered: "Pay no attention; I myself didn't know that this magazine is still being published. And as far as we can figure out, there is just one subscriber in all of Capital City, the St. Jerome University Library. Nobody reads the sheet."

"I don't think, Patrick," said Allessandri in the bantering tone which he only used when he was in deadly earnest, "you'd call His Excellency the Nuncio a 'nobody.' He has read the editorial and is quite perturbed by it.

"But that's not the main reason why I'm calling. Patrick, Rome wants to know about this editorial and what's going on at St. Jerome. You may be right about the unimportance of *The Voice of Reason* in the United States. I admit I myself had never heard of the magazine. But in Italy and Spain and Portugal, and especially in the Soviet bloc countries with large Catholic populations—Hungary, Poland, Czechoslovakia, and East Germany—*The Voice of Reason* is still widely quoted and considered the liberal conscience of the United States, its one 'progressive' publication and the true voice of the repressed proletarian masses of America. This editorial is bound to be picked up and reprinted widely; it's just too convenient for those, in Poland, for instance, who want to discredit the Church's demand for a bigger say in higher education. Of course it won't matter if that happens in the daily press. But if the intellectual monthlies of the left in France or Italy run with it, it could do a good deal of damage—and it couldn't come at a worse time than now when Rome, for the first time, sees a chance for a dialogue with the intellectuals on the left."

Monsignor Allessandri paused ("He's consulting his notes," Bishop O'Malley thought), then continued in a brisker tone. "I would have called you up anyhow, Patrick, to give you good news. Your request to Rome to raise Capital City to an archbishopric is doing much better than I dared hope. You were right: Rome has wanted to do this all along and was just waiting for the proper moment.

"But if you don't do something to show that there is no substance whatever to this attack on a leading Catholic university and a prominent American priest—both in your diocese—well, Patrick, you know how timid the Curia is.

"I'll tell His Excellency the Nuncio what you've told me about *The Voice of Reason*, and I'll pass it on to Rome, of course. But, Patrick, what is the name of that brilliant young diplomat, your secretary?— ah yes, Father Tom Martini—one of your good Irish names, I take it. Why don't you put this young man on the job to extricate yourself and this Father Heinz Zimmerman, and to find a solution that shows this attack is a lie and there's no scandal brewing at St. Jerome University, and no unseemly quarrel among the priests in your diocese?"

• • •

"I don't really know how to explain it," a deeply disturbed Tom Martini said three days later to his Bishop. "There's something terribly wrong at St. Jerome. But I can't figure out what it is. The little that's tangible is all trivia. I was reminded the whole time of when I was twelve or thirteen and my sister and I used to bitch and scream at each other: 'You've used my scissors without asking my permission!' It's all on that level. It's one man's wounded ego and another man's envy and gossip and backbiting. But it's sick, very sick. Dean Ritter holds the place together, sort of; but he's hanging on for dear life and doesn't seem to know what to do, or even whether to do anything.

Yet the place is losing its self-confidence and decency and cohesion by the hour.

"Everyone blames somebody else for starting the trouble. The priests blame the lay faculty, and both blame the Order's General or the chairman of the Regents. And everyone protests that he himself, of course, is totally blameless and has done nothing but pour oil on troubled waters."

"'And Brutus is an honorable man,'" Bishop O'Malley said, half under his breath.

"And the worst of it," Tom Martini continued, "is that every one of these great scholars and good Christians blames Father Zimmerman. And when you ask them what Father Zimmerman has done to be blamed for, they say in effect: 'He hasn't done anything but shouldn't have done it.' I felt like throwing up the whole time I was out there.

"And yet," added Martini after a short pause, "I just can't figure out what all this nastiness is about. The only specific complaint— if you can call it that—is that Father Zimmerman disregarded etiquette and phoned directly to a neighboring women's college to find a job for a middle-aged professor whose contract won't be renewed, instead of going through the department chairman. Everyone admits he did it out of pity for the man, but says he shouldn't have done it."

"'And Brutus is an honorable man,'" the bishop muttered again.

"But the worst of it, sir," Martini went on, "is Father Zimmerman's having given up. He's a defeated man, and no one can figure out why. He sits in his office, leaving everything to Dean Ritter; he hardly speaks to people.

"Dean Ritter asked me to have a word with a friend of his and of Father Zimmerman's, a Dr. Bercovitz, a psychiatrist. He's the State Commissioner of Mental Health. Do you know of him, sir?"

"I've heard he's a competent man," the bishop answered. "What did he tell you?"

"He called the Holloway Affair a 'storm in a demitasse'—rather clever, I thought, and quite apt. Of course, he's right. It's a petty business. But to use his metaphor, it's cracked the demitasse to where it can't be glued together again. I don't see how Father Zimmerman can ever again truly run the place the way he used to and the way it should be run. Not because St. Jerome won't accept his leadership. I agree with Dean Ritter that it wouldn't take much to get the St. Jerome faculty to return to sanity and self-discipline, if only Father Zimmerman took the lead and asserted himself. The faculty itself, I'd say, is quite scared of the mischief it's been making. But I don't see Father Zimmerman recovering. Whatever ails him, he seems to have lost his self-confidence and his belief in himself and what he's been doing. He hasn't been dethroned; he abdicated at the first challenge."

"All these trivia you describe," said the bishop thoughtfully, "are just symptoms, I'd say. The real issues, I am convinced, go much deeper. Twenty years of mushroom growth has pushed everything out of alignment at the university, so that no one can really know what the rules are. Worse, there is still the unanswerable question of what a Catholic university has to do in order to be first-rate, or a 'first-rate university' has to do to be Catholic—you remember our talk a few weeks back?

"But, Tom, no matter what the real issues are, we have to help Heinz Zimmerman. His only offense is in having yielded to the temptation to do good and behave like a Christian and a priest rather than a bureaucrat."

"I don't know, sir," Martini replied, "what we could do. The place is so totally demoralized. Do you remember Hemingway's *Farewell to Arms*?"

The bishop nodded.

"The rout of the Italian Army after the Austrians smashed it in World War I? I read that chapter over again last night to make sure I remembered it right. That's what St. Jerome reminds me of: a lot of defeated and leaderless people running away in all directions, united only in their hatred of their own High Command."

"And do *you* know, Tom," the bishop said with sudden animation, "what stopped that rout of the Italian Army after Caporetto? Of course you don't; I don't think it's in the novel. What made the Italians become an army again were the big naval guns of the English and French fleets in the Mediterranean. They were hauled on land and began to bombard the retreating Italians, who were left no choice but to turn around and fight the enemy again.

"Well, in the Church, the bishop is the big gun. It's my job to stop this poisonous rot at St. Jerome. After all, this is *my* diocese, not the diocese of the Nuncio or Monsignor Allessandri. And the priests at St. Jerome are priests in *my* diocese. I am responsible for their behavior. I don't know precisely yet what I'll do. But at the very least I'll call in the St. Jerome priests one by one, read them the riot act, and threaten them with everything I can think of unless they rally behind Heinz Zimmerman. I'll be the naval gun; I'll make such a noise that they'll have to listen!

"I know, Tom, you'll remind me that I'm critical of Father Zimmerman and very dubious about his whole policy. But that's got nothing to do with it; it's a matter of common decency and conscience. What's going to happen later at St. Jerome, we'll see. But first it's my duty to protect Heinz Zimmerman."

"The Nuncio and Monsignor Allessandri will hardly like this," the startled Tom Martini said. "What will it do to your request to have Capital City raised to an archbishopric?"

"The good Catholic people of Capital City," the bishop said with something like a smile in his voice, "will just have to survive without it for another ten or twenty years. The Nuncio might not get to be proto-Secretary of State and a cardinal when he returns to Rome in a few years. And Allessandri might have to wait a mite longer for the bishopric he wants so badly he can taste it." ("And you, Tom," the bishop added to himself, "might end up a vice chancellor rather than a bishop.") "But I haven't taken an oath to further the Nuncio's career. My duty is to this diocese."

"You make it sound very grim, Bishop," Tom Martini said. "Don't you see any way out?"

"There's always one," the bishop said. "It's called a miracle. Sure, I'd rather not have to wade into this sewer and play the heavy, and no one is going to thank me for it either, least of all Zimmerman. It would be nice if the Lord sent down a fiery chariot for Heinz. But miracles, Tom, don't happen just because you and I want to avoid unpleasantness.

"No, we'll have to fight this one out—never mind *The Voice of Reason* and Rome and the Nuncio and Monsignor Allessandri. Why don't you go downstairs and huddle with Bernie Murtagh and work out a plan of action—no one around here knows politics as well as Bernie. And then I'll go to work. I don't think we can wait for Providence to do the job for us."

But Providence did in fact intervene, although Bishop O'Malley was to wonder more than once whether the miracle had been sent from above or from below.

Bernie Murtagh was on the telephone when Tom Martini entered his office. He was talking in the exaggerated Irish brogue—a vaudeville actor of the twenties would have been ashamed to affect it—he only used when speaking to politicians. But he cupped a hand over the receiver and muttered, "Won't be a minute," while waving Martini to a chair.

"Faith, Timmy-me-lad," he said heartily into the phone, "you're in a fine pickle. But we'll find a solution, trust me. Give me a while to think and I'll be back at you."

"Quite unimportant and can wait," he said in his usual voice when he had hung up. "Now, what can I do for His Efficiency?"

"You know anything about the troubles at St. Jerome University, Bernie?" Martini began. And when Murtagh shook his head, Tom started to tell him the story. At first Murtagh listened in silence. Then he began to ask questions, got Tom to repeat parts of the story, wanted more details, and became more and more interested. And when Tom finally got to telling him what the bishop had said about "a miracle," Bernie Murtagh burst into loud laughter. "So, His Efficiency doesn't believe in miracles! Maybe what we have won't quite satisfy the canon lawyers and the theologians, they're so picky. But it's miracle enough for me."

Martini stared at him with wide-open eyes.

"I was talking to Timothy Doyle when you came in, Tom," Murtagh said. "The name mean anything to you?"

Martini shook his head.

"Officially he is State Highway Commissioner. He's Governor Ewing's political adviser and his campaign manager.

"You know anything about the politics in this state, Tom, or do you only read the *Diocesan Messenger*? Okay, let me brief you. You know this is normally a Republican state?" Martini nodded. "And you do know that three and a half years ago we elected a Democrat as Governor in the backlash against Watergate, for the first time since New Deal days and with a greater majority than the one with which Jimmy Carter carried the state? And I imagine you know that Governor Ewing comes up for reelection this fall, and that the state is rapidly moving back into the Republican column, even though Ewing himself is remarkably popular?"

Martini nodded a few more times.

"But I bet you, Tom," Murtagh continued, "that you do not know that our last Republican governor, Colebrooke, who will try for a comeback this fall, created a Civil Rights Commission in a bid for the votes of the liberals and the minorities and especially the blacks the year before he was defeated for reelection? You ever heard of it?" Martini shook his head.

"You and the other seven million citizens of this great state," commented Murtagh.

"I bet you also never heard of the Reverend Thomas Langley Gould of the African Methodist Church? No, you're too young. Fifteen, twenty years ago he cut quite a figure in the state—a friend of Dr. Martin Luther King, a participant in the March on Selma, prominent black orator, invited by the Kennedys to the White House, and so on. A pompous windbag, actually, and he never did anything but chase publicity. Governor Colebrooke made him chairman of the Civil Rights Commission and its one and only full-time paid commissioner with a fat salary and a big staff. Of course, you don't know any of this—you weren't meant to. For Gould wasn't appointed to *do* anything. His appointment was intended to satisfy the blacks without upsetting anyone else. And everybody was perfectly happy to have him do nothing except make a few speeches and travel the state accompanied by three or four very young, very lush secretaries."

"You're a cynic, Bernie," Martini said.

"No, Tom, I am not, otherwise I'd have gone into real estate rather than politics.

"But let me go on with what Tim Doyle was telling me when you just came in. Everything was hunky-dory. The governor was going to reappoint the Reverend Thomas Langley Gould to another five-year term as chairman at $62,500 a year when his appointment expires next month—I think Doyle said the date is April 15. Then, to use Doyle's words: 'The bastard double-crossed the governor and suddenly died,' three weeks ago. And now the governor is on the hook. What should have been routine has become a life-and-death matter. There are more than enough candidates for the job. But to appoint any one of them would cost our governor the election sure as God made little apples.

"The blacks want one of their own again, of course. And they do have a candidate: Ralph Christenberry of the state AFL-CIO."

"Oh no," said Martini.

"Oh yes," said Murtagh. "I see you *do* read something beside the *Diocesan Messenger*, so you know that Christenberry as AFL-CIO state director made headlines a few months ago by coming out for the PLO and against Israel, and by that violent attack on the Jews in which he called them 'Sheenies,' 'Shylocks,' and 'Yids.' I don't have to tell you what the reaction of the liberals and the Jewish business community would be to having *him* appointed chairman of the Civil Rights Commission. The governor desperately needs the campaign contributions from the Jewish business community, the Fynemans and Kesslers and the rest of them.

"But what you can't know, Tom—unless you also read *La Causa*, the Spanish-language weekly—is that Mr. Christenberry also attacked the Chicanos in the state, accusing them of taking jobs away from decent American workers and demanding an end to immigration from Mexico and deportation of all illegal Mexican aliens. I don't know what Christenberry's game is. I suspect he plans to run for Congress from the solidly black district on the south side of town. But in any event he can't be appointed—and yet he refuses to withdraw, and the blacks refuse to nominate another black for the job.

"The Hispanics have nominated a Professor Fernandez—he teaches at one of the state colleges—who has come out against busing and accused the state government of favoring blacks over Hispanics. And the liberals have a candidate of their own, supported by the business community. He's Judge Rosenbaum, of the State Court of Appeals, who was chairman of Americans for Democratic Action in the state and is married to one of the department-store Fynemans.

"Do you see now why your Father Zimmerman is a miracle? He'll get everybody off the hook—not just you and the bishop and St. Jerome but the governor and everyone else. You tell me he was on President Johnson's Civil Rights Commission? Wonderful. We have a thirty percent Catholic population in this state. He's a distinguished educator and he's never before taken part in local politics and has no enemies. He couldn't be better!

"Let me just check back with Tim Doyle. Of course I'll tell him it would be a miracle if Father Zimmerman were willing to accept the job. And then let's go to work—we have very little time."

Tom Martini could never remember much of the next few days. They were a blur of endless telephone calls, meetings at odd hours, hasty conferences, and improbable "crises." He could not recall having gone to bed at all during those days, nor having eaten. Most of the time, it seemed to him, was spent sitting in Sister Renée's conference room (it had become their command post) and waiting, waiting, waiting.

"I don't think we can get the ideal," she warned, "a public offer of the job to Father Zimmerman, which he could then turn down but which would show everyone inside and outside the university that there's nothing to these vicious rumors. Tim Doyle is too shrewd to go out on that limb. But if we get an offer at all—and I think we have a chance—and Father Zimmerman can be persuaded to take it, I'd say a hundred Hail Marys."

Sister Renée immediately mobilized her contacts in the state government, the governor's press secretary and the social secretary of the governor's wife, both alumnae of St. Mary in the Plains and both enthusiastically willing to help. She also dispatched Tom Martini to enlist Seymour Bercovitz, who in turn talked to his friend, the governor's counsel, and got his support. A contrite, remorse-stricken Dennis Levecque, pathetically eager to undo the damage he perceived he had done, talked his friends in the labor movement into supporting Zimmerman's nomination; his compelling argument was the almost certain loss of the governorship to the Republicans should the civil rights job go to anyone but a distinguished and neutral outsider.

But the decisive move was sending Dean Meyeroff to talk to his brothers-in-law, the Kesslers. When Bobbie Kessler, that year chairman of the State Chamber of Commerce, telephoned Tim Doyle to tell him that Judge Rosenbaum had withdrawn his candidacy and that the business community of Capital City would support Heinz Zimmerman and no one else, the battle was won.

Or almost won. As Sister Renée had predicted, Tim Doyle refused to have the governor offer the job unless Zimmerman would declare his acceptance beforehand. And no one, of course, had even mentioned the job to Zimmerman, let alone obtained his consent. But who could talk to Heinz Zimmerman and persuade him to take the offer?

There was only one person who had a chance to be listened to: Erwin Ritter.

It took a whole morning to persuade him to take on the mission. Then Ritter disappeared into the president's office and they all waited endlessly, saying nothing, in Ritter's conference room. What happened between the two no one was ever told. Ritter was gone for two hours or more.

When he reappeared, he looked a very old man, said simply, "He'll take it," and vanished into his office, firmly closing the door behind him.

It took another week to work out all the details. But the following Monday morning the *Capital City Gazette* carried on its front page a four-column article:

ZIMMERMAN NEW CIVIL RIGHTS CHAIR

At a hastily called press conference last night Governor Willie Ewing announced the appointment of Father Heinz Zimmerman to a five-year term as Chairman of the state's Civil Rights Commission. Father Zimmerman, 56, has been President of Capital City's St. Jerome University for almost twenty years. He will be sworn in as Chairman of the Civil Rights Commission on April 15, with Bishop O'Malley of the Roman Catholic Diocese of Capital City administering the oath of office.

"I know of no one more qualified to fill this important position than Heinz Zimmerman," Governor Ewing said. "He is one of our nation's most distinguished educators and one of the state's most distinguished citizens. He has served the cause of civil rights with great distinction on a Presidential Civil Rights Commission. And he has the full support of all groups in the state."

Father Zimmerman's appointment is indeed being widely applauded. "We have full confidence in Heinz Zimmerman, his objectivity, his knowledge, and his humanity," declared Mr. Ralph Christenberry, state director of the AFL-CIO and chairman of Capital City's Black Caucus. "An outstanding Christian and a fine choice," was the comment of Rev. George Hammond of Park Avenue Congregational Church and chairman of the City's Ministerial Council. "This appointment should satisfy everyone," declared Professor Carlos Fernandez of Buffalo Junction State College and state director of *La Causa*. "The state can be congratulated on this appointment," we were told by Mr. Robert Kessler, chairman of the State Chamber of Commerce; "we are fortunate indeed to have so distinguished a man in our midst."

The state's Civil Rights Commission was created by former Governor Colebrook in 1975. Its first chairman was the Rev. Thomas Langley Gould, whose sudden death a few weeks ago created the vacancy Father Zimmerman has now been appointed to fill. The job pays $62,500 a year.

And on the front page of the paper's second part with the local news there was another banner headline, with an even longer article:

PREXY LEAVES ST. JEROME U.

St. Jerome University announces that its long-time President, Father Heinz Zimmerman, has resigned, effective immediately, to accept appointment as Chairman of the State's Civil Rights Commission (see also front-page story).

"We are unhappy," the chairman of the university's Board of Regents, Mr. Jack Mulcahey, declared, "to lose Heinz Zimmerman. He has made St. Jerome University what it is today. But we realize that our claims must take a back seat to those of public office. And we are proud that Heinz Zimmerman has been selected to fill so important a position."

Father Zimmerman has been on the St. Jerome faculty since 1952, when he received his doctorate in Logic from Freiburg University in Germany. He became the university's Acting President in 1960 and its President two years later, in 1962. Under his leadership St. Jerome University has grown from a student body of fewer than 2,500 to 12,000 students today, has gone fully co-educational, has increased its faculty from 120 to almost 1,000 members and its endowment from $4.5 to $59 million. When Father Zimmerman took over as Acting President, St. Jerome University had a Law School and an Undergraduate School of Business in addition to the Undergraduate College of Arts and Sciences. It now has a full Graduate School of Arts and Sciences offering masters and doctors degrees in all academic disciplines; a Graduate School of Management; a fully accredited Engineering School offering both a bachelor's and a master's degree; and professional schools in Nursing, Dentistry, and Pharmacy. It has achieved national stature and is considered to be on a par with leading research universities such as Chicago, Yale, and Stanford.

Father Zimmerman's achievements have been recognized by many honors and awards, including honorary doctorates from Columbia University in New York City and from Notre Dame University. He has twice been featured on the cover of *Time* magazine.

Pending selection of a new President, Father Erwin Ritter, 63, has been appointed Acting President. Father Ritter has been Dean, Executive Dean, and Chief Academic Officer of St. Jerome University since 1954. He has agreed to serve as Acting President to the end of the current calendar year. "I am convinced," he told our reporter, "that we will have selected a new President by Christmas. The Board of Regents has already appointed a search committee headed by Mr. Jack Mulcahey, the board's chairman. We shall look both inside and outside the university and at both lay people and religious. We already have several very promising candidates in mind."

In a related action, Mr. Jack Mulcahey, the university's board chairman, announced that he was making a donation in the amount of $1.5 million to establish a Heinz Zimmerman Distinguished University Professorship in Philosophy at St. Jerome University. At Father Zimmerman's request, Acting President Erwin Ritter has agreed to become the first occupant of the new chair upon stepping down as the university's Acting President at the end of 1980.

"Do you believe me now, Martin?" Lisa Holloway asked her husband when he came dashing into her bedroom, woke her up, and excitedly showed her the announcement of Heinz Zimmerman's resignation as president of St. Jerome University in the *Capital City Gazette* he had just picked up outside the door. "I told you I'd make them pay.

"And don't tell me again," she continued, "that I was unfair to him. You didn't believe me that he knew we were being persecuted by a Godless, anti-Catholic conspiracy. But if he hadn't had a guilty conscience he wouldn't have made that telephone call to Harriet Beecher Stowe to get a teaching job for you. That proved he knew that he should have reappointed you and was just too much of a coward to do it.

"You were appalled when I said aloud that the relationship with Agnes Muller is a scandal and immoral. Remember, you told me it wasn't true? But do you really think they would have panicked the way they did if there hadn't been something to it? When they immediately put a typist into the office where those two had been together so cozily, I knew I was right. If they'd been innocent, they wouldn't have done that.

"Well, at least I've spoilt their fun and games and brought a little truth and decency into the stinking mess that's St. Jerome."

"Yes," said her husband meekly, "I admit you were right and I was wrong. Thank God it's over.

"But, Lisa," and he suddenly grew animated, "I have wonderful news! You know how depressed I've been about not landing a job yet for next fall. My resume has gone to every Catholic college in the country and we didn't even get a single nibble. And the St. Jerome checks will stop coming in three months.

"Last night after you'd gone to bed, Boglund called. He's lined up a job as senior scientist in the testing lab of a big pharmaceuti-

cal company in Chicago. I'll get a formal offer within a day or two—
and the job pays more than twice what I've been getting as assistant
professor."

"*Martin Holloway*," she screamed, "you must know I'll leave you
the moment you take a job in industry! I won't live with a man who
helps capitalist swine make filthy profits out of poor people's sickness. You were nothing but a tool of those exploiters when I first met
you, and a heathen to boot. You go back to your vomit like a dog. I
won't follow you!"

"Lisa, Lisa," he groaned, and tried to take her hand in his, only to
have it snatched back when he touched it, "you know I need you. You
know I love you. I realize how much I owe you—how you led me from
my wasted, Godless life to the true faith and into the true Church,
and how you slaved for me for four years typing in that dreary office
so I could give up my job and go back to graduate school.

"But, Lisa, I've told you often enough that capitalists and capitalism had nothing to do with my work in industry. No matter what the
system or who runs it, somebody has to do what I was doing—and I
did it better, I daresay, than I've done my teaching. Whoever does the
job, wherever it's done, it's got to be done the same way: make sure
that the water is pure and the ingredients uncontaminated, that the
right yeast strains go into the fermentation tanks and the drugs that
come out are pure and potent. I wasn't exploited, no matter who else
might have been. I was paid well and treated right."

"Martin Holloway, I forbid you to talk such drivel," Lisa said, sitting bolt upright in bed. "You are not going back to industry—not as
long as I'm alive.

"But don't worry, Martin," she added in a quieter voice. "I have it
all worked out. Remember the Catholic Commune in the New Mexico mountains, the one I told you about where I lived for two years
in the late sixties before I went back to Cleveland to finish college
and met you? I've written to the priest who runs it. He's forgiven me
for leaving ten years ago and is willing to take me back and have
you join—there are still a few people left there. It's going to be hard
work; we try to raise all our own food. But we lead a Christian life
like the early followers of Jesus. And at least we'll have the one hun-

dred and sixty dollars a month extra from the trust fund my father set up when I first went off to college. I wrote Father Joseph to expect us around the first of June."

Holloway started to say something. Then he looked at his wife's face and thought better of it.

Agnes Muller was sitting at her desk on which lay a copy of the *Capital City Gazette*, with her head buried in her arms and sobbing, when Heinz Zimmerman arrived at the office that Monday morning. She did not even look up when he came in and wished her good morning, nor did she return his greeting. "Agnes," he cried, thoroughly alarmed, "what is the matter? We've known of my leaving for a week, there's nothing new. Why has the announcement upset you?"

And when she did not respond, he said: "I didn't want to talk to you about it until my appointment had become official. But Agnes, my dear, I count on you to continue as my partner in the new assignment. I plan to appoint you the Commission's staff director the day I take office—I've already cleared it with John Lindstrom, the governor's counsel."

"No, Heinz," she muttered in a weak voice. "No, please, no.

"Heinz, please don't scold me, I couldn't take it. But Erwin Ritter came to my house yesterday and I accepted his offer to become vice president of Administration and Budgets for St. Jerome. He's going to appoint Sister Mary Annunciata from the Women's Campus to work under me as my assistant and the university's budget director. I didn't want to take it—all I want is to get away from St. Jerome and Capital City as fast and as far as I can. But Erwin pleaded with me to stay and help him preserve what you've built here and to continue your work.

"Oh, Heinz," she wailed, "I didn't want to say yes, but what else could I do?"—and she buried her face in her arms again and began to cry wildly.

"Don't desert me, Agnes, please. Agnes, I need you." He put his hands in a tender gesture on her shoulders and awkwardly, clumsily tried to caress them.

But she shook his hands off, almost violently.

"Don't touch me. Don't touch me!" Her voice rose to a pitch of hysteria. "It's too late." But she calmed down right away. "Don't worry about me, Heinz," she said. "I'm used to being a widow."

A mulish look, the look of a pouting ten-year-old, came over Heinz Zimmerman's face. Wordlessly, he left Agnes, walked through the door into his office, and began to take down the honorary doctorates from his trophy wall.

"I'll leave on a three-week vacation until I'm sworn in on the new job," he said aloud, as if talking to no one in particular.

At this moment, his telephone rang. He hesitated a second. But Agnes made no move to pick it up, so he answered it himself.

It was Seymour Bercovitz.

"Heinz," he said, "I'm calling to give you my very, very best wishes for the new job. I suspect you consider it a comedown. But you'll find you are wrong. The job was just waiting for someone like you, someone courageous and dynamic and imaginative, to become a key position in the state. You're just the man for it.

"And, Heinz, I'm calling to convey an invitation from my two children—and I concur in it wholeheartedly. You know we have a much bigger house than the three of us can use. Years ago we converted the top floor into a separate apartment—three rooms, kitchen and bath, with its own entrance from the street. We thought we might rent it out but we never did. It's fully furnished. The kids and I should be honored and delighted if you were to move in as our guest and stay as long as you want to—at least until you've found a permanent place to live.

"But," Seymour went on, and his voice dropped a whole octave to become a whisper, "that's not really what I'm calling about. I know, Heinz, you have other things on your mind, but I would be immensely grateful if I could have a few minutes of your time to tell you something personal. I have to talk to you about it. May I?"

When Zimmerman still remained silent, Bercovitz continued:

"Do you remember, Heinz, my telling you a few months ago why I dropped out of the seminary when I lost my faith in God? I still haven't regained it. But now, after what has happened at St. Jerome, I know that there is evil. No, I don't mean that wretched creature, that woman, who started it all. She is only sick—and I still expect medicine to find a cure for her disease, or at least a treatment that makes the likes of her realize that they are deluded. I mean all the others, the sane and normal ones, with their pettiness, their meanness, their delight in inflicting pain, their hurt vanities and inflated egos and their cowardice. Now I know that there really is evil—and then one needs God."

Seymour had become agitated; his voice had risen and he was talking so fast he almost slurred his words. When he stopped, Zimmerman could hear him taking a few deep breaths.

He continued at last in quite a different voice, low-pitched, and so slowly that it sounded almost like a chant:

"What I called to tell you, Heinz, is that I went on Friday to Father Neeley at St. Anne's and asked him to give me instruction in the Catholic faith. I don't know whether I can regain faith, but I do know I need it."

"We have betrayed him," said Bishop O'Malley, when Tom Martini brought in the morning paper with its news of Zimmerman's appointment as chairman of the State Civil Rights Commission and of his resignation from the presidency of St. Jerome University. "We have thrown a good and decent priest to the wolves."

"With due respect, Bishop," said Martini, "I disagree. We have saved Father Zimmerman. He made himself hopelessly vulnerable when he couldn't resist the temptation to do good and put through that impetuous telephone call to Harriet Beecher Stowe. And then all the tensions, all the conflicts, all the contradictions you saw so clearly when this sordid business first started with that poisonous letter from that wretched woman, all of them came out into the open. Every one of them was petty and mean and despicable. But the real issue is not. And it's the real issue that has defeated Father Zimmerman—and you and me. What we've been able to do not only saves Father Zimmerman and gives him a new sphere of contribution and effectiveness. It also gives St. Jerome University the breathing space it needs to straighten itself out."

"Quite a speech, Tom," said the bishop, and he made a little mock bow. "I bet you practiced it before you came in here today."

"That isn't quite fair, sir," protested Martini. "The university is going all out to honor Father Zimmerman. There's the Distinguished University Professorship in his name Mr. Mulcahey is endowing. The Administration Building is going to be renamed Zimmerman Hall. And—though Father Zimmerman isn't supposed to know it yet— he'll be given an honorary doctorate at the June Commencement."

"That's making it up to the victim of judicial murder by giving him a first-class funeral," growled the bishop.

"Don't get me wrong," he continued in a milder tone. "I do not criticize you—quite the contrary. You pulled off a near-miracle, I admit; and I've already told Bernie Murtagh how much I admire what the two of you worked out. You sure got St. Jerome off the hook on which they were trying so hard to hang themselves. Of course, it doesn't solve the problem Zimmerman wanted to ignore—how St. Jerome can be both a great and a Catholic university. I don't envy Heinz Zimmerman's successor; no matter how good a man he is, he won't last three years. Either Willy Huber or the faculty or the two together will kill him off. But, then, that wasn't your problem and it isn't ours. What you did was a virtuoso performance. I haven't seen a better one and I'm full of genuine admiration.

"But that doesn't alter the fact that we betrayed a good man and a fellow priest whose only fault was that he exercised a little Christian compassion. Instead of defending him against libel, slander, and petty intrigue, we took his life's work away from him and kicked him upstairs into a meaningless non-job where he won't have anything to do except listen to the complaint of a black cop that he should have been given fifty extra points in the sergeant's exam because his grandpappy was a slave."

Tom Martini was still wondering how he should answer the bishop—indeed, whether he should answer at all—when the telephone rang.

"It's Monsignor Allessandri from Washington," Tom said, as he handed the receiver over. "He wants to speak to you in private," and Martini got up and left the room.

"Good morning, Patrick," said the familiar voice in its beautiful Oxford English with the almost imperceptible trace of an Italian accent. "I hope I'm not disturbing you, but I do need ten minutes of your time. What I have to say shouldn't wait, especially as it's all good news.

"First, I have been instructed by His Excellency the Nuncio to call the American bishops with whom I've worked and tell them that I have been called back to Rome. I shall leave here by the end of the week. I have been appointed Papal Nuncio to Colombia and will be raised to Bishop before Easter. I am supposed to take over in Bogotá by early July. And I need a few weeks to be briefed, to brush up on my Spanish—it's been almost fifteen years since I last used it in my first diplomatic assignment as a junior secretary at the Nunciatura in Buenos Aires—and to learn what 'Liberation Theology' is all about.

"And so let me say thanks for all your cooperation during my four years in your country. I can't tell you how much I appreciate your friendship and your many kindnesses to me. I am particularly grateful to you for what you taught me about organization, management, and developing people. I shall consider myself your student and in your debt the rest of my career. No, Patrick, I really mean it.

"And now," Allessandri continued, "I have a second, more important message for you from His Excellency. He just read in the Washington morning papers how superbly you handled that awkward affair at St. Jerome University. Don't protest—who else but you and that young Father Martini of yours could have found so elegant and perfect a solution? My congratulations, and His Excellency asked me to add his thanks. You have averted what could have become a damaging scandal and have done so by advancing and strengthening the moral position of the Church, and moving a prominent and widely respected priest into a visible leadership position in public service. '*Bravissimo*,' that's what His Excellency said when he read the news, and you know he is not the enthusiastic type."

There was a pause—Allessandri, O'Malley thought, was consulting his notes again—then he continued:

"I haven't forgotten our talk about your secretary, Father Martini, and his future, nor your telling me that you had entrusted the St. Jerome problem to him. And I must admit the way he worked it out fully justifies all you told me about his being an extraordinary young man. So I am delighted to be able to tell you that the Nuncio has accepted your recommendation. As soon as you telephone me that Father Martini will accept, the Nuncio will announce his appointment as American attaché at the Washington Nunciatura. It's usually a three-year appointment, as you know. Afterwards Martini should be able to choose between joining the papal diplomatic service permanently or moving over to the National Conference of Catholic Bishops as an associate secretary. I am only sorry I won't be here when he reports for duty. But I do expect you to phone me his acceptance right away—today, I hope. I want to call him myself before I leave to congratulate him."

O'Malley was overwhelmed and started to say so, but Allessandri cut him off.

"One moment, Patrick," he said; "I'm not quite finished. I have kept the best news for the end.

"It gives me exquisite pleasure to inform you on the instructions of His Excellency the Nuncio that the Holy Father has acceded to your petition and will raise Capital City to an archbishopric and establish within the archdiocese a new bishopric and diocese at Palmer. His Excellency has charged me to convey the Holy Father's hope that you will accept elevation to Archbishop and serve in Capital City until you reach retirement age, if the good Lord preserves you in life and health until then, as all of us hope and pray. May I be the first to congratulate you, and to say how delighted I am that my period of service in the United States concludes with such a happy, such a blessed event?

"I know, Patrick, you suggested that Monsignor Sullivan be put into Palmer. Frankly, His Excellency the Nuncio feels—and Rome agrees—that a new diocese needs a younger man, who can stay in the post a good many years. The Holy Father has therefore decided to raise your Vicar General Monsignor Corrigan to the rank and title of Bishop of Palmer, and to appoint Monsignor Sullivan to become your auxiliary bishop in Capital City. You are overloaded and need help, especially with ceremonial duties.

"The Holy Father will announce these appointments in the week after Easter—the date set is April 10. You will then be asked to come to Rome as soon as possible, no later than the first week in May, to receive the Archbishop's pallium. Corrigan and Sullivan will be asked to accompany you and to be consecrated at the same time.

This means that I'll be seeing you soon—I'll plan to be in Rome then. Rome further suggests that you plan your formal enthronement in Capital City to take place on the Feast Day of Saints Peter and Paul—June 29. May I be so presumptuous as to invite myself to the great occasion? I have to be in Bogotá around July 3 or 4 and can easily make the detour to Capital City. And the following Sunday, Rome suggests, you formally install your two new bishops.

"Again let me say," Allessandri added with a flourish, "how happy I am that I can finish my American tour of duty by bringing such good news to a dear friend, and how delighted I am that I don't have to say 'Goodbye' but 'arrivederci.' And don't forget, please, we'd like to get Father Martini's acceptance as soon as possible. Do you think you can phone it in today?"

"I am overwhelmed and more than grateful, sir," Tom Martini responded when Bishop O'Malley gave him Monsignor Allessandri's message a few minutes later. The Bishop saw that the young priest had tears in his eyes and was close to choking on his emotions. "I know this is the most fabulous and most exciting opportunity that will ever come my way.

"But, Bishop," Martini continued, "when Monsignor Allessandri called, I was just about to tell you of my own plans and to make a request. My term as your secretary is about ended; I know your four-year rule and I've been here more than three and a half years already. Of course I never dreamed of anything so grand as the Washington assignment you got for me. Don't protest, sir; *you* were the one that procured it. I thought you might offer me a position as a department head under a vice chancellor here in the diocese or at most a vice chancellorship.

"But, sir—and I do hope you can forgive me—I have decided to ask you respectfully to relieve me of my administrative and executive duties, and to assign me instead to where I can minister to individuals—to a parish or as chaplain to a prison or a hospital—though I hope you won't make me a chaplain at a university and a faculty member right now. I hope you don't think me ungrateful. I know I could never hope for a kinder boss or for one from whom I could learn more. But I'm determined to become a pastor and stop being an executive."

"When did you reach this decision, Tom?" asked O'Malley in a very soft voice.

"I started thinking about it a few months ago when I realized that my four years as your secretary would soon be up. But what really made up my mind was our first talk about Father Zimmerman. Do you remember, Bishop, what you said about people who don't know that they are ambitious and how endangered they are, that morning when Mrs. Holloway's letter arrived?"

"But, Tom," the startled bishop protested, "I didn't mean you."

"I realize that, sir. I know that you'd be direct if you wanted to talk *about* me. Still, you talked *to* me, whether you meant to or not. It was quite a shock, I must say. But I needed it; and I'm grateful."

"You realize, Tom," the bishop said—and now his voice was stern—"that your going into parish work would be a wicked waste of your gifts. You are so very good as an administrator and executive, and so few are. There are dozens who can do a decent job in a parish or as chaplain. If ever I saw anybody with a true vocation for being an executive, it's you."

"I'm deeply grateful for your praise, sir, and flattered. But it's just because I'm good at it that I want to leave while I still can. I enjoy it too much. I know that if I don't get out now, I never will. And it's not what I went into the Church for."

There was a pause. Then, "Very well, Tom," said the bishop. "Of course, you've earned the right to go where you think you belong, although both Allessandri and I will be very disappointed. But you are making a serious mistake. Tell me, have you given any thought to where you'll be if it doesn't work out, if you find that your vocation is not pastoral work and being a parish priest? I hope I'm wrong; but, Tom, I'm almost sure that in a few months you'll be bored stiff and find the life humdrum and pretty frustrating. You're used to so much bigger a world than the four walls of a parish."

"I wouldn't be surprised, sir, if you're right, although I hope you aren't. But I'm determined to find out. I'll give myself two years. If after two years I find that my vocation is not to be a pastor but to be an executive, I still wouldn't want to be an executive in the Church.

"I would want to stay a priest, I believe, but I'd look for my career elsewhere than in the Church. I don't think I've ever told you, sir, that my parents have been quite successful in their business. They've built up the small neighborhood grocery store my dad inherited when he came back from the service in World War II into a profitable chain: five Italian supermarkets in and around Capital City—they're called 'Alberto's'—and each has a trattoria attached to it that serves Italian meals, and a gift shop. My father always wanted me to come into the business and was very disappointed when I went into the seminary instead of going to Business School. If I don't make it as a pastor, I'd rather go in as an executive with my father. I am sure I could build the family business into a national chain; all right, it won't be another McDonald's or Kentucky Fried Chicken—but in ten years it should be a sizable company. Alberto's has the right formula. What it needs is management—and that, sir, you have taught me.

"With all due respect for you and your great office, if I have to be an executive, I see more scope and a greater contribution for me in a business than in the Church. Here it's all rules and regulations and paperwork. The main task is to preserve, to prevent change, discourage innovation, and not go in for experiments. To do reasonably well what has been done so much better many times before. And most of the administrative work is so petty. Do you realize, sir, how much of your time and energy goes into taking care of alcoholic priests? And then the politics! No, Your Excellency, if the Lord has meant me to be an executive, it's not in the Church, no matter how much I love it.

"So, please convey my gratitude to Monsignor Allessandri and accept my thanks for all you've been doing for me and have tried to do for me. I know how much I owe you. Tell Monsignor Allessandri, please, that I am most sensible of the honor. It's very tempting. But I am determined to resist the temptation."

"Tom is wrong," Bishop O'Malley thought after the young man had left. "Doesn't he realize that the parish priest and the prison chaplain can do their job only because there's someone who sits where I sit taking care of the paperwork and worrying about alcoholic priests and petty politics and teaching people and developing and placing them? He'll be in for one heck of a surprise if he thinks there's no routine and no politics and no worrying about alcoholic or dishonest store managers in running Alberto's. It's quite unthinkable to me that he can turn down the Washington offer—it's tailor-made for him, and there's so much good he could do in the job. But perhaps, after what he's just seen at St. Jerome, it's understandable that he wants to resist the temptation to do good.

"But what about myself?" Bishop O'Malley asked himself suddenly. And such a wave of black despair rose in him that he had to steady his head with his hands to fight the nausea and dizziness. "I have failed in my duty as bishop, failed miserably. Of course the Order of St. Jerome and its university are outside my jurisdiction. But I am the diocesan and the guardian of Faith and Morals in my diocese. And if what happened at St. Jerome was not gross, flagrant immorality, I wouldn't know what is. What they normally mean, of course, when they talk of immorality are the sins of the flesh. But the sins of the spirit are as much or more immoral: the sins of pride and envy and of bearing false witness against one's neighbor. I've not fought against them but have given in to them and sacrificed a good man, a good Christian and a fellow priest, to avoid controversy, unpleasantness, criticism from the Nuncio, and adverse publicity. And instead of being punished for my failure, I am being praised and rewarded by being made Archbishop.

"Of course, I could refuse and retire. I am sixty-three years old, after all." But the bishop knew that he would not refuse and would not retire.

"To be sure," he said to himself, "I can always tell myself that it's the right thing to do. Capital City should have been an archbishopric years ago. I can tell myself that I'm doing it for my clergy, and for the faithful in the diocese to whom the news will bring such joy and pride. It's true, but not true enough. I know I want it—and what's worse, I know I'll enjoy it."